Secrets Echoed
The House of Phoenix Chronicles Book II

Secrets Echoed

The House of Phoenix Chronicles
Book II

by
Kurt W. Oster

All Genders Press

an imprint of
Perceptions Press
Victoria, BC
Canada

2023

Secrets Echoed
The House of Phoenix Chronicles Book II

Copyright © Kurt W. Oster

Revised and published in paperback and e-book in 2023

First published in paperback and e-book, Wilhelm P. Ostir, All Genders Press, ISBN 9781990096723, 9781990096747, 2022

Cover Design: Margot Wilson (Midjourney)
Illustrations: Kurt W. Oster (Canva Pro)

ISBN: 978-1-998924-75-2 (Paperback)
ISBN: 978-1-998924-76-9 (Kindle E-book)

Published in Canada by
All Genders Press
www.allgenderspress.ca

an imprint of
Perceptions Press
www.perceptionspress.ca
Victoria BC
Canada

Contents

Preface

One flash of light. Then, nothing, just darkness holding the space. Finally, a small flickering orb of light flashes and floats around in the darkness. Then, just like that, it disappears. Quietness is the only thing left holding the space.

Then again, another orb of light, this time glowing blue. It pops and multiplies into ten separate orbs, floating in the darkness. Then, all of them go out. Again, darkness is the only thing left holding the space!

A third flash of light, then another, and another. Images appear floating in the air, image after image of the Arcane fighting back the darkness throughout the years, the entire story of time, playing out, dancing around the room. Stories echo and ring throughout the space. The chatter of each story grows in volume, one decimal at a time, until the sound becomes unbearable. A half-visible orb emerges out of the ground and levitates into the air as hundreds of images explode, filling the space as they dance across the walls and ceilings. The noise continues, unbearable, and the commotion makes the space sound like a busy city in rush hour traffic.

Then, absolute silence.

The room falls quiet as the last orb darkens, dissolving, dust falling to the floor, leaving only a golden pocket watch, the legendary watch itself, all too familiar from the stories of time, but never seen like this.

The watch spins slowly, the hands frozen at twelve o'clock. A flash of purple light and the second hand begins moving—tick, tick, tick. A blue flash of light illuminates the space. Then, the minute hand begins moving, spinning out of control. Then, suddenly, it stops.

The watch flies across the room and lands in the hand of a cloaked figure. Turning, they throw the watch into the air as they disappear. Reappearing, they walk across a frozen field, time completely stopped. Looking around, the figure examines the Arcane frozen around them, suspended in time. When the figure reaches the leader of the Arcane, Noel, they reach into their pocket, pull out a small bag, and dump the contents into their hand. Raising their hand, they blow dust around them. The dust begins to spin, shifting the nature of the story.

Definitions

Arcane: known or knowable only to a few people, secret, mysterious, obscure, esoteric, magical, a mystical, an enigmatic force in the world, heavenly or spiritual, arcane magic entails forces or phenomena that somehow transcend the natural laws that govern the world by directly manipulating unknown energies that bend the fabric of reality to create a desired effect.

Arcane of Mystical Experience: an individual of secret, mysterious, and mystical force in the world that may not necessarily be magical but still transcends the natural laws that govern the world by directly manipulating unknown energies that bend the fabric of reality to create a desired effect. May include: dwarfs, vampires, centaurs, animagus, and mystical creatures. Individuals may be seen as having only a percentage of magical or mystical heritage.

Arcane of Mundane Experience: an individual known or knowable only to a few people, secret, mysterious, obscure, esoteric, a magical, force in the world of arcane magic or non-magic, entails forces or phenomena that are of this earthly world, relating to, belonging to, or characteristic of the earth, earthly, in relation to the immediate concerns and activities of human beings and has resided among humans and is part of their daily life. May include: particular houses in which the individual may have grown up in the Mundane world, known of or having magical powers. Includes members of the Houses of Phoenix and Pendragon. Individuals may be seen as having only a percentage of magical or mystical heritage.

Arcane of Magical Heritage: an individual known or knowable only to a few people, secret, mysterious, obscure, esoteric, a magical force in the world of Arcane magic. May include: Fairies, Elves, and certain Wizards and Witches. Includes the Houses of Ignatius, Drake, Phoenix, and Knight. Individuals may be seen as having only a percentage of magical or mystical heritage.

High Arcane: applies to an individual known or knowable only to a few people, of magical force in the world, heavenly or spiritual, Arcane magic entails forces or phenomena that somehow transcend the natural laws that govern the world by directly manipulating unknown energies that bend the fabric of reality to create a desired effect and is considered to immortal. Includes: The Nobles.

Mundane: of this earthly world, relating to, belonging to, or characteristic of the earth, earthly, in relation to the immediate concerns and activities of human beings.

Prologue
Rising from the Ashes

For one to come to understand this story, one must know one word—"love." To know this part of our story, you must understand two unique magical forms: love and time. You see, over the centuries, the Arcane became focused, consumed, and obsessed with the sheer power of time. Many tried to find ways to control and channel it. Others looked to cheat death and prolong life. Covens sought to control time as a weapon against their enemies. Then, there was one Arcane, in particular, who was so consumed by the magic of time that they nearly destroyed the story entirely. But you know about them—Merlin, that old, cranky warlock wizard, hell-bent on world domination.

But to truly understand this story, you need to know about the other form of magic—that of love. A compelling magical form, love, much like time, is bizarre, a magical form only mastered when two individuals fall in love. Sometimes love is so powerful and so feared that the Mundane and Arcane alike have worked to ban certain forms of it. Claiming that certain forms of love is unnatural, many fear what it means, what it could fuel, and how it could enhance the sheer power of some individuals.

But, then again, I believe it is mostly feared because of what happens when love meets time. If love and time fall in love with each other, and the two combine in magical form, they become… well… What is the word to describe it? Oh, yes—unstoppable. Now, one mustn't forget that they are supposed to live happily ever after, or so one might think. But living happily ever after is only found in fairytales. You see, to understand this story, you have to know something about time as well, and what caused it to shatter. To put it more simply: time has shattered, and now, we must journey to put it back together.

So, in order to understand this story, you must understand time. Would you like to meet time? I am sure you would. Hold tight. Our story begins when time is as young as it is old, when time is in motion even as it stagnates. Unfortunately, time is a unique conundrum that behaves and misbehaves and through time's misbehavior, the ancient artifacts of the past became lost—many believe kidnapped, stolen, traded, and sold—never to be seen again. These artifacts are so powerful that they give the user unrestrained magical potential. Let's just say that they amplify the power of any magical user but, with some of them, at a high cost.

There is not a single being of Arcane ability who has not heard of the existence of these magical artifacts. But to many of the new generation, the artifacts are the stuff of fables. Many younger Arcane have lost touch with tradition. Some have even adopted technology. Magic is powerful, but when one adds a device, such as a wand, staff, orb, elfish arm blade, or magical sword, that item becomes an extension of magic and, thus, amplifies the power of the wielder.

You see, when Merlin rose to power, he sought out these powerful artifacts. Then, he hid, stole, killed, and lied for them. He took them from Arcane and Mundane alike. No one knows where these items are currently, their whereabouts unknown to any of us. Only a story, here and there, remains. There has been a rumor of a hidden magical bunker, which adds to the complexity of the fable. Many believe that Merlin used his status among the Knights of the Roundtable to do his bidding. Thus, the stories of the artifacts have emerged, twisted, died off, and spurred adventurous quests. Passed from one generation to the next, the stories form the basis for the great philosophies of the Arcane texts, which survive from a time that only a few living individuals still remember. Still, one Arcane remembers that time all too well, the only one who walked through the story, and has passed their knowledge on to a new Arcane leader—me!

Time, an eternal loop and, in its infinite wisdom, still as bizarre as ever, plays its games, many of which remain unknown to any of us. But time itself is such a powerful form of magic that it can be bent to the will of certain powerful individuals once it is channeled. I have learned this all too well. You see, my journey begins and ends in the exact same moment. You could say that I am stuck in a never-ending loop, trying to figure out how to bring the story to a happy ending. When you have traveled through time for the past eighty years, as I have, you learn a thing or two, and that makes you well-qualified to speak on such a rich history.

Shh! Can you keep a secret? Please do not tell anyone, but I stole something. Well, I kind of borrowed it for my travels throughout time. It is a neat little magical device with precisely what is needed to move the story forward or freeze it, replay it, or alter it. You ask why one would want to freeze time. While that is an interesting question, it is not as interesting as turning back time, thus allowing time to play out repeatedly and, in the end, altering the story's outcome altogether. This way, a story continues to change, shatter, then reassemble.

Throughout our story, I have broken time. Actually, time broke itself first. Then, I broke it again. Then, I restored it, only to break it again. But then, with the help of the others, I finally restored it. But when time was restored, it played out as a different story altogether. In the new version of the story, Merlin and the legions of darkness he commanded could not anticipate what was to come. The best part was that they were not able to see what would happen next.

One needs a simple but rather complicated piece of magic to alter time—a watch. But not just any watch, the pocket watch that the Magical Three found. It had frozen their family's home. Among its many features, it is the only watch in existence that causes time to come to a sudden halt.

Please don't judge me when I show you, but I have that pocket watch. Of course, this particular version of the watch is the one that works with full magical powers. But you are probably wondering why I would borrow such an artifact, particularly from the Queen. And yes, when I say, "the Queen," I am referring to Queen Roslynn herself, the one and only Arcane whose magic can stop anyone in their tracks.

You see, to save time, I needed to understand how this pocket watch works. It is a rather complex piece of technology. For any Arcane who touches this watch, it is relatively simple. It merely freezes time. However, something different occurs for me. The pocket watch acts—how do I put it?—differently. Not only can I freeze time, but I can control it, turning it forward and backward, making it stop, making it skip, erasing the timeline, and rewriting it, a power only held by a select few Elders. So, while everyone thinks that Lady Mora and Queen Rose are the only Arcane who can control time, they are not. A half dozen Arcane have this unique magical ability. Mora's grandfather, Noble Elder, can control time, a form of magic that he learned from his old friend Elder Yule.

On the other hand, no one truly knows or, I believe, understands, where Queen Rose learned to master time control, but that is a part of a story that is still unraveling.

❧

Now, where was I? Oh yes, the story of Elder Yule. A unique fellow, Elder Yule is as strange as they come and fascinated with making time do weird things. Many of the texts note that what he did was for fun, and he was known for turning back time just to let it play back over and over for sheer amusement. So much so that when Merlin cornered Elder Yule and tried to take the pocket watch for himself, Elder Yule hid it. Then, he changed the timeline, hid it again, dangled the watch in front of Merlin, and then, just for fun, hid it again, and continued to alter the timeline repeatedly, every day, for an entire century. So, you see, our timeline is so tangled that we have to sort it out. Not just fix it but restore it. But where do we begin?

Now, time is as young as it is old and it teaches us how to find what is lost and reveals the mystery of the truths we seek. Here is something for you mere Mundane to ponder. How does one fix a broken story? Give up? It is relatively easy. You must fix time itself. But time is always tricky, never still, always moving and, thus, evolving. Time is—if you remember, or need I remind you?—what we call an "echo," a continuous loop with no beginning or ending. The question that arises is how to find the point, the exact moment, where our story begins, the point at which only one timeline existed. But to find that bizarre point, one must understand how the realms, the timelines, and magic have collided over the past few centuries, thus never making sense. So, to find the beginning, one must find the most bizarre point of the story and let it play out.

However, before that point is chosen, you do remember, or should I remind you, that the evil sorcerer warlock, Merlin, taught us that magic has rules that are meant to be followed. He put these rules in place as a way to, more or less, justify his lust for absolute power. You see, if magic was bound by rules, Merlin believed it would give him the ability to control anyone who would attempt to stand against him.

Magic is not the same for me as it is for other Arcane. In fact, my magic is quite different. Okay, I lied. It is freakishly different and scares many. Who am I, you ask? Someone you would normally never know. Yet, the story is around. You see, I am the story. And then, again, I am not. To know my story, you also have to know the story of the Houses of Phoenix and Ignatius and those other houses that intersect these two great houses.

But my magic is different. It is as old as time itself, the kind of magic only told of in stories, the kind of magic from which fairytales are made. A story so old and powerful, it haunted the great sorcerer warlock, Merlin, until his death, after which only his son knew of it and never speaking of it, sealed it away for all time. My story scared everyone and, if revealed, would bring about the destruction of the darkness. To reveal my story would be to admit that Merlin was not as powerful as everyone thought.

You may have been led to believe that the magic of the Magical Three transcends all rules. Now, while that is true, it is not the whole story. We know that magic, which does not follow the rules, has its pros and cons. But, ultimately, compelling magic to follow or be bound by the rules, causes the timeline to become confusing and, in some cases, very hard to understand.

Inevitably, you will discover that magic is so complex that it has to be separated from time. How, you inquire? Well, that is where the story begins, and yet, where it also ends. Time is there one minute and gone the next. The watch, protected by the child of Elder Yule, seems to control all time and, as such, controls that very moment, that moment when time itself would forever be changed, then returned to normal, then altered again.

To understand the story that I am going to tell you, we must first jump forward to the point that will send us backward in time.

"Quickly! Put the coffin down. This is going to be the most exciting moment of my career, the crowning achievement, finding the burial spot of the lost treasure of the great wizard Merlin. It was hidden where no one dared to look. It took years to find this spot, the last of the Celtic temples from the times of Arthur, a remnant of a time long past. My students and I, mere Mundane, who study history, have waited for this moment when the Mundane finally take back the earth from those "Arcane." To find such a prized treasure will be the crowning moment of salvation for the Mundane. This burial site is said to hold the last of the Curpendulums. Without it, those Arcane will never be able to enslave us. Without the Curpendulums, the very fabric of their society will unravel, and we Mundane will be safe from the unfavorable practices of the magical arts," the man declares loudly as he motions for his students to lower the coffin gently. "I have waited my entire career for this moment."

And then, one loud thud. As the coffin hits the ground, the pine box breaks open. Nothing but ashes fall out. The professor runs his fingers through the ashes and finds nothing. Nothing but ashes.

"How can this be?"

"Professor? What does this mean?" a student inquires.

"That the hunt for the Curpendulum continues."

As the last word emerges from the professor's mouth, he and the student fade and the room begins to spin. Then, time fast forwards and comes to an abrupt stop.

Ah, give me a moment. I need to fix the story. Fascinating, I know. A coffin filled with ashes. But, at least, this time, it is ashes. The last four versions of this timeline have been nightmares. First, there were snakes, hundreds of them. Next, the garden of never-ending mazes. Indeed, a maze as wicked as that could hide the Curpendulums. But, no, it was just a massive headache of dead ends.

Then came the house of a million dolls. Now, dolls are creepy enough as it is, not to mention in this place. They were all possessed and attempted to hurt or kill anyone within their vicinity. Finally, there was the House of the old lady on Pearl Street with a unique touch. Three weeks later, you awake from your trance to find that you are still sitting at her dining room table as she drones on about the cute kitty cat that she is petting over and over. Of course, if you try to leave the table, the old lady will hex you. Do not ask how I escaped that one. Let's just say that when I teleported, I left her and the cat in a field full of cows. But if I have learned anything from all of this, it is that, as always, time is bizarre.

In the version of the story, which we are currently exploring, we have a coffin filled with ashes. I can only imagine what sick and horrifying thing may have been in the coffin this time. Believe me, when I say that it was a pain to get all those ashes gathered up. But you will learn of that hiccup in a few moments. Now, if you think that the professor was dismayed and displeased to learn that the Curpendulum was not there, you have not seen anything until you see my reaction.

Trying to find these Curpendulums is like looking for a needle in a haystack. I have spent the past eighty years of my life traveling through time, jumping from one timeline to the next, being dumped here and there, only to discover that, yet again, it is another dead end. But, as always, time, with its quirky sense of humor, is not making sense one second, and then, in the next, is making perfect sense.

In all of this, the one thing I have learned is to examine everything. Whoever came up with that idea should have their magic revoked. Examine everything, huh? I am still finding ashes in my nice cloak. But where were we? Oh yes. The coffin was found, hit the ground, broke apart, then only ashes. Then, the student asked, "What does this mean?" Please do not judge me for this next part.

↎

"Professor, are you okay?"
"No. The coffin was said to be the resting spot of the last of the Curpendulums. Everything we knew, everything

we discovered, all the maps, all the research, pointed to this very spot. Then nothing!"

"Then do we continue to look?" one of the students suggests.

"My career is over. I have spent hundreds upon thousands of dollars of research money to fund this dig, and now, I will be heading back to the university empty-handed. That, though, is not the worse part. In the midst of all this madness, that cloaked figure ran through the camp. The next thing we knew, we were all tied up, and every last container of ashes was gone, along with all of my documents, everything. I am ruined!"

⋙

Actually, he is *not* ruined. Well, okay, maybe a little bit. I did feel badly. So, I put a small bag of ashes back in his lap with an "I am sorry" note, right before I unfroze time. I told you that this watch has its practical uses and comes in handy.

I will say that I am not proud of stealing the ashes, but please remember what I said a few moments ago—we have to examine everything. Now, if my mother were here, I would be dragged across that camp by one of my pointed ears and told to put everything back. In her charming way, she would even have made me clean up everything with a hand broom and dustpan. Then, she would insist that I make dinner for those lovely students and their professor, mend their socks, and build them a log cabin, all without the use of magic.

Why steal all the ashes, you ask? That is easy. I am also looking for the Curpendulums. I have several of them, thus far, in my collection. Please do not roll your eyes. I know what you're thinking. What do the ashes have to do with the Curpendulums? Everything. You see, Merlin was such a cranky, grumpy, old man. Nothing we have learned about him surprises me in the least bit. So, I stole the ashes to check them. I tried multiple tests. First, I tried to restore them with multiple spells, then I converted them to the natural elements, earth, fire, water, and wind. Then, when all else failed, out came the potions. At first, the potions yielded no results, but then, something happened. A note appeared.

A journey that began many centuries ago will shape the very fabric of time. Yet, it shall also not affect time the way many thought it would. Time, in its infinite power, remains as bizarre and complex as it has been for these many years. Let this note serve as a clue, Time has presented a new way of stopping the darkness. A dream and two individuals' love shall stand at the heart of every hero's journey. Challenges will arise that will test their resolve, new friendships will be forged, and unexpected secrets will be revealed. At the forefront of the journey is love, a form of magic that is so powerful it is known to alter the very fabric of time itself.

How delightful! The dream of Merlin stands at the heart of the journey. Tell me something I do not know already. Blah, blah, blah. As always, the reference to the dream but nothing more.

I ran my hand through the ashes, and then, an idea came to me. Ashes! That's it. Where is it? Why did I not think of it before? I know it is in my bag somewhere. Hum. Oh yes, *The Liber of Animalia et Creaturae (The Curpendulum of Animals and Creatures)*. Now, this is where the story gets even more enjoyable. You see, I am not supposed to have this grimoire. It was locked up, and if the head Arcane librarian knew that I took it from under her nose… well, I would hate to see what would happen. But, in this case, it may hold the answer. Besides, I replaced it with a duplicate. The original libers should remain hidden and are, more or less, held in my private collection. Some of the texts note one or more things about Arcane powers, magical spells, and creatures.

P-h-o-…. Phoenix, here it is.

The Phoenix is the most ancient Arcane beast, next to the dragon, dating to ancient Egypt and China. The Phoenix is considered one of the original four mystical Arcane beasts and the great guardian of time. The phoenix lives for several hundred years before it bursts into flames and is, then, reborn from its ashes.

Ashes. The ashes of any burned substance can be used to re-awaken the epic phoenix. All one must do is find a place of calmness, mix a dragon fang, the feather of a phoenix, and the scale of a turtle, and then, wait. This will allow for the reanimation of the ashes, and thus, awaken the great phoenix.

Reborn of its ashes. This should be interesting, but it cannot be done here. So where? To reanimate the ashes and raise the phoenix, it has to happen someplace away from all Mundane and Arcane.

With that, I have an idea. One that, if caught, would get me into heaps of trouble. But surely, no one would dare venture there. One quick wave of the hand and presto! The ancient ruins of wisdom and the goddess Athena. Now, to wake this bird and find out what is hidden in these ashes.

The ingredients: a fang of the dragon, a feather of the phoenix, and a scale of the Turtle. Interesting, it appears that the grimoire does not indicate how they should be used. So, this is where, as always, time decides to rear its nasty head and play a bizarre twist.

Let us fast forward, shall we? First, I spent three hours figuring out how to wake the bird. The *Liber of Animalia et Creaturae* (*The Curpendulum of Animals and Creatures*) said nothing about how to use these items, only that you need them. Finally, frustrated, I threw everything down, turned, walked away, and that is when the three items combined with the ash and, poof, a billow of smoke, and there, a small bird of orange, red, purple, and yellow arose. A charming little creature.

But that is beside the point. As I looked around at the ashes, I found exactly what I was searching for. Starting to sparkle, the ashes transformed into the Curpendulum. The professor was right, and the coffin did hold the Curpendulum—*The Liber of Naturae et Elementis* (*The Curpendulum of Nature and the Elements*). It was just hidden from Mundane eyes.

Oh, forgive me. Where are my manners? "Curpendulum" in Arcane means "grimoire or spellbook." The Curpendulums are very ancient *scripti* (texts) of magical teachings. Many believe that the Nobles wrote them. Others believed it was the Celestials. So, perhaps I should tell you that story.

☙

Thousands of years ago, when the earth was still young, the Celestials, ancient immortal beings of extraordinary power gave earth magic. Magic was created from all things, and in its creation, several families emerged. They were divine, magical beings. "The Nobles," as they were known, created the Curpendulums as the balance in the world and, ultimately, contain the teachings of all magic. The Nobles wrote down every step and form of magic given to the earth by the Celestials. As such, it was known that the Nobles could see thousands of years into the future, and when they discovered that Merlin would seek out these grimoires to gain absolute power and dominion over the Mundane for himself, they hid them.

Now, the Nobles usually made it a point to not interfere with Mundane and Arcane affairs. So, they decided, in that very moment, to appoint the Council of Light and placed one of their own, a young child, on that council. The child was none other than the Lady Mora.

The Nobles were concerned with the grave vision of Merlin stealing the grimoires and decided never to let him have them. As a result, Noble Elder and Elder Yule opened a portal, stacked the numerous Curpendulums, one on top of another until all fifteen stood to the height of their shoulders. Then, holding up their hands, one by one, they launched the Curpendulums, one after the other, into the portal. The Nobles hid the grimoires throughout time and, in doing so, created fifteen separate timelines. Thus, imitating time's bizarre and unusual behaviors.

Now, here comes the twist. Noble Elder entrusted me, of all Arcane, to find each of the Curpendulums and return them to the Sanctuary of Legends and Lore. As I have mentioned, the Nobles, like the Celestials, have never interfered in Arcane and Mundane life, but Noble Elder broke this ideology when he entrusted this task to me.

Oh, by the way, if you have never teleported, I would recommend you hold on to something. And 3-2-1... presto! Please mind your manners and touch absolutely nothing, particularly the other Curpendulums. At this time, I hold ten of the fifteen. The last five seem to have eluded me. Previously, I would have said the last six, but, with this new one, only five remain to be found.

I have been one of only a few Arcane who can find and utilize the Sanctuary of Legends and Lore. No one knows how Noble Elder, and I met or how I gained access to this place. But that is a story for another time. For now, we must find a point to re-engage the story of the life and times of the House of Phoenix.

Mind yourself. I would recommend standing back. The viewing globe is relatively large. Do you think Esther is the only one who can watch everything?

Shall we see where time has decided to drop us? Ah, yes, nearly seventy years ago, this should be interesting. I was not even born yet. Shall we?

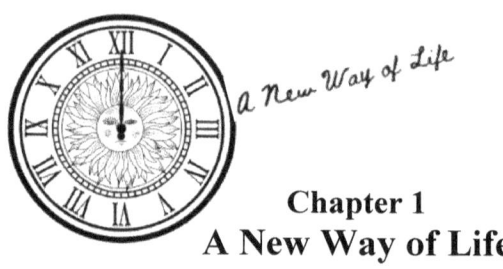

Chapter 1
A New Way of Life

"I know it is here. Where is it, Alezander? Have you seen my diary, or did one of the kids pick it up and move it?"

"It is on your desk where you left it, Hun."

"Zander, have you seriously seen what my desk looks like?"

"Rose, if you would clean up, you would be able to find things."

"Now, you sound like my mother."

"Is that it?"

"Yes, my love, it is. Thank you."

Zander shakes his head as he picks up Vivian and walks out of the room. I sit in the armchair at my old oak desk and start writing.

Dear Diary,

Things here are ever-changing. Nearly ten years ago, my dear brothers, Oliver and Ethan, and I became known as The Magical Three and stopped the very forces of evil and darkness. Yet, with each passing day, time continues to play its bizarre tricks, and we never know what will happen next. Over the past decade, the world has restored its downed cities, and everyone is living in peace. However, every now and then, the remnants of the darkness continue to attack. Today has been hectic like any other day, and I am happy to take a much-needed break to write.

While peace has existed between the Arcane and Mundane for the past decade, we have remained in hiding;

our leaders called upon to advise Mundane world leaders and the world powers. But our leaders feel that the world is not ready to integrate fully.

Over the years, I have become aware that the Mundane have come looking for us. Today was interesting. Two Mundane crossed the barrier and, in the process, lost their minds and went mad. Try explaining to Arcane guards that there is no need to hurt any Mundane who appears to be babbling incoherently.

The Arcane have started to live among the Mundane and go about living everyday lives. With each passing day, and as Arcane interact with Mundane regularly, safety concerns for both sides have lessened. My father, Lord Kelvin, continues to serve as the President of the Arcane and serves as the Arcane ambassador to the United Nations. Cousin Bethany originally served in that role until she earned her Doctorate, at which time, she and Phineas moved, when she accepted a more exciting and promising role. She is now the head of The Arcane Ignatius Institute at the University of Arcane and Mundane Studies. Through her appointment and Father's role, partnerships have begun to form. Mundane can now learn about Arcane History. The children of Mundane families, who demonstrate Arcane magical ability, finally are attending school at our Arcane institutions, which are equipped to handle their magical teaching.

Throughout all of this, Mother and Father appointed the council as the new parliament of the

Arcane, and many individuals of the community now work for our growing government. Father spent the first two years overturning many of Merlin's policies and has worked to create an inclusive society for all to live, work, marry, and raise families.

Every day, more documents arrive from the castle and worldwide. Merlin had stashed documents, manuscripts, and grimoires in secret rooms in the castle and hidden in various secret spots around the globe. While many of the texts have been located, many ancient artifacts and relics have yet to be found to date. This creates a continued and alarming concern about these items floating around in the Mundane world and the possibility of people getting hurt. Through my continued studies and now in my role, as Assistant Headmistress and keeper of records in the library, I have learned that my great grandfather did not look favorably upon the Mundane. Rather, he despised them! Although Merlin was a powerful sorcerer, I found that he has not been spoken of favorably in either the Arcane or Mundane texts.

Mother and Father are currently traveling and are in New York. Father is meeting with multiple delegates at the United Nations, and, as always, Mother is close by, helping him and enjoying the city. While Father and Uncle Wade decided to dissolve the Royal Arcane Monarchy, Father notes that he feels the monarchy still exists with extended powers because of his role. Father spends most of his time talking with world leaders about what magic is and is not. When he is home, he loves to share the stories of some of the world leaders' bizarre, yet amusing, concepts of magic.

The fun part of all of this has been dear, charming Father's interaction with technology. Unlike Oliver, Ethan, Zander, Olivia, and I, Mother and Father have not spent time in the Mundane realm for many years. Hence, they are concerned about adapting to technology and Mundane society. While Mom has caught on fast, dad, on the other hand, is a different story. All of us remind our mother, every chance we get, to keep Dad occupied with his work to avoid another technological blunder. Let's just say that Dad and cell phones do not get along. He still prefers to send Fairy messengers or orbs. So, while Mother has settled into the world of technology, Ethan, Oliver, and I laugh together that, one-day, Dad will get so mad that he will use his magic to make all technology disappear.

Oh, and then, there are my dear brothers. Not much has changed as the two are still causing problems. Sebastian is not a fan of Ethan and Oliver working together because he always has to save them. Oliver, Olivia, Ethan, and I completed our undergraduate studies and are glad to have that journey over. Oliver notes that he is now at a point in his career where he wishes to return to school to pursue further studies. Olivia and I both shake our heads and laugh at the thought of him doing another two to four years of schooling, books flying everywhere, quills all over the room, writing paper after paper, and poor Cedric having to climb over piles of papers to clean.

Of course, what is the easiest way to annoy your Vampire Butler? Simple. Just leave piles of papers lying around. I will never forget the look on Oliver's face the day he came home from class to find that Cedric, being his usual self, made a dumpster appear outside on the ground, then opened the second-floor window, and threw the entire study into the dumpsters and did it in a record time of fewer than two minutes. Let's just say that being a vampire and possessing the speed he does was helpful. While Cedric laughed and noted that it solved the problem, Oliver was beside himself.

The castle has been transformed into the Arcane headquarters and now stands at the heart of the village. Oliver and Olivia live in the village, within walking distance from the headquarters. Both Oliver and Olivia work for the parliament. Olivia loves her job serving as the Chief Advisor for Mundane Affairs, and Oliver serves as one of the heads of Arcane Investigations and Magical Enforcement.

Oliver and Olivia were the last two to start having children and currently have twin girls two years of age. My dear nieces, Gwen and Madelene, are adorable and are very in tune with their magical powers. It is always interesting when their daughters are together with Zander and my four, and Ethan and Sebastian's son. Let's just say that we all have master clean-up spells with the help of Cedric.

Oliver, in his role, often travels, visiting various parts of the world. While Olivia and the girls travel with him, he often objects because he worries about their safety. The nice thing that Oliver, Ethan, and I have come to love is having the dragons and fairies around, as they are wonderful babysitters, who keep the children safe. Gwen and Madelene are staying with Uncle Wade and Aunt Destiny as Oliver and Olivia are in Europe following up on a lead about an old, Arcane artifact that has caught the antiquities community's attention. Unfortunately, this artifact has attracted some much unwanted attention for our people. We are afraid that if the Mundane have their way, it will be sold to some private collector at a rather considerable price.

Although Olivia is Mundane, she always seems to be the one, out of any battle, incident, or attack, who is not touched, hurt, or bothered by any form of magic. So, the only conclusion we can reach is that it has to be her Arthurian bloodline that protects her. Yes, recently, we learned that Olivia, her sister Brooke, and their cousin, Claire, are descendants of King Arthur. So, they are members of the Pendragon family.

The covens remain throughout the world and have come to respect the parliament. Now, they state that they do not feel so disconnected from the Arcane as they once were. They also assist Olivia when she travels, and many members of the covens have been known to hex those who mess with her.

While the last elfish village remains up in the mountains, Zander and I serve as their King and Queen. Many elves have moved into the village to connect with the Arcane community. However, Zander and I still know that while the elves are spread out, the highest-ranking members of our people, including the council, healers, and remaining royal family members, remain in the mountain village.

My brother-in-law, Sebastian Knight-Phoenix, serves as the head of the elite Arcane investigations team and works with Oliver. If you remember, Sebastian and Ethan's son, Matthew, who they rescued during the battle nearly ten years ago, is now eleven years old and is in the sixth grade at the Arcane School of Magical Teaching. My dear sweet Ari is a year behind him, and the two have formed an incredible bond and tend to get in trouble. Ethan originally started teaching at the school in sports but soon came to love science and took over as the head of the science program. While he works down the hall from my office at the school, I have considered utilizing a relocation spell as the latest explosion from his classroom still has my staff cautious and uneasy.

My dear mother-in-law, Mora, is close by as she reopened the magical school ten years ago. I serve as Assistant Headmistress and keeper of records in the library. Zander teaches defensive spells, and our dragon/dog, Autumn, is always close by. Mora traveled with Zander and me to the Elfish Village when Merlin first fell from grace. The people welcomed their queen and were very pleased to have her home. However, after about a month of being there, she slipped out of the back gate as she grew tired of being treated like an idol. Every time she opened her cottage door, the elves cheered and started celebrating.

Three years ago, Zander, Mora, and I donated a substantial amount of money as an endowment to The Arcane Ignatius Institute at the University of Arcane and Mundane Studies, where there is an entire building dedicated to college studies in the Arcane arts, anthropology of magical and Arcane, history, and anything Arcane-related. Bethany serves as the director of the research center on Arcane, and Phineas teaches in the Arcane agricultural program there. They are expecting their first child in about three months. The institute serves as the only place of higher education where Mundane and Arcane study together. Zander and I split our time between our country manor estate in Ireland, the Elf village in the mountains, and here at the school.

Zander and I are excited as the days grow closer as our last-born, Rusty, should be arriving anytime now. Ari is in the fifth grade, Theo is in third grade, and Hope is now in first grade. And, of course, there is dear Vivian, who already, at the age of three, is a firecracker. The children love being at school together, but as Ethan and I have discovered, it is hard to have them all together as their magic can act in bizarre ways, particularly during tantrums and meltdowns. Nevertheless, I am happy to be close here at the school. Let's just say that I have had to deal with a few rogue spells here and there that Ari, Matthew, or Theo have decided to cast on either their teachers, peers, or some object in the school.

While magic is a fascinating tool, I have also come to learn of its many mysteries. Over ten years ago, my brothers and I learned of our true magical heritage and fought the darkness to save the Arcane. Throughout our journeys, we have met some extraordinary individuals, but one still eludes all of us, Noel, an interesting Arcane of genuinely extraordinary power. His magic is... well, how do I put it? As bizarre as time itself. While Zander and I know that Noel and his sister, Willow, are both elves, there is no reference to them in any of the texts. Zander was very curious about Noel. Several years ago, he and his mother time jumped twenty-five and then forty years into the future. Both returned very perplexed as they were unable to find any reference to Noel. Yet, we know Noel is powerful, so powerful, in fact, that he makes the combined magic of Oliver, Ethan, and myself look like a cheap stage trick.

Further, we know Noel's sister, Willow, is an elemental witch, one of the most powerful ever seen. Most recently, we have come to learn of two others who are traveling through time with him. One is an Arcane by the name of Minnie, who we are still trying to figure out. It has been of interest how she fights. Her fighting style is similar to that of Cedric. But, of course, he has made no comment on the matter. Zander and Mora note that her *magic comes across like that of a Noble. Then, there is an elf, named Isabella, who fights just like Vivian did ten years ago. The more intriguing thing about all four is that they fight with both magic and technology. Finally, Noel has robots, almost like nano-bots, that can do anything he commands them to do. All of us are fascinated because, when least expected, one or all of them will arrive to help fight the darkness.*

So, for now, I must go, Zander is having lunch with us, and it appears that dear Vivian has just discovered how to transfigure her teddy bear.

~Rose

I pick up Vivian and wave my hand as a tray flies behind me, and the diary closes. Then, with one quick motion, I change the dump truck back into Vivian's teddy bear. Vivian becomes very excited to see her toy back to normal.

In the distance, the wind howls as the school, shielded by magic, sits on the side of the hill overlooking a small, bustling village. The school looks as if it is rising out of the side of the mountain. In the distance, brooms with wizards and witches speed by, dragons graze in the field, while Centaur's hooves are heard thundering over the land. The mermaid's songs are particularly powerful this day as children can be seen picnicking on the hillside. Rising over the land is the highest tower of the castle. The double doors of a central balcony fly open, and, with Vivian in my arms, I stroll out, the tray of food floating behind us. As we sit down, the tray lowers onto the side table, and food magically appears. A loud pop echoes over the balcony as Zander reappears.

I kiss Zander on the cheek as Vivian climbs up into his lap, clapping with excitement. We begin to eat when, suddenly, a scream echoes from below, ringing out over the land as dark shadows rise out of the ground, attacking the students. I grab Vivian from Zander and run indoors as Zander jumps over the balcony railing, and flies twenty stories down the side of the castle, landing on his feet, sword in hand, and striking out at the dark creatures.

Suddenly, Ethan emerges out of the ground and casts a lightfield around the grounds, protecting the students as Zander strikes multiple dark creatures. A phoenix flies overhead as Ethan throws an orb into the air in one quick motion, then catching it again. The orb takes off down the side of the hill toward the village. As Ethan turns to open a portal, multiple dark shadows fly backward away from him and Zander as I reappear through the door at the tower's base. My eyes are glowing silver as light explodes from my hands, throwing the darkness back and causing them to scream as they explode. Raising them off their feet, I tear the dark shadows apart with my magic and throw their dead, lifeless bodies out of the way.

The darkness charges as I launch an orb in the air. Two beings of solid light appear, casting a magic lightfield around the school and fighting off the darkness. Then, spinning my hands, I thrust my magic into the ground as a shockwave causes light columns to ignite from the ground around the courtyard, bringing the darkness to their knees as they rapidly, in waves, explode.

The two defend the school as I shield several first graders, ordering them to follow the staff and faculty inside to safety. Within seconds of casting the shield to protect the students, a roar causes the air to vibrate as Autumn lands, grabbing one of the dark shadows by its head, shaking it, snapping its neck, and throwing it into the air, over the walkway, and down the hill. Belinda, rearing back, lands, crushing three dark shadows while bellowing fire at five more.

In one quick motion, spinning my hands in front of myself, I seal the grand entry doors to the courtyard and raise a lightfield, protecting the entry to the school. The darkness strikes the lightfield, trying to reach the students. A pop echoes over the land and a bright ball of light emerges. Then, the area is illuminated as Destiny walks up with orbs flying around her. The group looks at one another as they hear the roar of three lions coming from the main bridge leading into the school. Disappearing from the back of the school, the group reappears in front as the dark army marches towards the bridge.

I raise my hands in the air and turn toward the school, casting a second lightfield to seal the school. Autumn and Belinda take to the air above the bridge as another loud pop occurs. Father, Mother, Oliver, and Olivia appear behind Leo, Lucy, and Leaf, who are standing on the bridge, ready to attack. Olivia turns and bolts for the school, picking up students along the way, hustling them into the school to safety.

My mother looks back at me, nodding as I lower my hands to my sides and take to the air.

Summoning light around me and the group, I spin my hands, separating the bridge from the land and halting the army that is advancing on the school. As the bridge separates from the land and floats into the air, the leader of the dark army raises their hand, halting the group. Then, tilting their head, they look at the edge of the cliff, and, with a snap of their fingers, re-creates the bridge out of pure darkness.

"Attack," the leader yells as the dark army lowers their spears and begins to charge over the bridge. Suddenly, a pillar of light hits the bridge and out steps Mora. Her arrival causes the dark army to hit an invisible barrier and disappear on the spot. With one wave of her hand, the dark army disappears, the bridge created of dark magic is gone, and the leader of the dark army lies dead on the ground. Mora disappears and reappears at the spot where the fallen dark general lay. At her side, Zander kneels and pulls back the hood of the general. When Mora looks down, her eyes widen as she shakes her head. Ethan, Oliver, and I, appear next to Zander as Mother and Father watch from the bridge.

"Mom, this is not good," Zander notes, leaning back so his mother can see.

"Bartholomew. I suspected the darkness had gained power and is trying to return, but I did not expect it to be this bad. The Council of Dark is trying to regain their following," Mora states, looking at the dark general.

Zander pulls his wand, points it at the dark general as the body bursts into flames. Mora turns on the spot, snaps her fingers, and the bridge reappears.

"Ethan, call the faculty together immediately. Zander, activate any of the remaining incantations around the school and the grounds, Rose..." Mora orders.

"Yes, Head Mistress!" I reply.

"My child, how many times...." Mora begins to ask as I nod my head towards a group of students who are looking around at the end of the bridge.

"Children, inside now. Please hurry. It is not safe," Mora instructs.

"Thoughts?" Mora inquires of me as my mother approaches.

"Yes, I have many thoughts about this, Mora. But give me a minute. Hi, Mom. I hope you and Dad are not missing anything important," I remark.

"No, I was falling asleep listening to several of the ambassadors droning on. Your father, well... you know him, fascinated by Mundane issues. For me, it is very boring. For him, he loves every minute," Nadia replies, motioning over her shoulder as Kelvin follows Oliver, asking him if he can get his phone to work.

"First, we never should have bought him that thing. Second, how did you know we needed help?" I begin to ask when I notice that my mother is wearing her bracelet.

"Never mind your bracelet. But Mom and headmistress, did you not find it bizarre that the darkness attacked at midday, during the afternoon sun? They hate the sun and the light," I inquire.

"Yes, they have become bold and daring. But why now? What do they want?"

"This is what I believe they might be after," Oliver remarks, walking up and lowering an old beat-up steamer trunk from his shoulder onto the walkway.

I move quickly and wave my hand over the lock as it flies open.

"Oh, most definitely, they would want this particular artifact. Get it inside and into the library immediately. Tell the students not to touch it and to leave it be. I will deal with it personally."

"So, the artifact drew the attention of the darkness. I am afraid as we continue to unpack Merlin's dark past, we may have some other challenges on our hands."

Now, if there is one thing Mora hates more than Merlin, it is having to clean up his mess. One of the worst messes we have had to clean up was a horrible sneer orb that was uncovered. The thing's screams were so loud it was ear piercing. It took Zander, Ethan, Oliver, Sebastian, Bethany, Dad, Mom, and I to subdue the thing. As a result, all of our ears were ringing for over two weeks.

As we all head inside to prepare the school for the changes to come, Mora and I get the students settled and review the new protection rules to ensure their safety. Then, I head to the library to handle the relic that has arrived.

Chapter 2
The Line-Up

You are probably wondering about that trunk taken to the library. But, before we get there, let me tell you about the school. We have come to discover and create new ways of living for ourselves. You have heard many of my stories before; of course, but do you remember the night young Mora and her mother escaped from the siege of the council chambers? They arrived on the hillside and created a village and school, and it, within seconds, stood in ruins. Welcome to the school restored.

So, the School of Arcane Magical Teaching is where those who are magical or those showing magical promise attend. The school is not only for the Arcane magical but for any Arcane of mystical heritage as this is a safe place for them. Situated in the English countryside, Arcane children from all over the world attend school here. However, to most Mundane, the school appears to be in ruins.

The school serves as a refuge. This is the first year in ten years of the school's existence when we have had a diverse Mundane and Arcane student body. The Mundane students who attend the school have demonstrated some Arcane power or are descended from one of the Arcane magical or Arcane mystical bloodlines. Yes, I know it is weird to understand that some Mundane children have Arcane parents and vice versa.

Our school halls are filled with students from five to eighteen years of age and all different levels of magical ability or mystical heritage. My mother-in-law, Mora, as I noted before, is the head of the school. Talk about a divine being. She is very patient and helps each student figure out who they are, whether magical, mystical, or not, something I wish my brothers and I had had growing up.

The three of us provide a different perspective to the school community because we grew up among the Mundane and bring that experience to what we do as Arcane. Five years after our school reopened, the Divine Priory of Time fell to the darkness. As a result, we relocated Father Francisco and his staff to the school grounds, to the very spot on the cliff, overlooking the sea, where the pale-skinned, red-haired woman in my dreams was unsuccessfully attempting to summon water to her.

The cliffs provide protection for the school being located on higher ground. At the bottom of the cliff is a valley with a river running through it. Many times, different mystical beasts can be seen down there grazing. The school's location is also ideal as it is near the village, which allows the council to have access to the school and the students and staff of the school often frequent the village. The hillside also provides a reasonable training ground where our young students learn how to manage various terrains, running, levitating, flying their brooms, or navigating the woods.

Now, enough about that. Let me introduce you to the critical faculty of our school. Over the past ten years, Mora has hand-picked an exceptional faculty that represents the times and supports the students' growth. We are a large school, but first, let me tell you about the core heads of each department or grade level.

৵

First off, there is my dear husband, Zander. He teaches one of the most popular classes, defensive spells. Now, every student wants to take this particular class as they hear the buzz of excitement about the various things being taught. They learn to control magic in defensive approaches and use various items in defense. Because of Zander's teachings, many students have learned to channel their magic ability against the darkness.

Zander also teaches *elfudo*, a fascinating form of martial arts. The elves have developed this combative, defensive approach to fighting that combines magical teachings, the use of magic, martial arts, and the ability of the user to channel magic into weapons. It is this same form of magic that I understand is what Vivian and Rusty used in battles when they helped us ten years ago. Zander and Mora note that it is an intense magical defense used by elves, vampires, and fairies.

Many of the students, when they first come to the academy, are afraid of their magic, but Zander makes learning fun. Although he is strict, the students quickly become comfortable with their magical abilities. Zander also serves as the head of our secondary division and many of the older students have come to respect the uses of Ignatius and Phoenix because of him. Zander only teaches part-time as he divides his time between his roles in the Aelfdene village and at the school.

৵

One of the students' other favorite teachers is one of my older twin brothers, Ethan. Dear brother Ethan teaches science for the Arcane. First, the students learn the basics of scientific principles, such as biology, physics, chemistry, environmental magic, and general science. Then, these subjects are expanded with magical understanding. On several occasions, the school has had to be evacuated because of some alchemy explosion in the science wing. Through all of that, Ethan maintains his composure and has become my go-to person for anything potions-related. Ethan has been known to mix some mean potions and is, genuinely, the potions master of the family.

❧

Then, there is Lady Marybelle. She teaches English and reading and is the one teacher who frequents my library more than any other. She has a way of making literature come to life, literally. Our library holds some of the most incredible bodies of literature, and, until Lady Marybelle, I never thought that I would have to hide specific stories.

Marybelle is an Arcane Witch of a long bloodline and a family of great magic and the texts in her class come to life, and her students have spoken with Shakespeare, Jane Austen, Walt Whitman, and even Ernest Hemingway, but some texts could have been far too dangerous for the students. So, for the students' safety, I have had to decide to not allow some specific texts to be readily available.

By the time Marybelle was fourteen, she had already read most of the classics and could animate any story. Her skills prove handy when distracting her enemies, as any book becomes a weapon by coming alive around her. She can command great armies at her fingertips or drown darkness in a flash flood of water coming from the texts. I have learned not to leave any texts lying around that cover the history of the Arcane as I am afraid that they could become real in the moment. Marybelle serves as the head of the lower grades at the school and is the Head of Arts and Humanities.

❧

The next teacher does not need any sort of an introduction. Professor Destiny, the one and only, our charming aunt, is always close by watching. She can be as weird as she wants and fits right in among the faculty. Clapping her hands together and the shutters slamming shut no longer causes alarm as it did when we were young, and she was our teacher. Also, her teaching of the history of the mystical arts holds a place of respect here at the school. I enjoy having her around as her knowledge, just like that of our Mom, is exceptional when it comes to the relics and texts of the Arcane.

On another note, Aunt Destiny still resides in the home my brothers and I grew up in, and it has become more of a family vacation home than anything. Mom and Dad use it regularly when staying in the United States. Aunt Destiny also married Uncle Wade about a year ago. Aunt Destiny serves as the Head of history education for all grade levels. Many of the students have come to love her, and she serves as the advisor to the History Club.

৵

Then, there is Prof. Giggle. Do not let Prof. Giggle's name throw you off. He is one of the eldest living dwarfs, and he won't let you forget it. He teaches economic education and is far from happy or giggly. Actually, he is the opposite. He was so grumpy one day that the students were hiding in the bathroom crying. While his teaching methods are spot-on for economics, he has a horrible classroom manner. Finally, he must constantly be reminded that we do not feed the children to the dragons.

I will never forget Mora's reaction two years ago, when a huge commotion broke out in the hallway. An eighth grader decided to utilize a multiplication spell to make some extra gold. Now, if you know anything about dwarfs, they are small in build but will fight to protect every last penny in the room. They believe all money is theirs. Prof. Giggle got so angry at the eighth grader that he hoisted the student over his head and marched down the hall, calling for Autumn or any of the other dragons he might find who would eat the child. Mora had to intervene and remind him that we do not feed the children to mystical creatures. Of course, you try explaining this to a grumpy dwarf, and you will understand why we all hate having to do it.

Mr. Bruin is Prof. Giggles' best friend. He is my assistant in the library, who has a stern wit about him and makes sure everything runs smoothly. However, being the opposite of his best friend, he is very gentle until you make him angry. Then he has a temper. His organizational skills are so complex that many do not like to work with him, but he knows where every text is located in the library.

৵

How do you scare the students and teach them about living in the dark? Give up? Let me introduce Mr. Wolf. He is a charming gentleman. No one knows how old he is. He is half-vampire and half-human. He teaches physical education. So charming, the students love him except the lower-grade students when they are crying over the class being held in the dark. Still, mostly, the students find him funny.

Mora and Mr. Wolf have had their moments. First, Mora has to remind him that it is cruel to hang a student upside down. Next, he protests that they should learn to sleep like vampires. Then, Mora reminds him that the children are not vampires. Now, here comes the fun part. How do you get under Mr. Wolf's skin? Have Cedric show up. Mr. Wolf has been heard grumbling every time Cedric comes around as Cedric is a full-blooded vampire and is quicker, stronger, and much more knowledgeable about everything.

Mr. Wolf works with Mr. Terran, a 6'8" centaur who handles sports for the students and has been known to bring in help from other mystical creatures. For the last three years, swimming has been a big hit with the students as he brings in mermaids to teach the students how to swim. The riding of mystical beasts, however, does not always go as well. The griffins do not take well to the students on their backs. Since Mr. Wolf and Mr. Terran have been life-long friends, Mora and I decided to make them co-Heads of the athletics department.

Mr. Terran, while sweet, has had his moments with Ms. Hoot, a shapeshifter who came highly recommended by Lord Leo and who taught Leaf, Leo's son, when he was a boy. Ms. Hoot, many believe, is as old as Belinda and Mora. A sweet lady, but do not let her sweetness fool you. In battle, she is one of the meanest Arcane around. You may guess, from her name, that she is an owl who shapeshifts into a short 4'1" woman with giant eyes. She teaches the students about mystical creatures and curates a zoo of unique magical creatures in the school's backyard. Often, you will find an Arcane creature roaming the halls with her.

On numerous occasions, she has been known to get into arguments with Mr. Terran about the amount of noise coming out of his class. You see, her classes are held in the evening, and she sleeps during the day. Unfortunately, his sports field backs up right next to her place, and you can imagine the conflict that has arisen. Mora has offered to relocate Ms. Hoot to more suitable quarters, but our Creatures Mistress has refused.

Then, there is Ms. Adwin, the Art and Choral Mistress, who believes that these are the only two subjects worth teaching. Ms. Adwin is much like Lady Marybelle in that she has been known to charm a painting or two, bringing them to life. Two years ago, the music program did the magical rendition of Romeo and Juliet. Instead of directing the production herself, she brought Shakespeare to life and had him direct the play. He constantly rambled on about how he cannot work with the students who hate musical theater and how the students spent more time hiding things from Sir Shakespeare than he was able to spend teaching them anything.

I remember one ninth grader telling me that he found Sir Shakespeare most helpful in honing his defensive spells. Ms. Adwin is a world-renowned artist, but it is unclear what she actually is. Some believe she's an elf, some believe she's a fairy, many of the students believe she is a vampire, still others think she is just plain crazy. Ms. Adwin has a unique magical power. Much like Lady Marybelle, she can bring paintings to life, she has a way to… well, how do I put this? She can control them like Lady Marybelle does with books. One day, the darkness attacked her and the students while they were on a field trip. The students came back drenched when she brought an ocean painting to life and while using the waves to wash away the darkness, failed to control them, thereby getting the students wet too. The students joke that if the darkness attacks, one can simply run through the school, throwing paintings at her, and they will come to life.

૭૦

One of my favorite teachers, Ms. Tulip, is a garden fairy who teaches the basics of earth magic, a friendly environment, and the power of the elements. The students all fight to go to her class. She is known for taking them to the fairy village. The students particularly love the shrinking magic that makes them small. Like Phineas, she is one of a few fairies who can take on a full size and hide her wings. If you met her in the hallways of the academy, you might easily mistake her for a student. Mora considers Ms. Tulip to be one of the critical faculty in terms of defending the school. When pushed, Ms. Tulip can enhance the grounds, trees, flowers, anything natural, around the school. And then, watch out. She has become a dear friend, and when I need help, she is always there. With a quick whistle, the fairies appear around her and my children, Ari, Theo, Hope, and Vivian have multiple babysitters. Ethan and Sebastian have also been known to call upon her and the fairies to babysit my dear nephew Matthew.

૭૦

Last but not least, everyone's favorite staff member—actually, no, she is far from anyone's favorite—Lady O is a somewhat helpful member of the staff, a witch who oversees nourishment for the students. An old friend of Mora's, she is not liked by the staff who swear she is trying to poison the students and themselves. She is very unconventional in her cooking. For example, the second graders are still scared of her eyeball soup, mainly when it screams at the students, "I can see you."

૭૦

How silly of me. I almost forgot one person, myself. I serve as Assistant Headmistress of the school, overseeing all grades. I also serve as the Chief Librarian and hold all of the knowledge of the Arcane. Our library is one of the most comprehensive magical libraries outside of the Sprite Library in the Aelfdene village.

While our library holds many magical texts, there are still many we are gathering, not to mention a number of missing artifacts. One of our biggest concerns is the number of missing elfish and other Arcane artifacts and relics.

We have discovered that Merlin hid these items in his attempt to gain absolute power. While there is concern about all of the relics and artifacts that remain unaccounted for, one of the more significant concerns is the "Curpendulums of Power."

What are the Curpendulums of Power, you ask? Easy, they are the fifteen magical texts that were hidden throughout the world by Noble Elder and Elder Yule. They are the fifteen Curpendulums of absolute magic that govern all magical power and its interaction with all life. Right now, we know of the existence of only one of the Curpendulums of Power. Morgana's grimoire of the dark, that wonderful, and yet dreadful, Curpendulum is one of the fifteen. Unfortunately, though, we do not know where the other fourteen are at this time. We have some speculation, but nothing is confirmed.

What is fascinating is how we discovered the secret of the Curpendulums. In the Arcane language, "Curpendulum" means "balance." Merlin spoke of the balance of magic throughout much of his writing. We all thought that Merlin used the term "Curpendulum" to refer to the pocket watch that controls time, but he did not.

Do you remember that I told you time is bizarre? Shall we take a trip? I promise there will be no bodies to climb over or the need for a cloak to stay warm, but I do have to say that I hope you are not afraid of heights. Follow me and try not to wrinkle the scroll that I have rolled out. To follow me, step carefully into the steps I take. And away we go.

Oh dear, where is that torch? Oh fiddle. Here we go. If you look at the paintings on this wall… Wait, this won't do. Hang on as I light the room better. With that, five orbs fly into the air and light the cave. This cave was discovered three years ago by Bethany and the fairies on a journey looking for some of Merlin's artifacts. When she stumbled over this cave, she immediately summoned us, and we all came as fast as our magic could bring us. On these walls are the stories of the Divine, the celestial beings who gave magic to the earth.

We know that after the Celestials appointed the Grand Council of Light, several members got upset with the council's beliefs. They separated and created the Grand Council of Darkness. And that is where the battle for light and darkness began.

The Nobles, as they were called, the five elders of the council, two of which are Mora's grandparents, cast a magical spell so potent that it opened a single portal, captured the 15 Curpendulums in the care of the council, and scattered them throughout the world. These five Nobles knew if the darkness found the 15 Curpendulums, the wielders of this magic power would be unstoppable.

At this time, not knowing where all of the 15 Curpendulums could, and could not, be is the challenge and the concern for us. The Curpendulums are concerning to Oliver, Ethan, and I because if these items were to be found and the people who find them do not know what they have stumbled upon or of how to deal with them, it could put the entire world in danger.

We learned that we have already found one of the more dangerous of the Curpendulums, the *Grimoire of the Dead*. I have a hunch that another one may be in our control, but I cannot prove it. One of the most significant challenges, as I have told you many times, is how time can act bizarrely.

At the very moment that the 15 Curpendulums were split, they were erased from time, protected, and all their knowledge was blocked from existence. No one has been able to find the vision of that moment in time, although, now and then, a clue turns up here and there.

What has become the focus in all of this is a conversation for another time. We have heard of a prophecy of a single Mundane so powerful that they alone hold the key to unlock all 15 Curpendulums. But, unfortunately, while we have searched the texts, and Lady Divinity has utilized her powers of divination, no one has found any information about who this Mundane is.

My brothers, Zander, Sebastian, and I agree that finding and protecting the Curpendulums is the first order of business. Then, locating this Mundane, who is discussed in the legends, is second. Why, you may ask, protect the Curpendulums and not the Mundane first? From my research, reading, and jumping in and out of time, and from the writings of the cave, I have discovered that the Mundane, who holds this knowledge and power, has not been born yet. Also, since my family controls the cave, the darkness does not know of this person, let alone being able to decipher the writing on the cave wall.

Watch your step, the cave is beginning to spin. We're going to move again.

&

Well, look at this. We have finally reached the library on our journey through the school. I warn you that our library is continuously busy: texts are constantly whistling, talking, and acting up. My assistants, the dwarfs, tend to the texts and do not mind their noise. One warning, however, do not cross the line behind the main desk, which has become a "battlement" because it holds many of the protected texts and artifacts. Oh, and unless you want to be babbling for the next fifty years and skipping around believing you are a five-year-old schoolgirl, do not go back there unless I have lowered the battlements field.

Chapter 3
The Chest of Nightmares

If time acting up isn't bad enough, there is worse—the artifacts of Merlin. We will take time acting bizarrely and misbehaving any day of the week over Merlin's nasty artifacts. Unfortunately, some must be destroyed because of the pure danger they pose.

"Ethan and Sebastian, please seal the doors. Oliver, close the shutters. Zander, please cast the seal of protection."

Walking to the far side of the circle where a podium rises out of the ground, Rose taps it three times and her magic grimoire appears. The grimoire has grown significantly, as Rose has learned and written more every day. Unfortunately, the grimoire has become so heavy that, now, she has to leave it on a pedestal.

Once the circle of protection is in place, and the library is sealed, Rose says, "Let's see what this nasty artifact is about."

With a simple wave of her hand, the lock on an ornate, wooden, steamer trunk pops, and the lid flies open. Then, waving her hands in a circular motion, Rose levitates the black crystal orb out of the box.

"Do not touch it for any reason. Oliver, be ready to light it up if it makes any aggressive moves toward us. Ethan, can you please give me a purification potion, preferably, something with a field of protection to contain the darkness."

Ethan has learned to concoct some powerful potions that contain various forms of protections, ranging from some that are fairly mild to some that are extremely strong. For the most part, those have become the most useful when dealing with the darkness.

Rose walks cautiously towards the orb, examines it, pours the purification potion over it, and steps back. The orb flies up, hits the containment field, and screams. Lightning shoots all over the room, and the darkness rises out of the crystal ball as Sebastian, Oliver, Ethan, and Zander move against it, sealing it in a new orb. Opening a portal, they cast it to the Neverlands.

But before they can cast it out, the creature breaks the orb containing it and advances toward Rose. Not pleased, Rose summons a lightfield around it. When it touches the field, it creates a prison and shrinks to the size of a small mirror. Rose picks up the mirror, walks to the portal, and throws it through as the portal slams shut. The orb remains, floating in the air. Circling it, Rose again examines the condition of the orb. Perfect. Not a mark! Now, orbs, much like time, behave bizarrely, and this one is no exception.

Orbs serve several purposes. They act as vessels to contain magical beings or creatures. They hold visions. They are used for viewing the past, present, or future. Or they can act as conduits of power to transfer power from one individual to another. They can also help enhance any spell. In the case of this one, it appears to be a vision orb.

"Shall we?" Oliver asks.

"No, Rose! You are staying here. The four of us will handle this."

"Zander, dear, I love you, but I am going."

"Rose, you are in no physical condition to go with us. You are due to have our baby any time. We do not need to be in a vision when you go into labor."

"Here is the funny part, dear. In contrast to the four of you, who have learned to control only various aspects of time, I am still the only one, maybe next to Ari, who can stop the visions altogether and rewind them."

"Problem solved then. Rose, what time is it?" Zander inquires.

"Alezander. No! You are not pulling Ari out of class. Not happening and not allowed," Rose snaps.

Before the conversation can continue, Rose grabs the orb.

"Zander, I know that you hate it when I do something like this. You always feel that way when I choose not to heed your safety warnings," Rose says as the five are pulled into the vision.

"Typical! More fog. This is getting old. Gentlemen, hold on to your wands. We have no clue where we are landing." With a quick wave of Rose's hand, the fog disappears.

Being pregnant never helps time jumping, particularly with the difficult landing and heightened senses.

"Gross, what is that smell?" Ethan asks, looking around at the others for answers.

"Hun, it appears it is rotten sewage," Sebastian notes.

"Rose and Zander, where and when are we?" Oliver asks.

"It appears we are in what looks like medieval England," Zander explains.

"Are you sure?"

"Yes, Rose, this must be medieval England because that castle up on the hill is Camelot. I recommend holding tight to your weapons. I am curious what this is about."

Quietly, we walk down the road, examining the village for any clues of magic gone awry or time acting bizarre. But things are quiet. Nothing seems to be amiss, no battles, nothing. But, of course, we all think this too soon. In the distance, we notice a cloaked figure who stops staring at where the five of us are standing and takes off running in the opposite direction.

"What is that about?" Oliver asks.

"I was wondering the same thing," Zander notes as he disappears and reappears, standing in front of the cloaked figure. Of course, our visions are often not entirely accurate as we watch things play out. However, that is not the case in this particular vision. The cloaked individual projects an elfish arm blade out from under their cloak sleeve and into his right hand as they attempt to strike Zander. Raising his arm, the blade strikes Zander's gauntlet. The blade flies back as the individual uses their other hand to control the blade. As the individual attempts to strike for a second time, Ethan catches the elf blade with the blade of Excalibur. The cloaked figure backs up and looks at Oliver, Sebastian, and Rose, as we point our wands. Then, the individual reaches for their hood and lowers it.

"May I ask you to lower your wands, please?" an all too familiar voice asks.

"Russell Ambrose Alezander Elderchild Ignatius. What are you doing here?"

"Hi, Dad. Sorry I did not know if you were real or the vision playing a wicked game," Rusty explains.

"Well, Sis, you called it. Time is really acting bizarre this time," Oliver states, half laughing.

"Uncle Oliver, I was about to say the same thing."

"Look, we can all catch up in a few minutes, but in about 30 seconds, the witch up the street is going to realize that her grimoire is missing, and we are going to have an all-out battle. So, please excuse me for a minute."

With that, Rusty raises his hand, and a pocket watch appears as he freezes time.

"I'm curious. If you five are standing here, then you must have found the dark moon orb. A nasty dark creature came out of it. Did you cast it to the Neverlands?"

"Of course, Rusty," Rose replies, looking perplexed.

"And Mom, all five of you did this at the library at the school?" Rusty inquires.

"Yes. Why wouldn't we?" Rose questions in a stern tone.

"Uh oh! Mom, you need to end this vision right now and get back to the library. Trust me, and do not let go of your wands," Rusty says, pulling his wand and looking concerned.

If there is one thing that Rose hates more than anything, it is taking orders. While she rarely takes orders from anyone, she has learned that if time is acting bizarre and she runs into older versions of one of her children, she listens.

With one quick movement of Rose's hand, they reappear in the library to find a dark griffin surrounded by the darkness attacking the dwarfs who have been able to contain the darkness to the library. At the heart of the battle, stand Matthew and Ari, magic spinning around them as a cloud of solid spinning light floats above them.

In the middle of the library stands the figure known to the group as Noel. His hands are spinning over his head as he holds the darkness at bay, shielding Ari, Matthew, and the dwarfs.

"Told you guys," Rusty smirks.

"Mom, these things are wicked, but this dark griffin is worse," Ari notes.

"Ari, you and Matthew, hold that shield. Mr. Bruin, protect the dwarfs," Rose commands.

The easiest way to piss Rose off is to be a dark creature coming after her nephew or children. Rose takes to the air, her eyes glowing, just as Zander reaches Ari and Matthew and pulls them away from the center of the floor. He quickly ducks under a table and covers both of their heads as Oliver and Ethan also take to the air, their eyes glowing. As the three raise their hands, beams of lights connect them, creating a pentagram around the creature. Books, texts, and manuscripts fly everywhere as Rusty spins his hands.

In the middle of this is Noel, wand in hand. As he spins it in front of him, a vortex opens. He walks over the open vortex as if strolling on air. Then, stowing his wand, he jumps into the air, flips, and dives into the vortex, grabbing the griffin by his back legs and pulling him into the vortex with him.

"Close the vortex, quickly," Noel directs as he disappears.

Rose, Ethan, and Oliver lower their hands toward their sides, helping to cast the dark griffin further into the pit.

Sebastian and Zander emerge, wands drawn as they spin lightfields around the space, and everything begins to return to normal until, once again, the griffin starts to ascend out of the vortex pit. The doors of the library blow in as dark creatures explode. Red orbs spin through the space, striking down multiple dark creatures simultaneously. Eventually, Nadia appears, walking through the door, red orbs flying around her. As she pulls her hands apart, the darkness explodes. She grabs the vortex like a rug, snaps it out, flattening it, and then throws an orb of bright light into the air. As it catches the vortex, it seals it and then, explodes—the wing of the dark griffin severed and landing on the floor.

"Cool! Ari, check it out!"

"Matthew, so help me, you will be grounded if you touch that thing."

"Oh man! Dad, you're no fun. I wanted to keep it as a souvenir. It's not every day that I get to see you guys take on the dark. Grandma is wicked."

Displeased with Matthew, Nadia crosses her arms, taps her foot, and scowls at him. "Wicked? Wicked?! First, wicked is such a gross term for a proper wizard to be using, and second, magic is not a toy. For an Arcane of your power, touching any part of the darkness like that could result in you being transformed and becoming dark yourself. Matthew, have you not paid attention to defensive magic? And why is Ari here?"

"Grandma, he called for help."

"Ari, is this true?"

"Yes, Mom. I came to the library looking for you, I forgot…"

"…Your lunch. And you stumbled upon that thing. Ari, dear, there is no reason to be embarrassed about forgetting your lunch but, please, tell one of your teachers or staff members to contact me next time."

"I understand, Mom, but if it were not for Mr. Bruin, the library would have been consumed."

"The dwarfs were awesome against the darkness."

"They fight like the…."

"Sorry, Mr. Bruin, I almost said it."

"Young Ari, you can say it just this one time," Mr. Bruin noted with a half-smile.

"You fight like the elves!"

The group laughed, as the dwarfs standing in the library muttered quietly to themselves.

"Mr. Bruin has, and always will, protect this library. These dwarfs who work in the library are the ones not driven by gold but, rather, by their thirst for knowledge. To them, that is their gold," Rose remarks, looking at Matthew and Ari.

"My Lady, the books *are* gold to us, and we are glad that we were here to protect young Ari and Matthew," Mr. Bruin states.

"And Matthew, may I inquire how you got here from class?"

"Dad, it was Ari."

"Hey, don't blame me."

"You were the one who sent out the shockwave of light. I felt it and came running."

"So, you left class? Matthew!" Sebastian snaps.

"Papa, I did not mean to. Ari needed help, and I did not know what was going on."

"Sebastian, it is okay. I am glad Matthew was here to help Ari and the dwarfs," Rose explains, trying to calm Sebastian as he and Ethan give her a stern look that indicates that she should stop butting in.

"Now, boys, both of you get back to class. Also, you both have detention after school. Report to Ms. Hoot!"

The boys nod and walk toward the door when Ari turns.

"Mom, that elf over there, is that…?" Ari begins to inquire when he is interrupted.

"Ari Ignatius, head off to class. Now!" Zander snaps as he puts the doors back on their hinges and re-attaches them to the archway.

"Zander, you cannot blame him for wanting to know."

"Yes, and now that they are gone, 'Are you kidding me?' You brought me back? Are you serious?" Rusty inquires.

"Rusty, did you think that your father, uncles, and I would stumble upon you in a vision, and then, just leave you there so that you can time jump back to whatever time you came from without getting answers first? I think not."

"Grandma, please talk some sense into her."

"Rusty, she is your mother. And no, I have learned when my daughter speaks, I do not challenge her, particularly when she is pregnant and at high power," Nadia replies, patting him on the shoulder in a gesture of good luck

"Start talking, kid! You were in the vision. Yes, we know of the catastrophic implications this has. Yeah, yeah. Now, talk," Zander demands.

"Zander, dear, don't be so hard on him. This is Rusty," Rose says, smiling and turning to Rusty.

"Thanks, Mom," Rusty replies with a smile.

"Russell Ambrose Alezander Elderchild Ignatius, explain yourself," Rose barks.

"'Don't be hard,' she says, and yet, she just snapped at the poor kid," Oliver laughs, nudging Ethan as Rose glares at them.

"Mom, let me ask you this? How do you make an entire room go quiet?"

"Rusty, this is not a game!"

"Give up?" Rusty inquires.

"Russell, what is that?" Rose asks, her eyes narrowing as she sees the grimoire in Rusty's hand.

"By the look of curiosity on your faces, I see that I have your attention," Rusty laughs, holding up the book.

"Can someone explain, please? How is a grimoire going to make a room go quiet?" Ethan asks, holding up his hands, confused.

"That is the *Grimoire of Antiquity*. It is older than Zander, and I combined," Nadia notes, moving forward and examining the grimoire in Rusty's hands.

"That grimoire is said to hold the most ancient of all knowledge of the magical, from before the time that the term Arcane was ever utilized," Zander explains.

"Rusty, would you care to explain why you sought this grimoire?" Rose asks.

"Well, Mom, I was hoping that you and Dad might be able to tell me that."

"Can I see it?" Zander asks, holding out his hand.

"Err, No. Mom was clear that if I found the grimoire, I was to come straight home. I am going to be in so much trouble."

"Russell, one thing I have learned is that if a grimoire from the past or future comes here and we acquire it, the timeline alters accordingly."

"Meaning when your father and I read that grimoire, it will be knowledge we will have in the future and can use to prevent time from acting bizarre," Rose explains.

"I have to object. That is not how time works," Rusty says, being cocky.

"And you would know how time works, Rusty?" Zander asks, crossing his arm and tapping his foot.

"No. No one knows, not even your mother, my grandmother, Mora. But holy smokes! Wait, what time is it? I have to get back," Rusty says, glancing at his watch.

"Not a problem, Rusty. It was a pleasure seeing you, dear. Now, hold on," Rose says, opening a portal and pushing him into it.

"Wait…" But before Rusty can finish speaking, Rose sends him back to his time.

"Sis, was it necessary to keep the grimoire?"

"Oliver, you heard him say that he is going to get into trouble. Besides, it is an ancient grimoire, and I am keeping it."

"Rose, do we dare read it? Or do we not?" Ethan asks.

"We can read it. But we should skim it to see what the contents are, in order to determine why my future self would have sent Rusty to find this grimoire," Rose suggests.

Aside from the concerned looks she is getting from her mother and Zander, the one thing that Rose is really not too fond of is when her mother, Nadia, tries to take control of an artifact or a piece of text because she is concerned about its power and the danger that entails.

"Rose, what is it?" Ethan and Oliver ask in unison when, after looking at the inside cover of the grimoire, Rose freezes.

"This grimoire has a handwritten name on the cover."

"Whose?" Nadia inquires, moving toward Rose to take a closer look.

Minda

"And it is written in beautiful, elegant handwriting."

"Rose, put the grimoire down carefully and step away from it slowly. Now!" Nadia exclaims with concern in her voice as she carefully levitates the grimoire off the pedestal and lowers it gently to the floor in the middle of the room.

The pages begin to fly forward, then backward. Finally, Nadia blasts the grimoire with light and then, nothing.

"It appears that the grimoire is safe, but I strongly urge the three of you not to explore the grimoire without me or Mora present. Is that clear?" Nadia asks.

"Yes, Mom," the three reply in unison.

"What is very clear, however, is that if Rusty stole that grimoire, he has invoked her. This means Minda will be coming to take the grimoire back. One simply does not steal from Minda," Nadia explains with a look of deep concern.

"Who is Minda?" Ethan asks.

Reading from one of the grimoires on the other side of the room, Rose responds.

"According to the texts, she is an extremely old goddess of the ancient ways, the one who balances all knowledge. She is also the keeper of wisdom and a great warrior. During battle, she can be invoked to aid the caster on battle strategy and logic. Her army is noted to be immortal and unstoppable.

Any who have tried to stand against her army have failed. The text further notes that she is symbolized by the owl, combat armor, and carries a spear. Her texts and grimoire are sacred and highly coveted items as they share insights into the worlds of both the Mundane and the Arcane."

"Oh great! So, in other words, Rusty stole from an ancient deity, who is someone you do not want to piss off," Ethan declares.

"Which is why I don't want any of you touching that grimoire," Nadia states as she secures the grimoire to the floor with a binding spell, so that it does not disappear.

❧

It is bad enough that Rose cannot get any work done with her brothers, children, and husband hanging around, but now, with Nadia sitting in the library all day, it will make the situation even more difficult. Finally, Zander heads off to teach his class. Ethan and Sebastian slip out the door with him, leaving Oliver and Rose to handle their mother.

Oliver goes to the third-floor balcony, where he can look down and watch the grimoire, while Nadia sits quietly, sipping her coffee and watching every move that the grimoire, Oliver, and Rose make.

"Mother, I cannot have a thousand-year-old plus grimoire sitting in the middle of my library floor. Shall we move it to the battlement?" Rose inquires.

"No, dear, it can stay right where it is," Nadia answers.

"But, Mom, it cannot stay out there, not with students coming in."

"Problem solved," Nadia replies, raising her hand, turning it, and sealing the library door. A giant "closed" sign appears on the outside of the door.

Several hours pass until Zander arrives with Ari, Theo, Hope, and Vivian, the kids running through the great oak doors of the library directly toward the grimoire. Nadia disappears from her spot on the second floor and reappears standing in front of the grimoire.

"Stop! Go around. Visit with your mother, but you're not messing with this grimoire."

"Mom, we are going to make dinner. Did you want to join us?" Rose inquires.

"Yes, I would love that, Rose."

"Oliver, dear, your sister is making dinner. Let's go."

If it was not already bad enough that Nadia has the grimoire chained down, but she also casts a lightfield around it. Zander and Rose regard each other, shaking their heads. When Zander quietly winks at Rose, she understands all too well what he means.

"Everyone, go ahead. I will be right there. I forgot to leave directions for Mr. Bruin," Rose says, walking behind her desk and writing some instructions on a magical piece of paper. One minute the message is there: the next, it disappears. Rose hands the note to Mr. Bruin, who waits for everyone to leave. Walking toward the door, he opens the note, scans it, and knows what has to be done.

Waiting for half an hour after everyone has left, Mr. Bruin pokes his head out of the door to the library to make sure the coast is clear. Then, he shuts the door and seals it as he motions for the two dwarfs guarding the backdoor to unlock it.

"Is my mother gone?"

"Yes, Masters Ethan and Sebastian. I see you have brought young Matthew with you. Your sister left this note for you."

"Thanks, Mr. Bruin."

"Ethan, what does it say?" Sebastian asks as Ethan smiles, walks over to the candle, lights it, and holds the paper over the flame as the text reappears.

"Sebastian, this is Rose we are talking about. First off, this is the way that she hides any messages that she does not want Mom, Dad, or Mora to see. Second, she reminds me that time is mine to control and to be careful. Third, she wants you to go with me. This is going to be interesting. She wants us to find and talk with Minda."

"Dad, Papa, am I staying or going with you?" Matthew inquires.

"I am sure Mr. Bruin won't mind watching you," Sebastian replies.

"I do not mind at all, Sir. But I'd rather not endure the wrath of your mother-in-law if she discovers your son here without either of you. However, I do have someone who can assist. They should be arriving anytime. Ahh, in the cabinet over there. Matthew, why don't you go see who it is?"

As Matthew opens the cabinet door, Cedric steps out.

"Ahh, young master Matthew. Good evening, fine Sir. Masters Ethan and Sebastian, it is good to see you both. Mr. Bruin has summoned me."

"Hey, Cedric. We have a little errand we need to take care of, but we cannot let my mom know."

"Ahh, is that why you sent your sister and twin brother to distract your mother? You do realize that she will catch on, Sir, and you will be in trouble. Please do not say that I did not interject and warn you. Besides, why else would you need someone to watch young Master Matthew?"

"Cedric, could you? Please? That would be great. You're the best."

"Master Ethan, I would love to, but you forget one thing. Your mother bound that grimoire. It will be next to impossible to get through her magic, even for you, Sir. It looks like your babysitter will be traveling with you. You see, Sir, if you have me with you, it counts as if she is here, traveling with the two of you. Besides, young Matthew shall be tended to. The lad needs adventure. It is a win-win for everyone," Cedric explains while Ethan and Sebastian shoot amused looks at each other.

"How do we get past the field?" Ethan asks, examining the lightshield that is protecting the grimoire.

"Master Ethan, it is rather simple. You walk up to the shield and politely ask it to let you pass."

"It cannot be that easy" Ethan and Sebastian say in unison, a tone of disbelief in their voices.

"Oh, but it is, Sir."

Watching, the two cannot believe their eyes as Cedric walks up to the lightfield, speaks to it, and walks right through it. Ethan, Sebastian, and Matthew stand there continuing to examine the shield in disbelief, when, suddenly, Cedric's arm comes back through the lightfield, grabs Matthew by his collar, and pulls him through, followed by Sebastian, and then, Ethan, who spins his right hand over his head, sealing the room as he steps into the shield.

The four examine the grimoire while Ethan waves his hand over the clasp, and the pages begin to flip. Fog fills the area, then everything around them begins to spin. Ethan and Sebastian pull their wands, wave them, and the fog departs. Cedric holds Matthew's hand tightly as the fog disappears, and the four are left standing in a field in the midafternoon sun, looking down an English country road toward a small, bustling village that is rising out of the hills in the distance.

Chapter 4
Rebellious Ethan

"Okay, Matthew, here are the rules. Number one, stay with Cedric. Number two, listen to all orders given to you. Number three, this is a vision. You cannot interact with the beings in it, and if you can, make sure one of us is always with you. Lastly, if Cedric, your papa, or I, tell you to run, do so and call your aunt, uncles, and grandmothers. Is that clear?" Ethan explains to Matthew.

"Yes, Dad," Matthew replies, imitating his dad.

"Master Ethan, may I remind you of the sun, Sir," Cedric notes as Ethan and Sebastian cast a charm over Cedric, so he is not affected.

Ethan looks at Sebastian nervously as they start down the path in the vision. This is the first time that Ethan is in charge as Rose has always been in charge in the past.

"This is cool," Matthew laughs, examining the area.

"Matthew, stay close," Sebastian says as his wand starts glowing. Ethan spins his wand over his head to accelerate the vision.

Looking around, carefully observing the area, they continue down the path. At the first house that they come to, located at the entrance to the small village, they find a woman sitting outside on her porch spinning yarn. As they continue to stroll down the path, looking around, Matthew points to the ruins on the hill.

"What is that?"

"Ruins, Master Matthew, from times past," Cedric explains as the group continues down the path, Ethan and Sebastian closely examining the area as they go.

A young girl runs past Matthew, but instead of running through him, she bumps right into him.

"Oh, I am sorry," the girl says as she continues on.

"What? Hey, girl, wait. Dad, Papa, Cedric, she is real. She is real and running down that path," Matthew points, very excited.

Sebastian stops and watches the girl, now skipping down the path, picking flowers and throwing them on the ground. Curious, Cedric walks over, reaches down, and picks up the flower.

"Yes, Master Matthew is correct. She is real, very real indeed," Cedric notes, holding the flower to his nose.

Sebastian and Ethan gaze at each other when they see Matthew reaching down to pick up the flower and handing it to the girl. The young girl's hand touches his briefly as he smiles, and the girl skips away from him.

As Sebastian and Ethan continue watching, they notice that she skips right through several villagers. After watching Matthew's interaction with the girl, they follow behind her. Finally, at the end of the path, she skips into the downed ruins of an old temple.

"Cedric, please stay here with Matthew. Sebastian and I will handle this," Ethan directs.

The two creep into the old temple, looking around cautiously, but no longer see the girl.

Suddenly, a dagger flies past, inches from Sebastian's head, as the young girl reappears out of thin air and stares at them.

"Whoa, whoa, whoa! We mean you no harm. I am Lord Ethan Knight-Phoenix."

"Blah, blah, blah. Yes, I know who you are. So, why are you here?" the girl inquires, twisting her head all the way around and then, looking at them.

"We wanted to know about a grimoire we found. There is a powerful being that was mentioned by name in it," Sebastian explains as the girl walks across the grounds, and parts of the temple reconstruct with each step.

"What is this grimoire?" the young girl inquires as she stops to feed some birds.

"*Chronicorum antiquitatis* (*The Chronicles of Antiquity*)."

"I understand, Lord Ethan. Let me guess. You come seeking answers," the young girl replies in a snarky tone of voice, rolling her eyes.

"Yes, we have. Can you help us? We are looking for the one they call Minda. Do you know her? May we ask your name?" Ethan inquires.

"You can ask my name, but I do not feel obliged to share it with you," the girl states, somewhat annoyed.

"Please, we mean you no harm," Ethan responds with a hand raised. "You know who we are. I think it is only fair that we know who you are."

"I won't tell you, Lord Ethan. Do *not* inquire again, or I will get ugly."

"Ha, you're a child."

"Want to try me, Lord Sebastian?" the young lady asks as she summons a plasma ball in her hand.

"You're Minda, are you not?"

Lowering her hand, the plasma ball disappears, and the girl looks directly at Matthew.

"How did you know?"

"My great aunt Destiny teaches about magical beings, mystical creatures, and pretty much all things Arcane. Minda is the girl who loves all knowledge, who knows all, who sees all, and is the balance of new and ancient wisdom," Matthew explains.

"Sharp young man. I like him," Minda remarks, smiling at him.

Now, they have grown accustomed to magic but what happens next is amazing. As Minda turns, the ruined temple around them transforms into a beautiful old library, with Greek columns reaching for the sky. The ceiling looks like clouds, and giant basins light the room. Bookshelves and cabinets run the full length of the library, filled with grimoires, scrolls, and papers.

Minda spins her hand and transforms into a young lady, decked out in armor, with a Greek-inspired helmet and spear. An owl lands behind her as she summons chairs for each of them.

"Wait! Why didn't we get it when Rose described her earlier from the texts? A lover of knowledge, surrounded by ancient texts, a spear, and an owl. Holy smokes, you're the goddess Athena."

"Young Ethan, you are wise and correct," Athena notes, smiling at them.

"My Lady, our respects."

"Thank you, Sebastian."

"Now, you are on a journey, looking for answers."

"Yes, the grimoire."

"Ah yes. The grimoire was stolen by that pointy-eared elf boy."

"Rusty," Ethan declares, looking at Cedric.

"Ah, yes. Master Russell tends to get into trouble more often than he should," Cedric comments.

"Indeed. He certainly stole the grimoire, and while I understand why, I have to ask, 'Why now?' Your sister has known about its whereabouts for over 20 years," Athena explains, annoyance in her voice.

"Wait! Rose. Twenty years? Oh no, the timeline."

"The timeline?" Athena inquires.

"Great Athena, the timeline has been altered. How do I put it? Time is acting bizarrely."

"I see. So, you, Matthew, are not forty-two?" Athena inquires.

"No, Ma'am, I am twelve."

"Interesting, thirty years before the prophecy. How can this be? The oracle Delphi always predicts how things will happen, but she must be wrong. But how? She is the great Delphi and is never wrong. The scrolls, where are they? This is just illogical."

"Cedric, what is Athena talking about?"

"Master Ethan, it appears she is operating from a perspective thirty years into the future."

Athena rummages through piles of scrolls, throwing them everywhere, until Matthew picks up a scroll.

"Can I help you, Ma'am?"

"Child, you are so kind, much like your fathers."

"Is that what you were thinking when you threw the dagger inches from my head?"

"I heard that, Sebastian. Do not think because I cannot see right now does not mean I cannot hear you," remarks Athena as Sebastian rolls his eyes.

"Great Athena, you thought we were older, and you mentioned a prophecy. Can I ask what is going on?" Ethan inquires.

"Time is bizarre. It is altering, changing, creating echoes, then changing again."

"We are aware of this. What is it about that particular grimoire that drew my nephew or, in this case, an older version of my sister to it?"

"The grimoire, Ethan, holds the most important of all knowledge, the story of Merlin's birth."

"What? Wait, his birth?" Ethan and Sebastian say, gazing at one another.

"Master Ethan, what seems to be troubling you?" Cedric asks.

"If the grimoire talks about Merlin's birth, then it could reveal where the Curpendulums are."

"You are correct, Ethan, to a point. But, then again, you are not correct."

"What does that mean?" Sebastian asks.

"Sebastian, hold that thought. Athena, are the Curpendulums discussed or not?"

"They are, and, then again, they are not. You see, to understand that knowledge, you must know something about everything, and everything is a hard something to understand, particularly if you are not ready for the truth. But, then again, humans are never ready for the truth. To understand Merlin, in this case, you must understand the darkness itself. But the darkness did not always exist. Rather, it was created, much like all magical things."

"What? That does not make sense."

"Yes, it does, Sebastian. I get what she means."

"Athena, if darkness was created, then Merlin created the darkness, and if so, why?"

Athena stops, glancing over the pile of scrolls. Then, she points at Cedric.

"Cedric, tell me. Where do vampires come from?"

"What does that have to do with the question about Merlin?"

"Master Ethan, I understand what Athena is asking," Cedric smiles. "Vampires were created when man thirsted for knowledge, and, in that thirst, they sought new ways to modify their blood, to become more powerful. One night, when the original vampire, Vlad, was afraid and worried about losing the war in which he was then engaged, and after watching a bat prey upon its victims for days, he bit the bat to see if it would give him the same thirst for control. To his surprise, it did. However, he also soon learned that the thirst came with a severe penalty."

"Correct! You see, Ethan, what Cedric is saying is that much like Vlad, Merlin was obsessed with power," Athena responds.

"The power he already had was sufficient. But he was not happy with it. He wanted more but at a great cost. You see, Merlin believed that the Arcane was the absolute power," Sebastian remarks.

"Possibly, Sebastian. But we know more than that, Athena explains, looking at the group.

"What more can there be?"

"Now, Ethan, didn't that charming sister of yours teach you anything?" Athena replies.

"It is the Curpendulums, is it not?" Matthew answers.

"Correct, young Matthew. But why?" Athena questions him, while she continues to throw multiple scrolls over her shoulder.

"According to Ms. Destiny and my grandmother, they hold power."

"Correct again. But there is more than that. Here it is, finally. My apologies for digging through the scrolls, but I needed to find the one that tells the story. Would you care to hear it?"

"Yes, Athena. Please share it," Ethan replies, while the others nod in agreement.

&

Long ago, when the earth was still new, and men and women were learning the ways of the earth, demons came to earth to play games with them, particularly incubuses—

demon men who tried to enslave Mundane women to do their bidding or to reproduce. One night, one of the incubuses succeeded, and Merlin was born nine months later.

A child born of Mundane and incubus blood is powerful, but one who could do magic was invaluable to the demons, because they feared the power of the light. So, to have a child who could control darkness and suppress the light was vital to their success and enslavement of all. Thus, as Merlin grew, so did his power until he was able to manipulate the power of time to do his bidding, including manipulating Arthur and Morgana-la-fay. Unfortunately, Merlin's manipulation of time had fatal consequences because to tamper with time is to tamper with fire.

The Nobles, who received their magic from the gods and goddesses, are ancient beings of great magical power. Over time, Merlin came to their attention. But, unimpressed by his power, they dismissed him, noting that his magic was relatively weak. Instead, they laughed and ridiculed him. You see, their magic was natural. It came from all around them. But Merlin's magic was the magic of rage and anger. Thus, it appeared unnatural in the eyes of the Nobles.

Angry, Merlin sought guidance and found help from the incubuses, who told him of the most prized form of magic, the Curpendulums, 15 libers of absolute power that would forever enhance the power of the person who controls them. They taught Merlin that if he controlled the 15 libers, he would become the most potent wizard alive. Obsessed to prove to everyone that his magic was the most powerful, Merlin stole one of the grimoires, the Liber Mortuus Caelum (The Grimoire of the Dead).

With this liber, he created the first army of Norminis Umbra (Shadows), an army so strong that they overwhelmed the armies of even my brother, Ares and my sister Artemis. Merlin's army was composed of the dead, demons, incubuses, and other wielders of dark magic.

Fearful of such an army, the ancient gods and goddesses fled, leaving the earth and magical to fend for themselves. Merlin's power frightened many, and rightfully so.

But this power was not enough to satisfy Merlin. He wanted more and he became so driven by his thirst that he continued to seek the other grimoires. But when the Nobles, discovered that Merlin had stolen the Liber Mortuus Caelum, they decided, as part of their sworn duty to protect the earth, that Merlin had to be stopped. Thus, the echoes of time were born. The Nobles opened a portal and distributed the other 14 grimoires throughout time, scattering them all over. They believed that, by doing this, Merlin would never find them, and thus, the Curpendulums would be preserved and protected. They knew that if he only had one grimoire, they could easily defeat him.

The libers, as the Elders knew, were bound to each other. If all 15 came together, they would confer unlimited power on any individual who controlled them. But separated, they would be simply another Cantamen Liber (grimoire).

The Elders were concerned about Merlin's abuse of the Liber Mortuus Caelum and how he learned to alter time. So, they also hid their two most valuable Nobles, ancient beings of great magic. One you have come to know as Mora and the other was Elder Yule. The Nobles entrusted one of the Curpendulums, the Liber Divinarum (The Grimoire of the Divine), to Mora.

This one grimoire was, more than anything, what Merlin desired. The Liber of the Divine is the answer to all immortality. He hoped that by taking a chunk of Mora's hair from the temple floor, the night that she vanished, he would be able to find her. When that failed, he came up with an even darker plan. He twisted and spun the timeline to create Morgana-La-Fey. We do not know how Mora lost her magic or how Morgana ended up with Mora's children, however, we do know that Merlin planned to use Morgana to find the Liber of the Divine.

The Nobles opened their special vault to entrust the rather bizarre pocket watch that freezes time in the Arcane realm with its creator, Elder Yule. However, the pocket watch was gone.

It took centuries to find that watch, and when it was found, it was broken. Merlin had used it so much that he had damaged it. So, while the watch has been found, to date, the Liber of the Divine has not. No one knows where Mora hid it. Many believe she still has it and waits for the one of which the prophecies foretold to become so *powerful that their magic alone will compile the 15 grimoires and restore the timeline. This being so, no one knows where they are, who they are, or if they even exist.*

◈

"Athena, do we know if Mora still has the liber?"

"Sebastian, why not ask her?" Athena replies as Sebastian mumbles under his breath.

"So, if we understand you correctly, the Curpendulums are 15 key grimoires?" Ethan surmises.

"You are correct, Ethan. They are the original texts about all magical teaching given to humans by the gods and goddesses. Merlin wanted them in order to create a race of magical beings, that would reign over and, if needed, kill the Mundane."

"Have any of these grimoires been found?" Sebastian asks.

"From my knowledge and the chatter that I have heard, Sebastian, you all hold the *Liber Mortuus Caelum*—well, what remains of it. I have also heard that you possess the *Liber Dryadalum Sequere Magicae* (*The Grimoire of Elfish Magic*)."

"Ethan, is that the one Rusty carried?" Sebastian inquires.

"Yes, Rose confirmed it to be that grimoire," Ethan replies, glancing at Sebastian.

"Correct. Your sister's discovery about the liber is correct. It is one of the oldest histories of the magic entrusted to the elfish race. Also, I know that the *Liber Vampiris* (*The Grimoire of Vampires*) and the *Liber Fairie* (*The Grimoire of Fairies*) are close by," Athena notes, winking at Ethan.

"Cedric, please tell me, you have the *Liber Vampiris*." Ethan says.

"No, Master Ethan, but I may know the whereabouts of it."

"Athena, thank you for sharing this information with us. Will you come with us to speak with Oliver and Rose?" Ethan inquires.

"Not at this time, but I will give you this story of Merlin and the Curpendulums," Athena hands the scroll to Ethan.

"Dad, Papa, Cedric, we have company."

As they turn, they notice warrior women, dressed like Athena, marching through the door.

"Great Goddess, Pallas Athena, darkness is here and moving against the sanctuary," one of the guards announces.

"They have found us. We must protect this place at all cost, Ethan. It looks like I may be meeting your siblings after all," Athena explains.

Peering out of the door, Pallas Athena counts the number of dark guards moving against her temple.

"Well, I may be the goddess of war, but there are too many of them for me to stop them all," Athena remarks, looking around.

"Cedric and Sebastian, we cannot let them get this knowledge," Ethan declares, pulling his wand.

"Sebastian, open a vortex portal back to the school. I need it to be the size of this building. Cedric, once the Vortex is open, take Matthew and go. Alert my family of what is occurring. Cedric, if any darkness comes after Matthew, finish it," Ethan orders.

"Ethan, we have never had darkness attack like this, in a vision before," Sebastian says as he starts to open a vortex portal.

"Rose has, Sebastian. She told me the stories. Sebastian, look at me. Protect Pallas Athena and her guards."

"Ethan, hun, what are you doing?" Sebastian inquires, looking concerned.

"My job, Sebastian. Now, open the vortex fully and stand back."

With a quick spinning of his hands, Sebastian opens the vortex portal to full size.

Ethan takes to the air inside the temple, his eyes glowing blue and his robes floating in the air, as a helix of light encircles him. Putting his hands together, and then, pulling them apart, an energy ball forms in his hands. As the darkness comes charging through the door on the other side of the sanctuary, they hit a lightfield as the vortex portal grows larger.

"Cedric, Matthew, now!" Sebastian yells as Cedric grabs Matthew by the collar of his jacket and Pallas Athena by the arm and jumps through the vortex portal.

"Sebastian, let go of the portal, take Pallas Athena's guards, and get them out of here. I have this," Ethan shouts in a deep, booming voice.

Looking at the warrior guards, Sebastian nods, and they all start jumping into the portal. Sebastian looks back as Ethan glows brighter, his power growing as grimoires and papers fly around him and the darkness explodes, one after another, when they hit the lightfield.

Back in the library, the room begins to shake. Tremor after tremor roll through the building. The dwarfs, tending to the grimoires, start scrambling as the pages of the *Grimoire of Antiquity* fly open. Finally, Cedric, Matthew, and Athena jump out of the grimoire.

"Everyone, quickly, secure the room. Secure the grimoires. Summon the Lady Rose," Mr. Bruin hollers as dwarfs circle the library, swords and hammers drawn, ready to attack any darkness that emerges from the portal.

The doors of the library begin to rattle as they explode open. Mora now standing where the doors once were.

"Destiny, Marybelle, Tulip, Lady O, maintain that field. Let no students pass," Mora commands as she spins her hands and her eyes glow blue. Oliver and Rose run past Mora, looking around to assess the situation.

"My library! Cedric, what happened?" Rose asks.

"We fell under attack, My Lady. Your brother has activated his magic," Cedric replies, holding tightly to Matthew and a woman. Rose notices the woman with Cedric and nods to her. Rose runs toward the grimoire. But, just as she approaches it, she jumps back as Sebastian and ten warrior guards emerge through the portal.

"Sebastian, where is Ethan?" Oliver yells.

"Going all freaky magic. I think he is trying to move the Sanctuary Library," Sebastian replies as he reaches Matthew and holds his hand tightly.

"What library, Sebastian?" Rose inquires, spinning her hands and containing the field.

"The library of knowledge of Athena," Cedric explains. Then, moving quickly, Oliver grabs Rose's hand as they raise their free hands, trying to contain the portal further.

"Move!" Nadia barks as she appears in the doorway. She levitates the grimoire from the circle and casts it through the window. The portal follows, and the group runs outside.

Clouds roll overhead as the winds pick up. Flashes of light streak across the night sky as dragons appear. They circle overhead as Oliver and Rose' eyes begin to glow, and the bottom of a giant stone foundation emerges from the portal. Oliver and Rose glance at one another, nod, and then, push their hands over their heads. The portal flies high into the air, revealing the Sanctuary Library.

Screams echo across the sky as dragons roar, snapping at the darkness that has begun crawling out through the edges of the portal. Oliver and Rose spin their hands, shrinking the size of the portal, trying to seal it when Ethan suddenly appears above the building. Light begins spinning around him and water from the river flies up the hillside, reinforcing his magic shield. Angry with the darkness's arrival, Ethan speaks,

Tueri Omnibus. Tueri hoc Aedificium. Tueri Schola.
Protect Everyone. Protect this building. Protect the School.

Ethan slams his hands together, then pulls them apart as the darkness screams and explodes on the spot. Orbs of light appear, flashing and exploding, one after another, around the darkness. A shock wave knocks everyone off their feet. Ethan's eyes begin to glow blue as the darkness spirals together and flies full speed toward him.

When the darkness is only inches from Ethan, a ray of light appears. Looking around, everyone notices Matthew, Ari, Theo, and Hope standing together, wands drawn. The darkness immediately turns away from Ethan and toward them.

"Hold tight and do not let go of your wands," Matthew states as other students begin to appear, drawing their wands and casting light.

Screams ring out as the darkness dives towards the students. Suddenly, a cloaked figure appears, holding the Noble Staff with the Elder Elfish Star. A middle-aged elf woman walks through the crowd, spinning her hands as energy bolts fly back and forth between her palms. When a second elf woman appears, vines explode out of the ground, striking the darkness. Regarding one another, the two women throw orbs into the air as the Elfish Star explodes with light.

As the light grows brighter, the darkness is gone with a flash. The figure spins his staff as they and the two elf women disappear and the portal closes.

Using his magic, Ethan settles the library on the ground. When it touches down, he flies over the roof and lands just inches from his siblings on the ground. When he collapses to one knee, Oliver races to help him up.

"Are you okay?" he inquires as Ethan struggles to stand.

"Yes. Just give me a minute to regain my strength," Ethan replies, balancing himself on his brother's arm. Rose rushes up to the steps of the sanctuary and starts to ascend when she is stopped by a series of loud pops.

Kelvin and various council members arrive, wands drawn, as Belinda, Drago, and Autumn land, scanning the grounds for adversaries.

This is followed by Mora, Destiny, and Nadia who also check for any remaining enemies while Marybelle and Lady O hurry the children to safety inside the school.

"Lady Marybelle, leave the Phoenix and Ignatius children. I wish to have a word with them." Mora remarks, looking over her shoulder at them.

"Oh, we are so busted," Ari declares as Theo hides behind his brother, and Hope runs off, chasing a bunny. Matthew stands quietly waiting, knowing they are all in trouble.

"Lord Ethan, thank you," Athena says as she hugs him.

"Pallas Athena, my goddess, you are not upset?" Mora inquires.

"Are you kidding me, Lady Mora? No, I am not upset. Lords Ethan and Sebastian were amazing, and so was the young Lord Matthew. Please go easy on him, My Lady," Athena asks as she walks past everyone and up the steps of her sanctuary. Stopping, she puts her hand on Rose's shoulder, nods at the children, turns, and walks through the doors of the great temple as her guards follow.

"Uh hum, children," Mora clears her throat.

"Yes, grandmama?" the three answer in unison.

"Yes, Ma'am," Matthew answers in unison with his cousins.

"What was that?" Mora inquires, walking back and forth in front of them with her hands behind her back, tapping her wand. Ari quietly raises his hand.

"Yes, Ari?"

"It was Noble Elder needing help. You always taught us that the Nobles are our friends, and the darkness is bad, so we helped Noble Elder," Ari explains.

"And you know that to be Noble Elder how?" Mora inquires, her eyebrow raised.

"Because the pretty lady with the energy bolts told us," Hope replies, holding the bunny she has caught.

Doing everything she can to contain her smile, Mora stops looking at Hope and glances toward Ethan, Oliver, Sebastian, Zander, and Rose.

"Cedric?" Rose says.

"Yes, My Lady?"

"Can you take the children inside, please?"

"Of course, My Lady. Children, follow me, please."

Cedric picks up Hope and the bunny and begins walking toward the castle.

"If that was the great Noble Elder, it would make sense," Rose remarks to Mora.

"In what way, Rose?" Lady Mora inquires.

"He has been around a lot more, and his presence is growing. If he continues to show up, then the darkness must be growing in ways that we do not understand."

Then, looking at the group, Rose walks into the Sanctuary Library.

The Museum

Chapter 5
The Museum

The students run through the grand entryway and file into the space the following day.

"Students, students, attention. Your attention, please! Okay time to quiet down," Lady Mora states.

"Remember, students, today's field trip is to allow you to experience Mundane culture. Now, the rules are as follows: no wand waving, no use of any magical items in front of the Mundane. And older students, you are responsible for maintaining order and helping the younger students," Mora explains as the faculty attempt to maintain order in the room.

"Everyone, please remember that the Mundane are going about their daily lives. Any use of magic in front of them could cause catastrophic issues," Rose explains, entering the room and walking toward the grand stairway.

"Your teachers will be with you today, and remember, have fun," Mora notes, hands in the air as a portal flies open.

"Youngest students will go through last, older students first. Remember our rules and have fun. Matthew Knight-Phoenix, a word," Mora demands.

"Yes, Headmistress."

"Matthew, you will be responsible for both of your younger cousins. And Matthew, give me your wand. Let's go," Mora says, holding out her hand.

"But, Headmistress, if we run into trouble…?" Matthew begins to interject when he is interrupted.

"You allow the faculty to handle that," Mora notes, looking sternly at him.

"I better go. I need to catch up with Ari and Theo," Matthew says, rolling his eyes and handing his wand to her.

"Lady Mora?"

"Yes, Ms. Destiny."

"Taking Matthew's wand won't solve the issue," Destiny notes, walking past her towards the portal.

"Emma, I understand, but it is a precaution, one that I'm afraid may not be enough," Mora explains as Emma crosses, followed by the Lady Mora.

When the students arrive at the museum, they are broken into groups. Of course, Matthew, Ari, and Theo are placed with Ethan.

"Remember, guys, we are here to look around. Touch nothing. And, Matthew, please don't enchant anything."

"Dad, I couldn't if I wanted. Headmistress Mora took my wand," he complains, looking displeased.

"Well, Matthew, after the debacle we had in the park three months ago, in front of the Mundane, I don't blame her," Ethan responds.

"Now, go, and stay with your cousins," Ethan instructs.

The three boys walk around looking at the various artworks until Theo stops to look closely at a statue of Apollo and asks, "Ari, do you think that the Greeks miss their statue?"

Matthew quickly answers. "A museum is a building full of artifacts, little cousin, many of them stolen from other cultures and civilizations. I'm sure Apollo knows that it's here. So, come on, let's be good boys and explore the armory."

As Ari and Matthew walk away, Theo looks around cautiously and, when he notices that no one is around, he waves his hand in front of him and the statue of Apollo disappears.

"There. Much better," he says aloud as he runs after his cousin and brother. As the three enter the armory, Lady Marybelle watches the students from the doorway.

Several rooms over, a considerable commotion breaks out.

"The statue! How does a statue disappear?" a voice rings out through the museum.

Lady Marybelle quickly walks into the armory, raises her hands, to get the students' attention and motions for them to follow her.

"Students, pay no attention to what is going on. Shall we?"

Quietly, the students leave the armory, filing out one after another. Matthew and Ari hold back toward the end of the group.

"Theo, please tell me you didn't touch that statue," Matthew inquires, looking very concerned.

"I didn't touch it, but I did make it disappear," Theo replies, smiling and skipping towards the other students.

"If our parents find out, we are so dead," Matthew says, looking at Ari.

They catch up with the rest of the group, who are exploring the vast collections in the Renaissance and Baroque galleries. Looking around quietly, Ari notices a strange man and recognizes a woman from his visions.

"That is Aunt Raven. But she is dead," Ari mutters quietly under his breath, ducking behind a display.

"Raven, when no one is looking, get the grimoire and get it out of here," the man demands.

Quickly, Ari runs toward the other side of the room, and when no one is watching, he pushes over one of the displays. As a loud crash rings through the hall, people scatter. Running toward the case, he observes the grimoire.

ᛚᛁᛒᛖᚱ ᛗᛟᚱᛏᚨᛚᛁᛊ

"Of course, the title is written in runes. I can only make out the word "liber." Why didn't I pay more attention in my Ancient Runes class? Where is Mom when I need her? She would look at it and know which Curpendulum it is," mutters Ari, scrambling to find the description of the exhibit.

The Liber Mortalis, believed to be a prized Arcane artifact, is the only grimoire of the 15 still in existence. The Liber Mortalis is the Grimoire of Mundane and holds many of the original ancient spells from a time past. The original witches of Salem used many of the spells in this grimoire, which led to the Salem Witch Trials. Unfortunately, to date, very little else is known about this grimoire.

Materials: Leather Bound with Stone and Rock Inlays
Date: Unknown
Author: Unknown
Origins: Central Europe

࿇

"Yes. Of course, very little is known about this grimoire by Mundane. I see why they want this grimoire, and this is not good. Think, Ari, think! That's it." Pulling his wand, Ari slides it up his sleeve, points it at the grimoire, and says,

Evaporate.
Disappear.

Moving his hand in front of him, he speaks again.

Apparent.
Appear.

The grimoire fully rematerializes in his hand just as screams echo throughout the room and multiple explosions go off around him. He ducks down, leaning over the grimoire to protect it, just as Raven reveals herself and Lady Marybelle moves against her. As screams continue to ring throughout the hallways, the students closest to the action pull their wands and start spinning them, creating lightshields, protecting themselves, their peers, and the Mundane.

Matthew notices Ari scrambling across the room toward him stooped over, protecting something.

"What is that?" Matthew inquires.

"It's a Curpendulum," Ari replies.

"Ari, what do you mean it's a Curpendulum?" Matthew demands.

Ari reveals the cover of the grimoire to his older cousin, *Liber Mortalis,* (*The Grimoire of Mundane*).

"Holy smokes, cousin! Give me your wand," Matthew demands.

"Theo," Matthew yells. Multiple older students cast a secondary lightshield as Theo reaches his brother and cousin. Unfortunately, the darkness strikes the first lightshield, causing it to explode as the older students tighten their grips on their wands.

When the darkness strikes the second lightfield, a scream pierces the space and dark creatures explode onto the ground. An elf appears, picks up his giant hammer, and throws it over his shoulder.

"Afternoon, my dear friends. My name is Lord Kells. Older students get these younger students through that portal immediately. It will drop you back at your school," Kells directs as he scans the room for danger.

"You three," the elf points at Matthew, Theo, and Ari.

"Yes?" the three answer in unison.

"Whatever you do, do not let go of that Curpendulum. Do you understand?" Lord Kells lowers his hammer, smashes the lightfield and takes out three dark creatures who are moving through the door.

The three glance at each other as Lord Kells points across the room toward the portal and strikes down two more dark creatures.

"Go and do not stop until you reach the Lady Rose."

The three bolt across the room, through the portal, and reappear in the back courtyard of the school.

"Ari, Theo, quick! Let's get that Curpendulum to the library," Matthew commands just as the three hear a loud crash. Gazing up, they see the darkness hitting the lightfield that surrounds the school.

"Let's go," Matthew yells as four dark creatures rise out of the ground. The three boys run toward the school's back doors just as Pallas Athena and her guards appear. The darkness runs right into Athena as she grabs two of them by the throat, smashing them into the ground.

"Ladies, protect those boys and get them to safety. I will handle this," Athena notes, spinning her spear and jamming it into a dark creature. The guards of Athena pick up the boys, run across the courtyard, and ascend the stairs to the mezzanine. The darkness continues to emerge as Willow and another elf woman appear out of the ground.

"Get them out of here. We have this," Willow yells at the guards carrying the three boys.

Willow's eyes turn green as she spins her hands down and then, pulling up, causes the dark creatures to explode. The woman with her grabs one of the dark creatures using ropes from her wand, smashing it into the wall. Running through the doors, Athena's guards set Matthew, Ari, and Theo down.

Dark creatures emerge from everywhere as the suits of armor tap their spears against the ground. Pulling their spears up to their chests, they turn.

"Boy, whatever magical artifact you hold, don't let go of it. Quickly, up to the library. We will hold them off," the head of Athena's guard states.

The three boys look at each other, nod, and run up the staircase. Athena's guards turn on the spot, holding their swords, shields, and spears at the ready, striking down the darkness as the suits of armor form a protective barrier across the stairway. Theo is the first to reach the top of the stairs, yelling for his mother and father, as Olivia emerges from the library.

"Boys, what is the meaning of this? Why aren't you at the museum?" Olivia inquires.

"Aunt Olivia, where are our parents?" Ari asks, winded.

"They went to the museum to help contain the darkness. They went looking for you three."

"Aunt Olivia, the darkness is here, and it's after this," Ari explains as he holds up the grimoire.

"Guys," Theo points at the ceiling as dark creatures begin crawling across it.

"Boys, get inside the library and activate the defenses. Go, quickly" Olivia shouts, pulling a charm from her pocket and throwing it across the hall as a lightfield raises and a phoenix appears, guarding the field.

An owl also appears flapping its wings.

"Madam Hoot, notify Rose that the school is under attack," Olivia directs as the owl takes off. The library's doors fly open and all three run through them into the library.

"Mr. Bruin, the darkness is here," Matthew calls, motioning for Olivia to also get into the library.

"Matthew, thank you. Quickly, activate the defenses," Olivia calls, helping Matthew to shut the doors.

"You heard them. The darkness will be descending upon this place. Lock it down!" Mr. Bruin yells as a dwarf throws a giant mace to him. Then, in what looks like a synchronized waltz, the dwarfs run through the walkways of the library, the bookshelves coming to life, and turning to secure the ancient texts. As the shelves turn, they reveal more suits of armor coming to life and stepping down off their stools, marching down the walkways, and assuming protective stances throughout the room.

"You three, is that a Curpendulum?" Mr. Bruin inquires, his eyes narrowing.

"Yes, Sir, it is," Matthew replies.

"That is what I thought. Quickly! To the circle, you three. That also includes you, Lady Olivia. Lord Oliver will kill me if something happens to you," Mr. Bruin declares, running toward the counter where he pushes the stone gargoyle on the floor, activating a giant lightfield that raises around the circle.

An explosion echoes through the door as it blows open, and the darkness enters. The suits of armor and the dwarfs strike the darkness and hold them back. Then, suddenly, a flash of light, then another, as, screaming rings out.

"Ha, Ha, Ha! Bad darkness!" Hope declares, holding her mother's necklace in her hand. The darkness charges toward her and strikes a lightshield that is protecting the child.

"Someone get the Lady Hope," Mr. Bruin barks, fighting off one of the advancing dark creatures. Then, as Hope continues to laugh, the necklace begins to glow brighter as the darkness charges Hope again.

"Matthew, we have to help my sister."

"We will, cousin," Matthew replies, grabbing the grimoire on the table next to them and throwing it up into the air. Tapping the grimoire, lightning strikes the floor, one bolt after another, until the room starts to fill with smoke, the wind picks up, and paper blows everywhere. Then, multiple roars shake every inch of the room as three dragons explode from the pages of the grimoire, snapping at the darkness, and circling the room. Fighting the darkness, the dragons bellow fire around the lightfield, protecting the group.

Concalo.
Summon.

Matthew points his wand at Hope as she flies through the lightfield and lands in his arms. Darkness flies backward in every direction and a column of light explodes in the center of the room as the Lady Rose, the Lords Oliver, Ethan, Sebastian, and Zander step out.

"Darkness in my library, attacking my children, my sister-in-law, my nephew, and the dwarfs? I think not! That was the wrong move," Rose declares, spinning her wand. Rose's eyes and the eyes of the others turn red.

Oblitero.
Obliterate.

The five say in unison, pointing their wands in various directions throughout the space as the darkness begins to shake and explode. Wave after wave of light beams explode from their wands striking the darkness, which continues to appear, until the space darkens, and, in one quick wave of darkness, Merlin steps out.

"Give me the grimoire, you wretched child!" he yells, stretching out his hand toward Ari, his wand clenched in his other hand.

As Rose and the other four blast Merlin across the library, Olivia steps in front of Ari.

Rising and spinning his wand, grimoires on the shelves begin flying around the room as lightning strikes Merlin. Furious, he attempts to move out of the way, only to discover that his arms are bound to his sides as a cloaked figure materializes.

Snapping their fingers, they speak,

Defaeco.
Purify.

The area grows bright, and then, returns to normal as Merlin and the figure disappear.

"Mom," Ari and Theo say at the same time as the field lowers.

"Are you all okay?" Zander inquires.

"We are fine," Ari replies as he continues to hold tightly to the grimoires.

"It appears we have a Curpendulum." notes Ethan, laughing as Ari nods.

Loud clapping fills the area as Merlin reappears, walking across the circle, then stopping.

"Ah. How sweet! They figured out that it is a Curpendulum. Hand it over, boy!" demands Merlin, holding out his wand.

Zander, Oliver, and Ethan step in front of the children, holding tightly to their wands. Merlin casts magic by spinning his wand. Suddenly, a light column rises around the circle. The cloaked figure steps out of the light column, looks at Merlin, and, raising their hands, multiplies. The multiples of the cloaked figure touch their palms together as they encircle the light column.

Angry, Merlin yells,

Oblitero.
Obliterate.

Magic ricochets back and forth inside of the column in which Merlin is encased until the cloaked figure snaps their fingers and the column grows brighter. Then, a second later, the column, the multiples, Merlin, and the cloaked figure are gone.

Chapter 6
The Kidnapping

Tossing and turning several nights later, Ari cannot sleep. At 3:45 AM, he awakens and sits straight up crying. Then, quietly, he tip toes down the hall to the family room and turns on the television and begins channel surfing. Eventually, he doses off to waken in a quiet mountain village. Leaves blow through the air as many of the elf children he knows run down the street where the streetlamps are lit with glowing orbs.

Walking down the street, Ari looks around but suddenly realizes that he is still in his pajamas. Examining the street, he recognizes the place as the elf village in the mountains when he sees the darkness lurking. As the darkness kills two elf guards, he yells for help. Then, the space around him begins to spin and he lands back on the floor of the family room. Getting up, he bolts down the hall crying for his parents.

"Mama, Papa," he yells, running.

An old mansion rises over the landscape in the village. Light flickers behind the windows, showing that someone is home.

"Maria, are you coming?" her sister yells up the stairs.

"I will be there in a minute, Alvina," the young lady yells back at her.

"Do you two always have to shout?" their mother asks, coming around the corner, drying her hands with a towel.

"Mother, Duke Avery is out for the evening at the academy, and Maria and I are about to head out. Are you sure you do not care to join us?" Alvina inquires.

"Alvina, thank you, my dear, but when you two leave, I am retreating to my study to write. But you two be safe. I will see you upon your return," their mother remarks, hugging her daughter.

The two sisters walk out the door and down the path to the gate of their yard. Their mother watches from the terrace. When the girls disappear out of sight, the woman turns and walks into her study, She sits down to begin writing.

Suddenly, a loud crash rings through the house, then a thud, a scream, then, silence. The house goes dark, frozen.

ॐ

Two hours later, Alvina and Maria return home to find the house in darkness and the door's glass smashed in. The door jamb is also smashed, and the door is barely hanging on its hinges.

"Maria?" Alvina inquires, looking at her sister as they pull their wands and blow the door off the remaining hinges moving it out of their way so they can enter.

"Maria, the staff," Alvina says, kneeling beside the maid, then, turning her over and checking her pulse.

"Dead," Alvina declares.

"Same here. All of the guards are dead as well, and, by the looks of it, they were attacked by vampires and demons," Maria notes, leaning down and checking their pulses.

"Mother?" the two girls call out, looking at each other and running up the stairs.

"Mother? Mother! Where are you?" the two young ladies yell. Running through the house, the tips of their wands light, as orbs of light fly toward the ceiling, lighting their way.

"Oh no, Alvina," Maria cries, standing in their mother's study.

"Mother? Every one of her scrolls, grimoires, and orbs are either damaged or taken," Alvina notes, examining the area while turning over burnt papers and scrolls.

"Sister? Who would do this?" Maria inquires.

"There is only one way to find out. Follow me," Alvina commands as the two descend the stairs.

Alvina reaches down and touches the forehead of the maid. Then, closing her eyes, magic flies around her as the home is reconstructed. Seconds later, Alvina opens her eyes. Maria stands looking at her, waiting for a response.

Walking into the parlor, Alvina taps the old chest, which flies open, revealing elfish weapons. Alvina reaches down and retrieves a bow and arrow as she throws a spear to her sister. The two nod, and Alvina walks out of the door. She pulls an arrow, nocks it against the string, and pulls it back. As she lets go, the arrow soars into the air. A giant gong can be heard in the distance. The gong sounds again, then again. Alvina turns as flashes of light appear, and multiple individuals begin to materialize around her and her sister.

"Cousin, what has happened that you are calling for aid?" Archduke Lukas asks, as he approaches.

"Our mother has been kidnapped," Alvina explains, leaning on the bow.

"Guards, search the house," Archduke Lukas commands.

"They will only find dead staff. Our mother's library has been ransacked and items destroyed, burnt, or missing," Maria remarks.

"Her works?" A woman inquires.

"All gone or destroyed," Alvina explains.

"Do we know who did this?" Archduke Lukas inquires.

"We do. It must have been Balimore…" Alvina replies.

"Guards, search every part of the village. Leave no stone unturned Make sure darkness does not continue to lurk. If you find darkness, destroy them," Archduke Lukas demands as he walks toward the gate.

"The city is to be locked down. Secure the library, the palace, and the weaponry. Immediately!" Archduke Lukas explains to the members of the elf high court as they all begin to disappear.

"Cousin?"

"Yes, Alvina."

"We must send word to the King and Queen," Alvina says. Lord Lukas nods as he disappears through the gate.

"Sister, get to the council chambers and find father. I will send word to King Zander and Queen Rose," Alvina says.

As Alvina walks down the path towards the gate, her outfit transforms into long elfish robes, her hair pulled back, as she stows her bow on her back. Her staff appears in her hand as a long riding cloak appears, flying behind her. Continuing down the street, elfish guards march behind her, more joining with every step she takes.

Upon reaching the guardhouse, Alvina calls for the captain.

"My Lady, good evening," the captain bows his head.

"Captain, you must send one of your fastest riders. We must get word of what has just occurred to the king and queen," Alvina commands, trying to hold back tears.

"My Lady, we have no one to spare. With Archduke Lukas putting us on lockdown, we have no extra guards," the captain explains.

"Then, Captain, I know of only one way to solve this," Alvina states, tapping her staff. Before anyone could respond, a beautiful black stallion runs up, snorting. Shortly thereafter, Alvina's brother, Duke Avery, materializes.

"You rang, sis?" Duke Avery inquires, looking at the big group of guards behind her.

"What did I miss?"

"Brother, you can ride faster than any living or dead elf. Unfortunately, we have no time to waste. Our mother has been kidnapped, and we must get word immediately to King Alezander and Queen Rose. King Alezander is not going to be happy to hear about this," Alvina notes as she follows her brother, who runs quickly out of the door, jumps onto the horse, his outfit transforming into elf battle armor.

"I will get help," Duke Avery declares, clicking the sides of the horse. As it rears up, lightning flashes across the sky.

"Duke Avery, do not stop until you find them. I am entrusting you with this responsibility. May the magic of our people protect you. The very fate of the Arcane rests with you, brother. Now go, and may all magic of our people protect you," Alvina states, pointing her wand as a portal flies open at the end of the street. Duke Avery clicks the side of the horse as it rears up and takes off at a gallop toward the portal and then, is gone.

A giant bell rings twice as students hustle throughout the halls of the Arcane Academy. As Rose ascends the grand staircase, she turns to acknowledge the students.

"Good morning, students. You normally get your greetings from the headmistress, but she is on a field trip with several faculty members. So, you will be seeing me a lot more over the next few days. Remember to have fun. Remember that magic is a beautiful thing. Open your minds and be willing to learn. Oh, and before I forget, one last thing, have a great day. You are all dismissed to class. Please hurry along," Rose remarks as she stands, looking out over the students, her hands resting behind her back.

Quietly turning, Rose peers down the stairs as Cedric approaches.

"Good morning, My Lady."

"Good morning, Cedric."

"I hope you don't mind. I figured I would come to assist for the next few days," Cedric explains, smiling.

"That is much appreciated, my old friend. Students, quickly, to class," Rose says as she catches fire pixies in her hand.

"Annoying little things, they are. Why they were ever created is beyond me," Cedric remarks.

"Indeed, Cedric, I agree," Rose notes as she and Cedric descend the stairs to the doors and head toward the front of the school to walk the grounds. As they begin to stroll through the gardens, hooves can be heard.

"Cedric, do you hear a horse?"

"I do, My Lady."

Just then, the stallion carrying Duke Avery comes into view as three demons fly behind him, diving at the horse and its rider. Moving quickly, Rose spins her hands, blasting one of the demons back as Cedric disappears and materializes flying next to the other two. He grabs them by their necks and slams them into the ground.

"Duke Avery, how are you?"

"My Queen," the young man says as he collapses, winded, his hand shaking as he hands her a letter.

Taking the letter, Rose raises her wand and the four dark shadows that are flying down the walkway toward them disappear through a portal.

"Cedric, quickly! Help me get Duke Avery up and inside," Rose says, stowing her wand and reaching down and offering the young elf a hand just as Mr. Terran gallops up.

Mr. Terran scoops up Duke Avery and runs inside with him as Rose opens the letter and reads.

೨

Dearest Queen Rose,

There is not much time. If you are reading this, darkness has fallen upon the Aelfdene village. My mother, Lady Otta, was taken. All of her prophecies are either gone or destroyed. I fear that Balimore is waging war on the Arcane. Help is needed, dear queen, please hurry.

Countess Alvina

೨

Rose turns the letter over in her hand several times, examining it carefully. Lady Marybelle and Destiny run down the walkway toward her, having seen Terran galloping through the school with Duke Avery in his arms.

"Cedric?"

"Yes, My Lady?"

"We are activating the Phoenix Protection Protocols for the school. Immediately!" Rose declares, spinning her hands as twelve orbs of light appear and circle her. Then, they fly into the air toward the school as lightfields explode out of the ground.

"Yes, My Lady. I understand," Cedric replies, lowering his hands to his sides and disappearing on the spot.

Rose regards the two women as they approach, then hands the letter to Destiny. Marybelle reads over Destiny's shoulder, then disappears.

Rose and Destiny nod to one another, then turn to face the school. Working together, they raise their hands as more lightshields explode into the sky, forming a protective barrier around the school. Destiny motions for Rose to go first. Turning, Rose begins walking across the ancient bridge as beings made of stone appear on either side of her and her staff appears in her hand. Walking the length of the bridge to the school, Rose speaks with the stone beings to the right and then to her left as they disappear into the ground. Moments later, the stone beings reappear in the courtyard, smashing the walkways and separating the school from the mainland. Destiny reaches the school's front courtyard just as Rose enters it. The bridge dissolves, falling into the ravine below, as two stone beings melt and form a stone wall that blocks the entry to the school where the bridge once stood.

Rose follows Ms. Destiny into the school. They part inside the door, reaching for the torches on either side. Pulling them down, the giant oak doors at the front of the school slam shut as vines rise up over the door, twisting through the iron as a lightfield rises up, sealing the door.

Rose and Destiny walk quickly into the grand foyer as suits of armor run past them, lowering their spears, and forming a protective barrier inside the door. Rose raises her wand straight into the air as a spark explodes, sounding like a gun going off to start a race. As the noise rings through the halls, a large bell sounds.

Gong! Gong! Gong! Gong!

Throughout the school, the students, in the midst of their lessons, are stopped by their teachers suddenly holding up one of their hands and pointing toward the ceiling, indicating that they should listen for a fourth gong. The teachers quickly rally their students. The hallways come alive as students bustle quickly through them, teachers and staff directing them to the main hall and the enclosed courtyard.

Vines rise out of the ground throughout the school, sealing every door and window. Finally, in the middle of the courtyard, Rose taps her staff, and a giant orb appears, floating over the ground. Image after image flashes across the surface of the orb as roars are heard and the glass ceiling of the courtyard opens, and three dragons soar into the space.

"Mr. Bruin, lock it down," Rose commands, her eyes running over the surface of the orb, watching the images displayed there.

The dwarf nods as he motions for the other dwarfs to follow as they start bolting throughout the courtyard, securing it even further. The students stand in amazement, watching the globe as Ethan pushes his way through them toward his sister.

"Rose, what is going on? Why are we activating The Phoenix Protection Protocol?" He inquires, standing next to her.

Rose looks up from the orb and hands the letter to Ethan.

"This is not good. Not good at all. Sis, where are Mom, Dad, and Oliver?"

"Ethan, I sent Cedric to retrieve them," Rose explains, walking around the orb.

"What about Headmistress Mora and Zander?"

"Unable to locate them, Ethan. They are too far into the forest, and I cannot track them. But I have called in reinforcements," Rose says, continuing to watch as Ms. Hoot appears.

"I hear that you needed assistance," Ms. Hoot states.

"Ms. Hoot, I need you to go with Belinda and find Mora and Zander. It is urgent. Tell them that the Phoenix Protocols have been activated," Rose says as her eyes turn purple.

"Understood, Lady Ignatius," Ms. Hoot replies as she transforms into an owl and takes off.

The students settle into the courtyard as Autumn and Drago circle the ceiling. Suddenly, screams ring through the hall.

"HELP! Aaaaah!"

Quickly getting to their feet, the faculty draw their wands.

Looking up, Rose flies over the orb as Theo comes barreling down the hall, carrying Hope in his arms. Matthew and Ari run on either side of them, wands out, as orbs fly around them, protecting them. Inches behind them, on their heels, is a giant, dark griffin, snapping at them. Immediately, Rose raises her wand and yells,

Oblitero.

Obliterate.

The creature explodes as four more dark creatures emerge. Ethan spins his hands, creating a lightfield. When the dark creatures hit it, they scream and explode.

"Ms. Destiny, take members of the faculty with you and check the school for any more rogue mystical creatures," Rose notes, stowing her wand, tapping her foot, and looking displeased. Just then, Theo runs up.

"Mom, that was awesome!" Ari declares.

"Explain to me why you are not with your class?" Rose snaps at him in front of the entire group. Before anyone can respond, Rose looks past Theo as Duke Avery enters the room, leaning on a walking staff.

"You four, we will finish this discussion later. Get to your groups now," Rose says, pushing past them toward Duke Avery. The two greet one another with a nod just as the giant orb, in the middle of the room, begins glowing and flies into the air. Ethan is standing close to the orb when a light beam hits the ground. The students move back quickly, examining it in awe, when Nadia steps out of it, spins her hands, and Ethan and Rose are decked out in armor. At the sight of Nadia, Autumn lands and bows.

"Autumn, please stay here and protect the students," Nadia asks as she turns, looking around the room. Rose quickly weaves her way through the students as Sebastian appears next to Nadia.

"My Lady, we must go quickly," he remarks as Ethan comes up, kisses him on the cheek, and the two disappear in the light beam.

Emerging from the archway, Destiny and Lady Marybelle look first at Nadia and then, at Rose.

"Keep the students safe. I will be back soon," Rose declares as Phineas and Bethany appear out of the light beam. Bethany places her hand on Rose's shoulder as the two nod. Athena and her guards appear as Nadia steps back into the light beam. Rose spins her hands and disappears on the spot.

꙳

Deep in the forest, several students are sparking leaves with their wands as others sit around bored out of their minds. One student leans over and whispers, "Professor Ignatius, how much longer do we have to listen to Headmistress groan on about the mystical water dews on the tree canopy?"

As Zander shrugs his shoulders, a scream rings out. Jumping to his feet, Zander draws his wand as two students run back toward the group, the darkness at their heels. Just as the students reach the group, the darkness suddenly stops in mid-air and starts flopping around like rag dolls. The two girls turn to look behind, as a cloaked figure emerges out of the ground, hands raised.

"Minnie?" the cloaked figure inquires.

"Yes, Sir," a golden eagle replies, landing next to the cloaked figure and transforming into human form.

"Get Lord Ignatius, the Lady Elder-Ignatius, and the students out of here. I have this," the figure says as he raises his hand revealing the two dark, cloaked figures that were hidden. Tilting his head, he lifts them into the air.

As Minnie approaches the group, Merlin rises out of the ground and grabs Minnie. Looking confused, Merlin flies backward past the cloaked figure that seizes Merlin with his magic and launches him away from the group and across the field.

"Minnie, I am not telling you again," the cloaked figure snaps as they cross their arms in front of themselves and slide backward across the ground as Merlin and the two dark figures throw magic, causing the cloaked figure to shield themself.

"Quickly, follow me this way," Minnie says, motioning for the group to follow. The students make haste behind Minnie when a loud hoot is heard, and Ms. Hoot appears, running next to the group.

"Professor Ignatius, I found you. Assistant Headmistress Ignatius has activated the Phoenix Protection Protocols. Mora stops, looks at Zander, and the two nod as Belinda soars down next to the group.

Zander yells toward the front of the group, "Minnie, take them and get them out of here. I have this."

Zander motions for Belinda, who grabs Mora and throws her up into the air onto her back. Zander turns, pulls his hair back into a ponytail as he pulls his sword, and runs in the opposite direction from the group, advancing on the darkness.

The students running close to each other are startled when a loud pop occurs, and two elves appear, flanking the group on the left side. Then, another loud pop sounds and two more elves appear, running alongside them, flanking them on their right.

"Keep a tight perimeter around them. The darkness must not touch them," one of the elfish women yells as the others nod at her. As darkness rises from the ground, two elves break from the group, sliding across the ground, and tearing apart the dark creatures with their magic. One of the elves spins his mace, striking several dark guards simultaneously as the woman spins her wand around her, magic flying around and hitting the darkness, causing them to explode.

As the group reaches the edge of the forest, they observe an older gray-haired man leaning on a walking cane, standing at the top of the hill. His hands rest on a hand-sculpted giant phoenix. The gentleman reaches into his vest pocket and retrieves a pocket watch that is broken and has a crack across its face. He places his monocle over his right eye and examines the watch.

"Dear me, it appears the time has come," the man remarks as an elf woman walks up, tilting her head to the right.

"They are an odd-looking group?" the woman notes as she lowers the different lenses in front of her eyes, focusing on something or someone. Then, one of the students in front of the group, Darren, yells "Look" and points at the sky as it begins to flash with various colors. Suddenly, a beam of light explodes from the sky, striking the ground as Nadia, Kelvin, Oliver, Olivia, Sebastian, Ethan, and Rose appear.

"Indeed, My Lady, you are correct. What an odd-looking group!" the Arcane man notes, snapping the pocket watch shut as he unhooks the watch from its chain and throws it into the air. Time begins to slow, then freezes completely.

Chapter 7
Introducing Time Themselves

Gliding down the hill, the Arcane man looks around then glances back up the hill to observe everyone frozen. He switches his monocle from his right eye to his left, then back to his right.

"It appears I have plenty of time," he notes, laughing to himself as he glides over the ground toward the cloaked figure, Noel. Examining Noel, he turns, then, observing the darkness approaching, his eyes narrow.

"Every time, we get to this part of the timeline, this always happens," the man remarks, walking up to the dark shadow general and examining the blade in his hand. Then, as he reaches up and taps the blade, it dissolves.

"Better. Besides, he might hurt someone with that blade," the man notes, rolling his eyes. Observing the area further, he disappears only to reappear on the other side of the field, examining the spot where Rose and her family stand frozen.

"What am I missing? Think Time, think," the man says, pacing the ground with his hands behind his back.

"Each time they appear, it is never the same," he notes, walking around looking at the members of the Houses of Phoenix, Knight, and Ignatius who have arrived.

"When Father and Noble Elder separated the Curpendulums throughout time, they created 15 unique timelines. If this battle has occurred 13 times already, then I wonder…? But it cannot be this easy," Lord Time Yule notes as an orb appears in his right hand. He spins his left hand over it and the orb begins to glow. When the glowing disappears, image after image play out.

"Hmm, each image contains a clue to the puzzle. But where to begin?" he asks, examining the orb, which when he threw it in the air, floated and projected 15 gold and silver lines across the field, scenes playing out on each.

Walking down the center of the lines, he watches the different scenes, all of the same battle, but each with different outcomes. Then, quickly, he glides above the ground to the 12th timeline.

"Here," he points as the scenes from that timeline spin around him, coming to life in slow motion. Turning his hand, the scene fast-forwards, then stops.

"In this particular timeline, Rose arrives separately from her siblings and parents. But in timeline nine, she arrives with Ethan only," he remarks, writing in a grimoire while tapping his quill against his chin, thinking.

"Differences? What do we know? When the Lady Rose arrives in each of the timelines, her arrival marks the point at which the darkness gets angry, their powers fluctuate. The fluctuations in their power causes Noel's power to grow.

"That's it—Noel!" Lord Time Yule says,

Moving his hands back and forth over each other, he works to align the battle scenes all to the same point, all fixed on Noel, who is frozen in time, darkness preparing to attack him. Quietly observing the 15 timelines, he unfreezes them to watch what happens. He freezes the story again as each scene plays out and walks the timeline, dismissing the lines' irrelevant aspects with a flick of his finger.

"This is it. This one right here. This is the time in which Noel receives help from his siblings. But why this time? Wait, that is this timeline," Lord Time Yule notes as he grabs the orb. Walking towards the field, the 15 timelines disappear when he drops the sphere and the area around him begins to spin. Then, summoning his cane, sand begins to fly around Lord Time Yule. When he leans forward on his cane, the sand disappears and there he stands in pitch black space, the only light coming from the eyes of the phoenix head on his cane. Walking across the space, one cauldron torch after another lights. The flames begin as a light blue flame, then turn orange as he passes. As the space lights, orb after orb can be observed as they float around.

࿇

Stopping, he reaches up, searching through the various sized orbs in the air, pushing several of them out of the way when he hears a voice.

"Hello, Brother."

"Hello, Sister," he acknowledges, rolling his eyes as he walks through the sea of orbs.

"Little brother, is that any way to greet me?" the Lady Time Yule inquires.

"If you are here to lecture me about meddling with time, I do not want to hear it," Lord Time Yule replies, his hand pushing an orb out of the way.

"I am not here to lecture you. What? Am I not allowed to visit with my little brother? Besides I bring news," says Lady Time Yule.

"Sister, a new coffee flavor at Dwarf Brew is not news. Wait! Let me guess. You have a clock for the shop," Lord Time Yule laughs.

"Ha, ha! Very funny, Brother. Noble Elder does not have much time," she remarks, looking concerned.

"And that is news, how? If you are referring to his expected passing in a half-century, I am aware," he notes, turning to look back at her.

"Brother, I am serious. Unfortunately, Noble Elder does not have much time," she restates with a sense of urgency.

"Remind me to send flowers when he passes or maybe a chorus singing praises of his passing. But if you are that concerned about him, then just turn back time for him. Several hundred years should work," Lord Time Yule notes, winking as he continues to rummage through the orbs.

"My dear brother, will you visit him?" Lady Time Yule inquires, waving her hand as a table and chairs appear, and she takes a seat.

"Why would I? He and I do not see eye-to-eye on well… anything," Lord Time Yule explains as he grabs an orb, examines it, and throws it over his shoulder.

Unfortunately, the orb shatters upon hitting the ground, dissolving to dust.

"Brother, do you know how old that one was?" Lady Time Yule asks, shaking her head.

"That thing old? They are all old. Blah! Why we keep these things is beyond me. We need to clean this place out," Lord Time Yule says, floating into the air and examining multiple orbs at once.

"Dear brother, we keep them as they are our stories, the great stories of time. Besides, what are you looking for?" she asks as she floats up into the air next to him.

"You would not understand," he states.

"Understand? Try me." she replies, handing him an orb.

"That is not it," he says, throwing it out of the way.

"Lord Time Yule, what are you looking for?" she shouts in frustration.

Lord Time Yule stops, takes a deep breath, and raising his head to look at the ceiling, lets out a sigh as he lowers himself back down to the ground.

"I have figured it out. I know how to help him," Lord Time Yule explains, looking at his sister as she also lowers herself down.

"Okay, and…?" she begins to inquire.

"It has to do with the secrets echoed," he says, walking across the room as he spins his hands over his head and the orbs fly up to the ceiling.

"I see, and what about them?" Lady Time Yule inquires.

Lord Time Yule throws an orb into the air as the room spins, and the two land in a field. Examining the area, Lady Time Yule spins her hands, and their outfits transform.

"Are you kidding me? Leather?" Lord Time Yule says, holding up his sleeves.

"I assume we are on a journey, and if we are traveling, why not in comfort?" she asks.

"First, leather is hot, and this is not the 1960s leather scene in the gay community. Second, we are watching from afar. We are not, and I mean we are *not* intervening, unless you are the great queen," he replies, spinning his hands as his regular clothes reappear.

"I like you better in the leather. You look so cute. Besides, I like it better than that monocle. I hate that thing," she says, walking past him.

"Geez, you are a pain," he remarks.

"Now, you were saying something about the secrets echoed?" she asks as they walk across the field.

"Yes," he replies as he waves his hand, and a door appears.

"Strange. This place looks different," she remarks as she follows her brother through the door.

Looking around, she gasps. "What happened here? Everything is burnt."

"That is what I am still trying to ascertain," Lord Time Yule explains.

Reaching down, Lady Time Yule scoops up a broken hat, examining the many different lenses on it that are shattered.

"I do not understand. This was Willow's. She would never have left this behind. What happened?" she inquires as Lord Time Yule steps over the downed planters, gets to the middle of the room, and raises his hands, turning them in a counterclockwise motion as the room begins to reassemble.

As the last item flies back into place, the two look around. Then, Merlin walks in.

"My Lord, it is not here," one of the dark guards says.

"Sir, no one is here either," another dark guard says, quivering.

"Burn this place down! Find me the prophecy! So help me, if that old crazy elf lied, she will be dead by morning," Merlin says, running his index finger along the leaf of the one plant as it turns black.

"Miraculous! I love that trick," Merlin states with a smile.

"Lord Merlin, we found this." one of the guards notes, handing the hat to him.

"Blah! Weird elves!" Merlin remarks, holding up the hat, examining it, then throwing it on the ground, kicking it, and cracking a lens.

"Burn it down. General, take whatever you want," Merlin commands, pulling a handkerchief out of his pocket, wiping his hands, and looking disgusted.

"Yes, Sir," the guards say.

"What Nimuway ever saw in elves is nauseating," Merlin states, stalking out the door.

Lord Time Yule watches as the hat slides across the floor. Then, he raises his hand, and everything comes to a halt.

"Brother, what is it?" Lady Time Yule inquires, her right eyebrow raised. Lord Time Yule walks over, takes the hat from his sister, and puts it on his head, spinning one of the larger lenses down in front of his eyes as he examines the room through the broken lens.

"I understand now. Magnificent!" he notes, peering around the room as he walks to the far end and moves a broken cupboard out of the way, revealing a box.

"It looks like Merlin did not find what he was looking for," Lady Time Yule remarks, moving closer to Lord Time Yule.

"No," he notes, opening the box and revealing a necklace with a giant phoenix symbol and, in the middle, an orange stone.

"Is that…?" Lady Time Yule begins to ask.

"This, Sister, is the necklace of Noel," Lord Time Yule explains, holding the necklace up by the chain.

"Brother, what does this mean?" Lady Time Yule inquires.

"That my plan has worked, Sis. Travel through time. Let Noble Elder know that I will be paying him a visit. But I have something I must do first," Lord Time Yule replies, placing the necklace in his pocket and picking up the small bag sitting in the box and stowing it in his other pocket.

"I will go, but before I do…" said Lady Time Yule, who stopped and hugged her brother. "I know what you are about to do, Brother. Our parent's died protecting time, and now, it is our turn to protect time. But, this time, we do it our way and not by the rules. We can fix things and make it right," Lady Time Yule notes, smiling at her brother.

"Thank you," Lord Time Yule says, hugging his sister back as Lady Time Yule reaches into her bag and hands him an orb.

"I believe you will need this," she explains.

"Actually, yes, I do. Where did you get this? You just saved me a journey," he notes, turning the orb in his hands.

"My brother, know this. A friend got it for you and has sent it as the way to take the next steps. He says it is time. Now go, my brother. May fate be with you. Oh, and Lord Time Yule, if you must break the rules, do so accordingly and, by all means, break time the correct way," Lady Time Yule says as she spins her hands and disappears.

Then, throwing the orb up and down several times in his hand, Lord Time Yule summons his cloak around him.

"Noble Elder, I may hate you at times, but you having this orb makes my trip easier."

෴

Teleporting on the spot, Lord Time Yule arrives back in the field, throws the orb in the air, and strikes it with his magic as lightning hits the ground repeatedly around him. In a flash of magic, he waves his hand, saying,

Magicae Temporis Lanuae.
Magical Time Teleport.

Leaves begin blowing around Lord Time Yule as he transforms into a young man, his hair done up, his monocle perched over his right eye, his pants gray, black knee-high boots with metal buckles running down the side, his overcoat hanging to the back of his knees, his striped black and maroon dress shirt accented by the purple and gray vest he is wearing. On each of his fingers, he dons a different ring, symbolizing the original ten houses of the Arcane. Then, as the leaves continue to spin, sand joins in the mix. Lord Time Yule is lifted off his feet, and in a flash of light and a poof, he is gone.

Landing on his feet, the leaves disappear as Lord Time Yule holds a top hat in his hand, snaps it up onto his head, and tilts it to the right. His cane appears as he walks down the path of the village.

"Time, you old fool, it worked. Phase one down. Now, on to the rest."

Laughing he throws the orb up, catching it, shrinking it to the size of a marble, holding it at eye-level, and gazing through it, before placing it in his pocket. Then, strolling down the path, he explores the area. Finally, there they are, what he was searching for, the five magical children playing.

"Even younger, they are always getting into trouble," he remarks, laughing and shaking his head.

"If I remember correctly, this is the time they were without a governess. Perfect," Lord Time Yule notes, continuing down the path to a large street and turning down it.

Walking through the gate of the giant mansion, he waves his hand as a piece of paper appears when he knocks. Stepping down onto one of the steps behind him, he looks around when a woman answers.

"Hello, can I help you?" the woman inquires.

"Good day, Mrs. Ignatius. The Governess agency sent me. I am Dalton," the man says as Lady Ignatius steps aside, welcoming him in.

"I did not realize the agency has male governesses," she remarks as they walk into the living room of the home and sit down.

"May I call you Lord Dalton?" the woman inquires.

"Yes, My Lady," he says, sitting back in the chair.

"I assume the agency explained to you about my children?" the woman inquires.

"They did indeed, My Lady," he replies, nodding his head.

"While my older children can look after themselves, my husband and I need someone to watch over our youngest, Lord Ambrose. He is a polite child but quite odd," the woman says, looking sad.

"So, seven children, six magical, and one who is not, I assume?" Lord Dalton inquires, raising an eyebrow.

"No, he is magical, extremely. But he never uses his magic. He is so magically talented that it drives my husband crazy. My husband sees that our son has raw potential in the magical arts, but Lord Ambrose does not care about it," the woman explains, rising to her feet.

"If you would follow me, I will introduce you to Lord Ambrose."

The two ascend the stairs. When they reach the top, Lord Dalton looks around and sees young Ambrose sitting peering out of the window.

"My son, what are you doing?" the woman asks.

"Just watching, Mama," the young Ambrose responds, turning to greet the man.

"Ambrose, this is Dalton. Lord Dalton, my son, Lord Ambrose. He is your new governor, my son," the woman notes as Ambrose rolls his eyes.

"Ambrose, do not be disrespectful," the woman scolds.

"It is okay, Mrs. Ignatius. I was the same way at his age," Lord Dalton remarks.

"Well, I will leave you two to get acquainted," the woman says.

When Mrs. Ignatius is out of sight, Ambrose turns and looks at Lord Dalton, studying him.

"Yes," Dalton acknowledges, observing Ambrose's reactions.

"You are an interesting Arcane," Ambrose says.

"How so, kid?" inquires Dalton.

"A hat, a monocle, a cane with a phoenix, it is as if… oh, never mind," Ambrose states.

"As if what, kid?" he asks.

"It is nothing, Sir. Have you met my brothers and sisters?" the young boy asks.

"Not yet. But I am sure I will later," Lord Dalton states.

"Five of the six of them are not nice. Rather, they are mean, foul individuals. If you have ever heard the stories of Merlin, they make him look good. But, on the other hand, you seem cool. So, just be careful. They like to hex our governesses. Our last one was spitting frogs for days. The one before that ended up in the hospital. They had her believing she was a four-year-old schoolgirl, who liked to play with dollies," Ambrose explains, getting up.

"They sound charming," Lord Dalton remarks.

"Charming? Far from it," Ambrose says, horrified.

"Can I ask how old you are, kid?" Lord Dalton inquires.

"I am seven, Sir," Ambrose replies.

"And you do not use your magic?" Dalton asks.

"No, Sir! I use very little as it scares me," Ambrose notes as he walks down the hall, Dalton following behind him.

"Why does magic scare you? Magic is a beautiful thing," Dalton suggests, stopping.

"Sir, you sound like my grandmama, the queen," Ambrose says.

"The queen?" Dalton responds.

"Queen Roslynn, High Queen of the elves," Ambrose notes, shaking his head.

"I see. But you still did not answer my question," Dalton says.

"My magic, Sir, is dangerous. It is uncontrollable. It has no limits. The stuff I can do would scare anyone," the young boy remarks, looking concerned.

Dalton lowers himself down to eye-level with Ambrose. "Young Ambrose, your magic is nothing to be afraid of. Your magic is a beautiful thing and will go on to help many people," Dalton notes as he stands and the two walk outside.

Ambrose and Dalton spend the next two hours wandering the grounds of the estate. Ambrose tells Dalton about the estates' history. As the two walk, Ambrose points out one of his favorite places, the old greenhouse. He notes that he loves to go there and meditate. Next, the two approach the giant pond in the yard when Ambrose takes to skipping rocks across the water as Dalton sits quietly reading when a magic whisp flies overhead and lands inches from Ambrose.

Before anyone can move, Dalton is on his feet, his hat over the whisp. Glancing around, annoyed, he sees the other Ignatius children standing up on the hill. Standing, Dalton brushes himself off, picks up his hat, brushes it off, and motions for the other five to come down the hill.

"So, magic whisps?" Dalton inquires, pacing back and forth. The five stand quietly, looking at him.

"Okay, so let me ask this. Who threw it?" he inquires, observing the reaction of each of them.

"Now, we can do this the easy way, and you all answer my questions, or we will have to do it the hard way," he remarks with his eyebrow raised.

"I did it, Sir," the one boy says, raising his hand.

"You? Name?" Dalton insists, knowing all too well which of the Ignatius siblings he is dealing with.

"I am Michael, Sir," he replies with a scared look on his face.

"Show of hands. How many of you wanted Michael to throw the whisp?" Dalton asks as the other four raise their hands.

"Okay, okay. I see. Again, show of hands. How many of you think Michael worked alone?" Dalton inquires as the other four raise their hands.

"Thanks. Throw me under the bus, guys," Michael says, kicking the dirt.

"Lord Michael, you, Sir, threw yourself under the bus when you threw the whisp," Dalton remarks.

"Are we in trouble, Sir?" Sophia asks, raising her hand. Suddenly, a screech sounds over their heads that makes everyone jump.

The five siblings immediately go back-to-back, pulling their wands, as Willow appears carrying a pot with a rather weird-looking plant.

"Seriously, where have you been?" Isabella snaps, looking at her sister.

"In the greenhouse tending to the plants," Willow answers as she walks up to Ambrose and takes him by the hand.

"I do not know what to do with you five. You leave poor Ambrose standing here with darkness coming," Willow mumbles as darkness encircles the group.

Dalton spins his hands together as a lightfield appears around the seven children. The darkness strikes the field and flies up into the air.

"Stay close and do not leave the field," Dalton instructs as he spins his hands and throws the darkness back. Then, raising his hand, two dark creatures fly into the air. When he pulls his hands apart, the creatures explode. Charging Dalton, two more dark creatures stop in mid-air and fly backward.

While the darkness flies back, hitting the ground, a black cat runs across the yard toward the magical field. Laughing, two dark guards reach down, pick up the cat and examine it. Before they can respond, they find themselves lifted off the ground as Ambrose stands outside the lightfield, his arm raised as his eyes glow purple. He points his index finger at the dark guards as a phoenix flies overhead, screaming. Running, Ambrose scoops up the cat and holds him tight as darkness dives on them. The six siblings gasp when they notice Ambrose is holding his right hand up.

The darkness hits a field of light as they are thrown backward. Ambrose rises into the air, raising the darkness off their feet. Quickly looking around, Dalton notices that the darkness is flying into the air as everything around him and the group levitates. At that moment, Dalton understands what scares other Arcane about Ambrose's power.

As the darkness rises in the air, Ambrose spins his hands over his head. A dark cloud appears, spinning over him. Closing his eyes, then reopening them, Ambrose's eyes turn solid black as lightning strikes around the group and a giant orb of glowing light appears in front of Ambrose.

Tilting his head, he looks around at the darkness, then smiles as they explode. Then, to protect themselves, the darkness hurls dark magic at Ambrose, who catches their blasts of magic and absorbs them.

A sinister laugh rings out over the area, sending chills down everyone's spine. Observing the space, the six notice three cloaked figures approaching. Raising their wands to defend themselves, the three dark figures fly into the air, crash into each other repeatedly, then are projected in opposite directions from each other. One of the figures raises their wand at Ambrose. As Ambrose lowers his hand and snaps his open palm into a fist, the figure's wand explodes. The figure holds its hand as it drops to the ground. Hitting the ground, the other two figures crash into them.

Then, the three figures hear something that causes them to start scrambling to their feet. From the air, Ambrose speaks,

Vocate Spiritus, Vocate Spiritus, Vocate Spiritus.
Summon forth the Spirits.

A scream lets out as one of the dark figures is pulled into the ground. The other two scramble to get away when both also disappear into the ground. Then, as more darkness appears, they are met with spirits flying around them. The darkness, confused by the speed of the spirits, tries to engage them in battle, but Ambrose causes an orb to appear, blasting light rays, causing the darkness to disappear. Then, reaching up, Ambrose touches his index finger to the orb's surface. It grows brighter, and the remaining darkness dissolves into dust.

Upon the last darkness disappearing, the six siblings lower the lightfield. Ambrose lowers himself down, his eyes returning to normal, and his cat jumps up into his arms. Then, the children's parents and grandparents arrive with a loud pop.

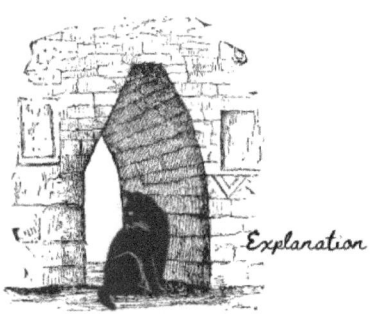
Explanation

Chapter 8
Explanation

"Mom, Dad, Grandmama and Grandpapa," the six siblings shout in unison, running up and hugging their grandparents. Ambrose turns away, petting his cat and walking away from the group.

"My grandchildren. Are you okay?" their grandmother inquires, examining them.

"Yes," they answer in unison when two dark figures move across the ground.

A scream rings out as the two shadows freeze on the spot. Ambrose tilts his head, then turns and walks away. He raises his right hand, snaps his fingers, and one of the frozen creatures explodes. The other dark creature begins to run when Mr. Cee jumps down from Ambrose's arms, transforms into a black panther, and chases the creature. Within seconds, Mr. Cee walks up, holding a severed head in his mouth. He drops it, then jumps into the air and transfigures back into a house cat.

As everyone watches, the eldest of the grandchildren responds. "As I said, Mom, Dad, Grandmama and Grandpapa, we are okay. If it was not for Mr. Dalton, fighting the darkness back and protecting us, we could have been hurt."

"Geez, do you hear yourself?" asks Willow, shaking her head as her older sister, Isabella, turns and glares at her.

"What are you shaking your head at?" Isabella snaps.

"You! Dear Ambrose played a part in saving us, but you do not recognize that," Willow replies as Isabella pulls her wand on her sister, and vines shoot up in front of Willow.

"Wands down. Now!" their grandfather commands, looking sternly at them as their grandmother pushes by them and walks towards young Ambrose. Standing quietly at this point and hiding behind Lord Dalton,

Ambrose peers around him, watching what is happening, all the while, petting his cat.

"I see Mr. Cee is happy and purring," his grandmother notes as she approaches, kneeling to his level, looking at him, then rising back to her feet as Ambrose nods.

"Dear me. Where are my manners? I am the Lady Roslynn," she says, extending her hand to Dalton.

"Nice to meet you, Great Queen," Dalton replies, shaking her hand and bowing his head.

Rose's eyes narrow and she turns her head slightly to the right as she smiles at him.

"Dalton, the pleasure is all mine," Rose says.

"Children, inside now. Wash up for supper," Dalton orders, walking away, trying to avoid Queen Rose's gaze. But unfortunately, he knows all too well of her magical ability.

"Zander, dear, take them inside. I wish to speak with Lord Dalton," Rose says, turning back looking at him, while removing her gloves and stowing them on her belt.

Zander nods, turning to take the children inside.

"That means you too, young man. Go!" Rose states as she holds out her hand to Ambrose.

The young man bows his head and walks past, carrying his cat. When the six reach the doorway, their mother begins to shoo them inside when a loud cackle rings out over the land. Zander, Rose, Rusty, Meredith, and Dalton all draw their wands. Rusty and Meredith step in front of the six children, along with Zander, as a dark cloaked figure floats above the ground toward Ambrose.

"My, my! What do we have here?" a woman's voice asks as Mr. Cee hisses and jumps out of Ambrose's arms.

Willow comes up alongside her brother and takes his hand.

"I am here, Brother, and I am not letting go," she says.

The witch's magic strikes an invisible barrier. Flames engulf it and cover the barrier, creating a fire dome.

"Ambrose! Willow!" their parents yell when they see the flames extinguish, and the two are standing, holding up their arms, light flying around them, pushing the dark witch back.

Rose and Dalton work together to fight off the dark guards who are emerging, when, suddenly, another cackle rings out, and a second dark witch appears, helping the first, striking the magic barrier that is protecting Willow and Ambrose. Zander, Rusty, and Meredith continue to fight back the darkness. Lord Zander has his sword drawn, helping to protect the other five children. Each magical blow to the field protecting Ambrose and Willow causes Willow to begin to buckle from the intensity of the continued attacks.

As Willow is pushed to her knee, Ambrose pulls her up as they are joined by their siblings, Kells and Sophia, who run up, grab their siblings' open hands, and join them in holding off the dark witches.

"We are here. We have you two," Kells and Sophia say, helping their siblings. The four hum as the magical barrier grows in power. As they hum, magical beams spin out from the field, encircle the two dark witches, and fling them across the yard.

The three eldest siblings work together, helping their parents and grandfather to hold off the darkness when Dalton and Rose appear with the four siblings who hold hands in front of the group as three more dark witches join the battle.

"Do they ever stop multiplying?" Sophia inquires about the five dark witches, who dive on the magic barrier, striking it repeatedly with their magic. Then, before anyone knows what has occurred, Ambrose yells,

Illuminare Ignire Accendo.
Illuminate and ignite the blaze.

A flash of light emerges from the clouds and fireball after fireball begin raining down, striking the five witches who create magical shields to protect themselves as four more dark witches appear. The nine witches soar into the air, acknowledge each other with nods, and combine their magic, striking the magical field. When their combined magic hits the field, the nine witches find themselves launched in various directions as Pete, Michael, and Isabella join their four other siblings. Holding hands, the seven siblings go back-to-back, their eyes glowing as they speak.

Per Potentiam de lux.
By the power of light.

Dalton spins his hands as the seven speak in unison. A light field appears in front of the group, then encircles the dark witches. Screaming, the nine witches repeatedly strike the field, as it encircles them with lightning, striking them. Ambrose's eyes turn white, and the nine, dark witches scream. Finally, the witches crash to the ground as the screams end, and all of them are dead.

The seven siblings look around and lower the light field. Willow is the first to hug Ambrose as the other five stand by quietly, watching. Ambrose embraces his sister back as Dalton walks up.

"The greatest lesson the seven of you have needed to learn is ways to work together. Although there will come times in the future when the seven of you will each be challenged, remember you all balance each other," Dalton notes.

"He is correct. Individually, magic can be powerful, but when you are with your siblings, it becomes unstoppable. Now, children, inside. Go and wash up," their grandmother, Rose, says, watching as the children head for the door.

"Zander, Rusty, and Meredith, I wish to speak with Dalton for a few minutes," Rose remarks as Zander bows and follows behind their grandchildren. Then, quietly, Dalton scoops up Mr. Cee, walks over to Ambrose, and hands the cat to him.

"Ambrose, you need to keep him safe."

"Yes, Sir," Ambrose replies, smiling and hugging the cat, as he moves toward the door.

"Ambrose?" Dalton calls.

"Sir?" Ambrose responds, stopping and looking at Dalton as his grandmother, Queen Rose, watches.

"Bud," Dalton says, kneeling. "You, of the seven Ignatius children, will have many challenges ahead of you. Do not be too hard on your siblings, okay? They are learning to work with you as you learn to work with them. You each need each other, for one alone is not enough to stop Merlin."

Ambrose nods, hugs Dalton, and disappears through the door. Rose walks past Dalton towards the gardens on the grounds.

Walking quietly beside the pond, Rose is the first to speak.

"Interesting, is it not?" Rose says.

"What is interesting, my queen?" Dalton asks, walking up alongside her as they start down the path into the flower garden.

"The fall lilies. Fascinating flowers. They grow all season and on the last day of fall in a very moment, time alters them," she says, touching the closed plant and walking toward the fountain.

Dalton's eyes narrow, watching Rose. Dipping her hand in the water, a ripple appears when she sits on the side of the fountain, observing the area.

"What do you see, Lord Dalton?" she asks, taking in a deep breath, as a bright light spins in the distance, across the garden.

"The garden, Ma'am," he replies, sitting down next to her.

"Silly me! That is not what I meant," Rose explains with a smile on her face.

"Then, what did you mean?" Dalton inquires.

Looking out over the garden, Rose raises her hand and points as a watch appears in the distance, spinning, then starting to glow.

Dalton rises to his feet, walks toward the watch, walks around it, and examines it as it spins.

"Interesting feat of magic," he notes, rolling his eyes at Rose as he continues to examine the watch.

"Indeed, it is. Only seen a half dozen other times and, every time, the same thing," Rose notes. Walking up and tapping the watch with her wand, it suddenly stops, time freezing completely.

Transforming on the spot, Rose grows younger, When she finally stops, a younger version of herself, from when she appeared with her mother and brothers on the hill the day Lord Time Yule froze everything and examined the fifteen timelines, is revealed.

Dalton backs up and examines the space when he suddenly finds his attire transforming into his time robes.

"Lord Time Yule," Rose says, bowing her head.

"What magic is this?" he inquires, holding up his sleeve and looking displeased.

"I knew I had to speak with you, so why not take a page out of your grimoire and time jump? Besides, every time you appear, so too does that watch, your signature calling card, the watch ever shifting the fabric of the story," Rose replies, tapping the glass of the watch as the area around them spins.

Lord Time Yule places his hands together, then pulls them apart as everything suddenly stops, and the two find themselves standing in the room of orbs. Lord Time Yule spins his cloak as he walks toward the table and sits down in the chair, placing his boots on the table. Rose walks through the room, exploring the various orbs. Whenever she touches one, it flies around her. Lord Time Yule sits back, holding his hands up in front of his face as he taps his fingers together, fascinated by the orbs' responses to Rose.

"So, this is the Room of Secrets," Rose notes as she strolls through the room, examining the orbs.

"Yes, it is, Queen Rose. But what I am curious about is how you know of this place?" Lord Time Yule remarks, tapping his index finger on the tabletop as two teacups on two saucers appear along with a teapot, sitting on a tray.

"Thyme Tea?" he asks, motioning for her to join him at the table.

Rose reaches into her pocket and approaches Lord Time Yule, pulling out a watch as she sits down. Then, holding it in her hand, she hands it to Lord Time Yule.

"Ha! A simple watch. It is broken. Why did you bring it to me? Did you think this clock master was going to fix it?" he inquires, tossing the watch onto the table.

"It is not just a simple pocket watch, and you know that," Rose retorts, pouring the tea. Lord Time Yule holds up his hand, and, from his palm, an identical pocket watch appears, floating.

"Queen Rose, you see, a watch like yours is simple. It is broken because of a moment, a glitch in time," he explains as he closes his hand and leans back in his chair.

Sipping her tea, Queen Rose comments, "A moment, a very odd concept, wouldn't you agree?"

"Time odd? Ha! You sound like Noble Elder or even my Father Elder Yule," an amused Lord Time Yule declares.

"Lord Time Yule, do you love him?" Queen Rose inquires, sipping her tea as Lord Time Yule rises to his feet and walks away from the table, his hands resting behind his back.

"Why do you ask, My Queen?" Lord Time Yule asks in a monotone voice, raising his hand and touching one of the orbs as it comes to life, image after image playing out of Ambrose aging through the years.

"Lord Time Yule, are you not the one with the ability to control time?" Rose inquires.

He turns his head and looks over his shoulder, nodding.

"Then, why not simply fix the timeline? Why continue with these illusions?" Queen Rose asks while leaning back in her seat.

"Easier said than done, Queen Rose. You see, when my father and Noble Elder altered time, they did so in a way that until a particular journey is complete, time will continue to repeat, divide, and then repeat. It is a never-ending story of twists and turns that becomes more complex with each passing day. The longer it takes to reach that particular moment in the journey, the one needed to stop this twisted story, the increasingly difficult it becomes to stop this nightmare," he notes as the orb begins circling his hand as his head tilts. At the same time, he watches a man fighting off the darkness.

"Noel?" Queen Rose inquires.

Lord Time Yule nods, then turns his attention back to the image.

"He can be saved, can't he?" Rose asks as she watches the image play out.

"He can, a new set of wheels have been put into motion, but throughout time, the same story continues to play out, except this one," he says, closely examining the orb that is flying around his hand.

"How do we fix the timeline?" Queen Rose inquires.

"It would require a feat of magic that I have only read about," Lord Time Yule explains, when suddenly Rose's grimoire appears. Placing the grimoire on the table and then, her glasses on the tip of her nose, Rose opens her grimoire and begins turning the pages, looking at Lord Time over the top of her glasses.

"No," says Lord Time, releasing the orb.

"You did not give me the chance to ask" Queen Rose remarks, annoyed.

"My Queen, however noble your intentions to help, your magic alone cannot fix a broken timeline," Lord Time Yule explains.

"What if my grimoire contains the spell? What if I give you that spell?" Rose inquires.

"Because, My Queen, the spell is not the problem," Lord Time Yule snaps.

"Then, what is it?"

"A magic more powerful than time. Magic that has eluded the great Nobles for years."

"Lord Time Yule, that is impossible. Nothing is stronger than time."

"Ha, there is one power far stronger than that of time. But it is magic that is tricky to master. I have traveled many timelines watching the same stories play out over and over, and the result is the same every time."

"If time is not the answer, then what is?"

Closing his eyes, Lord Time Yule takes a breath. When he opens his eyes, he says, "Love!"

"So, you do love him?"

"Yes, and no, My Queen," Lord Time Yule replies, pouring another cup of tea.

"It cannot be both," Rose states, tapping her foot and crossing her arms.

"I love him unconditionally, My Queen. I have been with him in every timeline. Our love for each other is unbreakable. But his love is filled with hatred. His childhood was nothing but trauma. He struggled growing up, and the people he needed to accept him would rather hex him than ever help him," Lord Time Yule replies, sipping his tea.

"Then, how do we help him?"

"We cannot. But who says that he has not been helped already?" he asks, sipping his tea again when he finishes speaking. "Noel's love is filled with rage, that is until the others learn to work with him collectively. Until the others put aside their differences, there shall be no peace, only darkness, much like your seven, charming grandchildren, who had to learn to work together with Ambrose."

"Yes, in that moment."

"Correct, My Queen, but they still have much to learn."

"Ha! That is easier said than done. Have you met my five older grandchildren, the children of my son, Rusty?" Queen Rose inquires.

Raising his hand, the orb from earlier flies to Lord Time Yule.

"As I have noted, it happens. Noel and his siblings learn to work together, and when they do, his magic grows much stronger, but at a great price," Lord Time Yule replies, peering into the orb as a tear rolls down his face.

"I won't let that happen," Queen Rose notes, placing her hand on his shoulder.

"My Queen, do not make a promise that cannot be kept," Lord Time Yule replies sadly.

"What if Zander and I raise the child?"

"It will not help. His magic is too strong. Wait!"

The orbs fly to the ceiling as a bookcase rises out of the ground and glides across the floor. Lord Time Yule floats into the air, takes a grimoire from the top shelf, and lowers himself back down to his chair.

"*Chronica Senioris* (*The Chronicle of Elder*)," Queen Rose says, trying to examine the grimoire that Lord Time Yule has chosen.

"My father spoke of a moment," Lord Time Yule explains, thumbing through the pages.

"Here!" he declares, pointing at the passage.

Rose is reading the page when Lord Time Yule speaks,

Magia Temporis Salire nos ad hoc Momentum.

Magic of time jump us to this moment.

The room begins spinning and they land with a loud pop, looking up from the grimoire.

&

"My old friend," the man says as the giant clock on his belt spins out of control

"Time," the other man says, pointing at the belt.

"Yes, it is broken. As usual, the timeline is acting up," Elder Yule complains.

"Then just fix it, my old friend," the gentleman replies, reaching into the air and revealing a wand out of thin air.

"Do you hear yourself, Noble Elder? Fix time! Ha! Fix time! Are you feeling okay? One cannot just simply fix time."

"Settle down, Elder Yule, and, yes, I feel fine. It is a simple fix, my old friend."

"Yes, you tell yourself that, Noble Elder," Elder Yule smiles, shaking his head.

"What is causing time to act so weird this evening?" asks Noble Elder.

"I was hoping you might tell me, my friend. I have heard of a secret, a secret so powerful that it echoes," Elder Yule remarks.

"Indeed, secrets echoed, that time itself has been fixed, but then again it was already fixed and working fine, but then it was broken. I cannot seem to remember," Noble Elder states.

Elder Yule shakes his head, resting it in his hand when the area around him and Noble Elder begins to spin and the two land in the dark of night in the middle of a field, the stars providing the only light to the area. In the distance, a young elf can be seen.

"Noble Elder, what are we doing here?" Elder Yule asks, watching the young elf.

"This is the moment in which time did not break," Noble Elder states, pointing at the young elf.

Quietly, the young man looks around and begins spinning his hands in front of him as he ages, then transforms to be young again, then ages for a second time.

The now elderly elf stands, holding a staff with a giant star perched upon it. He taps it on the ground as the sky spins, and seven cloaked figures appear.

Watching, Rose and Lord Time Yule look at each other, then back at what is happening.

> *As the seven approach the elf bows. The leader, in the middle, raises their hand as they lower their hood.*

"Willow," Rose says as she begins to approach, but Lord Time Yule catches her by her shoulder and shakes his head, indicating that she should not proceed.

> *"My dear sister," the elf says, bowing and then hugging her.*
> *"My love," the elf says as he pushes past Willow and hugs one of the cloaked figures. At that moment, the area spins back as Noble Elder smiles and walks past Elder Yule smirking.*
> *"You altered it?" Elder Yule inquires.*
> *"Actually, it was not me. It was your son, my old friend, and, of course, Noel," Noble Elder replies.*

As the area begins to spin, Rose raises her hand, and she and Lord Time Yule rise into the air then land back on their feet, watching the image.

"How did you do that?" Lord Time Yule asks Rose with a puzzled look.

"Like you, Lord Time Yule, I have many secrets," she replies, half smiling at him.

> *"Noble Elder, if what you say is true, that my son and your successor, Noel, can restore time, then I must ask, 'How?'"*
> *"Ah, your son figures it out. Smart lad that he is, he altered time every chance he got until that one moment when he got an idea. That idea was so powerful that it transformed the timeline and story altogether. It took all but a moment when he decided to help a young child, Lord Ambrose," Noble Elder explains.*

Rose raises her hand, and the area around them spins and they land back in the field where time stands motionless.

"You see, your act of love for him, for them, is what saves them," Rose says, raising her hand and pointing out over the frozen field, while looking at Lord Time Yule.

Nodding, Lord Time Yule walks down the hill, examining the area. Then, he raises his hands over his head, and a giant bright orb appears, floating above him. Lightning strikes the ground repeatedly as a door appears.

"Queen Rose, this is where we depart," Lord Time Yule declares, carrying the orb.

"Where will you go?" Rose asks.

"I will go to where the horizon's meet. I am sending you back to the moment when time froze, and Noel appeared. But you must promise me, you will raise him, keep him safe, and when the time is right, give him this," Lord Time Yule replies as he shrinks the orb into a small gem and places it into a necklace. As the gem merges with the necklace, it flashes, revealing light. Then, it returns to normal. Lord Time Yule hands the necklace to Rose. She nods and accepts it.

"I will make sure he stays safe," she promises.

"Thank you, Great Queen, that necklace will be the key to his knowledge, to his power, for him to find me, and for him to save time," Lord Time Yule notes, turning and walking toward the portal that has opened.

"Dalton," Rose calls as Lord Time Yule freezes and looks back over his shoulder.

"Yes, Queen Rose," he replies.

"Do be safe, old friend!" Rose says, bowing as Dalton Time Yule, disappears on the spot.

જ

A loud pop echoes through the space as Lord Time Yule emerges out of the portal and descends down the hallway of the dungeon. Several dark knights run towards him but drop to the ground, dead. Turning the corner, two more advance on him, but he raises his hand, revealing a magic outline of a clock. Time freezes and the guards fly off their feet, levitating into the air. Lord Time Yule quietly walks through the floating guards. Then, he raises his hand, snaps his fingers, and they all fall to the ground, also dead.

"Why do they feel they must always attack?" he remarks, rather disgusted as he steps over their lifeless bodies.

With that, he turns his attention to a door. Spinning his hands together, the lock explodes, and the door flies off its hinges. There, sitting in the cell, is the Lady Otta.

"You came for me?" she asks, raising her hands as the chains hold her at the table.

"No," Lord Time Yule replies as he raises his hand and the chains tighten, pulling Otta back down into her chair.

"You dare not help me? Why?" demands Otta.

"Because, My Lady, it is your prophecies that nearly destroyed all of the Arcane. Never again, witch. I, Lord Time Yule, hereby strip you of your magic. May you live out your days as a Mundane. No Arcane of magical power shall be able to restore your magic," he declares as he turns and walks through the archway created by the door flying back on its hinges.

Standing on the other side of the archway, he enters into the realm of time where beautiful columns rise from the floor, and dragons, fairies, and birds buzz around the columns with magic flying around them. Turning back to Otta, Lord Time Yule remarks, "Oh, by the way, your prophecies will never affect any of the timelines again. Darkness will not rule. Only light and only Noel." His voice ringing back into the cell where Otta remains, he raises his hood and dematerializes with a loud pop.

The Truth

Chapter 9
The Truth

In the field, time stands frozen as Rose raises her hand and disappears, returning to the library. Then, she quickly runs toward the spiral staircase, glancing around as she ascends.

"My Lady, good evening. What is the hurry?"

"Mr. Bruin, I need the *Chronicles of the Elders* as told by the elfish priestesses, please?"

"That would be to your left, three shelves up."

Grabbing the grimoire, Rose slides down the ladder to the floor as she races to the table. There, she discovers a young girl hiding under the table.

"Hello," says Rose, extending her hand. But the girl pulls away from her and then, pulls a wand as Rose and Mr. Bruin back up.

The girl crawls out from under the table, wand in hand. As Rose begins to spin her hands, a flash of light blinds her momentarily, causing her to back up. Rose blinks a few times, and as she begins to regain her sight, the girl transforms into an older woman, sitting at the table.

Finally able to see again, Rose inquires, "Who are you?"

The woman laughs, glancing around as she speaks. "How do you not know who I am?"

"Am I supposed to?" Rose inquires.

"In all of your studies, how do you not know me? I am Anwara, the Luminous."

"If you're Anwara, then, you're a Celestial. You are far more powerful than any living or deceased Elder."

"Correct and then incorrect," Anwara responds as she motions for Rose to sit.

"Okay, so there is more to your visit than meets the eye?" Rose inquires as Anwara nods.

"Would you care to explain?"

"Indeed, I came to speak with you about the timeline," Anwara says.

"I already know," Rose states.

"Know what? I have not had a chance to tell you what I came about," Anwara replies.

"Then, you are not here about Lord Time Yule altering time?" asks Rose as Anwara looks shocked.

"Wait! What do you mean 'altered the timeline?'" she shouts, jumping to her feet and beginning to pace the floor, mumbling to herself.

"That would explain why the timelines are acting up. But why would he do such a feat of magic, and without the permission of the Celestials or the Nobles? Hmm. Do the others know? This is alarming. What is your ploy, Dalton?" Anwara inquires, stopping her pacing

"Lady Rose, this is very important. Did he say how he altered it?"

"The only thing he said was that he was making it the last version of time, that, this time, it would all be different," Rose replies, standing and leaning against the table.

"The last version of time and it would be different. Hmm. He refers to a moment so out of context that it would not make sense to pursue," Anwara remarks as she walks toward the middle of the library. She waves her right hand over her left hand and the small pearl in her hand transforms into a viewing orb.

"If what you say is true, then we are running in time backward. Hmm, what a bizarre move. What is Lord Time Yule up to?" Anwara asks, peering into the orb.

"If it would help, it has to do with Noel," Rose says, watching the response on Anwara's face.

"Noel? Interesting. How did none of us see this?" Anwara inquires.

"Us?" Rose responds with an eyebrow raised.

"The Celestials, the divine council of all life and death," Anwara explains, looking up from the orb.

"Great, Anwara, what brings you here?" Rose inquires.

"Well, I had come to speak with you about some knowledge you will need to stop the darkness, but things have changed," Anwara says as she moves her hands on either side of the orb and the images change rapidly.

Rose approaches, watching the images play out in the orb when the room begins to spin. The two land in an old priory where a cauldron explodes in flames. A cloaked figure walks into the room, carefully observing the space. It is a cloak that Rose immediately recognizes.

"Nimuway? Where are you?" the cloaked figure inquires.

"Ahh, Lady Mora. How are you?"

"My dear friend, the earth trembles," Mora remarks, lowering her hood.

"Yes, I know. So, here they come," Nimuway remarks, pointing up as five other cloaked figures appear.

"What is this about?" one of them asks.

"Calm down, everyone. We shall wait for Noble Elder to get here," Nimuway explains as a loud pop sounds throughout the space and an older man appears.

"It is about time you got here," the figures in the space say in unison.

"Hush, all of you. I ran into a hiccup getting here," Noble Elder says, revealing that his cloak is burnt.

"Darkness?" Nimuway inquires.

"Of course," Noble Elder responds.

৵

Quietly, Rose freezes the vision and walks through the space, examining everything. Anwara floats on the air, legs crossed, observing Rose. After retrieving her glasses, Rose puts them on and walks around Noble Elder, then Nimuway and Mora.

"Interesting, I set them in the early years of the Arcane," Rose says as her eyes narrow on something. Then, walking across the room, she stops in front of one figure, then walks around them, and stops again.

"Hmmm, you are odd-looking," Rose remarks out loud.

"Indeed," Anwara agrees, walking down invisible stairs.

"A blip in the timeline?" Rose ponders.

"Yes, it just happened recently. However, we believe it to be Lord Time Yule himself," Anwara states.

"So, you all believe it is him, or you all know for a fact that it is him?" Rose asks, peering over her shoulder.

"We cannot prove it. The figure never lowers their hood during this entire interaction," Anwara states.

"How new is he in this vision?" Rose asks, pacing around the figure.

"The original vision is hundreds of years old, but the addition of this new figure is about a week? Also, the figure's attire does not match anything from that time," Anwara explains.

"What is the purpose of this vision?" Rose asks.

"It is the discussion about the youngest Celestials," Anwara says.

"The youngest Celestials?" Rose asks.

"Yes. Mora, your husband, Zander, and Noel," Anwara responds.

"Wait! I expected Mora to be ancient, but Zander? A Celestial? Is that a joke?" Rose asks, half laughing.

"No, he is a Celestial and a powerful one. Only one living Celestial is more powerful than him, and that is Noel. But, you see, no one knows the extent of Noel's power. We know he does not need a wand or staff. He can cast spells without a single spoken word. He has great telepathic power. He is telekinetic, and he has a power that scares the Celestials and Nobles," Anwara notes.

"What is this power that scares everyone?" Rose inquires.

"Rose, his magic is so strong that he can dissolve anything into dust, and he can cause the elements to do things that no one has ever seen. Let's just say that he can combine the four without any questions," Anwara says, looking concerned as she summons her staff, taps it on the ground, and causes the area to spin.

The two return to the library, just as dark guards are overrunning it.

Furious, Rose's eyes turn black, and the two guards drop to the ground dead. Turning, she raises her hand. A giant clock appears, and everything freezes on the spot. Throwing her hands out, everything explodes. Her eyes change from black to purple as she turns her hands in a counterclockwise motion and the giant hands on the clock turn backward and everything in the library flies back onto the shelves.

The dwarfs emerge from various hiding spots around the library, as a dark cackle rings out, and Mr. Bruin flies off his feet. A dark witch floats in the air, holding on to Mr. Bruin's shirt collar.

"Put him down. Now!" Rose screams as her eyes turn white and she rises into the air, the wind blowing around as a cyclone begins to form.

"You will never succeed. Lord Time Yule thinks he can stop me, but no one can stop me, I will have the Curpendulums. They will be mine, and I will give them to Master Merlin," the witch laughs. Mr. Bruin drops from the air, landing on his feet, as the witch suddenly finds her arms bound to her sides. Rose spins her hands as the witch spins in the air and the curtains shred into strips of fabric that wrap around her as she falls to the floor.

Screams echo as nails can be heard being dragged across the wood bookshelves as Morgana appears walking from behind two shelves, laughing. Morgana continues to laugh as she blocks blast after blast of magic as Rose lights the space with flying orbs directed toward her.

"You are still weak, and I will take great joy in destroying you," Morgana declares as she flies across the room and backward out the window. When Rose looks down, there is Noel, who lowers his arm and nods at his six siblings, who run past him and engage the darkness in battle.

Mora, Zander, Sebastian, Oliver, Olivia, Ethan, Kelvin, and Nadia also appear with a snap of his fingers. Stepping back, Noel takes to the air and shoots through the broken window, landing on his feet outside. Under his cloak, his eyes could be seen glowing silver as he walks up to Morgana and lifts her off the ground by her throat. The dark witch flies through the window, still bound, and lands on her back next to Noel. As he looks down at her, she dissolves on the spot. Turning his attention back to Morgana, he tilts his head, and the broken glass of the library window flies back into place. The six cast a field of magic around the building and window as soon as they saw Noel taking to the air. In a flash of light, Noel is gone, as are the six.

Landing back on the floor, Rose spins her hands, and the papers disappear, and the grimoires and other items return to normal.

"Well?" Zander inquires.

"Well, what, dear?"

"What did you learn?"

"Hold that thought, please," Rose glides across the room, grabbing the ladder and sliding it across the bookcase as she climbs up, disappearing into the bookshelves. She reappears a second later, sliding to the floor with a giant grimoire stowed under her arm. As she reaches the floor, she opens the grimoire, flipping the pages.

Finally, she replies, "What we've always known is that Merlin and the darkness are working together. I learned that they did kidnap your aunt, but her whereabouts, at this time, are unknown. Zander, you and I need to speak about something you are keeping from me."

Seeing Anwara, Zander nods. But, when he starts to speak, he is interrupted.

"Sorry, but what would the darkness want with Zander's aunt?" Ethan inquires.

"My dear sister-in-law is a mighty witch who is also a gifted seer. All of her prophecies and all of her visions, to date, have been true. So, if the darkness kidnapped her, then they are seeking answers," Mora says, looking concerned.

"Answers?" Ethan and Oliver inquire in unison.

"The type of answers, my dear brothers, that involve all of our children," Rose says, slamming the grimoire shut and walking across the library as her podium rises from the ground. She places the giant grimoire on the podium, then reaches into her bag, retrieving an old tattered leather-bound grimoire.

"Our children? What do they have to do with anything?" Oliver asks, looking at his sister, then around the room for answers.

"Everything," Anwara answers, making another grimoire appear and handing it to Rose.

"*The Liber de Tempus et Oraculum* per Domine Nova Astira Yule (*The Grimoire of Time and Prophecies* by Lady Nova Astira Yule)*,*" Rose reads the cover.

"The darkness is seeking answers, and while they have the Lady Otta, they failed. They thought she made the prophecies in this grimoire, but she did not. This grimoire was hidden safely away. It was written by the mother of Lord Time Yule, Lady Nova Astira Yule," Anwara explains. Thumbing through the grimoire, Rose notices a dog-eared page and turns to it. Examining the page, Rose places the grimoire on the podium, taps an orb against the page and the room spins.

ॐ

The group looks around as a thick fog fills the area. Sand spins around them as they all land in a river.

"Really?" Nadia exclaims as she waves her wand over her head, and the group disappears from the water and reappears on the riverbank.

"What happened?" Oliver asks as he waves his wand over Olivia, drying her clothes and then, himself.

"It appears the vision has had a mishap," Rose explains.

"Guys, listen!" Kelvin says as he motions for everyone to quieten down.

Then, separating the plants and looking around, the group observes several Elders.

"It appears the vision dropped us exactly where we needed to be," Rose says, pushing by the others to listen.

"Noble Elder, you must understand," Lady Nova Astira says.

"Please understand, my old friend, that what you are telling me is impossible," Noble Elder explains as Lady Astira walks over to the firepit and throws a powder into the flames, causing them to explode into the air, dancing, as images begin playing.

"There will come a time, when time themself, will not be able to stand against the individual that will be born. They will be so powerful that time will bow to them. The child, when they grow, will be the only one to control the Curpendulums, and they will become known as the Master of the Curpendulums. The child will not only control them, but he will use them. Combining their knowledge, he will stop Merlin, but at a cost. You see, Noble Elder, he is your successor. When you transcend to join the Celestials, this individual will take your place as the new Noble Elder. It is believed, as foretold by the stars, that the new Noble Elder's powers will be unlike anything ever seen," the voice of Nova Astira rings out over the fire as images continue to play out, showing a young elf man transforming into Noble Elder.

"Lady Nova Astira, he is an elf. Big deal!" Noble Elder states, laughing.

"Silence! He is not a joke. The blood that runs through his veins makes him a Celestial. The power of time fears him, and he is a Grand ArchSorcerer who is not light. Nor is he dark. Rather, he is both. He will answer to no one, and he will be the one to bring down Merlin."

The area spins around them as Rose's eyes turn white. The group lands back in the library as the fog lifts, and a cloaked figure glides backward to avoid the group. Rose and Nadia raise their hands together, pointing them at the figure.

"I would advise lowering your wands. I mean you no harm," the figure says, walking across the floor and stopping to pick up different artifacts, examining them, then putting them back. Rose watches as the individual demonstrates a particular way of setting the items back and adjusting them in the same way that she does.

Oliver and Ethan laugh, "Rose, it is your twin."

"Not funny, you two," Rose replies.

"You have been following me for some time now. Why?" Anwara demands.

"That explains why you were hiding here," Rose notes, stowing her wand as Oliver and Ethan glance at each other but remain close to her.

"To answer the Lady Anwara's question, I am not following her. Rather, I am watching, observing. Making sure that she, of all people, remains safe. You could say that I am keeping an eye on things," Noel notes, his attire changing as he rang one of the chimes of the giant gong.

"What is it that you're watching?" Mora inquires, carefully following every move of Noel.

"Ah, the great Lady herself? My respects to you," says Noel, bowing.

"That did not answer the question, and you sure dodge a lot of questions," Oliver says, looking annoyed.

Laughing, Noel replies, "Oliver, I see your sense of humor has not improved."

"Humor?" Oliver declares, spinning his wand and blasting Noel who catches the blast and absorbs it. The group backs away at the sight of Noel absorbing the magic.

"Arcane and their magic," Noel says, sitting down at one of the far tables.

"What does that mean?" Ethan inquires.

"It means that he does not find us any sort of threat," Rose remarks.

"Ah, yes and no. There are a few in this room, who frighten me, but I also know they would never raise their magic against me," Noel remarks, being very cocky.

"You must not have learned any manners. Your parents must not have taught you any. You are very disrespectful," Nadia states, sitting down at one of the tables.

"Your insight, Lady Nadia, is always wrong," Noel replies.

"Wrong? How so?" Nadia demands.

"First off, my parents and my siblings abandoned me. They were so afraid of my power that they wanted nothing to do with me. So, manners, yes, I have them, but I reserve them for special occasions, as the folks who raised me knew, in many ways, that all of you will judge in the future," he remarks, snapping his fingers and disappearing.

Looking around, the group finds Noel on the other side of the room, reading the grimoire. Rose raises her hand, motioning for the group to stay where they are as they observed the actions of Noel, who reaches up and, with his sleeve, appears to wipe his face, which is hidden within his hood.

"The darkness will definitely be after this grimoire," Noel notes as he raises his hand over the pages, and they begin flying around the room.

"What is he doing, Rose?" Ethan asks as the group watches Noel phase in and out, continuing to turn the pages.

"Ethan, while I have seen many Arcane who read rapidly by flipping the pages—we all do this, of course—I have no clue what the fading in and out is about. I have never seen anything like it. The magic he utilizes is different than anything I have seen. Well, let me rephrase—magic any of us have seen," Rose replies as the room spins, then crashes down.

"Is everyone okay?" Nadia inquires.

"No, Rose is missing," Oliver says.

"This is different. This is not how it happened before, which means he is aware of and changing the narrative," Lady Anwara says.

Spinning her wand over her head, Rose comes to a sudden stop, standing in an ancient library.

"Fascinating," she says, strolling over to the bookshelves and skimming the titles.

"*The Encyclopedia of Dragons, The Almanac of Gardening with Fairies, The Scientific Study of Atlantean Artifacts*, a six-book series on demon magic," she reads the titles out loud until she suddenly snaps around, her wand in hand.

"Sorry for taking you from the group, but I find it easier to talk with one person than having to answer to all of them," Noel states, pulling the chair out for Rose.

"Thank you. Now, what would you like to talk about?" Rose inquires, sitting down as a tea set appears.

"Time," replies Noel as he pours a cup of tea.

"I am listening," she says, accepting the cup from Noel.

"Queen Rose, as you know, Merlin wants the Curpendulums."

"So, I have heard," she notes, taking a sip of her tea.

"Otta missing, Anwara showing up, it is as if time has… well broken and not in the way we expected," Noel says.

"I am not following what you are getting at," Rose remarks.

"Time has changed. The stories have stopped playing over and over. It is as if they do not exist, Great Queen," Noel says, looking concerned.

Sipping her tea, Rose sits in silence, looking around. "Lord Time Yule mentioned about a Mundane who could stop Merlin."

"Ahh, the prophecy of the boy. The one that frightens everyone," Noel states.

"Why would a Mundane frighten everyone?"

"Because he is not Mundane. Nor is he Arcane. He is… well, unique. How do I put it? He is just different. His knowledge, his ability to fight, his understanding of science, of math, of the earth, of mystical and magical powers," Noel says, rocking in his chair.

Getting up, Noel begins to pace the floor, then, reaches into his pocket and retrieves the pocket watch. He turns it over and over in his hand, examining it.

Eventually, he approaches Rose and asks, "You mentioned Lord Time Yule, which means you met him. Did he give you the pocket watch?"

"Yes," Rose replies, pulling the watch from her blazer pocket.

Surprised, Noel backs up, holds up his watch, examines it, and nods.

"Queen Rose, it appears that the journey for the Curpendulums has begun. Lord Time Yule made a promise many years ago that he would never tamper with time unless he knew we could win. It appears that he has discovered the truth," Noel explains, opening his hand as the pocket watch flies into the air.

"Great Queen, this is where I depart. For once I leave, time will return to normal. The timelines will no longer exist, and time will play out normally with, of course, a little extra help from me. I have to make sure something that happened prior to this does not happen moving forward. I, of course, have two things I must do before I leave. But, My Lady, I entrust with you the last watch of time. Once, the watches are combined, time will be restored and it will guide the way," Noel says, handing his watch to her as he steps back, and turns away.

"Oh, and Queen Rose, there will come a day in about forty years when that watch will be needed. Please forgive me as I will possibly be stealing it if time breaks, and we start back on this rollercoaster. I promise, however, that I will bring it back."

Noel nods and, in a flash of light, he is gone. There sitting in front of Rose is a chest with a note on top of it.

꙰

Queen Roslynn,

Time is as old as it is young. Time has been stagnating, but it has been active. Time is a unique puzzle. Soon, a young man will arrive, and he alone will be so powerful that the darkness will fear him. You must find him, protect him, and guide him. He will need your teachings, your knowledge, but especially your caring nature. He has a rough road ahead, filled with many positive and opposing challenges. He will be the one to save Arcane and Mundane alike in his lifetime, but he loses many in the process. In altering the path of time, I hope to have changed this young man's path and given him the ability to write a new destiny for himself.

My Lady, good luck in your journeys to come. There are three items in this chest that I hope will aid you accordingly.

~Noel

꙰

"I hate mystery boxes. So, here goes nothing," Rose remarks aloud, pointing her wand at the box as it flies open. Looking inside, she finds that peculiar helmet worn by Willow in the visions. The second item is wrapped in a purple bag.

"Oh dear," Rose exclaims as she slides two grimoires out of the bag.

She examines them over and over, knowing all too well what each one is and what they mean. Carefully, she runs her hand over the clasp of the first grimoire as it flies open. The pages begin flipping until they finally stop, and she begins reading. As she reads, the area around her begins to spin and she finds herself standing by a fire pit, the light of the flames dancing across Noel's face as he sits on top of a boulder, writing.

Chapter 10
The Final Entry

Dear Journal,

My days have begun growing into my afternoons. They grow into evenings. All of them are confused and seem to blend. The confusion arises from an epic clash around times, actions, or lack thereof. As I have noted many times before, time is as bizarre as ever. I should know as I have spent many years searching for answers, and, to my surprise, I have come across a few recently.

While I understand that time being broken creates many moments of growth for all of us, there have been instances along the journey when I wish Lord Time Yule would have just fixed time. But, unfortunately, in his infinite wisdom, he seems to lack any urgency in helping me locate the Curpendulums.

For me, life is ever-changing, the seasons have changed yet again, and this marks another year of not finding the last few Curpendulums. To be exact, it will be my ninety-sixth year of jumping through time, landing here and there, looking for those grimoires. In my life, and in my years of travel, I've seen many changes, We have celebrated many successes within the Arcane community. We've seen the crowning of a new king and queen of the elves, the retirement of King Zander and Queen Rose, the growth of Arcane and Mundane acceptances, and so much more.

The grandeur of the Arcane Academies has grown, and magic has become a central part of community life. We have seen the changes in how magic is taught, how it is used, and how it is understood. Much of those successes are attributed to the work of the Magical Three.

Although successes exist, the great battle against darkness that began centuries ago continues to run rampant. There are times when I have questioned if we will ever find a way to stop Merlin and the Council of Dark. But then, I know from firsthand experience that Merlin was not always evil. Indeed, when we begin to think that all faith is lost, it has a way of proving to us that things are ever changing.

Something interesting, something miraculous, has happened. For once in my lifetime, time is fixed. It is not as bizarre as it has been in the past. For once, I can say it is behaving. And, if time is behaving, my love must have found the answers to fix it.

You may ask why I would need to or even want to save my siblings? That, dear journal, is the million-dollar question. I have always been different from them, I have been a child of two worlds, a child who loves everything about the Mundane, but I am also Arcane and hold magical powers. My siblings, except for dear Willow, have been difficult. Their sense of entitlement has caused many challenges over the years, some good and some bad.

Yet, I have seen the very moment in time when the seven of us will work together to stop the darkness and will end, forever, this never-ending nightmare with Merlin.

So, while I had little respect for five of my siblings, they are, after all, my siblings, and that perspective on them has changed over the years. Their stubbornness will help drive our success against Merlin and the darkness. I am the most powerful ArchSorcerer, but that does not mean anything. Now, if you ask my sister, Isabella, she would note that she is an ArchSoceress and would fly sky banners overhead, just to rub it in people's faces.

Though we all have had our differences, the one thing we all agree on is that Merlin has been a challenge for all of us over the years. But, I say this, he can be defeated. He can be stopped. And he can be destroyed. His magic is fueled by raw hatred. Yet, his magic is not pure darkness. When you learn more about him, you'll discover that his magic has been at the heart of many conflicts over the years. His influence is driven by greed, hatred, and the lust for absolute power, all attributes which I am afraid to say I may have influenced. But that is a story for another time.

Anyone who stands against him, he sees as a threat. He steals the Curpendulums, the weapons of Arcane, and the weapons of Mundane, not because he is a collector but because he knows that his power will become even more potent with those weapons. He lusts to be unstoppable, to be immortal. Because he is not immortal and has lived a long life, his magic has weakened. What scares him more than anything is losing his ability. For Merlin, life is not life without magical power.

I often laugh because I have always hated magic. I hate it because of how powerful it is and the things it can do. Try being an average child growing up, but when you get angry, things fly, furniture dissolves around you, and you hurt others, just by your thoughts. That is not magic. That is chaos. Great Queen Rose credits my magic as equal to the raw chaos magic of the incubus. But Queen Rose says that the difference between their magic, and mine is how I understand and use it. Yes, my magic scares me, but my passion, my heart, my love of all things, and the knowledge I hold is what keeps it in check.

The current timeline is the one that Lord Time Yule speaks of, the one that he has been waiting for. So, it will be this timeline when the seven siblings will learn to put their differences aside and grow together in magical balance and respect for one another.

As I write this entry, I sit on top of this boulder at the phoenix's nest, overlooking the majestic sea, and knowing that everything has an end. But much like the lifecycle of a phoenix, we all are reborn from the ashes and come back even stronger.

So, to you, I say, I hope you all will learn to channel your magic, not for evil, but rather, for good. When you see this, my siblings, please know that our lives have always been in turmoil, mostly because of the responsibilities that have fallen to us because of who our parents and our grandparents are. I do not blame them for the responsibility thrust upon us, but, I say this, my fear of my magic fuels your fears of me and my magic, along with the responsibilities we all have.

My hope in all of this is that, even in the darkest of moments, when you think that my magic is to be feared, remember that it will be my love, my joy of life, and my connection with all of you, that will keep my magic in check and will help us, once and for all, to save the ones we love. I have come to see who each of you will be. Each of you are my siblings and, together, we are part of something greater.

Know this, at this very moment, I have 12 of the 15 Curpendulums under my protection and care. However, the last three still elude me. Time, the one and only charming time, in its most infinite wisdom, is still as bizarre as ever, but I believe that I have found the final key, the way, the moment that will restore time, once and for all, and will save you, my siblings, my family, and everyone.

May this journal serve as a beacon of hope, power, knowledge, and, lastly, strength for the Arcane. This serves as my last entry that any Arcane will have the pleasure of reading. Then, much like Noble Elder before me, I too shall join the stars and watch over the past, present, and future. Once time is fixed, more than one version of any persons cannot exist. Therefore, while I must leave to take what will be the final journey for the Curpendulums, my knowledge of the darkness of Merlin shall live on.

May my infinite knowledge guide me in this time.
Though, I am not born yet. I will leave the final answers
needed to stop Merlin. Whenever you find this, know that
this book, this journal, my writings, may serve as a guide to
stop Merlin.

Yours truly now & always,
Noel

As Rose closes the journal, she observes Noel waving his hand over the seal, locking the journal while spinning magic around to secure it. Then, descending from the rock, Noel stands holding the journal. Taking a deep breath, he opens a portal. Examining the grimoire, one last time, he levitates it toward the portal, then he speaks.

Tempus vetus amicus et amor meus. Exaudi me.
Hanc scientiam tuere, hunc librum tuere, eamque in
posterum Noel huius timeline custodi.
Cum hoc timeline restitutus est nucn tempora fati
requiescat in hujus libri praesidio.
Tempus, mi amice vetus tibi hunc librum committo.

Time my old friend and my love. Hear me.
Protect this knowledge, protect this grimoire, keep it safe,
guide it to the future Noel of this timeline.
With this timeline restored, now let times fate rest in the
protection of this grimoire.
Time, my old friend, I entrust this grimoire to you.

As the last words of the spell come from Noel, the portal flies open as an arm emerges. Upon the hand touching the journal, it closes around the spine, and, like that, the journal, the hand holding the journal, and the portal are gone in a second. Leaning on his staff, Noel smiles, looking up at the stars as he waves his hand and the elfin star lights at the end of his staff. Then, observing the glowing star, he reaches up and removes the star from the staff's tip. Turning it over in his hand multiple times, he examines it for the final and last time.

Magia, audi me. Baculum meum et dryadum stellam incolumem in posterum serva.

Magic, listen to me. Keep my staff and the elfin star safe for the future.

As Noel throws the star into the air, the night sky explodes around him, stars spinning and the planets circling him. Picking up speed they all spin around Noel so quickly that they become blurred balls of light. His staff dissolves into dust as the wind carries it away. Then, as he reaches up, the star flies back to Noel. As he closes his hand around the star, both he and the star disappear.

Once the visions from the first grimoire are done, Rose retrieves the second one and opens it.

Chapter 11
The Libers

"This is interesting. What do we have here? *The Liber of Animalia et Creaturae* (*The Grimoire of Animals and Creatures*)," remarks Rose, while examining the cloth and noticing the marking of a phoenix on it. "Hmm, I have seen this before. In the castle."

Stowing the watches in a small bag, she places them in her side-saddle, then slides the grimoire in as well, and spins her hands. Fog swirls around her, and she lands in the castle. Two maids jump back as smoke fills the foyer as Rose steps out, cautiously observing the area and then, running up the stairs.

Moving down the hall, she examines the tapestries., Then stops, her eyes fixed on one tapestry that matches the one she holds in her hand.

"They are identical."

"What is identical?" a voice asks as Rose turns to see Cedric standing behind her.

"Good evening, Cedric. What is the story of this tapestry?"

"Ma'am, that is the crest of your family, of course. Why do you ask?" Looking down, he notices an identical copy in her hands. Backing up, his eyes narrow. When he reaches forward, Rose places the tapestry in Cedric's hands.

"Fascinating," Cedric says as he holds the fabric to his nose. "Hmm. Fascinating indeed," he remarks.

"What is fascinating, Cedric?"

"My Lady, where did you get this?"

"Noel gave me a chest, and in that chest was a helmet and this cloth, along with a Curpendulum." When Rose flips open the flap of her bag, Cedric jumps back.

"Oh my, a Curpendulum? Which one?"

"The Liber of Animalia et Creaturae."

"My Lady, that is four accounted for, at this point. Of course, your family will want to see that Curpendulum. But back to this tapestry, you said the Curpendulum was wrapped in it?"

"Yes, why?"

"During the years, when the castle was frozen, many items went missing. This particular tapestry, which is hanging before you, was brought over from the mansion. But I am curious as to where this one came from."

"I do not know. I know the Curpendulum was wrapped in it," Rose replies, placing her hand on top of his.

"Well, this is the original tapestry, the one that belongs here. It smells of the ancient walls of this place," he notes, folding it and handing it back to her.

"I will make sure it gets back to this place safely," Rose promises.

"No, take it to the library. If a Curpendulum was wrapped in it, then the tapestry will be endowed with magic, and that is something we do not want to leave lying around," explains Cedric with a concerned look.

"Why do I not like that look?"

"It is nothing, Ma'am. When you return to the school, I suggest you seek out the Lady Athena. Show her the tapestry. She will know what's going on and be able to explain further," Cedric suggests as he steps back. Rose's hands light and, with a flash, she disappears.

"Gillian? Where is the scroll of divine knowledge?" Athena asks.

Lightning hits the open space in the library as the papers, texts, and scrolls begin spinning around. Stepping out of the lightning, Rose brushes herself off as Ari and Matthew run up to hug her.

"Mom."

"Auntie Rose."

"Hello, boys. Ari, be a love and get your father. Matthew, will you go get your fathers and find your uncle Oliver, please," Rose asks as she turns, holding the tapestry in her hands and looking at Athena.

"Where did you get that?"

"Long story, but Noel gave it to me, and it was used to protect this," Rose explains, revealing the Curpendulum in her bag.

"Oh my, a Curpendulum."

Athena moves out from behind the table when a loud pop is heard, and Zander arrives.

"Rose, are you okay?" he asks, hugging her.

"Hi, Hun. Yes, I am fine," she replies as Oliver, Ethan, and Sebastian arrive.

"Are you okay?" Oliver and Ethan inquire in unison.

"I am fine. But we have work to do," Rose replies as Athena starts laughing.

"I assume there was a helmet with this?" Athena inquires as Rose retrieves it from her bag, looking perplexed.

Athena places the device on her head and starts clicking the dials, making different lenses drop down in front of her eyes.

"Gillian, clip the tapestry up for me, please, so that it can be read," Athena says.

She steps back and waves the back of her right hand at the tapestry while, logs in the fireplace behind it burst into flames. Taking the helmet off, she hands it back to Rose, who places it on her head and starts to look through the lens. Raising the lens, she looks at the tapestry then lowers the lens again.

"There are hidden runes on it," Rose remarks as Athena nods.

"Runes?"

"Let me, see, Sis."

"Oliver, stop. Let me examine it first."

❧

Carefully examining the runes, Rose begins to read them aloud.

ᛘᚠᛏᛂ ᚼᛗᚱᛍ ᚠᚷᚠ

"Many years ago…"

ᛏᛁᛂᛘ

Hmm, I believe that is the word "time."

"However, I cannot make that one out," Rose remarks, walking toward the tapestry. Pointing to the spot where the word is, she hands the helmet to Oliver.

ᚹᚠᛏᛖ

"That first word is 'fate,'" Oliver says. "It appears to be talking about the fate of the libers.

ᚹᚠᛏᛗ ᚠᚹ ᛏᚻᛗ ᛝᛒᛗᚱᚻ

Oliver takes the helmet off and hands it back to Rose.

"Sis, can Oliver and I inquire where you got that tapestry?"

"Long story, Ethan, just know that Noel has something to do with it."

"What I am curious to know about is the fate of the Curpendulums," Sebastian remarks as the others exchange glances, nodding in agreement.

"How are you feeling?" Zander inquires of Rose.

"I am feeling fine if you are trying to decide if I should go," Rose responds, looking annoyed.

"Go? Go where?" Athena inquires, tapping her foot, causing her armor to appear along with her spear and shield.

"Great Athena, I have a sneaky suspicion that my wife is about to take us to discover the fate of the Curpendulums," Zander notes as he summons his traveling attire. Sebastian, Oliver, and Ethan follow suit.

All of them watch Rose as she spins her hands. The wind in the Library of Athena picks up and paper begin flying around them. Then, in a deep tone, Rose speaks.

Magicae Temporis Lanuae.
Magical Time Teleport.

Sand and dirt fly around the group as Rose sits down, crosses her legs, closes her eyes, and goes into meditation as the others look around. Then, after what seemed like hours but are only minutes, orbs of bright, white light appear flying around Rose as she levitates into the air.

"What is she doing?" Ethan asks, looking annoyed.

"Time meditation," Zander explains, tightening his grip on his staff as the group begins to see land coming into view beneath them.

"Rose, it is time to come to," Zander suggests as she opens her eyes, and they all find themselves standing at the edge of the forest.

"How lovely! You have dropped us in a graveyard, Rose," Sebastian says, looking displeased.

"I thought you like dark things." Rose winks as she walks past him.

"Then, you are gravely mistaken," Sebastian retorts.

"Where are we?" Oliver asks as Athena and Zander examine the area.

"It appears to be an ancient graveyard and not very well taken care of, if I may add," Rose remarks, looking at Sebastian, then at Ethan.

Standing beside a toppled headstone, Oliver tries to read the inscription.

"Guys, you might want to see this. The writing on it appears to be in runes," he says.

ᚱᛁᚼ

ᚼᛗᚱᛗᛁ ᚠᚾᛒᚱᛗᚤᛘ ᚼᚼᚱᛗᚼᚤ

ꫯꫯoo ᛏᚱ ᚠ ᚠ

ᚼᚱᛗ ᚼᛗ ᛏᛁᚼᛗ ᚹᚱᚱᛘᚾᛘᚱᚠ

ᛒᛗᚱᚾᛘᛉ ᚼᛗᛁᛏᚱᚱ, ᛏᛗᚠᚴᚼᛘᚱ

ᚤᚾᚼᛘᚱ ᚤᚱᚱᚴᛘᚱᛘᚱ, ᚠᛁᛉ ᚹᚠᛏᚼᛘᚱ

"You're kidding me, right?" Rose inquires.

"What does it say?" Oliver asks, lifting the headstone.

RIP
MERLIN AMBROSE PHOENIX
1100 to --
May He Live Forever!
Beloved Mentor, Teacher, Super Sorcerer, and Father

"It appears that Merlin has a headstone," Athena laughs, slapping her knee in amusement.

"Is he that egotistical that he gave himself a headstone?" Zander inquires, looking around.

"It appears, Lord Zander, that Merlin is even more egotistical than I, the Great Athena, Goddess of Wisdom, foresaw. This is classic. He makes my father and uncles look tame," remarks Athena as everyone begins searching the area.

"Ethan, Rose, and Sebastian, please check the other headstones," Oliver commands as he drops the headstone back on the ground, face down.

Walking around, the group light their wands as light orbs fly around them. Sebastian reaches down, places his palm flat on the ground, and closes his eyes.

"Anything, Hun?"

"Ethan, shh. Give it a minute."

Sebastian opens his eyes and looks around, noticing a spirit pointing down the hill into the distance. Sebastian motions for the group to follow. Walking down the hill, he approaches the edge of the forest, then flicks his wand, and orbs of light fly in between the trees.

"Look," Zander says, pointing to a cave and downed ruins.

"That cave wall has writing on it" Rose remarks as Athena, Sebastian Ethan, and Oliver examine the area, holding tightly to their weapons.

"Rose, what does it say?" Oliver asks over his shoulder as she runs her fingers over the markings.

"It appears that it is some sort of tomb," Rose replies.

"How do you know?" Ethan asks.

"Because the runes say, 'The Crossroads.'"

ᛏᚼᛗ ᛚᚱᚠᛋᛋᚱᚠᚾᛋ

"Why do I not like the sound of that?" Ethan inquires as Oliver and Sebastian both nod in agreement, watching him closely.

Walking cautiously behind Rose, Ethan, Sebastian, Oliver, and Athena reach the cave opening and enter behind Rose and Zander. Holding up their wands like torches, they examine the cave. Advancing further into the cave, the group stumble upon a giant open space.

"Guys, it looks like the last visitor did not make it," Ethan notes, looking displeased and kicking a skeleton with his foot.

"It looks like there was a great battle here," Athena suggests, reaching down and picking up one of the swords, which she immediately threw down again.

"Lady Athena, are you okay?" Zander inquires as she falls backward into his arms.

"It was horrible. The anger, the darkness, the hatred," Athena explains as she reaches up to touch Zander's hand on her shoulder.

"Careful, Rose," Zander cautions as she approaches the sword.

Raising her hand, she levitates the sword and moves it across the space toward the middle of the room. Tilting her head, her eyes turn yellow as she chants,

Per via temporis, revelat arcana echoos,

Per via temporis, revelat arcana echoos,

Per via temporis, revelat arcana echoos.

By the ways of time, reveal secrets echoed.

Rose levitates into the air as she spins her hands. Images appear, then she disappears, and an image emerges and plays out.

"Where is it?" Noel asks, annoyance in his voice as he throws stones out of the way. A bone-chilling laugh rings through the space. Turning, Noel finds Merlin standing on the other side of the room.

"Noble Elder, you old fool, do you think you can stop me? Now, give me the Curpendulums," Merlin barks, holding out his hand.

"No!" Noel steps back as he pulls his wand.

"A wand? It is so unlike the Great Noble Elder to use a wand," Merlin remarks, clapping as multiple dark creatures rise out of the ground. Twelve of them advance on Noel. He stows his wand, closes his eyes, and when he re-opens them, the dark creatures dissolve into dust.

"Is that all you've got, Merlin?" Noel sneers, polishing his nails against his shirt.

"You think that will stop the darkness? The Curpendulums, Noel, or they die," Merlin declares as multiple elf guards appear bound with rope and chains, and choking.

Furious, Noel crosses his arms in front of himself in an "x" as the guards drop, disappear, but then, reappear. As the guards rematerialize, Merlin strikes Noel with one blast of dark magic after another. Noel holds him off, but then, Merlin raises his hand and blows dark magic into Noel's face. Backing up, blinded, and trying to see, Merlin strikes Noel with another blast. Merlin raises his hand and captures the guards again. Demons appear and consume the life force of each guard, causing them to drop to the ground. Merlin begins to approach Noel as his eyes turn black and he drops to his knees. Magic flies around him, as he clasps his forearms and screams, causing the entire room to shake as everyone dies on the spot leaving only Noel standing.

৵

Rose reappears and lowers herself down to the stone circle, catching her breath.

"It appears that Merlin pushed his luck with Noel," Ethan laughs.

"Yes, he did," Oliver agrees, smiling.

"I have only ever seen him do that one time before. This is now the second," Rose says, shaking her head.

"What is that magic he uses?" Oliver asks.

"Magic, unknown to any, including the gods and goddesses," Athena remarks.

"I take it that is what makes him different?" Sebastian inquires.

"Very much so. Noel is the master of many forms of magic, some that can be explained. Others that cannot," Athena says. Then, when she looks past Sebastian, she notices that Rose's attention is fixed on something on the wall.

Oliver and Ethan also notice Athena's gaze and inquire, "Rose, are you okay?"

"Yes, I am just curious," she said, standing and walking into the center of the circle, and levitating into the air. Then, reaching up, she touches an extended stone as the room begins to shake, and runes appear all over the walls, glowing.

"Interesting!"

"Hun, what do you see up there?"

"Zander, move over a little to the left, please. Very Interesting."

"Sis, what is it?"

"Oliver, do not step back. If you look where your right foot is, there are runes about the Curpendulums there. But wait, the circle speaks of different Curpendulums," Rose says, floating around the space. "It appears the floor is set as a key to not only direct the placement of the different grimoires, but it acts as a guide of what they are," Athena says as everyone looks down, examining the runes.

Floating around the space, Rose starts calling them off,

"Here is the

ᛗᛒᛖᚱᛢᚱᛆᚠᛖᛚᚢᛘ

ᛋᛖᛚᛈᚢᛖᚱᛖ ᛘᚠᚴᛁᛚᚠᛗ

Liber Dryadalum Sequere Magicae (The Grimoire of Elfish Magic)."
"I have the spot for the

ᛗᛒᛖᚱ ᚢᚠᛘᚻᛁᚱᛁᛋ

Liber Vampiris (The Grimoire of Vampires),'" Oliver notes.
"Athena, what do you have?" Rose inquires.
"It appears to be the spot for the

ᛗᛒᛖᚱ ᛚᚠᛗᛚᚢᛋ

Liber Caecus (The Grimoire of Arcane)," she says.
"Guys, this is the spot of the

ᛗᛒᛖᚱ ᛗᚨᚱᛏᚠᛚᛋ

Liber Mortalis, (The Grimoire of Mundane)," Zander exclaims.
"Ethan, dear brother, you do not look too happy. What is it?" Rose asks.
"I've got the place for the

ᛗᛒᛖᚱ ᛗᚨᚱᛏᚢᚢᛋ ᛚᚠᛖᛚᚢᛘ

Liber Mortuus Caelum (The Grimoire of the Dead). Delightful!" Ethan notes.
"Rose, I have the spot for the

ᛗᛒᛖᚱ ᛚᚢᚤ

Liber Lux (The Grimoire of Light). Next to it is the

ᛗᛒᛖᚱ ᚢᛁᛏᚠ

Liber Vita (The Grimoire of the Living), and it looks like the

ᛗᛒᛖᚱ ᚾᚱᚠᛚᚠᛁᛘᛋ

Liber Dracones (The Grimoire of Dragons)'" Sebastian says.

"Ethan, if Sebastian, has *Dragons*, *Light*, and *the Grimoire of the Living*, what is over there next to *Liber Mortuus Caelum*?" Oliver inquires.

"To the right, we have the

ᛗᛒᛗᚱ ᚠᚨᚾᚠᚱᚢᛘ

the liber of what?" Ethan asks.

"'*Nanorum*,' are you reading it right?" Rose asks, floating over to look down and examining the runes.

"I have no clue what that word is. Zander?" Rose says as Zander flips through a grimoire about runes to make sure the translation is correct.

"You are both reading it correctly. '*Nanorum*' is an old Latin term for dwarfs," Athena explains, walking up, holding a grimoire in her hand, reading from it.

"Got it. So, the *Liber Nanorum* is *The Grimoire of Dwarfs*," Ethan noted.

Rose lowers herself down and continues walking around the runes, examining them.

"Here is the *Liber Fairie*,

ᛗᛒᛗᚱ ᚹᚨᛁᚱᛁᛗ

(*The Grimoire of Fairies*)' and the

ᛗᛒᛗᚱ ᚠᚢᛁᚾᚠᛚᚠ

ᛗᛏ ᚲᚱᛗᚠᛏᚢᚱᛗ

'*Liber Animalia et Creaturae* (*The Grimoire of Animal and Creatures*),' Rose remarks, pausing.

Reaching into her bag, she retrieves the Curpendulum holding it over the spot remarking, "It appears they will be a perfect fit."

Finally, the group finishes finding the three remaining spots for *Liber Naturae et Elementis* (*The Grimoire of Nature and the Elements*), *Liber Caligo* (*The Grimoire of Dark*), and the *Liber Divino* (*The Grimoire of Divine*).

"If I counted correctly, that is 14 Rose says, looking around.

"I thought there were 15?" Oliver asks.

"The last is the *Liber of Orbis Terrarum et Universi* (*The Grimoire of the World and Universe*)," an all too familiar voice says as the group turns, wands drawn.

"Ah, you would attack an old man?" Merlin asks, smiling as he throws a dagger at them, but it stops in mid-air, exploding as Rose's eyes turn green, and with her hand extended, she takes to the air.

As fast as dark creatures rise from the ground, they begin screaming and exploding. Merlin encircles the room in darkness, then flies backward as the darkness disappears. Rose, Oliver, and Ethan join hands and create a field of magic.

The wind in the space begins picking up. Zander pushes against the wind, finally reaching the Lady Athena and pulling her down. Furious, Merlin spins his hands and throws a beam of dark magic at the three, which is met with a countering beam of light emanating from them.

Looking back, Rose notices a portal opening as Noel emerges. He grabs Sebastian and pushes him through. Then, he rolls an orb across the floor. It flashes, and two beings of light appear, grab Merlin, and drag him across the floor.

"Guardians, secure the area and take that trash out," Noel yells over the wind as he reaches Zander and Athena.

"I have to get you out of here," Noel says.

"Take Athena, I need to get to Rose," Zander replies.

"My King, no, I will get the Magical Three," Noel explains as he pushes Athena and Zander through the portal.

The guardians grow brighter as the three hold each other's hands tightly.

"You will not succeed. I will reign supreme," Merlin screams as his eyes turn black.

Turning, Noel captures the portal in his hand, seals it, and turns back to Merlin, pointing his finger as Merlin drops to the ground, screaming.

"Guardians get them out of here," Noel commands, running up the steps of the stone circle.

"We are unable to touch them. Their magic is too strong," the two beings echo in unison.

"Then, I will handle this," Noel declares as he spins his hand and the Magical Three disappear.

"You will not win. I will be the supreme wizard," Merlin exclaims, climbing to his feet.

"That is if you can figure out what happens with time," Noel replies.

"You tampered? How dare you! Who do you think you are? I will be in charge," Merlin stomps his foot, raising boulders magically over his head and throwing them at Noel.

Raising his hands, the boulders transform into bubbles.

"Bubbles! Bubbles? Ba ha ha ha! Really, Noel. Bubbles?, Your magic is a joke," Merlin sneers, throwing dark lightning bolts at him.

Laughing, Noel kneels, places his right palm on the ground, and snaps his fingers as Merlin freezes and disappears and a piece of glass falls to the ground. Getting up, Noel brushes himself off and walks over to the piece of glass. Peering down, he observes Merlin pounding on the glass from the inside. Shaking his head, Noel stomps the glass with his boot, shattering it into a thousand pieces. Then, as he waves his hand, the broken pieces of glass dissolve into dust.

"Every time you create a new multiple of yourself, Merlin, I will be there to stop you. Magic of earth give me strength," Noel declares as he disappears.

Chapter 12
Where are We?

Where are We?

Within several seconds of disappearing from the cave, the Magical Three land with a thud on the ground in a field.

"Ouch! Does anyone have any idea where we are?" Oliver asks, rubbing his arm as he helps Rose up.

"No. We are somewhere in time, maybe our own time, maybe somewhere in one of the timelines," Rose explains, retrieving a map from her bag. Unrolling it, she lays it on the ground, examining it.

"Look, we are in Vermont," Ethan explains, peering at the map over Rose's shoulder.

"Yes, but this looks like the Vermont map from six years ago," Oliver notes as Rose nods.

"We need to get out of this field before we draw attention to ourselves. According to the map, there is a road up ahead. If there is a road, then there is a town," Rose says as Ethan holds up his cellphone, looking for a signal.

"Weird, I have perfect reception. What I wouldn't pay to have this type of reception," Ethan notes.

"Whatever you do, do not answer it until we can determine if we are in our time. Remember, any interaction with anyone in a different time can alter the very fabric of time and cause chaos," Oliver exclaims.

"By the way, Rose, what is this about a town?" Ethan inquires.

"Here, oh, and hold on," Rose says, pointing to the map as the three teleport and arrive in a back alley. They walk toward the street, looking around.

"It appears to be fall here and, by the look of the decorations, around Halloween. Look, a place to eat," Ethan exclaims, motioning toward a diner as Oliver picks up a newspaper out of the rack.

"October 25th, 2016," Oliver notes, reading the newspaper as the three are seated in a booth at the diner.

"Hello folks, can I start you with drinks?" the server inquires.

"Three cokes," Oliver replies.

"And can we get three cheeseburgers, with lettuce, tomatoes, onion, and fries?" Ethan orders.

"Sure thing, I will have your drinks out in a few minutes and then your food," the server replies.

"Thank you," the three say in unison. They watch as the server disappears behind the counter and through the door into the kitchen. Then, they return to their conversation.

"So, 2016. We are still in college," Ethan notes.

"Yes, but why would Noel drop us here?" Oliver asks.

"I have a feeling it is not by accident either," Ethan states as the three grow quiet at the return of the server.

When the server is, once more, out of earshot, the three start talking again.

"Rose, you're quiet. Any ideas?" Oliver inquires.

"Multiple, but you are not going to like any of them," Rose states.

"Not like them? Rose, what is going on?" Ethan inquires.

Rose retrieves the pocket watch from her bag. "The hands have frozen, which means we have to find the pocket watch in this time to get this one to work in order to get back to our time."

"Wait, the pocket watch," Oliver notes, slumping in his seat.

"That means the library, which means the school, which means running into ourselves," Ethan remarks.

"Shhh," Oliver cautions as the server delivers their food.

"Thank you," Rose says as the server walks away.

"Rose?" Ethan asks, taking a bite of his burger.

"No, there is no other way around this," she explains.

"Well, we have an issue. We cannot just walk into the school. You are pregnant. That won't go over well. They'll think they're mad. You weren't pregnant at this time," Oliver remarks.

"Dear brother, I am exhausted and want to get home to rest," Rose replies, taking a bite of her food. While she is eating, Rose's cell phone starts chiming.

"Wait!, What? You got a text message?" Oliver asks.

"Yes, it appears I did," Rose replies, holding up her phone to read the message.

Rose,

Do not forget, you and Zander are invited for dinner at mine and Ollie's place tonight. So, bring your books.

We have midterms to study for. By the way, I hate our
professor and the horrible test they are giving. We have
to catch up tonight. See you then.

Olivia

"Weird! So, we can get texts. Ha! This should be interesting," Ethan notes.

"Wait! If we can get texts, then I have an idea. Quickly! Let's finish," Rose says.

The three finish their meals, pay the bill, and head for the door when Rose remarks that she will be right back.

"Oliver, we have a slight problem," Ethan says.

"I know. If she goes into labor in this time, we have a major problem that would make this child older than some of her other children," Oliver remarks.

"Weird! So, whatever we need to do, let's do it and get her home," Ethan declares.

"I agree," Oliver says as Rose comes back.

"What's the plan?" Oliver and Ethan inquire in unison.

"Follow me," Rose says as they go out of the door and turn down the street leading back to the alley.

ॐ

Holding out her hands, Oliver and Ethan each take one, as the dirt begins to spin around them and clouds form overhead. In a voice that both Oliver and Ethan know to be her casting voice, Rose speaks.

Accipe nos as Prioratus Temporis, Accipe nos as Prioratus
Temporis, Accipe nos as Prioratus Temporis.
Take us to the Priory of Time.

With a flash, the three are gone and, within seconds, are standing in the middle of a street looking up at the stained-glass windows of the old priory.

"We made it," Rose remarks.

"You know what, sis? I hate this place," states Oliver.

"Yeah, I am not a fan either. This place is, well, downright creepy," Ethan grumbles.

"Hush, you two, Father Francisco will be able to assist us. Now, shall we?" Rose inquires, walking to the door as the priory crumbles before their eyes. They observe a middle-aged man making haste down the street, examining the area. Curious, they follow, watching what is happening when he is gone. Seconds later, screaming occurs as the man runs out of the bookstore carrying a grimoire.

"Someone stop him! Thief! Stop him!" a woman yells. The man, not paying attention, runs right into Ethan, stops, backs up, and looks at him as Ethan reaches down and picks up the grimoire.

"You know, stealing a grimoire like this, no matter how noble, is not a good idea," Ethan notes, tilting the grimoire for Rose to see the cover.

"Give me that. I bought it," the man says, reaching for the grimoire when, suddenly, he flies backward.

"No," Rose barks, holding her hand up and casting a field of magic.

"Ethan, take that grimoire and get it out of here., Now! Curpendulums do not belong in the general public," Rose demands as the man opens his mouth and a black fog comes out, encircling him. Backing up, Ethan tucks the grimoire into his bag, closes the flap, and then reopens it.

"Secured," he notes, pulling his wand as Oliver and Rose get ready to fight.

As the fog lifts, there stands Merlin.

"Why is it you three are always in my way?" Merlin demands, spinning his wand and causing multiple buildings to burst into flames.

"Ethan and Oliver! The flames. Quickly!" Rose shouts, tightening her grip on her wand as Merlin hurls dark magic at her.

Catching the magic, she deflects it into the ground, causing the magic to travel under the street and explode inches in front of Merlin, throwing him off his feet.

"Give me that grimoire!" Merlin demands, holding out his right hand as he spins his wand over his head, causing the sky to darken and dark creatures to emerge.

"I do not have time for this, and I am sure as hell not in the mood," Rose remarks, rising into the air as the dark creatures explode and an orb flies from Rose's hand and circles Merlin.

"Ha! What a scary orb! Oh look, a single orb. What are you, Noel?" taunts Merlin when a sudden flash of light occurs, and he is gone.

Rose lowers herself down, walks over and picks up the orb, and examines it. Annoyed, she opens a portal and throws the orb into it as both disappeared.

"Nice touch, capturing Merlin in an orb," Oliver notes as Ethan comes up, wiping his forehead.

"Fires are out now. I believe we were heading to the priory?" he inquires.

"Yes, and that is a prison orb" Rose declares, winking at Oliver as they walk back toward the priory when members of the council begin appearing.

"Shoot! It is the council," Oliver notes as he pushes his siblings through the oak doors of the priory.

ം

"Get back," Rose says, placing her palms on the door as a field of magic rises over the door, followed by vines, sealing it.

"That should keep them out for a while, but we had better hurry," she exclaims, sitting down and holding her stomach.

"Is the baby acting up?" Ethan inquires with a concerned look.

"Yes, try being eight months pregnant and running through time," Rose replies when her eyes narrow, and she motions towards the altar.

"Hello, my old friends," Father Francisco says, smiling.

"Hello, Father. How are you?" Oliver asks as Father Francisco shakes his hand and looks at him.

"There is something different about you," he notes.

"Different? How so?" Oliver inquires when Father Francisco catches sight of Rose.

"I see," he says, raising his hands clapping them together as magical barriers rise over the windows and the doors seal.

"I am going to sound like the Lady Nadia, but time travel, no matter how noble, is dangerous. Are you three mad?" Father Francisco inquires.

"Father, no! Noble Elder sent us here," Rose replies.

"Great! Did the great Noble say why?" Father Francisco asks.

"Unfortunately, No!" Ethan and Oliver answer in unison.

"Well, now that you three have rested, off you go back to your time. Hurry along!" Father Francisco says making shooing gestures.

The three glance at each other.

"Please tell me that is a 'let's go home look,'" Father Francisco remarks, shaking his head.

"Yes and no. We are ready to go right now, but...." Ethan begins to explain when Father Francisco raises his hand to stop him.

"Quickly! Get behind the altar and not a word," Father Francisco commands as he waves his hand, and the three disappear. A pop rings through the temple as members of the council arrive.

"Sorry, Father, we did not mean to bother you. We see you have the place secured," members of the council note.

"Yes, just trying to keep the priory secure. Good day," he replies when another pop rings out.

"Sir, the place is secure," one of the council members declares.

"Thank you, I will take it from here, I wish to speak with Father Francisco. Run along. Go help Lord Kelvin and the Lady Nadia," Cedric replies. Then, as the council members disappear, Cedric turns, raises his nose in the air, and begins sniffing.

"Cedric, old chap, to what do I owe this visit?" Father Francisco inquires nervously, watching Cedric.

"Just checking all the spaces," Cedric remarks, walking down the far side of the priory, his fingers dancing across the wood arms for the pews.

"What were you doing?" Cedric inquires, as he stops at the front pew and walks over and sits down right where Rose had been sitting previously.

"I was just keeping the space...." Father Francisco begins to answer when he is interrupted.

"Father, we will take it from here," says Rose, as she and her brothers reappear.

"How interesting," Cedric remarks, placing his monocle over his left eye. Then, getting up, he walks over to the three and circles around them.

"Hmm. Older versions of themselves, Merlin attacking a city, the buildings on fire, the spotting of three who look like Rose, Oliver, and Ethan, and, oh yes, the queen is pregnant," Cedric notes, lowering his monocle.

"How are you, Cedric?" Ethan inquires.

"I have been better, Master Ethan," Cedric responds.

"You do not look pleased," Oliver remarks.

"Well, I will be pleased when we get you three out of here. So, start talking," Cedric demands, tapping his foot.

Rose explains what had happened.

"I see," Cedric replies. Then, he disappears.

"What was that about?" Oliver asks when a loud pop rings through the space, and Cedric reappears carrying a box.

"Cedric, you are the best," Rose says, hugging him as she takes the box from him.

"Awesome! We have the watch. Let's merge those bad boys and get out of here," Ethan declares. Opening the lid of the box, Rose's eyes narrow as she holds up the pocket watch.

"Wait. The hands are frozen on this one also," Ethan exclaims, looking rather annoyed.

"I do not understand," Oliver states as he examines the watch.

Frustrated, Rose continues to sit in the pew, digging through her bag to retrieve her grimoire.

"What does this mean?" Ethan asks, looking over Oliver's shoulder.

"It appears that your journey has just begun," Cedric explains.

"Journey? Oh no, Cedric. We need to get back to our time. Have you seen Rose? She looks like she is about to pop. No offense, Sis. But, seriously, we cannot be here," Ethan remarks.

"Master Ethan, I understand, but time has spoken," Cedric replies.

"Then, can we talk to time?" Oliver asks as Rose grits her teeth.

"Baby?" Oliver asks.

"No, it is not. How do I put it? Time kind of joined the Celestials," Rose replies.

"Wait. When? Rose, why did you not say anything?" Ethan shouts.

"Ethan, everything has been happening so fast. We have not had a moment to talk about everything," Rose snaps back at him.

"You are telling me that we have no way to jump-start the watch?" Ethan asks, shrugging his shoulders.

"You do," Cedric says.

"How?" Oliver and Ethan inquire in unison.

"Go get whatever it is Noble Elder sent you here for, and then, be on your way," Father Francisco suggests.

"It is not that easy, as we said previously. We do not know why he sent us," Rose explains, observing the space until her attention is drawn to the altar area.

"Ethan and Oliver, be loving brothers and help me up?" Rose asks as the two help her to her feet. She ascends the stairs and reaches for a small ball of light that begins flying around her. When she raises her hand, the small ball lands on her extended finger. It grows brighter, then takes to the air. Zipping around her, the small ball of light flies down the center aisle of the priory, then shoots into the air and explodes. After that, a funnel cloud appears in the ceiling and begins pulling everything into it.

"What is this?" Oliver yells over the noise of the wind and items crashing as they fly around the room.

Cedric and Father Francisco are lifted off their feet and pulled toward the cloud.

Funis.

Cords.

Suddenly, two ropes appear around each of their wrists. Oliver and Ethan pull down on the ropes securing Cedric and Father Francisco to the ground. The wind continues to pick up speed as Rose strikes the cloud with magic causing it to multiply.

"What are you doing?" Ethan yells, looking back over his shoulder at Rose.

"What do you think? Trying to close it," she responds.

"Masters Phoenix, let go of the rope," Cedric demands.

"Cedric, are you crazy?" Ethan inquires.

"You three have always trusted me. So, let go of the rope," Cedric remarks.

"Rose, trust him. They are not part of this journey," a voice says.

"Let the ropes go," Rose orders.

"What?" Oliver asks

"Rose, no! You are as crazy as Cedric." Ethan exclaims.

"Ethan, they are not part of the journey. Let go of the rope. They will be fine," Rose declares.

"Master Ethan, Father Francisco and I were meant to bring you this far. Now, you must do the rest on your own. Remember your teaching. Remember all that you have learned, and, above all, remember your magic together is stronger," Cedric declares, pulling a knife and cutting the rope of Father Francisco and then his own. The two are pulled into the cloud. When they disappear, multiple lightning strikes hit the ground as the three feel an earthquake shake under their feet and the priory begins spinning in the air.

Looking back, Ethan and Oliver notice that Rose's eyes had gone white as she speaks,

Si iter nostrum futurm sit, da nobis protectionem

et viam nobis monstra.

If our journey is going to happen, give us protection and
show us the way.

Moving quickly, Ethan and Oliver reach Rose take her hands, and their eyes turn white as they also begin speaking the spell.

Si iter nostrum futurm sit, da nobis protectionem

et viam nobis monstra.

*If our journey is going to happen, give us protection and
show us the way.*

With a pop, the priory feels as if it is free-falling but then comes to a
sudden halt, hitting the ground, throwing all three of them off their feet.

Chapter 13
The Arcane Ordeal

"Rose, are you okay?" Ethan inquiress as he and Oliver assist Rose to get to her feet.

"Yes, and thank you for helping me up," she remarks.

Carefully, Oliver approaches the door and pushes it open.

"A field," he notes, glancing back at his siblings, confused.

"It looks clear," Ethan says as he steps out the door.

The three emerge from the ruined priory, looking around.

"Ideas?" Ethan asks when he sees Rose spinning her hands and their outfits are transformed.

"Well, there are two things we have not seen in forever," Oliver laughs as he taps the handle of Gabriel, while Ethan examines Excaliber.

"How do we tell where in time we are now?" Oliver asks as Rose makes her grimoire appear.

Rose sits down on the downed step of the priory as her brothers look around cautiously. Oliver spots a village in the distance.

"Ethan, Rose, look?" Oliver points.

"Should we?" Ethan inquires

"Yes, but we take it slow," Rose comments.

"Agreed," Oliver replies.

The two brothers help Rose to her feet. Ethan takes her bag and Oliver walks next to her.

"Wait. Before you get too far ahead of me," Rose explains, tucking a small brush into her belt.

"Really?" Oliver asks.

"Hush, you never know when you may need your broom," Rose replies. The three approach the small village where they can see the attire of the villagers.

"Rose...?" Oliver begins to inquire when he looks over and notices that his brother and sister are dressed appropriately for the time.

"Ugh, we look like pilgrims," Ethan complains.

"I think you mean puritans?" Oliver exclaims.

"Shut up! Let's find whatever we need and get the hell out of here," Rose says, continuing down the path. As they reach the edge of the city, people are bustling about.

"Hello, you three must be lost. I am Ginger," the teen girl says, smiling creepily at them.

"Ginger?" a woman calls to her.

"I am here, Mother," the young woman replies, skipping up to Rose.

"Ahh, dear. There you are. But, dear me, three more! Did you three also get displaced by that witch?" the woman gasps.

"Yes," Oliver notes, playing into the woman's question.

"Ginger, run along and tell your father. And hurry. That horrible witch is at it again," the woman remarks, taking Rose by the hand and walking towards one of the houses. As Rose and the woman reach the door of the log home, a woman behind them screams as a small dragon appears, landing on the ground near them, snarling.

"Oliver," Ethan says, the two looking at each other as everything freezes. Then, the two shake their heads as they gaze at Rose whose hand is up and her eyes have turned green.

"I am not in the mood," Rose says, walking past her brothers and up to the dragon, pulling her wand. She holds her wand to the dragon's throat as reins appear around the dragon's neck and mouth.

"Brothers, if you would please," she says, turning her hand and the dragon unfreezes. Backing up, the dragon spreads its wings and growls.

"It's okay. We won't hurt you. I am Rose. This is my brother, Oliver, and that is my brother, Ethan," Rose explains as she pets the dragon's nose. The creature starts to snap but Rose gives it a stern look.

"Gentle," she says, looking at the creature. Carefully, Rose slides the rope off the dragon's mouth as it lowers its head.

"It is calm, like Belinda," Oliver notes when the three notice that the dragon is bowing.

"Belinda," Ethan says as the dragon keeps its head down.

"Guys, you will want to see this. I thought I recognized this dragon's eyes but these marks confirm my thoughts," Rose states, examining the markings on the dragon's scales.

Oliver steps up next to Rose.

"Well, who do we have here?" Oliver laughs.

Then, Ethan smiles at the dragon.

"Can it be? Autumn?" Ethan asks when the dragon springs to its feet and starts running around in circles.

"She is young," Oliver notes.

"Yeah," Rose agrees.

"Autumn, can you take us to Queen Belinda?" Rose inquires.

The dragon stops, looks at her, then runs and hides behind a barrel.

"Wait, Autumn. Come here!" Oliver says as the dragon pokes its head up from behind the barrel, then hides back behind it.

The three feel the hairs on the back of their necks standing up. Rose turns slowly to see a giant silver dragon breathing on them.

"Queen Belinda," Rose says, half bowing.

"Ugh, what a fat little human," the dragon replies, snarling.

"Autumn, home now. You know better than to interact with Mundane," Belinda snaps as the three back up.

"Are you not the great Queen Belinda?" Oliver inquires when the dragon wrinkles her nose at him, then stops and looks down at him.

"Interesting," she says, picking him up by the hood of his cloak and holding him at eye level while she examines his belt.

"That sword? Where did you get it? Answer me or so help me..." she snaps.

"Seriously, I am not in the mood right now," Rose remarks, rolling an orb across the ground as image after image of the past 15 years play out as Autumn runs out from behind the barrel to observe.

"What magic is this?" Belinda asks, dropping Oliver to examine the orb, snorting on it as the images disappear and time unfreezes.

Screams of the villagers ring out over the land as Rose reaches up and freezes time. The great dragon backs up and trips over her tail as she falls backward into a sitting position.

"The sword of Gabriel, an orb with images, and now a witch who freezes time," the dragon remarks, snapping at the three as she gets to her feet.

Autumn is sniffing the orb when Ethan disappears from where he was standing and reappears, kneeling and touching the orb as the images begin to play again.

"Curious, aren't you? Is this what you were like when you were young?" Ethan inquires, petting Autumn on the neck.

"What she was like when she was younger?" Belinda asks in a confused tone.

The great dragon starts pacing back and forth, talking out loud. " I do not get it, three magical beings, one has the sword of Gabriel, the other has

Excaliber, and the girl stops time completely with her magic. How fascinating, and they know my daughter, it can not be. No, no, no. It is too early! They are not due for another three-hundred years at the minimum. Time what are you doing with your crazy game?" the dragon muses, stroking her chin with her talon.

"Rose, what is she talking about?" Oliver inquires.

"Rose as in Roslynn?" Belinda asks when Rose spins her hands, and the images in the orb advance to the night when the three first met Belinda.

Rose motions to Oliver, and he reaches into his bag, retrieving a pouch. The dragon's eyes narrow as Oliver retrieves the horn.

"Delightful, it looks like that pointed ear elf was wrong on her prediction. Ha! For once, an elf was wrong," Belinda laughs, rolling on the ground. "I win the bet!"

"Queen Belinda," Rose says, bowing again.

"Yes, Roslynn?" the dragon replies.

"Great Queen, I am sorry, but what year is this?" Rose asks.

"The year is 1605. Why?" Belinda replies.

"Rose, Oliver, did I hear her say 1605?" Ethan inquires, standing up.

"Oliver, hand me my bag, please?" requests Rose.

"Sis, what is going on?" Oliver asks.

"If we are in 1605 and we have young Autumn, then the only answer to all of this has to be a Curpendulum," Rose replies when Belinda bends down level with Rose.

"What did you say?" Belinda inquires as smoke billows from her nose.

"A Curpen...." Rose begins to say when Belinda interrupts.

"Do not say that word."

"Why?" Ethan inquires.

"Not here. I assume you know how to ride?" Belinda inquires.

"Yes, we do," the three reply in unison, nodding at each other.

"Then hop on and hold tight," Belinda directs as Rose walks over, picks up the orb, and hands it to Oliver, who places it in the bag. Oliver and Ethan assist Rose to climb up onto the dragon's back.

"Autumn, go. I will see you at home," Belinda states as Autumn takes to the air.

"One last thing. In two minutes, time will restore, and they will have no memory of us being here," Rose says.

"Great! Can you erase their minds about some witch?" inquires Oliver.

"A witch?" Belinda exclaims, half smiling and half laughing.

"What's so funny?" Rose inquires.

"It was Autumn playing games on them. Remember that she can transfigure. She did that to scare the villagers," Belinda explains, motioning for Oliver and Ethan to get up on her back. Then, looking around, Rose points her wand and an illuminated watch appears as Belinda pushes off and takes to the air.

The three observe the ground below as Belinda dives and lands in an outcove near the water. Oliver and Ethan are the first to dismount and help Rose down just as other dragons appear.

"Our Queen, who are they?" one of the dragons snaps.

"Humans! She brought us food," another remarks as Belinda snaps at them.

"Touch them and you will deal with me. They are the Magical Three," Belinda explains as the dragons back up and bow.

"Our Queen, we apologize," the dragons say, bowing and watching as the three explore the area. As they walk around, Rose's eyes narrow and she points to the wall.

"The story of time," remarks Belinda, smiling.

Quickly, Ethan and Oliver teleport across the space to stand next to Rose and examine the wall.

"Again, the same story as before, seriously boring," Ethan remarks, displeased and rolling his eyes.

"No, Ethan, it is different," Rose replies, running her hand over the runes.

"She is right, Ethan. This story tells a different tale," Oliver notes, looking at Rose.

"Rose...?" Oliver begins to ask when she raises her hand to stop him.

"Queen Belinda, can you translate, please?" Rose inquires, glancing back at the dragon.

"Of course, it is written in ancient dragon form," Belinda explains.

> *Long ago, when the earth was young. The great Elders lived among the Mundane. They worked, lived, fell in love, married, raised families, just like their mundane counterparts. However, any Mundane who married an Elder would gain magical power, and thus the Arcane were born. Now, as you may know, the Elders' leader was a man named Noble Elder, an ancient being of immense magical power, who chose to live among the Mundane. Noble Elder was wise beyond his years and taught the Mundane many*

things, including farming, living from the land, hunting, and much more. Noble Elder is immortal and was the bridge between the gods and goddesses, and humanity.

Also referred to as the Great Sorcerer, he made friends with everyone he met. One day, the other Elders decided to join him. As a result, Elder Yule also came to earth to live among the Mundane. Now, Elder Yule was second in power to Noble Elder. The two were dear friends and became like brothers, doing everything together. Each married, started families, and ruled over the Arcane for many years. They are the original leaders of the Arcane. They watched the passing of seasons until, suddenly, Noble Elder fell ill. No one could explain it. No one knew what had happened. The Elders were baffled by the immortal's illness and hunted high and low for answers for how an immortal could become sick.

At this time, Merlin had already been cast out, and the warlock wizard, being hell-bent on destruction, seized the opportunity to attack the Elders.

Drawn into battle, Elder Yule led the army against Merlin. During the battle, Merlin killed Elder Yule and Lady Nova. In a rage, their son, Lord Time Yule, the successor to Elder Yule, summoned forth the magic of time and restored Noble Elder to full power. Within seconds, Noble Elder appeared and engaged Merlin in battle. Furious, Noble Elder did something that no one was expecting. He multiplied and a second form of him appeared.

Confused, everyone tried to understand what Noble Elder was doing. Then, it was revealed. Before Merlin could engage Noble Elder or his copy, the copy disappeared and then, reappeared behind Merlin, seizing him in a broken piece of glass and disappearing.

Immediately, upon Merlin disappearing, Noble Elder glided across the ground to check on his friends whose life-forces were beginning to fade.

"My granddaughter, can you save them?" he inquired of a young girl who was approaching. The young girl nodded and snapped her fingers. The second copy of Noble Elder reappeared, lowering his hood, and, at that moment, the Elders learned who Noble Elder had named as his successor, a young man from the future. The young man walked over, scooped up Elder Yule and Lady Nova, nodded his head, and disappeared.

Days passed into weeks, weeks into months, and months into years and the elders went about their lives. Then, one evening, the second Noble Elder returned. Now older, he walked across the plaza and gazed out over the land. The other Elders awoke when Noble Elder appeared. Quietly, they all emerged watching what he was doing, each keeping their distance when Lord Time also appeared.

As the second Noble Elder walked across the ground, he transformed again into a young man, touched the face of Lord Time, and the two at that moment became partners of time, the protectors of the eternal loop.

"For heaven's sake, Ethan, this is not school. Lower your hand," snorts Belinda.

"Sorry, Belinda, I did not want to be rude and interrupt in the middle of the story," Ethan explains.

"Your hand was up. What is your question?" inquires Belinda.

"What is the eternal loop?" asks Ethan.

"Let her finish the story. I am sure she will tell us. You are as bad as Matthew," Rose remarks, smacking Ethan in the arm.

"Thank you, Rose. Now, where was I? Oh, yes."

The eternal loop is the loop of infinite time. Only a few can control it. It is said to be ancient magic, controlled by the Yules. Now, as I noted, Noble Elder and Lord Time, in that moment, became partners in eternal time, the protectors of all magic and the past, present, and future of time. Under the full winter solstice moon, at the first snowfall, they married and restored time.

A week later, they were gone, disappeared. The earth begin to die. The plants wilted. The rivers and bodies of water began to dry up. At that moment, Noble Elder and the Elders discovered that time had broken again, but this time it was worse than the first. The Arcane worked tirelessly, using every magical skill they had to restore the earth to what it once was, but the magic weakened with each passing day. Then, finally, spring came, but the earth did not spring back to life as many had hoped.

Noble Elder left to speak with the gods and goddesses, leaving earth, the Mundane, and Arcane unprotected. This was an unwise move and when Merlin heard of Noble Elder's absence, he saw an opportunity to launch an all-out attack. Burning everything in his path, he laid waste to the land. He was joined in his rampage by the demons who hailed him their hero.

The Elders and Arcane fought to protect all they could while Merlin engaged Lady Mora in battle. Having used nearly all of her magic, Lady Mora grew weaker as she fought Merlin. Finally, Merlin thought that he had won when, suddenly, the earth began to come back to life.

The land bloomed as plants grew, the trees came back, and animals rose from the dead. Time turned back as the magic of earth flew around them.

"What is this? Destroy everything!" Merlin yelled at the demons as the wizard warlock was struck with a Curpendulum. The darkness screamed as it took to the air. It dove toward the other side of the field, racing towards the ground, when a column of light appeared and leveled the darkness. There stood the young Noble Elder-Yule, his partner the Lord Time Yule, and seven Arcane beings with all fifteen Curpendulums spinning around the group. They were joined by a single Mundane, a Pendragon, who, although they had no magical powers, had forged weapons with science and nanofairies, robotic fairies that could be destructive. Gliding across the land, this group joined in the fight against the darkness, and, within seconds, the darkness, the demons, and Merlin fell. Thus, time was restored, and like that, the earth became new, and the group disappeared.

ॐ

The fires in the cove die down as the images disappear, and the runes stop glowing. Rose, Oliver, and Ethan stand examining the space, then turn to speak with Belinda. Rose was the first to disappear from where she had been and reappear on the other side of the cove, examining the pedestal.

"I do not believe it," Rose says, picking up the pocket watch as the second hands tick second by second.

"Oliver, Ethan, you two might want to see this," she says, holding the watch in her hand and looking down at the other item on the pedestal.

"I do not believe it," Ethan declares as he looks at his siblings.

"*The Liber Dracones* (*The Grimoire of Dragons*)," Oliver exclaims.

"Entrusted to me when I was a young dragon guardian, and now, I entrust it to you. Magical Three, our paths will cross again. Be safe. Keep the Curpendulum safe. And promise me, promise me, when the time comes that you will protect Noble Elder. He is powerful, but he needs love. Without it, his magic will not exist. There will come a moment, a period of time, when he will turn his back on everything. Be patient. Lord Time Yule holds the key to save Noble Elder, and so do you three. Your faith in him will give him the strength and hope he needs," Belinda says, nodding as the three nod back to her and each other.

Oliver picks up the grimoire and slides it into Rose's bag as Rose begins spinning the dials on the pocket watch as Ethan hands her the other one. As the two watches come in close contact with each other, they merge, and the pocket watch flashes.

"Guys, it is ready," Rose says as the three step back.

"Oliver, Ethan, and Roslynn, two things before you go. Take the bag hanging on the pedestal. It will aid you in future journeys," Belinda explains.

Ethan opens the bag, revealing multiple scrolls, a dagger, and several items wrapped in cloth.

"Second, and hear this, there will come a point when Noel has to decide to save time or the earth. Tell him, tell him both can happen…" the voice of Belinda fades out as Oliver, Ethan, and Rose find themselves in a whirlwind of sand. Within mere seconds, the three land back on the ground as the whirlwind disappears, revealing Zander, Sebastian, Cedric, Nadia, and Kelvin waiting. As the sand departs and the three fully materialize, Rose collapses.

Chapter 14
Rest

Two hours later and in what seems like a blur, Rose awakes in the school's hospital wing

"Careful, you collapsed," Destiny says, smiling and handing Rose a cup of tea.

"Thank you, Aunt Destiny. Where is everyone?"

"Your brothers went back to their places to rest, Zander is with the kids, your mom has been out, and your dad is outside guarding the door," Destiny explains.

"The baby?" Rose inquires.

"Safe. Lady Mora and Dr. Irvin delivered him. Russell is fine, but your energy has weakened. Your mom drove your poor brothers up a wall about you guys time traveling," Destiny explains.

"I should probably thank them for dealing with Mom being upset," Rose remarks, sipping her tea.

"Little secret. Your brother, Ethan, stood up to her and told her off. I have never seen my sister so angry, except for that time when I burned her teddy bear when I was five, and she was seven," Destiny chuckles until she notices that Rose's attention is fixed on something across the room.

"My bag. Aunt Destiny can you get me my bag, please?" Rose asks as Destiny gets up, strolls across the room, and brings the bag to Rose. Quickly shuffling through it, she finds what she is looking for, removing a large item wrapped in purple cloth. Unwrapping the item, she reveals the grimoire.

"*The Liber Dracones*," Destiny says.

"Yes," Rose replies, running her hand over the cover.

"How did you get it?" Destiny inquires.

"Long story," Rose replies as she grabs her bag and starts rummaging through it.

"Rose, what is it?" Destiny inquires with a puzzled look.

"Where is it? The watch," Rose says.

"You mean this watch?" a voice asks.

Destiny is on her feet, her wand drawn.

"Aunt Destiny, no!" Rose says, motioning for her aunt to lower her wand.

"Who are you?" Destiny demands, tightening her grip on her wand.

"My apologies for startling you, Lady Destiny. I am the Lady Time Yule," she replies, bowing as Destiny lowers her wand.

"My Lady," Destiny bows.

"What can we help you with, My Lady?" Rose inquires.

"Everything," the Lady Time Yule says as she begins to cry.

"Lady Time Yule, what is concerning you?" Rose inquires.

"I was ready for this moment, but then again, I was not," she explains, sitting in the chair by Rose's bed.

"The Lord Time Yule, as you know, has joined the Celestials, Then again, him joining the Celestials has altered time in a good way but in a way that I do not understand. It is as if it has restarted time and now it is playing out differently," Lady Time Yule notes, weeping into her hands.

"Rose, what is she talking about?" Destiny inquires with a curious look on her face.

"Aunt Destiny, Lord Time Yule joined the Celestials to save time and, in doing so, has restored the great timeline," Rose explains as Destiny puts her hand on top of Rose's to comfort her.

"Are we on our own then?" Destiny asks.

"Yes and no," Lady Time Yule replies, sighing and wiping her face.

"I am still here, and I will fight to my last breath. My brother fixed the timelines to give Noel a way to stop Merlin and find the Curpendulums. No Elder has ever returned to earth after joining the Celestials," Lady Time Yule explains when a knock occurs on the door. Destiny gets up, disappears from where she was, and reappears at the giant oak double doors just as Hope and Vivian bolt through the door.

"Mommy!" the girls shout in unison as Zander walks in behind them with Ari and Theo.

"My girls," Rose says, hugging them both as Vivian climbs down off the bed.

"Hello," Zander says. Then, he notices the visitor. But before he can say anything, the group hears Vivian.

"You are pretty. You are the Lady that does neat tricks with time."

"Aren't you a sweetie? Yes, I am, and you are the warrior princess elf who can fight with any item," Lady Time Yule replies, summoning a bow and arrow and handing them to Vivian.

"Thank you, Lady Time Yule. But Vivian, no, you are too young for that," Zander says, trying to grab the bow and arrow from her as she runs out the door.

"Ari, will you watch your sisters please?" Rose asks as he nods and runs after them.

"You too, Theo," Zander states sternly.

"Ah, man, you never let me hear the good stuff," Theo says, strolling out of the door as Kelvin pops in.

"A bow and arrow? Vivian is going to put her eye out," Kelvin says, laughing as he bows at the sight of Lady Time Yule.

"I assume, My Lady, that you gave her the bow and arrow?" Kelvin asks, still bowing.

"Lord Kelvin, I did indeed. A child with her power and her bloodline should begin early," Lady Time Yule replies, coming up and hugging Kelvin, then hugging Zander.

"Rose, I assume if the Lady Time Yule is here, there is an explanation for this?" her father inquires, leaning down and kissing his daughter on the cheek.

He is the first to notice the Curpendulum on her lap, followed by Zander, who upon seeing the Curpendulum, picks it up.

"*The Liber Dracones*," Zander states, turning the cover and looking at Rose with an eyebrow raised.

But before anyone can say anything, a loud pop echoes through the room as Mora arrives with Nadia, holding baby Russell. Quietly, Zander slides the Curpendulum behind him and steps in front of the Lady Time Yule as Destiny stands next to Zander. Destiny reaches behind Zander, who slips the Curpendulum to her as she tries to slide it quietly into Rose's bag.

"Dear sister, if you think hiding a Curpendulum from me is going to stop me from questioning Rose, you are mistaken. Put the grimoire down and step away from it," Nadia says smiling and glancing at her sister as she hands Russell to Rose.

"*The Liber Dracones*," Mora says, picking up the grimoire and examining it. She holds it up to her nose and sniffs the spine.

"I date it to be from New England, 1590's, No wait. A hint of oak, burnt lavender, and do I get maple wood? I put it at 1605. So, you saw Belinda, which means you know of the Arcane Ordeal," Mora notes, looking displeased.

"Hello, Mother Mora, and, yes, you're good. It was 1605. And, yes, it was Belinda," Rose states.

"Excuse me. I may be the leading Arcane historian but what is the Arcane Ordeal?" Destiny inquires, perplexed.

"Only one of the bloodiest battles ever, and, of course, Noel let Merlin get away," Mora remarks.

"Get away? No, Lady Mora. He saves time. He saves Noble Elder. He saves the earth," Rose declares as multiple suits of armor crash outside the door.

"I swear if you do not get out of my way, I will barbeque you. But, while I will not eat the Houses of Phoenix, Knight, Pendragon, or Ignatius, all other Arcane are fair game," a voice snaps as one of the guards lets out a yell.

"Dragon, are you crazy? You are too big, and I am not allowed to let anyone in," the guard declares, a tremble in his voice betraying his concern.

"Zander, or Dad, please stop Belinda before that poor guard gets eaten or cooked," Rose says.

Just as Kelvin and Zander begin to disappear, the hospital's doors fly open, both guards fly back through the door, and Autumn storms through the door.

"Mother, for once in your life, will you shrink down?" Autumn inquires.

"I will be fine," Belinda replies, backing into the room.

"Mother, you are the queen, and the biggest dragon. Arcane and Mundane structures are not designed for us big dragons. Please, shrink down," Autumn barks.

"I'll be fine," Belinda says, turning and knocking a row of beds out of the way.

"Hello, my dear friends. I see you have the grimoire. Good, good," Belinda says, smiling and sitting down.

"You gave her the Curpendulum?" Mora shouts.

"No, Lord Noel did. I simply facilitated a story that they needed to know," smiles Belinda.

"A story I hear was told wrong," Mora notes, tapping her foot.

"You're incorrect, Mora. I have waited thousands of years to say that just once to you," Belinda laughs.

"Incorrect? I am the granddaughter of Noble Elder. I am not incorrect. But, if I was incorrect…" Mora states suddenly freezing as she examines the pocket watch floating in front of her.

"It works?" Nadia asks, rising to her feet.

"Yes, it works. All of them do. However, if we are in one timeline and the watch breaks, then we have to find and seek out the pocket watch in that time as it is the only way to restore the present one," Rose explains.

"Wait! Do you mean to tell me that the story has changed? The Arcane Ordeal? I do not understand," Mora states.

"Lady Mora Elder Ignatius, Belinda is correct. Noel and my brother entrusted the Curpendulum to Rose, fixed the watch, and changed the timeline for the better. We are running now in real-time," Lady Time Yule says, holding up her pocket watch as it projects a clock in space, revealing time ticking away.

"If we are in real-time, then does that mean the timeline is gone?" Kelvin asks excitedly.

"No, the other timelines still exist, but what happens in them will no longer have a bearing on this timeline. My brother ensured that," Lady Time Yule explains.

"By the way, how is your brother, Lady Time Yule?" Mora inquires.

"He has joined the Celestials," she notes as Belinda lowers her head respectfully.

"If Lord Time Yule joined the Celestials, then we are not only running in real time, but it means he altered the timeline in a way not seen by many, including our seers," Mora notes, pacing the floor.

"That means every prophecy can be disregarded and thrown out," Destiny states, trying not to show her excitement.

"Exactly," Nadia and Mora say in unison. Before anyone could say anything more, multiple guards run into the room and begin forming a protective barrier as horns sound.

"What's going on?" Kelvin inquires as Cedric appears carrying an injured Phineas.

"Cedric, what has happened?" Nadia and Kelvin inquire, rushing to help with Phineas.

Rose starts to get up, but Mora tells her, "No. Rest. We have this."

"Darkness has grown in numbers. It has been attacking both Arcane and Mundane," Cedric explains as another loud pop rings through the space and Leaf, Sebastian, and multiple council members appear, carrying injured elf soldiers and fairies, lowering them onto the empty hospital beds.

"Rest is far from it at this point," Rose says, getting up and spinning her wand around as she struggles weakly to her feet.

"Child, you are going to fall," Destiny says, trying to support Rose.

"Aunt Destiny, take Russell and get to mine and Zander's chambers. Activate the security protocols to secure the space."

Destiny nods, picks up the baby, and disappears. Two more loud pops ring out as Oliver appears with Olivia and Ethan.

As the horns sound again, Mora spins her hands, and the school comes to life and multiple light fields rise around the school.

"Another loud pop is heard as the witches three arrive.

"Our Lady Mora, it is horrible. The darkness has been kidnapping Arcane and Mundane alike," the three say, their voices echoing through the space.

"Do we know who they took?" Nadia asks.

"Yes, Bethany, and my mother, multiple fairies, also…" a weak Phineas explains.

"They have my father as well," Leaf says.

A whistle echoes as Mr. Bruin appears.

"Yes, Lady Rose?" he inquires.

"Mr. Bruin, secure the library immediately. The Arcane and Mundane are under attack," Rose notes as Olivia supports her to stand. Then, looking around, Rose nods, and the two disappear.

"I hate when they do that," Oliver remarks as the group begins to disappear on the spot.

Reappearing in the courtyard, they find Rose floating in the air over an orb.

"Zander, she needs to rest," Mora declares, looking perplexed.

Zander shrugs and nods his head.

Spinning her hands, Rose, speaks.

Ostende nobis omnes Arcanum et Mundanum qui desunt.
Show us all the Arcane and Mundane who are missing.

Image after image flash of Mundane and Arcane who have disappeared at the hands of the darkness.

"Leo, Queen Amaryllis, Divinity, Wade, Bethany, countless fairies, dwarfs, elves," Nadia gasps.

"It looks like the dark has been busy," Kelvin notes when Sebastian breaks the silence.

"Liam?" he inquires.

"Why would the darkness take your brother?" Ethan inquires.

"That does not make sense," Sebastian notes.

"The darkness takes those who pose a threat, those who they have easy access to, or are of the light. Your brother must be one of those. Otherwise, the darkness would have no reason to kidnap him," the witches three say.

"But why would Liam pose a threat?" inquires Ethan.

"His virtue towards the darkness faulters, and Merlin has grown concerned that Liam will join the side of light. But, if Liam does, Merlin is afraid he will reveal too many secrets," the witches three explain in unison.

"I do not mean to interrupt, but does anyone have any ideas about how we might find them?" Leaf asks when small orbs begin flashing around the space.

"It looks like the fairies have arrived," Mora notes as a loud explosion echoes throughout the hall and suits of armor fall to the floor.

"Help!" they hear as Rose flies over the orb, landing, and gliding over the ground as the group hears the cry for help again.

"Help, I need help," a woman's voice rings out.

Entering the archway is Lady Marybelle, carrying Willow. Lowering herself down, Rose walks over to the young elf and places her hand on Willow's forehead.

"Lady Marybelle, where did you find her?" Rose inquires, closing her eyes.

"She was with that guy called Noel. The darkness attacked and when he fought to hold them back, Merlin attacked her, and Noel went weird freaky magic on him. The area got very cold, and all happiness left the space. Dark magic spun around him as spirits rose. Then, an older blind elf appeared. He could have been Zander's twin. He opened a portal, told me the elf's name was Willow, and pushed us through," Marybelle explains as Oliver, Ethan, and Zander look at each other and shake their heads.

"Rusty," they say, simultaneously. Then, the group hears a voice at the top of the stairs.

"Is she okay, Papa?" Hope inquires as she levitates over the banister and touches down.

"Your mom is trying to help her," Zander replies as Hope runs over, picks up Willow's hand and begins humming. Suddenly, everyone in the room flies backward.

"Zander?" Mora says, looking at him in shock.

"What is she doing?" asks Rose, who is being helped up by Lady Marybelle.

"She is an elf healer," a fascinated Mora explains. As the group watches, Vivian runs down the stairs to join her sister, while Ari and Theo appear next to their father.

"Neat trick," Theo remarks. Then, the room explodes with glowing, spinning, golden, magical dust. Vivian and Hope hold hands as magic flies around Willow. As the two close their eyes, Willow awakens and sits straight up. She smiles at the two and hugs them.

"Oh dear, if you two are kneeling over me, and I am waking, then... Oh no!" Willow says, rubbing her head and rising quickly to her feet.

"Are you okay?" Rose asks as Willow glides past her.

"The orb?" Willow asks as she walks up to it, spins her hands, and an image of Noel appears.

"Where are the others?" she asks as images of five other elves appear. "Oh dear! This won't work. They need help, and I have to hurry," Willow declares.

"What is she doing?" Leaf inquires.

"Lord Leaf, the timeline has altered. They have never been separated. This is not good. Alone, they will fall; I must help them," Willow says as she holds up her hands, and lightning begins to form an energy ball. Then, raising her hands above her head, she and the ball of energy disappear. The group watches the orb as she appears standing next to one of the elves, the ball of energy striking down the darkness as suddenly the six emerge in the same image as Noel. Then, the orb goes dark.

"It appears they accomplished their mission," Nadia states.

"Rose, bed. You need rest. Zander and Cedric, take a group and locate the kidnapped Arcane and Mundane. Oliver, you and Leaf take a second group. Ethan and Sebastian, you two take the third group. Do not stop until you have found them all. Kelvin, convene the council. This threat is only going to worsen," Mora orders.

"Before I rest, Lady Time Yule, the library is a safe place. You are welcome to remain there," Rose remarks, leaning on Olivia.

Then, as the groups begin to disappear, Olivia looks at Rose, "Do you think they will find them?" Rose asks as Lady Time Yule takes Rose's other arm, helping Olivia balance her as the three walk back into the hospital wing.

❧

Rest, they say. Ha ha! Easier said than done. Laying there, Rose dozes in and out of sleep. Jumping in and out of one dream after another. Rose remembers each dream. Some of them have clear stories. Others are as confusing as trying to decipher runes. But all of them end with Noel stopping time, then restarting it as snow falls around him as he walks down the street of a town on a cold winter evening. If the disappearances and kidnappings are not bad enough, Rose has a hunch that Noel is stuck in a time-loop somewhere. What is worse is that Rose hates when dreams have no apparent meaning, as it is next to impossible to figure out where Noel could be stuck.

Chapter 15
A Peculiar Moment

a Peculiar Moment

Walking through time, the scenery changes rapidly. An old cobblestone street appears under Noel's feet as he walks among towering two- and three-story buildings with thatched roofs, each materializing as he passes. People are bustling about, the smell of old sewage and food vendors filling the air. Next, the image flashes, and Noel finds himself walking down a deserted street made of sand in an old Arabian town. Vendors are selling goods in the bazaar, then, a bridge leading over a lotus pond, the cherry blossoms lining the way as pagodas can be observed on the horizon while. In the distance, fireworks erupt in the air. With each step, orbs of various sizes and colors fly around him, spinning and lighting up.

Noel stops to watch the various stories on the orbs around him play out. Examining each, he observes the area around him, watching the stories playing out until one vision catches his attention. He stops and watches from afar, pushing his way through different orbs until he reaches up and touches the orb and is pulled into the story. Then, flying through a cloud of smoke and sand, lightning strikes around him as he lands in the middle of the street, looking around. Strolling down the street, he stumbles upon a memory from his childhood of which he is not particularly fond. "This should be interesting to relive," he mutters aloud as he disappears from the street and lands in the hallway of an old manor.

☙

The only light in the room is the glow of the flames burning in the fireplace and the twinkling lights on the Christmas tree. The shadows of the stockings dance across the walls. A crash is heard ringing throughout the old manor as the helmets of the suits of armor turn their heads to the left, watching the young man running down the hallway, spinning his hands in front of him, his cloak appearing on his shoulders as he pulls the hood up over his head while he quickly descends the stairs.

Carrying his small traveling bag over his right shoulder that reaches down to his left hip, the head of a black cat appears out of the side of the bag. As the young man continues to run through the long main entrance hallway, the candles in the candelabras pop on and the lights of the home light. When the young man bowls an orb across the floor in front of himself, a portal flies open, and he disappears. Immediately, a pop rings throughout the space as Cedric, Rose, and Willow appear, all three running toward the portal. When the portal seals, they stop, looking around the space.

Willow raises her hand, "Ambrose?"

"Cedric, notify the others immediately," Rose commands as her attire transforms.

ॐ

Seconds later, the portal flies open and Ambrose steps out onto the sidewalk next to a large rod iron fence, a park on the other side.

"It worked," he says, looking pleased as he wraps his scarf around his neck and snow begins to fall. Then, quietly walking through the park gates, he smiles, looking around at the bustling city rising out of the landscape in the distance. Then, he pulls up his collar tightly around his neck and walks down the street, disappearing into the snow.

Stopping the vision, Noel spins his hands and magic begins spiraling around his arms. The vision accelerates around him with each turn of his arms. When the vision finally stops, he carefully observes the area and, stopping at a particular moment, he pulls the pocket watch which reveals that it is 11:35 PM. Central Park stands quietly that Christmas Eve, with only a few people here and there. Then, walking through the park, Noel comes upon the part of the vision he is searching for.

"There you are," he remarks, and, raising his hand, he unfreezes the vision.

Sitting and observing the area from the walkway, a black cat sits quietly observing the park, his eyes narrowing as a portal opens, and twenty-five wizards and witches appear, looking around and examining their location.

"It smells horrible here," one of the witches' remarks as Olivia walks past her.

"That would be the smell of the city. It appears we are in Central Park," Olivia explains, looking at Zander, Rose, and Mr. Bruin.

"My Lady Ignatius, the magic signature is radiating from this park," Mr. Bruin notes, holding up a pendulum that is spinning wildly on its metal base.

"Everyone spread out and look for him. It is beginning to snow. We must move quickly to find him," Zander directs. When he looks over to speak to Rose, he finds that she has already walked away from the group. Stopping and glancing around, Rose closes her eyes and raises her hands, listening to the wind howling as the snow falls. Magic begins spinning around her as she moves her hands in the air as if conducting a choir. Finally, the spinning magic flies out into the park.

"What is she doing?" Olivia inquires.

"Listening, observing, searching. She is using her magic to see if she can locate Ambrose, a fascinating feat," Zander explains as Cedric approaches.

"You three, you take a right. You four, down the middle. You two, take the left. All teams report in if you find him, and everyone do mind yourselves. Mundane are not used to magic," directs Cedric as the other Arcane begin to spread out.

Cedric and Zander acknowledge each other, then Cedric begins to speak, but stops to observe a portal opening as Ethan, Sebastian, and Oliver step out.

"We got here as soon as we heard," Oliver and Ethan say.

"Good evening. I told you not to come. You are supposed to be spending Christmas with your children," Rose remarks, walking past them.

"Good evening, Sister. When have we ever listened?" inquires Ethan smiling.

"Point taken," Rose responds, pulling her smock up around her neck.

"What has happened?" inquires Oliver.

"Michael instigated a fight with Ambrose," Zander notes, looking displeased.

"Are the children okay?" Ethan inquires.

"Peter is spitting feathers. Isabella's hair was lit on fire. Michael was punched in the face repeatedly, and Ambrose took off," Zander explains as Rose turns back and nods in agreement.

"It isn't anything that magic can't heal. However, the words that Michael said to his brother, there is no magic to fix that," Rose says as Cedric approaches.

"Excuse me, everyone, I don't want to be rude, but, My Lady, the Lady Esther is calling," Cedric says as he hands an orb to Rose.

"Thank you, Cedric. I'll take it," Rose acknowledges, walking away from the group.

"Esther, what do you have?" Rose inquires as she rolls the orb across the ground and Esther steps out of the orb and appears in front of Rose.

"Grandma, his energy signatures are coming from the park, but, somehow, they are different. They're strange. It is nothing I have ever seen."

"Strange in what way?" Rose inquires as she stops and listens carefully.

"Grandma, I don't know how to explain this. I have Ambrose, and I have his general location, but I am getting multiple readings of him as if he has multiplied," Esther remarks.

"Multiples of Ambrose?" inquires Rose, eyebrows raised as the vision suddenly freezes.

&

"Well, this makes sense. The magic of the Queen and the Lady Esther has always been something out of the book of weird," Noel laughs to himself.

He stops, observing a small ball of light flickering in the background that opens into a portal. He ducks behind a shrub as he continues to watch. Stepping out of the portal is Rose, who looks around cautiously.

"Frozen! Good, I won't be affecting the timeline," she remarks, walking around the older version of herself and examining the image of Esther standing beside the older Rose.

"Central Park. Snow. Humm. This must be the Christmas Eve vision of Ambrose running away," Rose states, tapping her foot.

Turning, she quickly walks back toward the portal. Stopping, she looks back over her shoulder and speaks.

"If one simply wants the snow globe of power, all one must do is simply come and retrieve it."

With that, she steps into the portal, and it spins shut.

"Ugh," Noel says, standing and brushing himself off.

Then, walking back toward Queen Rose's frozen image, he shakes his head.

"So, you are the one who ended up with the snow globe. Lord Time Yule, I swore to you that fixing the timeline would make a mess of things. How could you allow Queen Rose to get Ambrose's snow globe? This is not going to turn out well. I hope this does not alter the timeline in ways we do not know," Noel declares, looking up at the stars as he waves his hand, causing the snow globe to appear.

"How this fascinating artifact could nearly cause the destruction of the Arcane community is beyond me. I should never have let Ambrose create the darn thing," Noel remarks as he raises his hand, and the snow globe disappears, and the vision unfreezes.

&

"Grandma, there are 14 magical signatures of Ambrose coming from the park," Esther says.

"Fourteen? Esther, please check the orbs. Have there been any changes in the timeline?" inquires Rose?

"None, Grandma. However, I am seeing that Noel has traveled, and his signature has vanished into thin air. It reappears when you arrive at the park, but then it is gone again," Esther explains.

"Esther, continue to watch and notify me of any further changes immediately," Rose says as Esther disappears, then reappears.

"Grandma, this is weird. Thirteen of the 14 Ambrose's have merged. Then, it gets really bizarre," says Esther.

"Bizarre how?" Rose inquires.

"The Ambrose that remains has just created an orb. A fascinating magical signature is coming from it. But he is gone now," Esther explains.

"Esther, where is the orb now?" Rose asks, pulling her wand.

"I am trying to track it, but the magic of the orb is too powerful," Esther notes with a look of concern as her hands run over an orb that is floating in front of her.

"Esther, not a word of this to anyone. Say nothing to your parents, your aunts, uncles, cousins, your grandfather, no one in the family. Also, immediately contact Lady Time Yule and explain to her what has happened, Enlist her help in tracking that orb. We must find it before anyone else does, even if we just put it away until the time is right. Quickly! Make haste! I have a feeling that I know how to find Ambrose," Rose commands as the image of Esther disappears.

Rose approaches the orb, scoops it up, and places it in her bag. Then, she raises her hand as water from the pond flies around her. Moving her hand through the water like a rhythmic dance, the water begins to spin and materializes into two beings who, nodding to each other and to Rose, take off running just as Cedric approaches.

"Zander asked me to check on you, My Lady," he explains.

"I'm okay, if that's what you're wondering. But, unfortunately, Cedric, I've learned some alarming news. Please make haste. I need my mother," Rose remarks.

"Indeed, My Queen, I will get your mother for you."

As Cedric turns to go, Rose places a hand on his shoulder.

"Thank you, my friend. Cedric, ask my mother to speak with Esther, please. Explain to Esther that I changed my mind. While I told her not to speak with anyone, tell her… well, tell her, 'Time Phoenix.' She will know what I mean by that. Ask her to bring her great-grandmother up to speed. Oh, and Cedric, one last thing, I need the bell."

Immediately, Cedric holds the bell between his fingers. He hands it to Rose, then disappears.

Observing the park, Rose watches as many of the Arcane, who traveled with her, hunt high and low for young Ambrose. Raising her hand, she levitates the bell. As she touches it with her index finger, it chimes. She stands quietly listening, and she hears another bell chiming in the distance. Again, she taps the bell with her index finger and, again, when the bell chimes, she hears a chiming in the distance.

"There you are," Rose remarks aloud. Snatching the bell out of the air, she disappears. Seconds later, she reappears at a bridge in the park. Looking around, she taps the bell with her finger once more and, once more, hears the other chime, this time underneath her. Walking to the edge of the bridge, she looks over the side, and she sees two green eyes looking up at her. Raising herself into the air, she levitates down over the side and onto the walkway underneath.

"There you are, Mr. Cee," Rose remarks as the cat approaches her, purring. As she reaches down to pet the cat, she pauses, seeing the images of the multiple Ambroses that Esther had referenced. Quickly, pulling her hand back, she tilts her head as a tear rolls down her face.

"Oh my! Mr. Cee, where is he?" she asks as the cat strolls towards an old man sitting under the bridge.

"Good evening and Merry Christmas, My Lady. Please come and sit by the fire to stay warm, since the snow is coming down," the man remarks.

"Thank you, kind Sir. Have you seen a young man?" Rose inquires, holding up her cell phone and revealing a picture of Ambrose as she lifts up the back of her cloak and wraps it into her lap as she sits down.

"Indeed, I have and a charming young man he is. The child ran through the park, crying, and a man was chasing him. The child turned with a stick and the man exploded. After that, the poor kid cried himself to sleep under this bridge. He's over there. I made this fire to stay close and keep the boy company. It is a wicked evening to be alone, particularly with how cold it is tonight. Are you his family?" The man inquires.

"I am, Sir. I am his grandmother. He and his siblings had an argument, and he ran out of the home. I have come looking for him."

"The young man was exhausted when I found him, and the cat was protecting him. He was holding this interesting snow globe. Finally, he was so weak that he collapsed."

"Sir? May I see that?" asks Rose, extending a hand. At first, the man is hesitant. Finally, he stops to examine her and then nods, handing it over. Turning it over in her hand, she examines it. The snow begins to spin inside of it. Then, her eyes narrow. Seconds later, she comes to. The man is sitting there, examining her out of the corner of his right eye.

"Kind and gracious Sir, thank you. How can I ever repay you? He means the world to me, and so does this snow globe," explains Rose.

"There is no need to thank me, My Lady. It is Christmas Eve, and your grandson gave me a beautiful gift this evening, the gift of conversation, someone to chat with. He was so kind. Once he somewhat got his strength back, it was magical. He waved his hand and made this fire and food appear. Santa has smiled down on me, and he sent a magical elf," the man explains, smiling and placing his hand on top of Rose's.

"Indeed, Santa has, Sir."

"My Lady, if he is your grandson, then you must be Mrs. Claus?" the man inquires.

"No, just someone magical."

"Well, he is truly magical, a child who can make a fire appear and food the way he did."

Rose nods, stands up, walks over to Ambrose, and puts her hand on his shoulder.

"I am here, young Ambrose, and I won't let this happen again," Rose declares as Mr. Cee purrs and rubs against Ambrose.

"Grandmama, you are here?"

"Yes," Rose nods, helping him up. She stows the snow globe and retrieves another orb and drops it in front of them just as Zander appears.

"Ambrose! There you are. You gave all of us a scare. You shouldn't run off like that," Zander scolds him as Rose shakes her head in disagreement, which Zander immediately understands.

"Zander, hun, please take Ambrose home. I will be right behind you. Mr. Cee, go with them," Rose says as a portal opens, and they disappear.

Observing the man who is still watching them, Rose speaks, "Again, kind Sir, thank you. Your kindness can never be repaid. I appreciate everything that you did for my grandson. Please take this gift as a symbol of my gratitude. Thank you."

As Rose disappears, leaving a box for the man, the vision spins as Noel lands in the middle of a street.

Chapter 16
A New Season

"Ugh, what is this? It looks like it just snowed. They freshly salted the street," Noel says, spinning his wand as his clothes transform. From his overcoat pocket, he pulls a watch, clicks the lid open, looks down, closes the lid, and stows the watch away. Walking down the street, he phases in and out of the town, examining the various parts of the story, laughing at the sight of people bustling about and grabbing some food on the way. Then, he stumbles upon a particular part of the story that he recognizes.

"Well, what do we have here?" Noel stops and looks through the front gate of a very dark manor that rises out of the ground.

"This place is still as creepy as ever. Lord Time Yule, my old friend, forgive me for what I am about to do. You have fixed the timeline, but you did not fix Ambrose. That is my job. This should be more interesting to relive then the last image," he states, spinning his staff and phasing into the upstairs loft of the home.

☙

"Master Ambrose, dear child, what seems to be bothering you?" Cedric inquires.

"Nothing, Cedric. This is just a horrible time of year. Every year, I am stuck here. My parents and siblings never come to visit," Ambrose explains.

"Master Ambrose, you have your grandparents, myself, and Mr. Cee," Cedric remarks.

"Old friend, thank you, and don't get me wrong, it's always nice having Christmas with you guys, but, of course, I miss my family. I especially miss my sister, Willow, and I cannot believe that I am saying this, but I am missing the other five," Ambrose remarks as he turns to look out the window overlooking the street, watching the snow start to come down again.

As he attempts to hide his tears, Cedric knows that more is going on than the young master is saying. Cedric thinks for a moment, looks around, and then breaks the silence.

"Young Master Ambrose, you always love to help me decorate at this time of year. Why don't you join me? I have some finishing touches to put on this place."

"Cedric, thank you, but not this time," Young Ambrose says as he stands and looks around.

"What good is it to decorate, old friend, if there's no one to spend Christmas with?"

"Master Ambrose, are you sure it is the holidays that are bothering you?" Cedric inquires.

Ambrose turns from the window and nods at Cedric.

"Cedric, life for me is different," Ambrose states.

"Different in what way, my good Sir?"

"I know, Cedric. I know who I am to become," Ambrose replies.

"Oh, and who might that be?" Cedric asks, tilting his head.

"Never mind, it is nothing."

❧

Freezing the image, Noel looks around.

"I'm not too fond of this time of year, Cedric, old friend, and you always were there. Breathe, Noel, breathe. When it all occurred to me, I took one look at the ring I was wearing and knew what had to be done. I know how to save time. Lord Time Yule, forgive me for what I am about to do, old friend. You are not the only one who can control time.

Noel spins his hands as the images move, quickly advancing. Then, he waves his hand and returns the story to average speed, finding himself walking through the local bookstore on Christmas Eve. Young Ambrose has snuck out and is strolling through an old bookstore.

Stopping the image again, Noel comments, "I remember that night, Ha! It was cold, and Grandma was furious with me for sneaking out. I remember it all too well. But wait, now I understand."

Let's see if this spell works. With that, Noel unfreezes the vision and can interact with it.

Accipe quod falsum est et fac verum.
Take what is false and make it true.

As the story comes to life around him, he says to himself, "I can't believe I'm doing this, I am about to break thousands of rules," and with a snap of his finger, his clothes transform, he becomes young again, and he watches the young Ambrose from the other side of the store.

Ambrose walks through the alley examining the different books on the shelves when the bookstore owner approaches.

"Are you just here looking, or are you going to buy something? It is Christmas Eve, and I want to close," the clerk inquires rudely.

"I am so sorry, My Lady, just browsing," Ambrose responds.

"Well, browse elsewhere," the clerk demands.

"Ambrose, there you are, little brother. I told you not to wander away," Noel remarks.

"Excuse me, Sir, do you know this child?" the lady asks, turning her nose up.

"Yes, Ma'am, I'm so sorry my younger brother seems to have wandered off. Come on, bro, let's get out of here. Besides, you do not want her books," Noel says.

"How dare you! Leave my store immediately," the woman demands as she stamps her foot, walks towards the door, opens it, and shows them out.

Whispering only loud enough for Ambrose to hear, Noel says, "Old troll."

Ambrose looks at him and smiles as the two walk out the door. Outside the bookstore, Ambrose draws his wand.

"Thank you, kind Sir, but I don't need your help."

"Wow, kid, calm down. Is that any way to show appreciation? Lower the wand, Ambrose," Noel demands, hands raised, trying to take control of the situation.

"Why?"

"Because, kid, it won't end well for you."

"Sir, I already don't like this time of year. Although I find your sense of humor funny, I don't like many people, and I'm not in the mood right now to deal with stuff."

"Believe me, kid. I get it. I understand. Sibling problems? Issues with the parents? And, ah yes, what about the epic dilemma about who you will become in the future?" Noel inquires, sitting down and inviting young Ambrose to sit with him on the edge of the fountain in the town center.

"To answer your question, yes and no. Not to sound rude, Sir, but what type of Arcane are you?" Ambrose inquires.

"Interesting question. I am an Arcane who is Mundane and who is not Mundane."

"In order to not be Mundane, you have to be Arcane. But to be Arcane, you must be Mundane," Ambrose replies.

"You are the first person in my ninety years of traveling who understands that."

"Ninety years? That means you have outlived a good majority of the Arcane community," Ambrose notes.

"Yes, I have seen many Christmases over my lifetime," Noel explains.

"That sounds horrifying," Ambrose states.

"It is not that bad. It grows on you over time. Why don't you like the Christmas season, kid?"

"It's a long, complicated story, one I hope to escape when I get into college," Ambrose states.

"I'm all ears," Noel says as he transforms his ears on the spot.

Young Ambrose scrambles to his feet, "You are… You are an elf."

"Yes, I am, and not the type that slides down the chimney with Santa either. Besides, I hate those children's stories. They make us sound so weird and weak. How many elves do you know that wear green tights and throw pixie dust everywhere?"

"I'm sorry, Sir, I don't meet many elves. A lot of them reside in the mountain village of Aelfdene and don't like to come down these days."

"Oh yes, I see. Many of them are still afraid of the Mundane Wars and another factor," Noel says.

"Yes, and you can say his name, Merlin," Ambrose explains.

"Merlin, ha! That cranky old coot! In ninety years of time travel, nothing has changed about him, I see. He is still causing problems, still trying to enslave, and still putting fear into the hearts of many," Noel laughs, while shaking his head.

"I do not know what is more horrifying, ninety years of Christmas or ninety years of dealing with Merlin," Ambrose states with a perplexed look.

"They are both equally perplexing. So, kid, tell me. What's your story?" Noel inquires, flipping the edges of his cloak up around his lap to stay warm.

"First, I am not a kid. I am fifteen. Second, I have been raised by my grandparents," Ambrose explains.

"Your parents are not around, I take it." Noel says.

"It is hard to explain. My parents are alive, but they are afraid of my power, so afraid that they sent me to live with my grandparents. I have six older siblings, five of whom I cannot stand. My one older sister is cool. My only family, next to Grandma and Grandpa, is my cat and my family's butler," Ambrose replies.

"Your butler?" Noel asks with a raised eyebrow.

"Well, I shouldn't say butler. He's more like a friend, right now, one of the only friends I have," Ambrose notes with a sadness in his tone.

"I see. So, are you not in school?" Noel asks.

"No. That's another long story. I'm not in school because my magic is too dangerous," Ambrose states.

"Too dangerous? There is no such thing. Magic cannot be dangerous. It is only dangerous in the wrong person's hands. Are you the wrong person?" Noel asks, leaning back.

"Not necessarily a bad person, just a person who does not use their magic. You see that fire hydrant?" Ambrose points as the hydrant dissolves, and a water geyser flies up into the air.

"Interesting. So, you can dissolve things. It is a rather handy form of magic," Noel states, raising an eyebrow and waving his hand, making the hydrant reappear.

"I hate magic! My magic is unnatural. It is weird. It is crazy. Besides, it caused my siblings to hate me and call me, 'the Freaky Merlin Twin,'" Ambrose says as a tear rolls down his face.

Noel sits back, remembering how cruel the five could be.

"Ahh, I am sorry to hear that. But the magic you explained to me does not sound freaky at all but, rather, what is needed," Noel says, handing Ambrose a handkerchief.

"Can I ask you a question, good Sir? You said you have traveled for ninety years?" Ambrose asks.

"I have," Noel responds.

"In your ninety years of travel, good Sir, have you ever met an Arcane who can fight without a wand? Who can do unspoken spells? Who can tear things apart with their mind? Who could bring the absolute destruction to the magical world?" Ambrose asks.

"Actually," Noel pauses, trying to choose his words cautiously so as not to alter time too much. Finally, he speaks, "Yes, I have."

"Really? Can I ask what happened to them?" Ambrose inquires with a look of hope in his eyes.

"The wizard's story is like anyone else's. They fall in love, go to college, create a family, and go to work, basically living a normal life," Noel explains, trying to keep a straight face as much as possible.

"They sound remarkable. They did not fear their magic?" asks Ambrose.

"Oh no, they feared it. They were so afraid of it they vowed never to use it," Noel explains.

"What happened that changed their mind?" Ambrose inquires.

"They met their partner, who showed them the world, who showed them that love, at least the love they held, is beautiful and powerful magic. It was their partner who convinced the siblings of this individual not to fear, but to join, them. So, you see, Ambrose, they lived an everyday life, and, in the process, they became extraordinary. You can become extraordinary as well," Noel explains, smiling.

"Me? Extraordinary? You're joking. Do you know what I would do to give up my magic? To live life as a Mundane, away from all of this. Maybe even escape to someplace like New York City?" Ambrose states longingly.

"I know. believe me, I know. Let me say this. Eight years ago, you met someone, a man, a governor. His name was Dalton, and he was extraordinary. His magic was unlike any that you have ever seen, and he had faith in you, a faith so strong, it shapes your future," Noel explains.

"Wait, how do you know Lord Dalton?" Ambrose inquires.

"There is not much that I do not know, or that I have not seen. But my journey is far from being over. It is yet to be concluded," Noel states, waving his hand as the snow flies like a cyclone playing out different stories until one story catches Ambrose's eyes.

"Wait, pause the image," Ambrose says, raising his hand as Noel waves his hand, and the image freezes.

"What catches your attention there?" smiles Noel.

"You know me. You are the one… the one I have sensed watching all those years but never interacting until now. Why?" Ambrose asks.

"Aye, I have traveled for so long that I have seen the many different timelines and have watched yours closely. You see, while magic is a powerful thing, there has always only been the one true you, no more, no less. But, unlike other timelines, you are only in this timeline with the power you pose. So, yes, I have watched, learning everything I can from you. I've seen what both the Arcane and Mundane can become. I have also seen what you become," explains Noel.

"What does any of that have to do with me?" Ambrose asks.

"Ambrose, when I was growing up, no one told me I would be anything. I grew up hating the world around me, both Arcane and Mundane alike. I did not care if the world was destroyed. I had made an oath in my youth, a very long time ago, that I would never save time, save people, save anyone, I just wanted to live a simple life away from everyone and everything. But then, I met someone. That someone was extraordinary. They loved me for me, and I'm not the same person because of it. So, your anger does not have to fuel your hatred. Why not channel it into something good?"

Noel finishes by taking his ring off, holding it up in his hand as it flies into the sky, and lights like a star.

"Wow, that is awesome," Ambrose says as Noel catches the ring again and holds it in his hand.

"You believe that you have no one who believes in you or your magic, but you are very wrong. Therefore, I give you this. When you do not believe, know that the faith of your people, your family, and who you are yet to become, will always be with you. But the ring is magical. If you choose to live an average life, that of a Mundane, then wear the ring, and, if your magic is needed, take it off. I am giving you something that no one gave me, a choice, a way to live the life you want. The person who gave this ring to me gave me a second chance to understand magic, and now, on this Christmas Eve, I give it to you," Noel says, smiling and handing the ring to Ambrose.

"Thank you, kind Sir," Ambrose says.

"You're welcome," Noel replies, rising to his feet.

"Sir, why me?" Ambrose inquires.

"Because, Ambrose, I believe in your magic. Dalton believed in your magic. Noble Elder believes in your magic. And believe it or not, your siblings will come to believe. The ring will protect you. Hold tight to it. In the times of greatest need, it will... how do I put it? It will light the way," Noel exclaims as he stands up and begins walking away.

"Sir, wait! Would you like to have Christmas dinner?" Ambrose inquires.

"Thank you but enjoy your holiday. Take the time to spend it with your family. But one last thing." Noel says.

"Sure. What is it?" Ambrose asks.

"Promise me, promise me, no matter how difficult life gets, how much you grow to hate magic, that you will never forget who you truly are and never lose faith. If nothing else, even if you choose never to use your magic, your faith will be the destruction of Merlin. Remember, as I said, Dalton believes in you. The Arcane believe in you. Your family, in their own funny ways, believes in you," Noel says as he reaches the street where he pulls out the pocket watch and throws it into the air.

"Sir?" Ambrose calls as Noel turns his head.

"Your watch, it is broken. The time-loop will keep you here. However, I think the academy library holds the answers you need. Just be cautious of the librarian," Ambrose says as Noel nods and snatches up the watch, disappearing into thin air. All that remains is a letter that flies in the wind.

Snatching the letter, Ambrose opens it and reads.

Ambrose,

Magic is light, magic is dark, magic is good, and magic can also be evil. When you become scared, when you feel like you are about to lose it, when you want to run away, open your eyes, examine the world around you, and look for new ways. Your faith in all things will be the downfall of Merlin. You may hate magic, but the fate of the Arcane rests on your shoulders. There will come a time when the world will need you. I know you do not like to hear this, but Merry Christmas and may magic guide your way.

~A Friend in Time~

Upon finishing the letter, Ambrose looks up into the sky and notices that the snow is beginning to fall again. Wrapping his scarf around his neck, he pulls his jacket collar up, and disappears.

Across time and space, Noel appears in the middle of a snowy street, crashing into shrubs and then, standing. He brushes himself off and examines the watch.

"I hate this thing, and how did he know it was broken?" Noel wonders.

"Interesting that it would dump me here," he remarks, pulling the other watch and examining the time.

"Seven o'clock. Just in time. I wonder what they are up to these days," he says aloud, snapping his fingers as his clothes transform into tattered rags with holes. His hair is long, and his beard is scruffy and unkept.

"One final touch," he laughs to himself as his walking staff appears and he leans on it.

"Huh, this is fun. Appearing to walk with a limp is more easily said than done," Noel notes, attempting to create a fake limp as he heads down the street until he observes an interesting sight.

Two elf males and one female lean on a planter bed, quietly waiting as a middle-aged woman appears with two more elves, one male and one female.

"Boys, have you seen your sister?" the woman inquires as the two boys shrug their shoulders.

"Willow? Willow?" the woman shouts.

"Mother, if she has wandered off, she will be back," Isabella says, standing up from the planter bed.

"Isabella, your job is to watch your siblings, a simple task," the woman snaps.

"Mother, we are all young adults or teenagers. Besides, it is not like she hasn't done this before," Isabella notes, rolling her eyes.

"You better pray that, for your sake, she does not get hurt or into trouble," the woman says, turning and walking away as the other four follow. Examining the area, Noel holds up his hand and closes his eyes as the magic guides his vision to where Willow is.

"There you are," he says, walking towards the old town center. Stopping, he observes the area until he catches sight of Willow moving in the distance. Approaching, he sees her walking down the street looking through the windows. Not paying attention, he trips, landing in the snow with a loud crash as he falls over some trashcans. People stop to watch what is happening. Willow also stops, then runs over to help him up.

"Dear Sir! Oh my! You must be frozen. How dreadful! Let me help you," Willow says, helping Noel up.

"Thank you, my kind lady," Noel replies, brushing himself off and standing up, very wobbly.

"Sir, I am Willow. It is a pleasure to meet you," she says.

"The pleasure is mine, and thank you again for helping me," he replies.

"What is your name?" Willow asks. Noel pauses slightly, thinking.

"I am Leon," he finally says, pretending to be weak and falling against the wall.

"Sir, you are weak. You must be chilled to the bone. Would you please let me help you? It is Christmas," Willow insists.

"It is okay, and I am just trying to find a place to eat, then off to find shelter," he replies.

"Sir, the restaurants have closed, and you say shelter? Are you without a home?" inquires Willow.

"Yes," Noel nods.

"This is Christmas Eve. This will not do. I insist you come home with me. My family has plenty of food, and my parents can help you find shelter," Willow says, offering her arm to support Noel.

"My kind lady, how do I thank you?" Noel asks.

"No need. It is my pleasure. May I ask, where is your family?" she inquires.

"Not around. It is an interesting and complicated story. I have seen the coming and going of the seasons and time playing its many games," he explains, leaning on Willow as they walk.

"You speak as if….," Willow begins, then she pauses.

"As if what? I am Arcane?" he inquires.

"Yes," she says, nodding.

"I understand what you mean by the passing of seasons and time," she states, stopping and looking toward the sky.

"Did something I say trouble you, My Lady?"

"No, kind Sir Leon. I cannot imagine what it must be like for you not to have any family around. But, unfortunately, my brother is not with us," she notes as a tear appears in the corner of her eye.

"Where is your brother?" he asks.

"My brother does not live with us. My other siblings are cruel to him. They would hex him. Then, finally, one day, his magic exploded and nearly killed three of them. He was so terrified that he ran away," she explains.

"Why did he run?" Noel inquires, knowing the story all too well.

"He was afraid of his magic. He was afraid of hurting others. So, he disappeared. My grandparents nearly sent the entire Arcane community out looking for him. He was finally found. He was sleeping under a bridge in Central Park in New York City. He was cold, tired, scared, and hungry. They spoke of the kindness of an older man who gave him food and protected him," says Willow as they continue to walk down the street.

"So, your brother is safe?" inquires Noel.

"Yes, my grandmama says that she remembers that the man was gentle and kind. But he was so worried about my brother. It was after that that my parents and grandparents made the decision that my brother should live far away from here," Willow says.

"I am sorry to hear that. Do you ever see him?"

"I would like to, but Mama feels it best not to visit him. She believes if we see him, she will not be able to protect him from the others. Mama says she feels the others did not learn from the last time with him. So, my mother blames herself."

"Willow, there you are!" a voice calls out.

"Yes, Mother, I am here," Willow replies.

"My dear, what are you doing?" her mother inquires.

"Mother, I was looking for a last-minute Christmas present for someone, and I was on my way home when I stopped to help Mr. Leon. He fell and is extremely weak," Willow says.

"Your daughter was kind enough to help me, and I enjoyed walking with her and talking," Noel explains.

"That is Willow for you, always caring for others," her mother remarks.

"Mother, he has no family around. I hope you do not mind. I invited him for dinner, and I was hoping that you and Papa could help him find shelter," Willow says, looking cautiously at her mother.

"My daughter, of course, as always, your heart is too big at times. Absolutely, Mr. Leon, if you have no family around, you are more than welcome to join us. No one should be without on Christmas. You may call me Lady Ignatius by the way," the woman says.

"Lady Ignatius? As in the queen?" Leon inquires.

"No, no, that is my mother-in-law, the Queen Roslynn Ignatius. I am the Lady Meredith Ignatius. You know of the queen?" Lady Ignatius exclaims.

"Yes, the queen is legendary, a gentle, kind-hearted soul. She has forever changed the way magic works," he replies, leaning on his walking staff.

"Fascinating. Willow, the gate." Lady Ignatius says, her eyes narrowing. Then, walking through the gate, the two help Leon up the steps of the old stone home and they enter the foyer.

"It is about time you got home. Mother has been worried sick," Isabella remarks, looking at Willow, then at her mother, and then at the man.

"Who is this?" she asks, wrinkling her nose.

"This is Mr. Leon," Willow explains.

"Charmed," Isabella remarks, texting on her phone.

"Isabella Roslynn Ignatius, where are your manners?" her mother snaps.

Willow walks with Leon into the parlor and helps him into the armchair.

"Ah, little sis, you have a boyfriend," Pete smirks.

"Peter Kelvin Ignatius, so help me, young man," his mother scowls.

Noel looks around, examining the place, and removing his gloves. Lady Ignatius returns carrying a tray with a teapot, a cup, and biscuits.

"Tea, Sir Leon?" she offers, placing the tray on the cart.

"Yes, please and thank you," he replies as the eldest of Willow's brothers appears.

"Funny looking fellow," Michael remarks.

"Seriously, Michael? You are as rude as Isabella," Willow snaps.

"Lady Willow, it is okay. Isabella and Michael remind me of my siblings," Noel remarks, accepting a cup of tea.

"Sir Leon, how many siblings do you have?" Lady Ignatius asks, pouring herself a cup of tea.

"A few," he replies, sipping his tea and trying to avoid giving a number.

"Why aren't you with them then?" Michael inquires rudely.

"Michael Cunnings Ignatius, manners," his mother complains.

"It is okay, Lady Ignatius. But, to answer your question, Michael, my siblings are not around," Leon explains, sitting back quietly.

"I am so sorry," Lady Ignatius says, placing her hand on top of Leon's. Immediately, she pulls her hand back, pausing and regarding him with a confused look.

"Michael, dear, will you set the table, please? Willow, will you help your sisters in the kitchen? I would like to speak with Sir Leon alone," she directs.

When the two disappear into their respective rooms, Lady Ignatius spins her hand over her head as the door slam shut. Looking around, she examines the room as Leon hands her the watch.

"Would this be easier?" he inquires, smiling.

Taken aback by the sight of the pocket watch, Lady Ignatius drops the teacup and saucer that she is holding. Raising his hand, Leon stops them in mid-air, preventing them from hitting the ground and shattering. Instead, they fly back up onto the cart as he transforms.

"Ambrose?" Lady Ignatius inquires.

"Hello, Mom," he replies, smiling.

"Ambrose, you are an adult," she remarks.

"I am, and I do not go by Ambrose. I have not since I was nineteen," he says, sitting back in the armchair as his mother sits across from him staring.

"Then, what name do you go by?" she asks.

"My apologies. I prefer to be called Noel," he explains.

"Noel?" she repeats.

"Yes, it is a nickname, short for Noble Elder," he says, sipping his tea.

"Wait! How?" she asks.

"Too long of a story to explain, but a story that I do not even know if it will happen," he replies, pausing.

"Not sure if it will happen? Do you mean the timeline?" she asks.

"Restored at great cost and sacrifice," he says, standing and walking over to the fireplace.

"Noel, if your siblings are not around, have they passed? Or are you still distant from them? You must be extremely old, I presume?"

"Yes, Mom, over ninety years," he replies, leaning one hand on the mantle.

"Ninety years is amazing. What brings you here?" she asks.

"I am stuck in a never-ending loop. When the timeline was restored, Lord Time Yule joined the Celestials. I had one last thing I needed to do. I have tried to jump and leave this time but ended up here, knowing where I landed. I took on the disguise of Leon. Interactions with any part of the current timeline could alter the current path," Noel explains.

"What do you need?" she asks.

"Hmm, that is hard to explain," he says, looking over his shoulder.

"Name it," his mother exclaims, placing her hand on his shoulder.

"Faith!" he replies.

"Faith? I do not understand," she says.

"When Lord Time Yule died, I lost all faith in everything, in the Arcane, the Mundane, myself, everything. The one thing that gave me power, I cannot find," he replies, pulling away from her and walking across the room.

"Ambrose, I believe it was fate that brought you here. If faith is what you need, then I am going with you to help you get back to the time you need to be in," she says.

"Mom, it is not that easy. Besides, you have your duties," Noel retorts.

"My duty is first and foremost as your mother. My other responsibilities are secondary," she replies.

Noel turns, lowers his head, and looks up.

"The time I come from, I would have done anything to hear that."

As he finishes speaking, glowing light fills the space. When he looks down, he notices that his left gauntlet is glowing.

"My gauntlet. But how?" Noel remarks, holding it as his expression goes from confused to understanding.

"Now, I understand. My final journey was not my only task. There is a second one. Dalton, you are always filled with mysteries. Mom, you can help me. What I need, I cannot access alone," he says.

"What is it?" she asks.

"Grandma's library," he replies.

"Understood. But I cannot leave your siblings. They will have to come along," she says when she notices Noel rolling his eyes.

"Fine," he remarks, looking displeased.

"What is at the library?" his mother inquires.

"The circle of power. If I can activate it, I can time jump," he explains.

"That circle does not work," she says.

"The explosion!" Noel sits down in the chair again, thinking.

"You know of the explosion? That was two years before you were born," she says, puzzled.

"Yes, but it is a story we all know too well. The circle fuels the power of the gauntlets and my elf jewels. The circle can be reactivated as it was when I was sixteen. A rather extraordinary feat of magic," he waves his hand, and a bag appears.

His mother carefully approaches, examining the bag, which is floating in the air. Noel reaches up, grabs it, and starts rustling through it.

"Where is it? Ah, here," he finally says, pulling out a grimoire and a small box. Reaching into the box, he reveals a ring with a giant phoenix head on it. He slides the ring onto his hand and the eye of the phoenix starts to glow purple, and what appears to be spiders emerge from the box and run across the floor, forming a pedestal for the grimoire.

"Eek, spiders! Really?" his mother shrieks.

"They are not spiders," Noel replies, slamming the heavy grimoire down with a giant thud.

"If they are not spiders, then what are they?" she demands.

"They have not been created yet, but they will be in about five years. It is called nanotechnology," he explains, peering up from the grimoire.

"Nanotechnology? Is that Mundane science?" his mom inquires, looking confused.

"I will say this much. There is more to me than meets the eye," he says, winking.

"You master science and magic?" she inquires.

"If you think about it, they are, in a way, the same. They use many of the same principles, something that Uncle Ethan believes will fuel the essence of magic. So, yes, I do both science and magic," Noel states, looking up from the grimoire.

"What are you looking for?" she asks.

"The time loop spell. Lord Time Yule could rattle them off like they were nothing. I, on the other hand, need to study them and put them to memory," he says.

Then, he freezes upon hearing a voice.

"Hun, kids, I am home," the voice calls.

"Lord, help me! This is going to be interesting," Noel remarks, tapping the grimoire, as it and the nanos disappear.

Lady Ignatius spins her hands, dropping the fields over the door and windows as Rusty enters, followed by his father, Zander.

The Impossible is Possible

Chapter 17
The Impossible is Possible

"Merry Christmas," Zander says, hugging his daughter-in-law when he notices the guest.

"I am sorry. I did not know you had a guest," Zander explains as he extends his hand.

"Grandpa," Willow yells, running into the room and hugging him. Noel quietly slides to the far side of the room, ready to teleport when Rusty asks him a question.

"So, Sir, what is your name?" he asks.

"Dad, this is Leon," Willow answers.

"He was injured, Hun. Your daughter brought him in for the evening," Lady Ignatius notes, looking over at Noel.

"What's going on here?" Zander inquires, and before anyone can respond, Noel is standing in the middle of the room, his eyes glowing silver as he holds Zander's wand arm.

"Good King, please stand down," Noel says when he finds Rusty's wand in his face.

"Let him go, or I will hex you," Rusty says.

"You were told many years ago that if you tried to hex King Zander, it would not go well. So, not only will I give you the same warning again, but I will add this, unless you don't value your magic ability, lower your wand," Noel replies, spinning Zander's wand in his hand and handing it back as he bows.

"A time traveler," states Rusty backing up.

"Yes," Noel says, raising cautiously from his bow, his hands raised, and backing up.

"Papa, do not do anything stupid," Willow cries, stepping in front of the man she believes to be Leon.

"Willow, thank you, but I have this," he reassures her, smiling.

Ligare.
Bind.

Before anyone in the room can respond, they find their arms bound to their sides, except for Willow and her mother.

"Dad, what is he?" Rusty inquires as Noel lowers his hand.

"To answer your question, Sir, I am an ArchSorcerer, stuck in a nasty time-loop and trying to return home before the timelines collide and cause havoc," Noel replies, looking displeased.

"An ArchSorcerer? Then your magic is strong. What can I do to help you? You said you are stuck, and I would be more than happy to help you get back to your time," Willow says.

"Thank you, but your mother has been kind enough to agree to help me," Leon replies as the magical bindings holding Zander snap.

Clipem.
Shield.

Noel holds his arm in front of him as the magic from Zander's wand is stopped in mid-air.

"Lord Ignatius, please, no," Lady Ignatius pleads, placing her hand on his arm and lowering it. Looking at his daughter-in-law, Zander freezes, recognizing the look in her eye.

"Release them, and I will take you to the library," Zander says, stowing his wand.

"Dad, are you crazy?" Rusty complains.

"Russell, enough. We stand down," Zander declares.

Raising his hand and waving as if dismissing people, Noel commands,

Libero.
Free.

"Dad, what is this about?" Rusty protests.

"He is Noble Elder," Zander says as the five Ignatius children behind them lower themselves to one knee, bowing.

"You are Noble Elder? You're too young to be him," Rusty exclaims.

"I am Noble Elder," Noel confirms.

"Rusty, hun, he is the new Noble Elder," Lady Ignatius explains.

"The new Noble Elder? What happened to the old one?" Michael asks.

"Still as stupid as ever, I see. In the time I come from, he died. You know that thing when someone falls over, their spirit leaves their body, and you bury them in the ground?" Noel snorts sarcastically.

"How can he die? He is an Elder!" Kells and Michael declare, looking around at the others for answers.

"He is an Elder who died and became a Celestial. But, before he did, he named me as his successor," Noel explains, taking a deep breath.

"Grandpapa, how is that possible? Noble Elder can die?" Pete asks, concern in his voice.

"Earlier, my father mentioned taking you to the library. Why do you need the library?" Rusty inquires.

"The circle," Noel replies in an annoyed tone, the same tone that Ambrose used, and that Rusty hated.

Backing up, Rusty observes him, his eyes narrowing.

"I see. The circle is broken," Rusty states in a snarky tone.

Noel holds up his gauntlets.

"I have the key to reactivate the circle. But the longer I stand here, the more the timeline will be affected, and heaven knows what Merlin will do," Noel declares as he raises his hand, motioning for everyone to stop. Then, looking around cautiously, he listens.

"Oh no! Don't tell me!" Noel says as he raises an orb and examines the image that is playing out.

The group can see images of the library where darkness can be seen moving around.

"Damn! Are you kidding me, Merlin?" Noel exclaims.

"Dad, if Merlin is in the library, what about Mom and the Curpendulums?" Rusty declares as the room flashes with light and Noel is suddenly gone.

The orb falls and rolls across the floor, hitting the sole of Willow's boot.

"I will not ask you again, dwarf! Where are the Curpendulums?" Merlin demands as the dark guards throw books from the shelves. The dwarfs cry out, watching the books being torn apart.

"I know not of what you speak," Mr. Bruin retorts as Merlin points his wand at one of the other dwarfs who immediately falls to the ground dead.

"I will kill them one at a time until you tell me," Merlin screams.

"Lord Merlin, Sir. We have scattered the library. None of the Curpendulums are here."

"They must be hidden," one of the guards says as Merlin pushes everything off the counter in a rage.

"Dwarf, what is the passcode for the secure section," Merlin barks, pointing his wand in Mr. Bruin's face.

"The passcode is 'you're old and cranky,'" a voice says from behind him as Merlin turns to find Noel standing there.

Clipem.
Shield.

A lightfield rises out of the ground in front of Noel. As he spins his hands and throws them forward, the field expands and flies across the floor, slamming Merlin into the counter. Working quickly, Noel causes multiple fields to appear, forming a box around Merlin and preventing him from moving.

"Mr. Bruin, get everyone out of here now," Noel yells as several dark guards charge forward but find themselves face-to-face with a giant, black panther.

"Mr. Cee, get them," Noel barks at the panther roars and tears into the arms of one of the guards as two others quickly dodge the beast. As the panther chases the fleeing guards, the doors of the library fly open. Willow stands in the doorway, wind spinning around her as her hair stands on end and static electricity is seen snapping between the ends. Looking around, her eyes turn green as she creates a shield of vines that allow the dwarfs to escape.

"Thank you, My Lady," Mr. Bruin says, bowing.

"Mr. Bruin, please find my grandmama," Willow says, walking through the door.

"What are you doing here?" demands Noel.

"I am helping you," she replies.

"Willow, the timeline has become unstable. The fate of the Arcane, of you, me, everyone, I cannot see it. I do not know the outcome of the battle. I cannot guarantee your safety," Noel cautions as Merlin pushes back against the lightfield.

"Fate brought you here, dear Noble Elder, to this moment in time. Why, I do not know. But what I do know is that we each control our own fate," Willow explains, lowering her hands down towards the ground, then pulling it up as if throwing someone in the air.

Vines explode out of the ground, destroying the dark guards. Four dark witches appear on the opposite side of Willow. But, when they simultaneously blast her, their wands explode. Hunched down, Willow looks up as the four witches crash into each other and fly violently around the room.

"I am so sick of you, Merlin! Ninety years of chasing you," Noel declares, pulling his left arm up as he slams Merlin into the ground with the full force of magic.

Coming from his left, three dark guards strike his gauntlet with their swords. They fly backward as one-third of the circle lights. Smiling, Noel spins his hands, lifting the three guards off their feet as his eyes turn black. Spreading his fingers, they explode.

"Seriously," Noel says as his eyes now turn solid white and three more dark guards dissolve into dust. Then, glancing back, Noel sees that Willow is fighting seven dark guards. He tilts his head to the left, and, with a quick nod, the seven dark creatures dissolve.

Two witches fly across the library, screaming, as Cedric appears, rising out of the ground, grabbing them by their ankles, and slamming them into the ground. Pulling her wand, one witch attempts to hex him. Cedric glares at her, and, in a split second, his fangs appear, and he sinks them into her neck. The witch's feet flail about as he drinks from her. Scrambling to her feet, the other witch tries to strike Cedric, but the panther snaps the witch's arm and drags her across the floor.

Turning back to Merlin, Noel spins his hands and encases Merlin in a lightfield, the walls of the field creating a cube prison. He is blasted backward as the cube drops and shatters, freeing Merlin.

"Master, are you okay?" Raven asks, suddenly appearing and helping Merlin to his feet.

"KILL THEM, NOW!" Merlin roars.

Noel looks up as twelve dark creatures move against him. With one quick wave of his hand, they also dissolve. Raven charges him with a dagger, but Noel catches the dagger's blade between his hands and kicks Raven in the gut sending her flying backward.

"I see you were trained exceptionally well," Cedric notes, smiling and slamming a dark guard through the table at exceptional speed.

Holding up his right hand, four marbles appear between Noel's fingers as he spins and throws them out in front of him.

When the marbles hit the floor, nothing happens immediately.

"Ha! Am I supposed to be afraid of marbles?" Merlin laughs when, suddenly, a giant rises out of them, grabbing Merlin and Raven by the ankles and throwing them across the room. The giant kicks three of the marbles back behind him and nods at Noel.

"Call for backup, now! I am done with him," Merlin barks as multiple figures emerge.

"The Council of Dark, Liam, Lord Aden, Lord Balimore, and your guards! Damn you, Merlin, you cranky, old coot, you really are serious about getting those Curpendulums," Noel remarks, flipping off his cloak.

As three dark council members, Liam, Aden, and Raven, attack him simultaneously, Noel holds up his hands, flipping them with his magic alone.

"Balimore, find the grimoires now!" Merlin barks as Noel casts magic but finds a lightfield dome over him.

"They cannot succeed! Secure the library! Secure the circle! And, for heaven's sake, do not let them destroy anything else," Queen Rose declares, picking up a torn grimoire as she, Zander, and the other five Ignatius grandchildren appear in the archway.

"Grandmama, what took you so long?" Willow yells across the room as she sits casually at a table, drinking a cup of tea as vines slam dark guards back and forth.

Scream after scream echo through the library as a hundred dark creatures and guards arrive. Raven screams, pointing her wand at Willow.

Finiendum Vitam.
To take the life of.

But her magic blast stops halfway across the room and disappears in mid-air. Suddenly, the magical blast reappears, redirected and striking one of the three Dark Council Members who falls to the floor dead. Angry, Merlin and Raven scream in unison,

Finiendum Vitam.
To take the life of.

This new magical blast flies towards Noel, who catches it in mid-air and absorbs the blast.

"Merlin, have you forgotten? The killing spell cannot kill me. Instead, it just amplifies my power," Noel remarks, his eyes glowing purple. When an ax of one of the dark guards strikes his gauntlet, another part of the circle lights. As the guard glares at Noel, the ax explodes in his hand. Then, the guard drops to the ground, screaming. Suddenly, he explodes when Ambrose appears spinning lightning between his hands, his eyes glowing white.

"Need help?" he asks.

Noel and Ambrose nod to one another and spin their hands as a dome of magic falls over them and the darkness, containing any further blasts.

"You know that I hate magic, right?" Ambrose inquires as the two work together to contain the darkness.

"I know you do, but your help right now is not only appreciated but has changed fate and the timeline," Noel remarks as the two stand back-to-back, their spinning hands holding glowing orbs.

Releasing the four orbs, they surround the light dome, causing a second lightfield to appear. Trying to stop Noel and Ambrose, Aiden points his wand at Noel and begins to open his mouth when his arm snaps multiple times and he falls to the floor screaming and holding his arm. Looking over, Noel backs up as Ambrose's eyes turn gray. Ambrose turns his head and looks at Liam, screaming as his leg breaks. Backing up, the two Dark Council members protect Raven and Merlin as they throw orbs, releasing demons. As the demons rise out of the orbs and begin filling the room, they scream and begin exploding as Ambrose turns his hand, destroying all of them at once.

Balimore is outside of the lightfield when Noel pushes his arms out, expanding the field and pulling Balimore into it.

"Grandmama, can you help them?" Willow inquires.

"No. This is not my fight. However, the six of you can help your brother. He needs you all to believe in him," Rose replies as she and Zander fight back the dark guards while the giant runs through the library, swinging a table and striking multiple dark guards.

Aden comes up behind Willow, without her noticing, and holds a wand to the back of her neck.

"Lower the field, or she will be babbling for the rest of her existence," he demands.

Turning, Noel's eyes narrow as Ambrose starts to run toward Willow. But Noel holds up his arm, blocking him.

"I will kill you, Lord Aden," Ambrose shouts.

"Kill me? You are just a boy. You have bigger things to worry about," Aden replies as Merlin blasts Noel.

Catching the blast, Noel drops to one knee as it pushes him across the floor.

"Ambrose, look inside. The magic is within you," Noel says, working to deflect Merlin's blast. Closing his eyes, Ambrose raises his hand, causing a giant illuminated clock to appear. Then, turning his hand to the left, time freezes.

"Wow, awesome! How did I do that?" he asks, looking at his hands in disbelief as Noel rises to his feet.

"Do not get cocky," Noel cautions as he pulls Aden's arm away from Willow and hugs her as he teleports her to the door.

In mere seconds, he teleports all six grandchildren to the door. Then, turning, he teleports back to Ambrose, grabs him, and teleports him to where the six are waiting.

"Ambrose, stay here with them. At the first opportunity, strike my gauntlet with your magic," Noel instructs them.

As Noel raises his hands, time begins to unfreeze. Everyone is moving relatively slowly. Watching carefully, Ambrose nods to his siblings and the seven begin to spin their hands simultaneously. The destroyed furniture begins to reassemble, and the grimoires fly back onto the shelves as the darkness explodes throughout the library. Seeing an opportunity, Ambrose grabs his brother's bow and arrow.

"Kells, I need to borrow this. Thank you," Ambrose says as he closes his eyes and pulls back.

Taking a deep breath, he opens his eyes and lets go the arrow, which screams across the room. When it strikes the gauntlet on Noel's arm, the last part of the circle lights, lightning hits the ground, and a magical column of light explodes, enclosing the circle. Spinning his staff, Noel slams it down and Merlin flies into the air, and Noel multiplies himself.

Containing any magic Merlin might try to cast against the others, Noel steps into the center of the circle as his doubles protect the perimeter. Noel nods to Ambrose and taps his staff on the ground as the eyes of the seven begin to glow. As the seven raise their hands, the room darkens, leaving none of them able to see. Suddenly, a crash rings out. Ambrose throws a light orb into the air and finds each of his siblings, in a separate part of the library with a weapon at their throats.

"Give us the Curpendulums, now!" Liam, Aden, and Raven demand in unison. Turning, Ambrose examines the space carefully, noting where each of his siblings are.

Summoning a grimoire, he lowers it to the ground, closes his eyes, and begins humming. The room darkens, and all that can be heard is the snap of fingers and the tapping of a staff. Then, a scream lets out.

"Aaaaahh!"

The room relights and the six find themselves standing behind Ambrose. They notice that they are decked out in armor. The dark guards are dead, and Aden, Liam, and Raven are left babbling in the corner. Reaching down, Ambrose takes Willow's hand. The other five follow, taking each other's hands. Then, raising their hands together, a flash of light blinds them as the room around them begins spinning.

"Ambrose...?" Willow begins to inquire until he squeezes her hand to let her know that he is there. The other five hold hands and as all seven of them combine their magic, the light column that had appeared around them grows bright. Finally, in one flash, it is gone and all that remains is the gauntlets, and a letter laying on top of them addressed to,

The Ignatius 7.

The seven disappear and reappear at the circle, examining it carefully. Ambrose picks up the gauntlets and is examining them when Willow, who had picked up the letter, hands it to her brother.

"Ambrose, what does the letter say?" his grandmother inquires.

Isabella, Peter, Michael, Sofia, Kells, Willow, & Ambrose,

In a moment, and it only takes a moment, I have seen time alter and for the better. The pleasure of seeing the seven of you come together was truly unique and magical. In my time as Noble Elder, I have seen many arguments. I have seen many moments of cheer & joy, and I have seen many moments of turmoil amongst the seven of you. Together, you will have your moments, but you are all the next generation of magic, of Arcane and Mundane alike.

Your magic is powerful. Each of you is unique and together you are the driving force that will save the world. Multiple magical bloodlines drive your magic but are also redefined by what is yet to come. So, may your magic

guide you. Magic is everything, and for you seven, the seven masters of magic, it is your life.

Lord Time Yule sacrificed himself to restore the timelines to normal to save everyone and everything. However, he waited decades before restoring time to the exact working moment, forever changing the story.

My mission is now completed, restoring the bonds amongst the seven of you. The bond between the seven of you is vital and will be needed in the many years & decades to follow. Your relationships with each other, as siblings, will have their moments. Some of those moments will be challenging. I implore each of you to learn to embrace the good and bad moments, learn and grow from them, and, above all, learn to be there for each other, no matter how bad the rift may be between you. Merlin can be defeated. I have seen it. He fears all seven of you. He will continue to time jump, trying to gain access to the Curpendulums. It is what fuels him. It is his drive and why he will stop at nothing to find them.

I will spend the rest of my time tracing and chasing him. I will buy the seven of you the time you need to find the Curpendulums. Merlin must not get them. I need not remind you what will happen if he finds them all.

I leave with you seven this gift on Christmas Eve, knowing that while each of you is different, you are also very much alike in more ways than any of you understand. Remember, when the seven of you put aside your differences, you will be able to stop him. The seven of you will become "The Ignatius 7," the greatest Masters of the

Magical Arts, whose magic will have no bounds, and no rules. Take a lesson or two from the Magical Three. They represent the history of our people. They are the present, and they are the future. Their sacrifices have set the way for you seven to succeed. Remember, anything that is impossible can become possible. In the darkest moments, if you hold faith, if all you do is simply have faith, then you will succeed.

To you, the Ignatius 7, exercise the powers of magic to guide you and keep you safe in your journeys yet to come. So, I say to you this Christmas Eve, Merry Christmas, remember this time of year, and may all magic protect all that you do.

Your dearest friend,
Noble Elder

When he finishes reading the letter, Ambrose looks around and smiles. He hugs Willow and the other five join in, hugging and smiling at one another.

"Would you like to come home for Christmas Eve and stay with us? While the seven of us are different, we need to put our differences aside. We promise not to hex you or do anything mean," Isabella says to Ambrose as the other four nod in agreement.

"I would like that," Ambrose replies, a tear rolling down his cheek as Willow takes his hand, squeezing it. Then, as the seven turn, a reflection of a spirit catches their attention. Watching, they see the spirit of Lord Time Yule bowing to them, then disappearing.

Avalon

Chapter 18
Avalon

The vision of Noel's journey spins as Rose walks out of the dust, looking around. *"Am I sleeping or am I awake?"* Rose wonders.

"Well, by my attire, it appears I am in my dreams still," she says aloud, spinning her hands and transforming her pajamas into her regular clothes.

"This is going to be a long night if I am going to have to do this in every dream. But where am I?" she inquires, walking along a shoreline, the stars in the night sky twinkling on the water. But, before she can go much further, she is pulled into a vision.

જ

A young man emerges from another room and walks through the old, ruined tower as he wraps his scarf tightly around his neck. Then, pulling his wand, he spins it in front of him and disappears. The next thing Rose knows, the vision has vanished but then, reappears, the smell of food filling the air. Looking around, she observes holiday decorations.

"This must be some sort of outdoor Christmas Market," she remarks aloud. Then, examining the area, she sees the young man from the tower again, and quietly watches as he walks through the crowd picking pockets and stealing anything he can find.

"How sad that the young man is homeless," Rose thinks, weaving through the crowd of people and watching him. Several booths over, Rose notices that the young man is sneaking around to the back and lighting a fire. Drawing people's attention to the flames, he runs back to the front of the stall and takes several roasted turkey legs.

As he runs off down the walkway, weaving through the people, he stops outside a book tent. Chewing on a turkey leg, he strolls through the tent looking at the various books. Then, he stops, looks around, and waves his hand over a book on the shelf, which disappears. Reaching the shelf, he picks up a small item and places it in his pocket. Rose watches as he does this several more times. Finally, the young man rounds the corner and bumps into two men.

"Oh, I am so sorry," the young man says apologetically.

"Watch it, kid," one of the two men says, raising a fist as if he is going to hit the young man, but his friend grabs the man's arms and shakes his head.

The young man exits the tent and begins walking along the other stalls, flicking his wand here and there, causing issues for many of the other shoppers. Laughing, he continues to walk along until a small flickering ball of light flies by him. The young man looks around, then points his wand.

Finiendum Vitam.

To take the life of.

Catching up to the young man and examining the area closely, Rose finds that the floating ball of light is a fairy lying dead on the ground.

"What a horrible, young wizard! No manners or remorse for any creatures. He struck down that fairy as if it was nothing," remarks Rose, shaking her head. The young man reaches the edge of the outdoor market, but when he starts to leave, he is thrown back. Upon seeing this, Rose stops and raises an eyebrow seeing that the young man has jumped to his feet, wand in hand.

"Stealing, making mischief, killing a fairy, and leaving it on the ground where the Mundane can see it. Kid, you are nothing but trouble," the two gentlemen from the tent note, both of them holding wands and aiming them right at the young man.

"Good evening, gentlemen," the young man says, motioning with his free hand as if tipping a hat to them.

"The books and various grimoires in your pockets, hand them over," the one gentleman demands.

"Ugh," the young man says as he pulls three books and two grimoires from his pocket and hands them over to the wizard.

"Nice, but that is only one pocket. We want the book that is in the other pocket," the other man remarks casually as the young man rolls his eyes.

"Hey, Vlad, he is a disrespectful one, isn't he?" one of the gentlemen remarks to the other.

"Yes, indeed, he is," Vlad notes, stowing his wand and smiling at the young man, revealing his fangs as he does.

Time freezes around them as Elder Yule approaches.

"The book, if you would please, young man," Elder Yule motions, holding out his hand.

"You know, I will have those grimoires one of these days, and Arcane and Mundane alike will bow to me," the young man says as Elder Yule snaps his fingers and the young man's mouth is sealed shut. The young man tries to spin his wand, but Elder Yule disappears from where he is standing and reappears, milliseconds later, grabbing the young man's wrist and taking his wand from him. Holding it up, he inspects the wand, then snaps it in half.

"No manners! Gentlemen, get him out of here," Elder Yule commands, raising his hands.

"Sir, what are you going to do?" Vlad asks.

"I'm going to clean up this kid's mess," remarks Elder Yule, spinning his hands as everything in the market begins flying around him, returning it to normal. Then, turning, Elder Yule points his own wand at various tents as they spring back to life.

"Sir, what of the boy?" inquires Vlad.

"Take him to Noble Elder. This kid has caused too many issues," Elder Yule notes, turning his hand as more items are restored to their normal state. As the two men disappear, holding the young man, Elder Yule turns around several times, magic flying around him, as he restores the last of the tents and items affected.

"Piff! Merlin, why do you always have to be so destructive," Elder Yule asks, looking in Rose's direction. Then, he winks, and the vision around her begins spinning, and she lands back on the beach.

Continuing the stroll along the beach, Rose notices a fire burning in the distance. Retrieving her wand, she holds it tightly as she begins walking toward the fire. A rustling in the bushes causes Rose to stop, then she proceeds quietly, examining the area closely until she notices that the water in the lake is glowing blue.

The water dances under the moonlight as it comes to life. Spinning, then stopping, the water ripples and begins spinning again. Watching this, Rose steps back as the Lady of the Lake emerges.

"Roslynn, my dear, how are you?" she inquires.

"Lady of the Lake, good evening. I am well. Just trying to figure out where I am. One minute, I am sleeping, then the next thing I know, I am in a vision. Then, I am here," Rose exclaims, bowing.

"Interesting, isn't it?" the Lady of the Lake says as she walks across the surface of the water toward Rose.

"You have something to do with this, My Lady?" Rose inquires.

The Lady of the Lake nods "I say it is time you know the truth, a truth your parents have not wanted anyone to know. But to know the truth may help us to stop Merlin," the Lady of the Lake replies.

"To stop Merlin? That will be the day! But wait, that young man was Merlin," Rose says, pausing and thinking hard.

"You are correct. Even as a child, he was difficult," the Lady of the Lake explains.

As she steps out of the water onto the shoreline, she begins transforming into human form. as the water spins around her, Rose can make out a blond-haired woman, wearing majestic blue, purple, and white robes, with a long, half-solid train made of water.

"How is that possible?" Rose inquires, smiling, her eyes fixed on the Lady of the Lake.

"It is possible because I am extremely old, and I will this form to be. Merlin cannot touch my magic. He has tried but failed," the Lady of the Lake says, smiling.

"My dear brothers, Ethan and Oliver, will never believe this story. Can you explain to me how it is that my great grandmother, the great Queen Nimuway, is also the Lady of the Lake?" Rose inquires, stowing her wand and joining her great grandmother walking along the beach.

"My child, do you think I would leave you and your brothers and your cousin to fight Mister All Pompous alone? Of course not," Nimuway explains.

"How long have you known about Merlin and his dark ways?" asks Rose.

"My entire life. I have protected the magic and ancient ways for centuries. I help to provide balance to the earth, a balance your great grandfather broke when he went mad. Actually, when I think about it, he broke everything, Time, the castles, my favorite tea set," Nimuway says as water flies around her spinning hands. When she throws it in front of them, a table and two chairs materialize. Rose stops and studies the furniture made of water until Nimuway motions for her to sit.

"Fascinating! Materialization of an element, such a highly advanced form of Arcane Magic, only spoken of in a few manuscripts and a half-dozen scrolls," Rose exclaims.

"A half-dozen scrolls? That is far too many! This type of magic should not be discussed," Nimuway declares, looking concerned.

"Why?" inquires Rose.

"There are some forms of magic, that well… How should I put it? Should not be documented," Nimuway explains.

"Understood. But may I ask, can you start from the beginning, please, and share what you know about Merlin?" inquires Rose.

"Of course. Oh, and Rose, I will answer all your questions at the end," her great grandmother says as the water flows from the lake and begins spinning around them.

As the water flies around them, Rose notices different visions playing out in the water before it flies back into the lake, and the two arrive in a field. The young man from the earlier vision sits with his face buried in his hands, crying.

Lying several feet away is a dead fairy, its wings missing.

"What a horrible child! No respect for that poor fairy. That is the second one he has killed," Rose remarks in an angry tone.

"Just watch," Nimuway instructs as the young man wipes his face, gets to his feet, points his wand at the fairy, and it bursts into flames. Rose attempts to enchant the vision when Nimuway raises her hand, stopping her.

"No. You must not interfere," Nimuway directs.

"Ugh, was he always this nasty?" Rose inquires as Nimuway nods and they follow Merlin, watching him skip down the path.

&

"Great grandma, why am I here?" Rose inquires, raising her hands, pushing them out, and freezing the image.

"As I told you, it is time you learn about a fascinating past, a past that will fuel the present and set the wheels in motion for the future. You know the story of time, and you know the story of the Curpendulums. But you need to know the true story of Merlin," Nimuway replies, looking out over the lake, her hands resting behind her.

"No one knows Merlin's true story," remarks Rose.

"That is because some of us kept it a great secret," Nimuway explains.

"Why hide his story? We all know he is a cranky, grumpy, old man, who is hellbent on world domination," Rose acknowledges.

"Indeed, you just saw him crying in the field. Your great-grandfather is misunderstood. The world never understood him. You see, being born an incubus, he was always mocked and picked on for being different," Nimuway explains.

"Wait, an incubus is a half-man, half-demon," Rose exclaims as she reads from her grimoire that has materialized in front of her.

Nimuway nods, agreeing with her great granddaughter.

"His mother was a mortal queen, the most beautiful, kind-hearted woman you could ever meet. Unfortunately, she was seduced by darkness and bore a child. Merlin grew up with every delight he could imagine and had a beautiful childhood. But then, he discovered his magical potential. His mother died when he was young, and he was on his own. His magic was the only thing that protected him. Some believe that he killed her. Others blamed the incubus and, eventually, he was cast out," Nimuway says.

"His father was not around?" Rose inquires.

"No. No one knows the true identity of his father. All that is known is that he was a demon, and that is where Merlin acquired his magic," Nimuway states.

"That explains much about his behavior," exclaims Rose, getting up and beginning to pace back and forth.

"His behavior stems from that, but also, he made a vow that he would use his magic against the world for taking his mother from him. The demons convinced him that the Mundane were to blame for her death," Nimuway remarks.

"So, that explains why great grandpa believed that the Mundane were his enemy, but it does not explain his hatred for the Arcane."

Rose stopped pacing, looking to Nimuway for answers.

"Actually, yes, it does. If you think about it. You see, his obsession with power fueled your great grandfather's hatred for the Arcane. His obsession for this power drove the wars to come. No one ever understood how an incubus could live as long as Merlin did, have the magical power he did, or how it was that he could not be killed. The magic that he uses is magic fueled by the dark. He tapped into the rawest core of the heart of darkness. He also vowed to use his magic against Noble Elder."

"Great Grandma, is that the reason he wants the Curpendulums so badly, to fuel his magic, and keep others from standing against him?"

"Yes, Rose. And, like every other incubus, he hates the light. But, then again, what incubus does not hate the light?"

"Ethan, Oliver, Father, Uncle Wade, Bethany, and I like the light. We embrace it."

"You are correct. But, then again, the demon blood in the bloodline of the House of Phoenix has been thinned out over time. However, your grandfather, King Titus, struggled with the light physically. The sheer power of the sun would burn his skin."

"True, but Merlin would be the strongest, as it was his parent who was the demon," Rose explains.

"Yes, indeed, however, there is one other who is believed to have a stronger tie to the incubus side of their powers than Merlin," Nimuway notes with concern in her voice.

"Who?" inquires Rose.

"That, my dear child, is a conversation for another day. Just know that they are on the side of the light," Nimuway explains trying to redirect the conversation.

"Delightful, like we need any more incubuses," Rose remarks.

"Now, shall we continue with the vision?"

Nimuway unfreezes the image, as the two continue to walk down the path following Merlin.

છ

Quietly observing, Rose pauses, watching Merlin throw stones into the lake when three other children come along and shove Merlin face-first into the water. Laughing, they walk away. When Merlin gets up, he brushes himself off, and his eyes turn black, and one of the children lets out a scream as his bones shatter and he falls to the ground.

"Freak!" the other two children yell, picking up stones and throwing them at Merlin. Although many of the rocks are too small to affect Merlin, one of the larger ones strikes him, causing his eyes to turn black for a second time. Demons spring from the ground and attack the child who threw the stone. Seconds later, the demons disappear, and the child lies on the ground, drained of his blood.

"Wait! Vampires?" Rose exclaims as Nimuway nods, and they both continue to watch Merlin.

"All your questions will be answered soon, to a point," Nimuway declares.

Merlin walks up to the remaining child, smiles, points his wand, and casts a spell.

Finiendum Vitam.
To take the life of.

They watch as the child's soul suddenly leaves his body.

"You will make a fine addition to the demon army," Merlin notes, smiling and patting himself on the back.

"I see you have added another one to the army," remarks a gentleman who walks up, applauding.

"Hello, Sir. How are you?"

"Merlin, I am fine. So, tell me, what is a young man, like you, doing out here?"

"Socializing," Merlin replies, smiling.

"That is good," the man says, smiling as the vision spins and Rose and Nimuway arrive back on the beach.

જ

"So, I do not know what is creepier, Merlin or that thin-looking man, with the weird scar down the whole right side of his face," Rose remarks.

"That is Lord Balimore Oblivion, and he is one of the heads of the Council of Dark, the closest thing your great grandfather had to a father," Nimuway explains.

"Eww! That is scary," says Rose.

"It is, yes, but that is not why I brought you here," Nimuway replies.

"Yes, I know the secrets of Merlin," Rose responds in a sarcastic tone.

"Rose, what do you know about Noel?"

"He is Noble Elder's successor. They say that he has weird magic, and that he is mighty. Why do you ask?"

"All of that is correct. Noel *is* Noble Elder's successor. But he is also the key to understanding Merlin," Nimuway explains.

"How is Noel, the key to understanding Merlin?" Rose inquires.

"Because when Noble Elder and Elder Yule sent the Curpendulums through time, that is when Noel emerged. The arrival of Noel pleased the Arcane. You see, now, they had their champion, the most powerful Arcane, who would become Grand ArchSorcerer. Noel's arrival meant the end of the battle between light and dark."

"So, the elders knew about him?

"Yes, Rose, they did. Mora believes that many Elders were more afraid of Noel than Merlin."

"Great grandmother, what you speak of is an alteration, a collision in time, if that's the right word for it. Noel is of the future," Rose acknowledges.

"Indeed, Mora was never able to explain it. The same collision of time, as you call it, created Morgana, which enraged and fueled Merlin's hatred. It is also the collision that sent ripples through time for years. It is also the very same collision that created the secrets echoed," Nimuway says, summoning a chair and sitting down.

"I understand that the secrets echoed, is the collision of each of the narratives on the collective timelines," Rose notes, smiling.

"Mora and I believe that, but we were unsure, until now. Rose, you must find Mora when you return and tell her she was right," Nimuway explains as Rose gazes out over the lake.

"Great Grandma?"

"Yes, Rose."

"Noel has broken thousands of the rules that bind Arcane principles, but you knew that he did that?"

"Why break the rules?" asks Rose.

"Because Mora, myself, and others of the younger generation of Elders, did not always agree with the Elder's rules or their teachings. But then, a vision occurred that forever shaped the future of all Arcane and Mundane. You see, Lady Nova had foreseen Noel's birth, but he was not just any child. Rather, he was a child of great power. His magic would save everyone and have no end. It was discovered in that vision that he was born a Celestial."

As Nimuway finishes speaking, she rises from her chair and walks toward the edge of the water and begins to dematerialize.

"Wait," Rose shouts as she runs towards Nimuway as she disappears into the water.

Walking along the beach, Rose tries to figure out where she is. Retrieving her map, she opens it only to notice a woman standing on the beach in the distance, watching her. Pulling her wand, she points it, then quickly lowers it.

"Grandma?" Rose says as she realizes where she is.

Turning away, the Lady Dawn strolls down the beach away from Rose. Rose chases after her and quickly follows her through a beautiful and majestic city until they reach the edge of a forest and Lady Dawn moves some vines out of the way, revealing the mouth of a cave.

"Interesting, that you are not trying to kill me," Rose says as the Lady Dawn stops, shakes her head, and points into the cave. Looking around, Rose notices several other women approaching. "This is Avalon, isn't it?" she inquires

Lady Dawn nods.

"Avalon is a safe place," Lady Dawn says.

"You are trying to get me home, aren't you?" Rose inquires.

"Yes, Lady Rose. The moment has come that all magic can rejoice. The timeline has been altered. Time has been restored. And now, the greatest journey of all Arcane is about to begin," the six women say in unison.

"You know what you have to do," a voice says as the women part.

"Are you Lady Nova?" Rose asks.

"I am, dear child. Yes. But, of course, you must protect the Arcane for they will need you and your magic. But not just your magic, but the magic of your brothers as well," she replies, smiling at Rose.

"Rose," Lady Dawn calls out to her. Turning, Rose looks back at her.

"My dear child, I owe you an apology; I was tempted and swayed by the darkness," she confesses, hugging her granddaughter.

"It is okay, and you are forgiven. Please come with me?" Rose asks.

"Child, my place is here, as a guardian with the Sisters of Avalon. We must protect the ancient ways. We must protect the balance of all magic, both light and dark," Lady Dawn replies.

Rose bows to show that she understands as Lady Nova approaches.

"You are my favorite of all the Arcane. Your great grandmother, the Lady Nimuway, has asked me to give this to you," the Lady Nova explains, handing an orb to Rose.

"Is this a time orb?" Rose inquires.

"One of the most powerful. My son entrusted it to the Lady Nimuway. Why, no one knows. All I know is that it is supercharged," Lady Nova explains, placing her hand on top of the orb.

"It is time for you to go home. Find your friends. Stop Merlin and protect the legacy of magic. Now go!" the women of Avalon say in unison as Rose nods, hugs Lady Nova, and stows the orb in her bag.

Then, just as she is about to step into the cave, she is stopped.

"Lady Roslynn Ignatius, you have a journey that you must take upon your return. To find your friends, you will have to travel where no other Arcane of Light is willing to go. It is a place of darkness, but you will find aid from an interesting coven of Arcane. They fear Merlin and will attack him to protect themselves. He has tormented them for years. But they will not attack you, not with this necklace. Hold tight to it, and you will know when the time is right to use it. They might be willing to make a trade," Lady Nova says, placing the necklace in Rose's hands and closing her fingers around it.

"I understand," Rose replies.

"Your journey to save the ones who have been kidnapped, you cannot be undertaking alone. You will need the help of the others. So, find your brothers, your husband, your brother-in-law, and seek the aid of your new friends. The orb will guide the way," Lady Nova directs as Rose steps into the cave.

Chapter 19
An Unexpected Visit

A cold breeze blows through the air as the Lady of the Lake materializes, walking across the water and taking human form when she reaches the land. Two dark creatures move to attack, but she strikes them dead where they stand. Stepping over their lifeless bodies, she approaches the priory and knocks.

The door swings open as she is greeted by a gentleman, "Go away. We do not want any of your kind here."

As he attempts to shut the door, Nimuway wedges her foot in the door and throws her hands in front of herself, blowing the door off its hinges as her eyes turn gray.

"Now, would you like to try that again, good Sir?" Nimuway asks, holding up an orb that shines, illuminating the space. The gentleman backs up, hissing.

"What do you want, My Lady?" he snaps.

"I am looking for Conrad," Nimuway declares as she holds the orb out in front of her.

"Fine, put the orb away and please note, Sir Conrad is not in a good mood. Do not say that I did not warn you, Lady. He he he," the man notes, turning and walking away from her.

Following, Nimuway looks around, examining the place, as multiple eyes follow her from the rafters and several individuals watch her from their hiding places behind various pillars.

"Sir! Sir!" the gentleman yells as Conrad grumbles, looking up from his grimoire. Then, suddenly, flying across the ground, Conrad greets his visitor.

"Lady Nimuway, to what do I owe this visit?" Conrad asks.

"I may have found a way to help you get out of the priory prison," she explains, sitting down on the bench.

"I am, as you humans would say, all ears," he remarks smiling.

"In less than thirty-six hours, a woman will travel here, a woman so powerful, her magic will break this prison," says Nimuway.

"A witch that powerful? There is no such thing," Crowley responds.

"Crowley, you fool! Do not question the Lady Nimuway," Conrad says, raising a hand to strike Crowley.

"Conrad, no," Nimuway commands, placing her hand on his arm to stop him.

"Fine," Conrad says, pulling his hand down.

"Remember, the enemy is out there, not in here. Your people need you to remain strong," Nimuway counsels.

"Remain strong? Ha! Tell that to the world. Your husband has tormented us for years here," Conrad replies.

"Conrad, you, your people, the witch who is coming, and her people all have a common enemy—Merlin," Nimuway notes, sitting down at a table.

"My Lady?" Crowley bows obsequiously.

"Dear Crowley, what is it?" she asks.

"You are a powerful witch. Why can't you break this place?" he inquires.

"Because, unfortunately, my magic is not strong enough anymore. You have all been my ally, but if I break you out of here, you will only end up in Avalon, when your home is among the Arcane and Mundane. Besides, to maintain the balance, I do not have enough magic to do that and break this prison of the lost," she explains.

"The prison of the lost. Bah! It is bad enough that Merlin tricked us into coming here, but then, he stuck us in this priory," Conrad complains.

"Yes, it is a horrible place, but it has kept your entire coven safe and also the item," Nimuway declares as she waves her hand over the table and by magic, a tray with cookies and tea appears.

"As long as I live, no one will ever have the item, Lady Nimuway. My father made me swear to protect it for all eternity, and I will never allow that filthy Merlin to get it," Conrad says as he spits on the ground.

"What if I told you there is a way to protect the item?" Nimuway asks while sipping her tea.

Several coven members emerge cautiously, approaching Nimuway and looking at the tray.

"Do not look at me. Ask her for the food," Conrad remarks.

"You all may have some cookies. That is why I brought them. I know you all like blood cookies," she replies smiling and taking another sip of her tea.

"You mentioned protecting the item, Lady Nimuway? I am listening," Conrad says while sitting on a large throne and tapping his fingers together.

"Indeed," Nimuway rises to her feet but begins to fall back weakly. Immediately, Crowley and Conrad are on either side to catch her.

"Are you okay?" Conrad asks, offering her a hand.

"Yes, my dear Conrad, but I am weak," she notes, sitting down again.

"Sir, we have never seen her this weak. Something must have happened," Crowley remarks.

"My dear friend, what is causing this weakness? Was it Merlin?" Conrad demands to know.

"Conrad, no, it is something more interesting. I was about to tell you the story," she explains.

"Lady Nimuway, if you are weak, then you must rest. Do you have a teleport orb?" Conrad inquires as Nimuway nods and hands the orb to him.

"Stand back, my friends," Conrad says as he throws the orb into the middle of the room as ribbons of water create a spiral column around the orb and multiple beings materialize.

"Sisters, quickly help the Queen Nimuway," Lady Nova commands as the ladies of Avalon run to aid her.

"My sisters, I am just a little weak. It is nothing major," Nimuway notes as she tries to rise to her feet but begins to fall back again.

"Can you help her? I have never seen her this weak in a very long time," Conrad remarks to Lady Nova.

"My dear Conrad, we can. Dawn, take this orb and secure passage for you, Nimuway, and the sisters, back to Avalon. I am staying behind to speak with Conrad for a few moments," the Lady Nova directs, spinning her hands as a portal opens.

Multiple coven members appear and help to carry Nimuway to the portal.

"Thank you, friends," the ladies of Avalon say as they wave their hands and food appears. As the last of the ladies exit through the portal, Lady Nova raises her wand and the portal disappears, and a small ball of light flies onto the tip of her wand.

"Very nice. I love what you've done with the place," Lady Nova remarks, picking up a broken bottle in one hand and looking at the torn drapes.

"Lady Nova, why is Nimuway so weak?" Conrad asks.

"Did she not tell you?" she inquires.

"She was about to tell us a story when she became weak," Crowley responds as Lady Nova paces the floor.

"I cannot believe that this is what your coven has been reduced to. The entire magical arsenal of Avalon could not destroy this place," she remarks.

"But yet, Nimuway told me that a witch is coming who can do that," Conrad says with his eyebrows raised.

"Oh yes indeed, a witch like no other," Lady Nova states, winking.

"Sir, why do I not like that wink?" Crowley asks.

"Because, Crowley, while Nimuway would never tell you who the witch truly is, I, on the other hand, will. Gather around my friends," Lady Nova says as she opens her hand, and an orb flies into the air.

Now, long ago, you all know the story of the Great Nobles, the divine guardians of magic and the Arcane. You know the story of how my husband and his best friend, Noble Elder, hid the Curpendulums and, in doing so, shattered time. In that very moment, time was, forever, altered.

No one truly knew if time could be saved, if it could be fixed, or if it would continue to act bizarrely. Seconds turned into minutes, minutes into hours, hours into days, days into weeks, weeks into months, and months into years. Finally, after the passing of many seasons, Merlin grew into power, creating a separate magical realm for the Arcane.

He knew all too well that this would be his last chance to gain any sort of control over the Curpendulums. So, he stole, killed, kidnapped, imprisoned, and tortured anyone who opposed him from the Arcane realm. Then, his plan backfired when he created the witch Morgana, the one witch who would oppose him more than anyone, but who was dark herself, corrupted by the Council of Darkness and pitted against Merlin in their sick and twisted game.

Merlin thought he would reign supreme, not realizing that his son, Prince Titus, held a secret that would forever shape the very fate of magic. Titus married Flora, a powerful witch, who knew about the various forms of magic. She was considered to be Titus' equal. Flora's father was the last student of my husband, Elder Yule, and Conrad's father, Lord Vlad.

Flora had been entrusted with a great secret, the ability to alter time, and, in doing so, she met the one Grand ArchSorcerer who could destroy Merlin. Flora told her husband of this Arcane, and Titus sought him out with the help of his wife.

When King Titus met this Arcane, he was seventy-five years old, of King Titus's line, and had come from over one hundred and fifty years into the future. You see, King Titus was the first wizard to meet the successor of Noble Elder, an individual known as Noel. King Titus and his wife were shown what would happen to the Arcane at the hands of Merlin, and it was in that moment that King Titus and Queen Flora vowed to stop Merlin, much like the Nobles had done many years before.

King Titus asked his wife to freeze time in order to study with Noel, breaking the rules of magic and time. By doing just that, the two learned everything they could under his guidance. When they were ready, now several hundred years later, they restored time, and what was years for them were mere seconds for Arcane and Mundane alike. Upon their return, they shifted their appearances and the minds of their subjects, who do not know that they had been gone for several hundred years.

Titus and his wife, Flora, had three children, their eldest was Lord Kelvin. Their second child, Lord Wade, and their youngest, the Lady Terra Phoenix, were all extraordinarily gifted Arcane who the Nobles believed were as powerful as they were because of the bloodline and their parents' knowledge.

A knowledge that Merlin sought for himself but would not come to possess. Years passed, and Titus and Flora's three children married and had their own children. Eventually, Kelvin's children became Nobles and became known as the Magical Three.

"My humblest apologies Lady Nova. Are these the same three my father spoke of when I was younger? The ones who would forever alter time?" Conrad inquires as members of his coven whisper amongst themselves.

"Indeed, they are the same, Conrad," Lady Nova explains as she raises her hands and advances the images of the story forward.

"So, they exist," Conrad and Crowley note excitedly.

"Yes, and now if you give me a chance, I will finish explaining," Lady Nova says, walking across the floor and fading into the image as it comes back to life.

∂

The Magical Three are the great Arcane, who can stop Merlin and inherited exceptional power from their grandparents. Years have passed, and now they are adults with their own families but still fighting the battle against Merlin.

None of them know or can explain how the girl, Roslynn controls magic much like her grandmother, my children, myself, and my husband do. What is believed is that she inherited the magical capability from her grandmother but was able to unlock it with the help of Noel.

So, to answer the question you have posed about why the Queen Nimuway is weak. You see, she entrusted her great-granddaughter, the Lady Roslynn, with her orb of time. But why did she do that, you may ask? It is because Lady Roslynn has a descendant who will be the one who will forever stop Merlin. That gentleman, the great Grand ArchSorcerer Noel, can not only stop Merlin but also controls the Curpendulums, hence he is also known as the "Master of the Curpendulums." The childhood friend of Conrad, my son, Lord Dalton Time Yule, figured it out. He fixed time and, in doing so, restored the timelines and gave his husband, the love of his life, his heart and soul, Noel, the way to save everyone and to stop Merlin once and for all.

Hence, when Nimuway said that someone is coming, it is the Lady Roslynn. Her husband, King Alezander Ignatius, her brothers Lord Oliver Phoenix and Lord Ethan Knight-Phoenix, and her brother-in-law, Lord Sebastian Knight-Phoenix, are the ones who are coming with her.

Their friends have been kidnapped, their people are frightened, and they have been thrown into battle again. Now, the time has come when Noel had planned to reunite the Arcane and give them the ability to restore the balance of magic. But, just like the Nobles, he also hopes that reunifying the Arcane will be what is needed to provide Noel with the power to stop Merlin.

Oh, and Noel also knows of the item and sends the person he trusts to retrieve it.

৵

The room returns to normal as Lady Nova reemerges from the vision and the image fades.

"Lady Nova, while what you have said is true, I am not releasing the item," remarks Conrad.

Then, the group freezes as a ghost-like figure appears, looking around.

"You see, Conrad, that is her. This is the Lady Roslynn. She seeks the item and will be the one who can protect it until Noel is of age," Lady Nova says as she opens a portal.

"Lady Nova, in your vision, you spoke of a friend of my father. Who are you speaking of?" Conrad inquires.

"Cedric!" she replies as members of the coven begin whispering amongst themselves.

"I see. Well, I will make a decision about the item when she arrives," Conrad says as Lady Nova turns back at the edge of the portal.

"I hope you make the right choice, dear friend. My son has put his trust in you, which means so will Noel. Do not disappoint them," she says.

"Lady Nova," Conrad calls, taking a deep breath.

"Yes, Sir Conrad?"

"If Lord Time trusts me, and Noel trusts him, then so shall it be. I will help the Lady Roslynn," he declares, shaking his head.

"You, my old friend, will not be sorry," Lady Nova replies as she disappears through the portal.

"Boss, do you think this Lady Roslynn can be trusted?" Crowley inquires.

"If the Ladies Nova and Nimuway trust her, then we have no choice but to trust her as well," Conrad replies, sitting back down on his throne.

Chapter 20
Time Restored

Waking from her dreams, Rose sits straight up in the bed, the orb and the necklace resting in her lap. Examining the room, she realizes that she is still in the hospital wing. Reaching for her phone, she checks the time.

"Ugh, it is 4:36 AM. How long have I been asleep?" she asks aloud as she gets up, snaps both fingers, and transforms her attire.

"Better," she says.

Picking up the orb, she holds it up as it disappears. She examines the necklace, and when she touches it, she knows who the new friends will be who will be aiding them.

"Fascinating! This should be very interesting. This is going to be a first," Rose exclaims as she examines the fang necklace and slides it into her pocket as she walks toward the door, which she quietly pulls open.

Then, heading down the corridor, Rose ascends the back staircase, rounding the corner to find that the library door is guarded by two dwarfs who bow when they see her.

"Feeling better, My Lady?" one of the dwarfs inquires.

"Yes, and thank you for asking," she responds as the dwarfs block her entrance.

"I am sorry, My Lady. We are not allowed to let anyone in," one of the guards explains.

"May I inquire why?"

"Yes. Noble Elder and the Lady Time Yule are meeting."

"Really? Can you two please move? My library, my rules," Rose replies, spinning her wand as she lands in the library.

"Rose, you're awake," Lady Time Yule says, coming up and hugging her.

"Noble Elder?" Rosed inquires with a puzzled look.

"You look confused, child." he replies.

"You are not Noel!" she exclaims.

"No, he will not be taking power for another thirty-five years," Noble Elder replies, chuckling.

"Then, time has been restored?" Rose asks.

"Yes, fixed by my brother and Noel," Lady Time Yule explains.

"What happened to them?" Rose inquires.

"As you know, my brother ascended to be with the Celestials and Noel, and his story has not been written yet," Lady Time Yule explains.

"Not written yet?" Rose repeats, pacing the floor.

A knock echoes through the library and the Lady Time Yule steps back as the doors open, and Nadia strolls in, carrying Russell.

"Good morning, everyone," she says as she approaches Rose.

"Good morning, Mother," Rose says, smiling and taking Rusty and gazing down at him.

"He has Zander's ears," Rose laughs.

"That he does," Lady Time Yule and Nadia agree.

"But his eyes," Rose pauses.

"He is blind, just as we suspected," Nadia says, smiling down at Rusty.

"No, it is not that. His eyes. I understand," Rose exclaims as she rocks Rusty to sleep.

"What is it you understand, my dear? Nadia asks.

"Everything. Mom, my job is that of head librarian, correct?" Rose inquires.

"Yes, why?" she answers, confused.

"The job of the head librarian is the keeper of knowledge. In my role, I maintain the library," Rose replies.

"What is she babbling about?" Noble Elder demands.

"The library, the temples, priories, time, magic, Rusty's eyes, it all makes sense," Rose says as she climbs the circular staircase to the third-floor walkway of the library.

"Mom, can you come to help me please?" Rose inquires as Nadia, Lady Time, and Noble Elder quickly climb the stairs. Then, Rose disappears around the corner, walking along the walkway, as the other three followed.

"This library is huge," Lady Time Yule remarks.

"Rose has always been amazing with expanding spells. So, as she started finding more Arcane texts, she expanded the space. The corridors of the library are never-ending," Nadia notes as the three emerge into a giant room.

"Impressive, her use of the expansion spell would come in handy in battle. Put her in an enclosed space and let her expand it. She would drive the darkness mad," muses Noble Elder.

"Welcome to the observatory. This is my private library and holds some of the most ancient texts," Rose explains.

Noble Elder stops, looking around and examining the grimoires on the pedestals.

"Fascinating! The remains of the *Grimoire of the Dead*. I see you also have the *Grimoire of Elements and Nature*, the *Grimoire of Dragons,* and the *Grimoire of Animal and Creatures*. Four of the Curpendulums, thus far," Noble Elder remarks as he notices metal-banded geo-spheres flying around the grimoires to protect them.

"You do realize that if Merlin wants those libers, he will destroy the spheres?" Lady of Time Yule says.

Rose turns and gives her a half-smile, laughing.

"What is that about?" Noble Elder asks.

"I would like to see Merlin try. Touching these spheres would not be the wisest thing," Rose states, rocking back and forth until Rusty stops fussing and finally falls asleep. Within seconds, Rose disappears, then reappears with Zander, Oliver, Ethan, and Sebastian.

"I take it you dropped Rusty off?" her mother inquires.

"Yes, he is asleep. Besides, it gives Cedric something to do," smiles Rose.

"What is this about?" Oliver grumbles, yawning.

"Rose, do you know what time it is?" Ethan asks.

"I do, dear brothers, and I am sorry, but I have news," Rose replies.

"What is so important that you must wake us so early in the morning?" Oliver asks in a grumpy tone.

"Time has been restored, not just restored, but adjusted. The story that was once foretold is now changed," she replies, reading from her grimoire.

"Wait! The stories have changed? If that is the case, Mom, what Rose is saying is that the prophecies are gone," Oliver replies.

"Yes, Oliver, that is exactly what I am saying," Rose clarifies.

"What does that mean for individuals like Otta?" Sebastian inquires.

"That none of her prophecies have any bearing. My brother made sure of that when he stripped her of her power before joining the Celestials," Lady Time Yule remarks.

"Stripped of her power? When?" Zander inquires annoyed.

"Lord Ignatius, you of all people should know that time is not something one should upset. You do remember the stories told when Lord and Lady Yule were killed?" inquires Noble Elder.

"I do. Magic nearly ceased to exist," Zander says.

"Exactly," Lady Time Yule agrees.

"That is all very interesting, but I am still not seeing what this has to do with anything." Ethan exclaims.

"Ethan, don't you see it? It is simple. We have Lady Time Yule and Noble Elder. We have four Curpendulums, and with no prophecies being told, we are in control of what happens next, fate, everything. We have the power to help locate those who are missing," Rose says smiling.

"Lady Ignatius, we dare not tamper with time. If it breaks again, there will be no way to fix it. I alone am not strong enough to fix it. I have tried. My brother held the knowledge to control it, to make it behave," Lady Time Yule states, puzzled.

"Then how do we get the others back?" Oliver inquires.

Frustrated, the group falls silent. Rose walks over to the edge of the room, peering out the giant window. Watching the sky, she notices a phoenix flying, soaring among the clouds, the great bird gliding effortlessly as rain begins to fall.

"Sun, moon, stars, past, present, future, liquid, solid, gas," says Rose, turning back to the group.

"What are you talking about, Rose?" her mother asks.

Rose turns, looks at the group, then turns back to look out of the window again.

"The powerful forces of magic, the sun as we know it, light or power, the moon, darkness, or the void, the stars, the fallen or passed individuals, whose power joined the sky and looks down upon us," Rose notes, smiling to herself as she turns, walks to the ladder, climbs it, stops, and pulls out a text from a shelf.

"You see, our magic, the magic of earth, and the magic of the universe, are fueled by the Nobles and what many would call the ancient Celestials."

Sliding down the ladder, she approaches a pedestal and places the grimoire on it. Then, she retrieves an orb.

"You know something that you are not sharing," Oliver and Ethan declare, looking at one another.

"Do you care to tell them? Or should I?" Rose inquires of Noble Elder.

Turning, Noble Elder points at an orb as it flies into the air and begins spinning.

Tempus est Secreti Participes.

It is time to share a secret.

Spinning, the group looks around as stories start to fly around them. Then, they land in the middle of a village, the smell of burnt wood lingering as everyone examines their surroundings.

"What happened here?" Nadia inquires.

"A terrible battle," Noble Elder says.

Kneeling, Rose picks up a burnt teddy bear. Turning it over, she examines it when a child comes into view. The child runs toward them but suddenly hits the ground, frozen. A sinister laugh rings through the area as a young wizard walks along, climbing over dead bodies, and wrinkling his nose at the sight of the fallen.

"Take all that stand against you and leave no remains," the wizard declares as Rose, Ethan, and Oliver, all from different parts of the vision, turn and advance towards the wizard, circling around him as the image freezes.

"Long brown hair," Oliver says.

"Blue eyes," Ethan notes.

"A scar down his right cheek," Rose remarks.

"The look of fire in his eyes," Sebastian confirms.

"The marks on his hands give him away," Zander declares.

"It is Merlin," they all say in unison.

"Typical! Killing everyone and destroying everything in his path," Rose says.

Then she stops, her eyes focusing on his hand. Lady Time Yule approaches Rose, but Noble Elder raises his arm to block her.

"She knows," he says.

"I would step back if I were you," Rose says as she spins her hands, and the image unfreezes.

Merlin, his followers, and the darkness march across the ground when two of the guards drop to the ground, dead.

"What happened?" one of the remaining woman villagers inquires.

"Nimuway, my dear," Merlin sneers as a blade flies past his head and strikes one of the dark guards in the face.

Fog encircles the village as Merlin spins his wand over his head. When the fog lifts, a cloaked figure stands across the way from him.

"Can I help you?" Merlin inquires as the figure lowers their hood.

"An elf. Guards, take him as well. Nimuway, my dear, you brought an elf? Of all Arcane creatures, an elf? Is this who is going to stop me?" Merlin laughs, dismissing the elf and turning to walk away.

"Merlin, the fate of the Nobles willed this many years ago." Nimuway replies.

"Fate? No one controls my fate," Merlin barks in response.

Kneeling and placing his palms flat on the ground, the elf looks up as his eyes turn black. Standing, he looks as if he is pulling vines from the ground. The darkness screams as roots emerge, striking many of them and killing them on the spot.

"What is this? He can draw on all the energies of earth and every living thing? Impossible!" Merlin exclaims, backing away and looking at the elf as Nimuway smiles and disappears. Merlin raises his wand and launches fireballs at several of the remaining villagers.

Magic flying around Noel catches the fireballs and dissolves them on the spot as Noel wraps his arm in one of the magical streams he just created, snaps it like a thread, and spins it, grabbing objects around him, and flinging them at Merlin. Unable to keep up, Noel successfully sweeps away all of Merlin's traveling party in mere seconds.

"An elf with this type of power is impossible," Merlin declares as a ring of fire explodes around him.

He begins drawing a pentagram in the air just as Noel clenches his hand into a fist, causing Merlin's wand to explode. Backing up and holding his bleeding hand, Merlin trips over a wooden bench and then notices that everything is slowing around him. Standing next to Noel, Lord Time Yule appears, a giant clock hovering in the air, the hands frozen.

Moving at exceptional speed, Noel comes up alongside Merlin, puts his hand in the middle of Merlin's chest, and as Lord Time Yule releases the clock, unfreezing time, Noel slams Merlin at full speed into the ground. Then, picking Merlin up by his hair, Noel raises him off the ground by his throat and, with his other hand, places his palm in the middle of Merlin's chest and launches him across the ground. Multiple animals and birds appear, flying and running around Merlin, hitting him repeatedly as Noel raises his hands and throws earth, water, wind, and fire at Merlin. The elements combine causing Merlin to be thrown back.

As Merlin rises to his feet, he finds himself slammed into the ground again repeatedly until he is spitting blood and reaches for his dagger. Finally, Noel draws up with his hand, clenching it into a fist and uses his magic to crush Merlin's other hand.

In an attempt to get Noel away from him, Merlin summons dark creatures and demons. But, as they begin to engage Noel in battle, they quickly vanish as Noel snaps his fingers, causing them to dissolve.

☙

Suddenly, the image freezes again. Looking around Ethan, Oliver, Sebastian, and Zander see Noble Elder, Lady Time Yule, and Nadia. But Rose is nowhere to be found.

"Am I missing something?" Lady Time Yule inquires with a puzzled look.

"No. Rose is not here. You are not missing anything," Oliver responds, walking around looking as puzzled as Lady Time Yule.

"Mom, do you have any ideas?" Ethan asks when the image begins to play backward in slow motion and the group finds itself back at the part where Nimuway appears with Noel. The vision unfreezes, then freezes again.

"Ideas?" Sebastian inquires when Rose suddenly pops back into the space.

"There you are!" Ethan exclaims.

But then, Rose disappears again.

"Mom, Zander, someone. What is she doing?" Oliver asks, looking to them for answers.

"Noble Elder, can you get us out of this vision?" Lady Time Yule inquires.

"Unfortunately, no. The magic that Rose is using is nothing I have ever seen before," he replies, waving his hand as a chair appears, and he sits down.

"Sitting? Are you serious? Aren't you going to do anything?" Lady Time Yule inquires.

But then, the image disappears completely, and the area becomes dark. Then, after a moment, the space brightens, the light coming from Nimuway and Noel.

Zander paces back and forth, examining Noel and Nimuway until, finally, he stops and focuses on Noel's crest.

"Noble Elder, when is this vision from?" Zander asks as Lady Time Yule pulls a small compact from her pocket, flips it open, and starts looking into it.

"The year is 1100, give or take ten years," Lady Time Yule declares as Rose reappears carrying a grimoire.

"Where were you?" Oliver asks.

"Trying something that I wasn't sure would work," Rose replies, walking toward Noel and examining his crest.

"Does this 'something' have to do with screwing with the vision?" Nadia inquires.

Rose looks up from the grimoire, smiles at her mother, winks, and turns her attention back to Nimuway.

"What is going on, Rose? Mom asked you a question," barks Oliver.

"Shh," she says putting her fingers to her lips.

She opens her bag and retrieves the helmet. Placing it on her head, she flips the lenses down in front of her eyes, one at a time, as she spins the dial, adjusting them.

"That's it," Rose finally says, slamming the grimoire shut as she levitates it in the air.

Looking at her, Ethan raises his hand, motioning for her to explain.

"Young Merlin, a thousand dark followers, a village, then Great Grandma arrives, then is gone, then comes back with Noel. She must have known about the time variances," Rose explains.

"Very good, very good indeed. I see you have figured it out. But this is also where I need your help," Noble Elder says, applauding.

"Wait! I am confused. What is going on?" Oliver asks.

"Brother, don't you get it? Although the time has been restored, somehow, Great Grandma Nimuway knew about it and time's bizarre behavior," Rose replies.

"How? Noble Elder, you and my father broke time when you hid the Curpendulums. Unless there is something you have not told us," remarks Lady Time Yule.

"Oh no, dear child. Time did break. But then, it was repaired. But it appears that your father taught a select few how to control time and, in doing so, gave them the ability to alter and change the path of time," Noble Elder exclaims.

"So, in other words, the story was to happen without Noel interfering," Ethan and Oliver note in unison.

"You two are correct. I need help in understanding how Nimuway found out about Noel. You see, Noel has not happened yet. He has not even been born, so how is he there in the vision? That's what I want to know."

"I think we should let the vision play out and see if it provides any answers," Rose suggests as the grimoire floats down into her hand.

Then, the room begins to spin, and the vision comes back into view.

Kneeling, Noel looks Merlin right in the eyes.

"You know, wizard, I have grown tired of you," Noel declares, pointing his finger at Merlin's face.

"My good Sir, I do not even know who you are! But I do know that I do not like you and find you rather annoying," Merlin laughs as Noel hoists him up by his shirt collar and launches him up into the air again.

"Lord Time Yule, check his bag," Noel says as Lord Time Yule grabs the bag and starts searching through it.

"What do we have here?" Noel asks as Lord Time Yule hands him a stack of grimoires.

"The *Liber Vita (Grimoire of Life)* and the *Liber Dryadalum Sequere Magicae (Grimoire of Elfish Magic)*. Merlin, you know that, by decree of the Council of Light, you should not have these," Noel accuses as his eyes narrow at the next thing Lord Time Yule hands to him.

"Where did you get this?" Noel demands, holding up the pocket watch.

"You will not succeed," Merlin declares as he spins his hands, blasting Noel in the chest with an energy ball, causing Noel to drop to the ground. Then, grabbing a branch off the ground, Merlin snaps a piece of it, turning it into a wand. Spinning it, he throws dark magic at Lord Time Yule.

Sliding across the ground, Lord Time Yule catches the dark magic in the open palm of his right hand, his left hand supporting his right and holding his wand. Angry, Merlin intensifies his magic but the new wand dissolves in his hand, and he is pulled into the ground by hands of spirits reaching up for him.

Glancing over, Lord Time Yule notices that Noel is gone from the place he had been. Then, he looks up to find Noel in the air, his eyes white as spirits continue to appear and fight against Merlin.

Eventually, summoning darkness to him, Merlin orders, "Bring me those Curpendulums."

Before anyone can respond, the Curpendulums fly into the air and begin spinning around Noel. As magic spins around Noel, one of the Curpendulums flies open in front of him, the pages exploding out and causing a tornado to appear. The winds spin violently as Merlin is lifted into the air. Then, like that, the tornado is gone, and Merlin hits the ground with a great thud.

Just as Merlin hits the ground, Noel speaks,

Vocate Spiritus, Vocate Spiritus, Vocate Spiritus.
Summon forth the Spirits.

Emerging from the ground, spirits appear for the second time, grabbing at Merlin as he runs, attempting to get away from them. Instantly, Noel appears in front of him, an orb in his hand. Merlin dissolves and reappears inside the orb. Walking across the ground, Noel throws the orb into the fire pit as screams are heard, and the orb dissolves in the flames.

"I see that you have handled the situation," Lord Time Yule says as he hands the watch to Noel.

"Indeed," Noel nods, reaching down into the fire and picking up a crest of the Templar Knights.

"The markings of the Knights," Lord Time Yule exclaims.

"Yes, and it looks like Merlin has more secrets than we know," Noel replies as Nimuway walks up to them.

"I see you have destroyed one of his copies," she remarks, smiling as she examines the crest that Noel is holding.

"If he has the crest of the knights, then I am afraid his power may have grown," Noel says as the vision begins to spin.

The light flashing from light to dark, the group finds itself back in the observatory.

❧

"The Knights? As in the Templar Knights of the Roundtable?" Oliver inquires as the space around them returns to normal.

"To date, we are still trying to figure that out," Noble Elder explains.

"Figuring that out? So, you do not have answers?" Oliver asks, displeased.

"Rose, are you okay?" Ethan asks as she flips through the pages of her grimoire, saying nothing.

"You're very quiet. Either you're reading, thinking, or you have found something of interest," Zander remarks.

"All three," Rose replies.

"Rose, darling, what did you find?" Nadia inquires.

"Noble Elder, how well did you know Lord Time Yule?" asks Rose.

"He was my closest friend's son. Why do you ask?" Noble Elder replies.

"You said your friend died?" Rose asks, turning a page.

"Yes, my father died and so did my brother," Lady Time Yule explains, looking at Rose, taken aback by her question.

"Lady Time Yule, thank you, but I was asking Noble Elder," Rose remarks, turning another page and glaring at him.

"I watched my friend die. I saw Merlin kill him and according to Lady Time Yule, her brother passed away," Noble Elder snaps in an angry tone.

Rose closes the grimoire, walks over to the fireplace, spins her hands, and a blue orb appears.

"Where did you find that?" demands Lady Time Yule, moving toward the orb.

Rose waves her hand, and it disappears.

"It is under my protection," Rose explains.

"What is it?" Ethan asks.

"A time orb," Sebastian answers, smirking.

"Why does Rose have a time orb?" Ethan asks, peering at Sebastian, then looking at Oliver and Zander for answers.

"Once, it belonged to Great Grandmother Nimuway, and now, as I said, it is under my protection," Rose explains as she watches for Noble Elder's reaction.

"It could be an orb of time," he says, waving his hand dismissively.

"But it is not. It is one that Merlin wants. Nimuway, by using it, broke the rules. It is the one that Lord Time Yule, himself, gifted to her," Rose explains as the orb reappears in her hand.

Lady Time Yule waves her hand and the orb lights.

"It works," she says, smiling as Rose nods to her.

"Tell me how to find them?" Rose says, holding up the orb but keeping her eyes on Noble Elder.

"I am not the one to ask. Time orbs are not my specialty," he remarks.

"You say the orb was Nimuway's?" Lady Time Yule inquires of Rose.

"Yes, why?" Rose responds.

"Rose, how do you have it? That orb was destroyed years ago," Nadia exclaims.

"Actually, no, it wasn't. And Nimuway is alive," Rose replies.

"Wait! How? Does your father know his grandmother is alive?" Nadia asks in shock.

"No, and we can discuss that later. Nimuway gave this to me but, right now, we have something bigger to worry about," Rose exclaims as she holds the orb out in front of her.

Lady Time Yule spins her hands over the orb. "The orb will guide you five, but I cannot go with you. I am afraid my powers would collide with the powers of the orb, and no one knows where, or when, you would end up. If that happened, I would be of no use to any of you, as I would lack the ability to bring you back," she says, bowing to Rose.

"Are you four coming?" Rose asks, continuing to hold the orb up in the air.

"We better go along to help her," Ethan and Oliver declare in unison, laughing as they transform everyone's attire.

"Lady Phoenix?" Zander inquires.

"Yes, Zander, I will watch the children," Nadia says, winking as Rose speaks,

Magicae Temporis Lanuae.

Magical Time Teleport.

The five look at each other as sand spins around them. Then, waving their wands, the tips light, providing light to guide the way.

The Lost Priory

Chapter 21
The Lost Priory

"Why are we standing about in knee-high water?" Ethan complains.

"Ethan, Sebastian, where are you guys?" Oliver's voice echoes through the fog.

"This is ridiculous," remarks Zander, spinning his wand as the fog begins to lift.

The five acknowledge one another and wade toward the bank. Oliver and Zander are the first out of the water and reach down to help pull Rose out. Then, they help Sebastian and Ethan.

"I thought this would take us to find our friends." Oliver mutters.

"Why is it always fields? Anytime we jump, we always end in a field somewhere," grumbles Ethan as he touches his wand to his clothes to dry them quickly.

"Zander, what do you think?" asks Sebastian as he looks to Zander for guidance.

"Do we wait for Rose to sort this out?" Ethan asks as he hands a chocolate bar to Oliver, Zander, and Sebastian. The four watch as, in the distance, Rose stands on a small hill, turning slowly and looking out over the land.

"Guys, look!" Zander points as Rose comes racing down the hill on her broom.

"Well?" Ethan and Oliver ask in unison.

"We are in Amesbury, England," Rose says.

"How can you tell?" Sebastian asks.

"Because, my dear Lord Knight-Phoenix, on the other side of that hill and down toward the far side is Stonehenge," Rose replies, pulling her hair back in a ponytail as her outfit transforms.

"Yuck, Mundane clothes. Are you serious?" complains Ethan.

"My dear Ethan, there is a tour bus and several hundred people wandering around the grounds of that place. We have to look like Mundane to fit in. Walking around in long cloaks with magical markings would only call attention to us," Rose explains.

"Rose, that is all fine and well, but why are we here?" Oliver inquires.

"Because, brother, this is where the orb brought us, and we go where the orb takes us," she replies, throwing her bag over her shoulder and starting to walk toward the hill.

"We had better follow," Zander suggests as he spins his hands, also transforming his attire. His ears transform to the standard human shape, and he stows his sword under his trench coat. The other three shrug as they also spin their hands, and their outfits transform.

"Ugh, I feel like we are back in high school," Oliver remarks, holding up his sleeves.

"I know," Ethan replies as the three follow quickly and catch up to Zander and Rose. Strolling toward the edge of Stonehenge, Rose reaches up, pretending to rub her head.

"Guys, look for anything suspicious, strange, or not normal. Look for anything that might catch your attention or draw the attention of the Mundane. We need to see what we can find, and we have to do it quickly," Rose says telepathically to the others.

The group separates, each strolling through the crowds of people. Stopping, Ethan bends down to tie his shoe as he listens to the groups around him talking. Finished tying his shoe and rolling his eyes, continuing to listen to the Mundane talk, a rune marking catches his attention.

Pulling his cell phone from his pocket, he snaps a picture of it and turns to walk toward Rose.

"Hey, you might want to see this," Ethan suggests as he hands his phone to her.

"E-A-R-T-H (Earth)," Rose notes as she gazes around the area.

"What did you find?" Oliver inquires as he shows Rose a picture of a rune he found.

"F-I-R-E (Fire)," Rose says, looking at Oliver.

"Earth and Fire. Elements?" Ethan inquires.

"Possibly," Rose and Oliver respond.

"Zander, did you find anything?" Rose asks telepathically.

"Yes, I have the rune for water," he responds.

"We have found fire and earth," she informs him telepathically.

Striding up Sebastian nods, and inquires, "Rose, the orb was blue, right?"

"Yes, why?" asks Rose.

"It is located by those rocks over there," Sebastian replies as the group breaks up, checking the area.

Zander stops watching the other four as Rose locates the orb. Upon reaching it, a portal opens between two of the stones. Quickly looking around, Rose picks up the orb, then steps through the portal. Zander weaves his way quickly through the crowd as Sebastian and Ethan arrive at the stones simultaneously.

"Should we follow?" Ethan asks, but Oliver walks right past them and steps through after Rose.

"I take that as a 'yes,'" Ethan remarks, shaking his head and following.

Zander and Sebastian are the last to go through finding themselves looking up at a priory that is rising out of the ground.

"What is this place?" asks Ethan.

"Someplace that only exists in legends," Sebastian remarks, gulping.

"Why do I not like the sound of that?" Oliver inquires.

"A legend? Is that what you call it, Sebastian? Tell me, dear brother-in-law, is this a bedtime story that you are reading to Matthew?" Zander asks with a half annoyed, half worried tone.

"No, this is way too creepy for him. Ethan and I would be up all night. The boogeyman under the bed is enough," Sebastian remarks as he and Ethan stand back-to-back, wands out, carefully examining the area.

"What is this place?" Ethan asks again.

"The Lost Priory. A sinister place. Keep a tight hold on your wands. This is likely not going to be pleasant. Merlin turned the priory into a prison for undesirable Arcane," Sebastian explains.

"Where is Rose?" inquires Oliver as the four look around cautiously.

"I am here," Rose calls, reappearing and stowing the orb.

"Where were you?" Ethan complains.

"Checking the area out, seeing what we are up against. A prison, by the way? Merlin is a loon," Rose states.

"I agree that he is a loon. Did you find anything?" Ethan asks, concerned.

"The dark energies that illuminate this area are enough to send chills down one's spine," Rose explains.

"So, what is the plan?" inquires Oliver.

"I guess we go in?" Ethan suggests.

"Yes, but Sebastian is correct. Hold on tightly to your wands. And be ready. This is the place nightmares are made of," Zander exclaims as he reaches for the door of the priory, which suddenly flies open, and a creepy-looking gentleman greets them.

"Well, hello!" he says in a sinister tone.

"Hello," Rose replies, looking him in the eyes as he backs up hissing and showing his fangs.

"Great! A vampire," Ethan exclaims.

"Fresh blood," the gentleman notes, licking his lips as he advances toward them.

Then, immediately, he backs up when he hears, "Crowley, let them in."

"Fine! But, I still want the fresh blood," the creepy man says, stepping aside and inviting the five into the priory.

Zander lowers his hand to his side as a wooden stake appears in it.

"Thanks, but no thanks. We will be keeping our blood today," declares Ethan as he turns to find vampires behind them. The five glance at one another out of the corners of their eyes as they walk cautiously through the doorway.

Slowly, the five move further into the building as more vampires appear all around them, and two shut the door, slamming a wood beam across it, and barring the way out.

"You could have told us there were vampires here," Ethan exclaims under his breath

"Hun, it is not discussed, at least not in any of the stories I have heard," remarks Sebastian.

As the group walks further into the priory more and more vampires come into view.

"I thought the vampires had been wiped out?" Oliver remarks quietly so that only the other four can hear.

Carefully, one of the vampires approaches them, nose up sniffing the air.

"The House of Knight. That will make a fine appetizer. The House of Ignatius and the House of Noble. Blah! They will do, but their blood is too rich for some. And what is this last one?" the vampire asks, backing up as he hisses.

"The House of Phoenix," Oliver and Ethan declare in unison as screams and screeches are heard, and the vampires all fly up into the air and disappear into the rafters, out of sight.

"What was that all about?" Rose inquires when she spies a gentleman peering out from behind a large stone chair.

"That name invokes fear," the man replies.

"Invokes fear? Of what?" Ethan and Oliver laugh together as Sebastian shakes his head, indicating that this is not the time for jokes.

"Leave this place, now," the gentleman demands, observing them now from the other side of the chair.

"Please, Sir, we won't hurt you. Can we speak with you?" Rose inquires as she stows her wand and raises her hands, motioning for the others to do the same.

"You are not afraid of us?" a voice asks from out of the surrounding darkness.

"No," the other four reply.

Then, Conrad cautiously emerges from behind the chair, his hands visibly shaking. Rose motions for her brothers, who are examining the space. Together, they sit down in the second row of pews, while Conrad slips down the steps and sits on the steps of the altar area.

"The House of Phoenix not aggressive? That is a first!" Conrad declares aloud. Then, as if reassuring himself, he says "No, it appears they are gentle. But we must be cautious." Then, he points around the area and, in a different, deeper voice, asks, "Why are you here?"

Then, cowering back down again, "No, wait! Do not answer that. Nimuway and Lady Nova have already explained," he says in a scared little child's voice.

"The Ladies Nimuway and Nova? Do you know them?" Rose asks politely.

"Possibly. But, then again, I cannot answer that. Yes. Maybe. No. I do not know," Conrad replies.

"Rose?" Ethan and Oliver say, looking at their sister and then back at Sebastian and Zander, who are behind them, searching for answers.

Shrugging her shoulders, Rose examines the space when she is standing and then, walks to the center aisle and sits down on the stone floor. Unfortunately, doing this puts her right in the line of sight of the gentleman. Several vampires appear in the rafters, hissing as they watch her.

"Is he their leader?" Sebastian whispers to Zander.

"It appears so," Zander replies, tightening his grip on the wooden stake in his hand and hidden under his cloak. The group sits quietly as the man rocks back and forth for a few minutes, mumbling to himself. Rose also sits quietly in meditation, her eyes closed, listening.

❧

"Merlin."

"Deception."

"The House of Phoenix are traitors."

"They are here to kill us, but what about the legend? Nimuway has never steered us wrong."

"They are friends of Cedric."

"Lady Nova said they would be nice."

"The light, the dark."

"The girl seems nice, but she has the blood of Phoenix. Yuck! What a gross bloodline."

"No one mentioned that the children were of the Phoenix bloodline."

"What brought them here?"

"They should pay for Merlin's crimes."

"Do you think they control... you know?"

The chatter of whispers from the dark rafters continue as Rose begins to levitate in the air.

"She floats on air. What is she?"

"Their blood smells fresh. No, we mustn't. We should not touch them."

"Remember the last time we tried to attack a Phoenix?"

"Who knows what will happen if we attack them this time."

"Why now?"

"What nasty game is time playing?"

"Are they here for the Curpendulum?"

As the last whispers echo down from the rafters, Rose opens her eyes.

Concalo.

Summon.

Magic flies around the space as Rose takes to the air, the walls start to rattle, the windows shake, and the vampires dive from the rafters, landing in the altar area, all of them trying to hold down the alter, as the stone table shakes violently.

"I remember," Rose says, pulling the fang necklace out of her pocket as she levitates it in the air and speaks.

Concalo.

Summon.

For the second time, the altar shakes violently again. This time, the altar flips over as a grimoire flies into the air. Both the necklace and the Curpendulum float in the air. Twelve more vampires dive from the ceiling, reaching for the grimoire and the necklace at the same time. Suddenly, the doors of the priory fly open, and a cloaked figure appears, arms raised as the tip of their wand glows. Turning, Rose looks back at the figure. Her eyes turn black as the figure flies into the air and is projected out of the door as it slams shut.

Concalo.
Summon.

The grimoire flies into Rose's hands as she lands, quickly retrieves her bag, opens the flap, and throws the grimoire into it. Then, raising her hand, the necklace flies across the room and floats above the gentleman, who is rocking back and forth on the steps.

"I believe these are yours," she says as she raises the necklace in one hand and the blue orb in the other.

At the sight of the orb, the vampires all back up. Rose turns, looks at them, and nods, her eyes glowing the same hue of blue as the orb.

"She is beautiful," one of the vampire women sighs.

"She is truly here to help," another says.

"Quickly, help master up. We must follow them," another vampire remarks as two of them scoop Conrad up off of the steps and a lightfield rises in front of the coven.

Crowley grabs the floating necklace and places it around Conrad's neck, "I hope it gives you back your strength, Sir."

In the back of the priory, a circling black cloud appears, as demons drop from it. Stepping up next to Rose are Oliver and Ethan, the Magical Three looking at each other as their outfits transform into armor.

"What is that?" Oliver asks.

"It is a cloud of destruction. You have angered the gods," one of the vampires replies.

"It appears that this is how Merlin keeps order here," Rose says, smirking.

"Rose, Oliver, and Ethan, you know what you have to do," Zander declares, walking through the lightfield and extending his hand toward Conrad. Sebastian is right behind him.

"Zander and Sebastian get them out of here! Ollie, Ethan, and I have this," Rose commands.

"Is there a way out of here? It appears that the cloud is blocking our exit," Zander inquires.

"Yes, there are catacombs under this place," several of the vampires reply.

"Let's go," Zander says as he takes control, supporting Conrad under his right arm.

Then, balancing Conrad, he follows one of the vampires.

"Oliver, Ethan, let's light them up," Rose says as her eyes turn green. Oliver's eyes turn red while Ethan's turn blue. The dark cloud at the back of the priory flies toward the floor as multiple demons step out.

Four demons charge the Magical Three when, suddenly, magical beams, each matching the color of their eyes, emerge from their hands. The three separate to take a different priory area as the demons descend upon them. Each strike the dark demons with their magic when the doors fly open again, and the cloaked figure reappears blasting magic at Oliver.

Deflecting the figure's blast, Oliver ricochets the magic off himself and sends it streaking back toward the figure. Reaching Oliver, Rose and Ethan joined him in the battle against the cloaked figure. Working together, the three join hands as the magic of light explodes around them and strikes the dark demons repeatedly. As they hum, white magic beams appear, spinning around the Magical Three as they strike the demons, transforming them into white spirits that bow, switch sides, and begin to fight back the demons.

"Whatever we are doing, let's keep it up. They cannot handle the power of the light," Oliver declares as the three continue to hold hands and more spirits rise around them, fighting the demons.

"At least, we have help," remarks Ethan.

"Yes, and, hopefully, that will be enough to stop the demons," Rose says as blast after blast of black magic ricochets off the lightfield in front of them. Annoyed, the cloaked figure increases the intensity of their attack as the ceiling explodes and the rafters rain down on everyone in the priory.

Continuing to work together, the Magical Three find the area filling with more dark creatures and demons.

"There can only be one explanation for this," Oliver declares as his siblings nod in agreement.

"So, how shall we do this?" inquires Ethan.

"Let's light this place up," Rose declares.

Illuminare Ignire Accendo.
Illuminate and Ignite the Blaze.

Light explodes around the three as torches pop on, one after the other, each lighting the area as a circle of fire explodes around them, throwing the advancing darkness back. Letting go of each other's hands, they stay close. They each spin their hands as they cast light throughout the priory. Disoriented, the darkness falls back toward the cloaked figure. Becoming even more angry, the cloaked figure, with the help of the demons, strike multiple light fields at once with lightning, their magic causing the lightfields to explode.

"Take them now," the cloaked figure snaps.

"Rose, Ethan, let's finish this," Oliver yells as their eyes start glowing.

Per Potentiam de lux.

By the power of light.

Light explodes around them, and the demons begin to scream. Some of them turn to stone, some vaporize, others simply disappear. Finally, as the area starts to return to normal, all that is left is the cloaked figure, breathing heavily. The figure lowers their hood.

"Why am I not surprised? Merlin? What copy is this?" Ethan inquires, sounding annoyed.

As the three tighten their grips on their wand, Merlin yells,

Oblitero.

Obliterate.

The priory begins to shake as the ceiling falls in and the three find themselves having to move quickly. Looking around, they find themselves in the altar area with members of the coven standing next to them. As various parts of the ceiling strike the ground, Merlin protects himself with a field. Then, lowering the field, he begins to laugh as he spins his wand, and the pews burst into flames.

"You will never succeed! You will be stuck in this prison with those filthy vampires, and I will rule," Merlin laughs until he is suddenly slammed face-first into the floor.

The Magical Three looked at each other and smile.

"I have just about had it with you, Merlin," Cedric remarks, picking him up off the floor.

"Cedric, my old friend. Release me, and I promise I won't punish you too much," Merlin says as he pulls his dagger and jams it into Cedric's arm.

"Guys, let's give Cedric a hand," Crowley suggests as he and the other two vampires standing with the Magical Three fly into the air and down the central aisle where they appear next to Cedric.

Merlin continues to fight, trying to break free of Cedric's hold until Cedric sinks his teeth into Merlin's neck. The other three vampires bite Merlin's arms and his right leg. As they feast on him, his body withers.

Eventually, Cedric drops the now withered body of Merlin to the floor as the other three vampires attack and tear it apart.

"Gentlemen, this is only a copy, not the true Merlin," Cedric remarks, wrapping his arm as Rose appears next to him.

"Cedric, let me help you," she says, pulling her wand as his wound begins to heal. Walking up, Oliver and Ethan look at the spot where Merlin's body had been but only a few bones remain.

"Well, that is one way to handle Merlin," Oliver and Ethan scoff in unison.

"I am glad you approve. A copy or not, he got what he deserves," Crowley smirks as the other vampires of the coven reappear. Zander and Sebastian also reappear with Conrad, who is now back to normal.

"Hello, old friend," Conrad says, extending his hand toward Cedric.

"Good to see you, Conrad" Cedric replies.

"You must be the Lady Roslynn." says Conrad.

"I am. It is a pleasure to meet you," she replies.

"Your husband and brother-in-law are truly remarkable wizards. They have restored my mind. I am indebted to you, all five of you, for what you did and for helping my people," he says when he reaches into his pocket and retrieves a small glass flask with a small grimoire in it.

"The *Liber Vampiris*," Rose says.

"Wait! Then, what was the grimoire from the altar?" inquires Oliver.

"A decoy, designed to throw Merlin or any dark creature off," Conrad explains as he hands the flask to Rose, who smiles and accepts it.

"You know, the Lady Nova Yule said you were kind," Crowley says.

"She did?" Rose inquires, stopping and observing what is left of the priory.

"Ethan, Oliver, we have one thing left to do," Rose remarks as she retrieves her orb and levitates it to the ceiling. The three take each other's hands, and as they raise them, the coven, Cedric, Sebastian, and Zander, all disappear.

The three look at each other as magic flies around them. They close their eyes. Then they disappear, and the priory explodes.

Chapter 22
The Search

One flash of light. Then, nothing, just darkness holding the space. Finally, a small flickering orb of light flashes and floats around in the darkness. Then, just like that, it disappears. Quietness is the only thing left holding the space.

Then again, another orb of light, this time glowing blue. It pops and multiplies into ten separate orbs, floating in the darkness. Then, all of them go out. Again, darkness is the only thing left holding the space!

A third flash of light, then another, and another. Images appear floating in the air, image after image of the Arcane fighting back the darkness throughout the years, the entire story of time, playing out, dancing around the room. Stories echo and ring throughout the space. The chatter of each story grows in volume, one decimal at a time, until the sound becomes unbearable. A half-visible orb emerges out of the ground and levitates into the air as hundreds of images explode, filling the space as they dance across the walls and ceilings. The noise continues, unbearable, and the commotion makes the space sound like a busy city in rush hour traffic.

Then, absolute silence.

The room falls quiet as the last orb darkens, dissolving, dust falling to the floor, leaving only a golden pocket watch, the legendary watch itself, all too familiar from the stories of time, but never seen like this.

The watch spins slowly, the hands frozen at twelve o'clock. A flash of purple light and the second hand begins moving —tick, tick, tick. A blue flash of light illuminates the space. Then, the minute hand begins moving, spinning out of control. Then, suddenly, it stops.

The watch flies across the room and lands in the hand of a cloaked figure. Turning, they throw the watch into the air as they disappear. Reappearing, they walk across a frozen field, time completely stopped. Looking around, the figure examines the Arcane frozen around them, suspended in time. When the figure reaches the leader of the Arcane, Noel, they reach into their pocket, pull out a small bag, and dump the contents into their hand. Raising their hand, they blow dust around them. The dust begins to spin, shifting the nature of the story.

From the dust, several figures emerge. When Rose, Oliver, Ethan, Sebastian, and Zander arrive, the dust spins out of control and lightning strikes the ground. Holding up his hand, Oliver redirects the dust flying around them to disappear, the last few pieces falling to the ground. The five examine the area where they landed. Then, they notice that time is completely frozen.

"Touch nothing. We do not need anyone frozen or disrupting any part of the story," Zander remarks, pulling his hair back into a ponytail while he watches Rose who walks quickly toward one of the frozen figures.

"Fascinating. This is Noel. It is as if we are running in a parallel time to what is currently happening," Rose notes as she observes Zander kneeling and touching a footprint on the ground.

"It appears we are crossing paths with this part of the story for a second. We need to locate our friends quickly," Zander declares.

"So, does that mean the individuals we are seeing as frozen are actually in a different aspect of the story, that it is playing out for them at normal speed?" asks Ethan.

"Yes, that is what appears to be true, Ethan," replies Zander as he points up the hill.

"Who wants to go first?" Oliver asks as the five examine the area for any concerns.

"The area appears clear," they note as they walk toward the top of the hill.

"Wow, that is not good. Did Merlin create a new land?" Sebastian inquires.

"It appears he has a castle in the middle of the field. However, it does not mean he created a new land, Hun. That would be well… too creepy," Ethan remarks. He pauses and thinks about it, "Although, you know, this is Merlin we are discussing, so maybe he did create a new land."

The five begin to laugh until they notice a small ball of light floating in the distance.

"Ethan and Oliver, remind me to speak with Dad when we get back about some way for the council to regulate any and all activities and actions of Merlin, past, present, and if necessary, in the future," Rose says in an annoyed voice as she looks at the castle.

While the five-are speaking, they notice the small ball of light land only feet from them. Then, it transforms.

"Lady and Lord Ignatius, Lord Phoenix, and Lords Knight-Phoenix, good evening. You all made it." Ms. Tulip remarks, bowing.

"Ms. Tulip, what are you doing here?" inquires Ethan.

"Watching the castle. Mora sent me to keep an eye on this place. It is the home of the dark. The place is crazy busy with people coming and going," Ms. Tulip notes as she motions for all of them to hide, after which Zander retrieves his spyglass and watches from the hill.

"I count, one, two, three, four… at least fifteen dark guards, twelve incubus generals, Balimore, and about a dozen vampires," Zander reports, handing the spyglass to Oliver.

"Conrad, Crowley, and Cedric are not going to like hearing their own are working with Merlin," Ethan acknowledges as Sebastian and Oliver nod in agreement.

"I thought the vampires despised Merlin," says Rose.

"How do we do this?" Sebastian asks.

"Not without backup," Zander states as Rose reaches into her bag and spins her hand around the top of the orb.

"I have an idea. Follow me and be quiet," Rose says as she quickly disappears over the hill.

The other five regard each other and quickly follow to find Rose waiting for them at the bottom of the hill.

"What's up?" Ethan asks when they reach Rose.

"You see that circular gazebo over there?" Rose asks.

"You mean, the monument to some Mundane queen? Yeah. What about it?" Ms. Tulip inquires.

"It is a safe distance from the castle and has some magic signature radiating from it that the darkness did not detect when it was arriving," Rose explains as she walks away from the group and retrieves her broom from her bag.

She throws her broom in front of her, jumps on it, and takes off, racing across the ground, flying toward the monument.

"I guess we follow?" Zander exclaims, taking off after Rose on his own broom.

Rose and Zander race along the rooftops, zipping by the chimneys billowing smoke. By spinning her wand, the smoke-filled night air provides cover for them.

"If you think that I am using a broom, you have another think coming," states Ms. Tulip as her wings appear. Then, taking off, Ms. Tulip soars down across the ground as Oliver, Ethan, and Sebastian suddenly appear flying alongside her. Finally, the four reach the monument where they notice that Zander is the only one waiting, leaning against the stone wall.

"Where is Rose?" Oliver asks.

"You know your sister. I recommend standing back," Zander replies, as flapping wings are heard, and Belinda appears with Destiny.

"Prof. Ignatius, Ms. Tulip, nephews," she acknowledges.

"Lady Destiny Phoenix," Zander replies, bowing his head.

"Time for chatting later. I recommend stepping back," Belinda suggests.

More flapping of wings is heard as Autumn shows up carrying multiple members of the fairy army, including Phineas and Leaf. The group quickly steps back as multiple bats land on the ground and transform into human form.

"Conrad, Crowley," Oliver and Ethan acknowledge them but Autumn interrupts.

"I would advise stepping back," she roars as Drago lands, carrying Kelvin, Nadia, and Cedric.

"Where is Rose?" Zander asks Nadia.

"Give her a minute. You know your wife," Nadia replies as Rose materializes with Athena, the Hippolytes, Lady Marybelle, and a pile of grimoires.

"The school is secure. Lady Ignatius Elder is with the students and the other faculty members," Rose explains.

"This is it?" Ethan asks, looking concerned.

"No, give it a minute," Rose says, pulling out the pocket watch as a portal opens and out steps members of the council, the elfish army, and Mr. Bruin with over a hundred dwarfs.

"Now, this is everyone," Rose says.

"We cannot just walk up to the front door. Merlin will expect that," explains Zander.

"Then what do you suggest we do?" inquire Oliver and Ethan.

"We break off into teams," Nadia suggests.

"I agree," Oliver says as his clothing transforms into long robes.

Smiling, Ethan and Rose regard each other as their attire also transforms.

Waving her hands over the ground, a giant table appears.

"Lords Conrad, Crowley, and, of course, Cedric, take members of the council and covens to form a protective barrier. Sister, you, Lord Leaf, and Lord Phineas, start enchanting those grimoires. Mr. Bruin, ready the dwarfs, and Countess Alwina, Archduke Lukas, and Duke Avery, it appears you are all ready to go." Nadia directs as the groups quickly go to work. Ms. Tulip rolls out a map for everyone.

As the groups start to split up, Kelvin inquires, "Zander, what are we dealing with?"

The two disappear and, seconds later, reappear.

"Everyone, we have a slight problem," says Zander.

"Problem? What sort of problem?" Ethan and Sebastian inquire.

"Kelvin, you want to tell them, or do you want me to?" Zander asks.

"No, Zander, I have this," Kelvin remarks, walking toward the table and making an orb appear.

"Dad, hold that thought," says Rose while she pulls her hair back, then suddenly stops what she is doing and gazes into the distance.

"Rose, sis, are you okay?" inquires Ethan.

Rose nods, disappears, and then, reappears at a distance from the group, running toward the protective barrier. Nadia and Kelvin watch Rose closely.

Spinning her wand, the barrier opens like two curtains being pulled back. An orb appears and flies through. They all draw their wands and point them at the orb. It flashes and multiple individuals step out. Waving her hand, Anwara closes the field, securing the area.

"Anwara," Rose acknowledges as Nadia materializes next to Rose and points at one of the women in the group with Anwara.

"Touch my daughter, and I will kill you on the spot," Nadia declares as Destiny appears behind her sister with her wand drawn.

"Lady Nadia, stand down. Your mother is on our side," a voice declares as the entire field of Arcane bow at the sight of Nimuway.

"Can it be?" Nadia inquires, backing up as Nimuway weaves her way through the crowd of women.

"Avalon has come to the aid of the three," explains Nimuway as she kneels on one knee, bowing to Rose. Out of respect, Rose bows back as Oliver and Ethan materialize next to their sister also bowing.

"Lady Nimuway," Zander says, bowing, helping her up, and kissing her hand.

"Help is always there when most needed. Besides, I owe the Magical Three a great debt. They destroyed the prison and saved the vampire coven," Nimuway remarks as Dawn comes up and hugs Rose. Oliver and Ethan both step back, watching.

"Grandma," Kelvin bows as she smiles and hugs him.

"President Ignatius," Nimuway greets him, then glides across the ground to hug Conrad.

"My Lady. You were spot on about these three, and thank you," he says, bowing.

"Conrad, no thanks are needed. We have to help those who need it most. The three were the ones who could help save you and the coven. For it was their power alone that could destroy the prison that held the coven," Nimuway remarks, winking at the Magical Three.

As the group walks back toward the monument and the table, Kelvin reappears, holding the orb as he clears his throat.

"Shall we?" he inquires as the group nods in agreement.

Kelvin taps the orb, and it floats across the table's surface as images begin playing out. As the group watches, they found themselves being pulled into the image.

ॐ

"Lord Merlin, we found the abbey," the knight declares as he and six other knights hold individuals from the abbey prisoner, with hoods over their heads so they cannot see. Merlin motions, and the knight to his right removes one of the prisoner's hoods.

"Blah! What an ugly and simple Mundane. But what is this?" Merlin remarks, digging his long finger into the man's nose as he examined the golden chain hanging around the man's neck.

"Sir, they are from the abbey up the road," the knight says.

"The abbey? A religious man. Ha! Do you fear the devil, good Sir?" Merlin asks, his eyes-narrowing as he turns and smiles at the man.

"I do not fear your false god, or you," the man declares defiantly as the knight pulls back on the man's ropes.

"Tell me then, priest, do you believe in god?" asks Merlin.

The man nods as Merlin backhands him across the face. The man spits blood as the knights stand by laughing.

"Gentlemen, raid the abbey. Find whatever artifacts, relics, whatever you can, and bring them to me. Oh, and burn the place down. Make sure the Mundane and King Arthur know it was Morgana who did it. And General, I will pay heftily if you find the Curpendulum in their abbey," Merlin directs as he walks through a portal.

"Sir, what should we do with these people?" one of the dark knights inquires.

"Keep them alive long enough for them to tell us what we want. Then, kill them," Merlin orders as the image begins to spin.

෧

Landing in the courtyard of a castle with sand and smoke flying around, they observe the knights from the previous vision.

"Kelvin, are they the Knights Templar?" Nimuway asks.

"They are indeed," Kelvin replies, walking across the space and through several of the knights.

Raising her hand, runes appear, floating in the air, as Nadia and Destiny begin sorting through them.

"I thought Merlin had wiped them out?" Nadia remarks as Rose nods in agreement.

"It appears more has occurred than we may have known," Nimuway suggests, motioning for the vision to begin again. A scream echoes around them, and then another, as everyone watches the vision play out.

෧

The knights run through the castle, trying to escape the darkness. Suddenly, vampires jump on the knights, sinking their teeth into them. Centaurs run through the area, killing all in their way.

Multiple dark witches and wizards appear. They raise their wands, tearing the knights apart as the vampires lick up the blood and scavenge the remains of the knights. The head knight runs up the outside stairs, fighting off dark guards. Swinging his sword, he takes more out with each step as he ascends. Finally, the knight standing on the walkway at the top of the castle looks down and points his sword at Merlin.

"You betrayed us," the knight yells as the dark, and all those following Merlin, turn their attention toward the knight.

Stepping over the dead bodies, Merlin looks up at the knight and snaps his fingers as stones fly out from the walls around the knight, encircling him.

"What is this?" the knight shouts, swinging his sword at the stones.

When Merlin snaps his fingers again, the stones smash into the knight repeatedly until his lifeless body falls to the ground below. A loud crack is heard as Merlin approaches the knight, looks down at him, and steps on his face. Merlin nods to one of his guards who picks up the body of the dead knight and throws it out of the way through a cast-iron gate. Merlin raises his hand.

Deleo.

Wipe Out.

The gate dissolves into dust as the guard enters the tower and emerges seconds later, carrying a grimoire which he hands to Merlin.

"It is mine, finally," Merlin mutters as the grimoire flies out of his hands.

At the same time the darkness flies into the air and over the walls.

"Sir, what is this magic? No one is here?" the guard remarks as Merlin spins his hands. Magic flies around him and the raindrops falling around him suddenly slow. A cloaked figure appears on the far side of the courtyard, the moon and lightning flashing overhead provide the only light to the area. Then, like that, the figure is gone, and spirits appear, throwing the remaining darkness into the walls.

The figure reappears in the middle of the courtyard, magic spinning around them.

When the image stops playing, Nadia and Destiny shake their heads in disbelief as members of the group whisper among themselves. Nimuway sits in silence, listening quietly.

"He was such a charming one," Rose says, her nose held up in the air.

"Please tell me that the castle we saw in that vision is not the one we are about to march into." Sebastian declares.

"Actually, it is," Kelvin responds.

"Absolutely not! Nope! No way. No how," Sebastian remarks, sitting down and crossing his arms.

"Hun, why not?" Ethan inquires.

"I think what your husband is getting at is that the spirits of that place will be protecting all aspects of it," Zander says, leaning on his staff.

"So, any rescue attempts are off?" Oliver asks.

"Not necessarily, but…" Zander begins to say when he glances over at Rose, who is rapidly flipping through the pages of her grimoire.

"Oliver, what my husband is getting at is that there are only a few who can fight the spirits," Rose explains, looking displeased.

"Who?" Ethan asks.

"You three, the vampires, and the Ladies of Avalon," Zander explains.

"Wait, we do not have you or Sebastian?" asks Oliver.

"Oliver, while we are Arcane, in a situation such as this, I would be ineffective at controlling them. My necro magic summons spirits for battles. It does not give me the ability to control spirits that are already in place. Also, Zander's elfin magic would not phase them," Sebastian explains as Rose shoots him an awkward look.

"Did we miss something, Sis?" Ethan asks, puzzled.

"There is one elf who could fight this, but they are not here, so it appears that Oliver, Ethan, and I will have to go in and rescue everyone," Rose says.

"My Lady, we will come with you," Cedric declares as he regards Crowley and Conrad.

"I will lead the elfish army against the castle. Nadia, you and Destiny be ready to open portals and get any of the injured out to safety," Zander commands.

"I will take Sebastian, Phineas, and Leaf, and we will create a diversion to buy the Magical Three and the covens time to get into the castle," Kelvin notes.

"Lord Ignatius, we have amassed a large army with the help of Lady Marybelle," says Ms. Tulip as the dwarfs run, continuing to open grimoires and placing them on the ground while figures rise from the pages.

Oliver, Ethan, and Rose nod to one another.

"You three be careful. Do you hear me?" Nadia exclaims.

"We will," Ethan and Oliver reply in unison as Ethan hugs Sebastian.

"At the first sign of Merlin, remember that the three of you must combine your magic, keep your heads up, be alert, and don't forget, you can stop him," Zander says, kissing Rose.

"If you need assistance, drop this orb," Nimuway says, winking at Rose as she, her brothers, Cedric, Crowley, and Conrad disappear.

Chapter 23
A New Way

Along with their vampire friends, the three materialize in an old cemetery at the back of the castle. Quickly, ducking down, they hide behind the headstones, looking around cautiously.

"Where do we go?" Ethan asks.

"We have to get into the castle and down into the dungeons. Follow me," Conrad says as he moves out from behind the headstone and runs toward the back wall of the castle.

"Crowley, the tower," Cedric says as Crowley scales the wall rapidly and jumps in through the window as the body of a dead soldier hits the ground.

"Wow, I am glad we have him with us," Oliver remarks as the group heard a faint click of the lock on the back door.

"Quickly! Get in!" Crowley hisses as the others enter through the door.

"Conrad, the dungeons are two floors down," Cedric remarks as Conrad nods. The six move along the back corridor, quietly observing every aspect as they proceed. Reaching the end of the hall, Conrad raises his fist, and the group stops behind him. Then, Cedric points in the direction they should go. Running down the old spiral staircase, they descend quickly into the dungeon of the old castle.

"Lovely," notes Ethan as he points with his wand at the skeleton still hanging by the chains from the wall.

"Let's find everyone and get out of here," Oliver says.

"Get out of here? No one is going anywhere," Balimore announces, appearing from behind one of the dungeon doors, wand in hand as multiple dark guards appear quickly surrounding the six.

"Rose, Oliver, and Ethan, you three rescue our friends, let Conrad, Crowley, and I handle this," Cedric says menacingly as the three bare their fangs and attack the multiple dark guards who drop instantly.

When Balimore attempts to raise his wand, he finds a hand clutched tightly around his throat as Cedric stares directly into his face. Cedric lifts Balimore off his feet as Conrad and Crowley continue to attack the dark guards. Then, with a snap of his fingers, Balimore disappears and reappears on the other side of the space, throwing dark magic at the Magical Three.

Blocking the magic, they activate lightshields to protect themselves as they spin their wands, blasting the dark guards back as more appear.

"There are way too many of them! We will never be able to stop them and save everyone," Ethan exclaims, striking three dark guards, at the same time, the light causing them to return to normal.

"We have to keep going. We cannot stop. We cannot give up. We can do this," Oliver declares, encouraging the others.

"Guys, where is Balimore?" Rose inquires when a sudden screech is heard, and four dark guards fall to the floor from the ceiling, blood running everywhere as vampires from the coven arrive.

"It looks like we have help," Oliver and Ethan say in unison, standing back-to-back to fight off the darkness. While the coven members are busy helping to put down the darkness, Rose and Cedric move along the cell doors in the dungeon, blowing the locks off the doors and freeing the Arcane and Mundane imprisoned in the cells.

Annoyed with the number of doors they have to open, Rose spins her wand over her head, causing all the locks to unclick simultaneously, and all the doors fly open. As the imprisoned Arcane emerge, Cedric appears next to Rose.

"My Lady, there are way too many of them. The darkness is overrunning this place. Even with the coven's help, we cannot stop them all," Cedric remarks.

"Not for long," Rose replies as she throws the orb against the ground. As the orb shatters, a tornado spins from the remains, and the space darkens. Then, a flash of light occurs, then another, and seven magical beings step out of the sandstorm and nods to Rose as they spin their hands and levitate the darkness into the air.

"Get all of them out of here," Noel commands as the others nod in agreement. The six figures standing next to Noel disappear and reappear in front of Rose as they lower their hoods.

"Hi Grandma," the six say as Willow and Kells begin catching dark magic.

"Need some help?" Isabella asks, walking up and raising her hands as more dark creatures explode.

"Yes, help us get all of the Arcane and Mundane out of here," Rose replies as she fights to hold back the dark. Finally, the six disappear and begin reappearing at various cell doors, moving quickly, to get the Arcane and Mundane out of the dungeon.

Rose bolts through the space, examining the different cells until she finally reaches the one she is looking for.

"This is no place for an Arcane like you," she remarks, extending her hand and helping Liam up.

"Thank you, Lady Rose," he replies, shaking her hand, then catching a black magic beam in his hand that Balimore had used to attack the two of them.

Rose's eyes turn blue as Balimore flies backward across the room.

Balimore grabs a lit torch and breathes in deeply as he gets to his feet. Then, he opens his mouth wide and begins breathing fire at the escaping Arcane and Mundane. The flames fly through the air until a wall of water explodes in front of him. There stands Peter, his hands raised and his eyes blue as the water spins around him, creating a wall that blocks the flames.

"Bella, that is our cue," Sophia yells as she spins her hands and wind encircles the area. Bella steps up next to Sophia, spinning her hands as the remaining flames that were not extinguished by the water begin to go out. She moves her wand, controlling the fire, while Willow kneels down, places her palms on the ground, and causes sand to fly everywhere.

"Michael and Kells, get everyone out of here now!" Bella yells.

"Oliver, Ethan, can you reach me?" Rose inquires telepathically as they appear next to her and a small ball of light whizzes around them.

"Queen Amaryllis, please help our friends to get out of here," Rose asks as the ball spins around them and immediately takes off. Rose looks toward her brothers, nods, and holds out her hands. as the three take each other's hands, time freezes. The dark is suspended in the space as the Arcane and Mundane look around anxiously.

"Get out of here now!" yell the three as the group hears,

Finiendum Vitam.
To take the life of.

Merlin hurls the spell across the room at the Magical Three, but his spell strikes a magical barrier and stops. Merlin waves his wand, unfreezing Balimore as the two back up and cast the spell again

Finiendum Vitam.

To take the life of.

As the final words come out of their mouths, their wands explode as the Magical Three take to the air, their eyes turning white.

Dark demons rise out of the ground as Balimore summons them for assistance. Light flies around the space as Noel spins his wand over his head. A portal opens as Queen Amaryllis assumes her full size, directing everyone out through the portal.

"Protect them," Noel says as the six disappear and then, reappear at the portal, raising lightfields to create a protective tunnel to get everyone out safely.

As the individuals move through the protective tunnel, the darkness grows in numbers, attacking the lightfield. Then, spinning his hands in a circular motion in front of himself, Noel releases magic against the darkness, causing them to disappear. Leo roars, exploding a group of dark guards that have appeared, trying to block the way out of the portal.

Dark guards charge over the rampart outside the castle and the elves lower their spears.

"Fire," Zander yells as the archers release their arrows and fairies charge the darkness. Multiple Arcane wizards and witches fly past Zander on brooms, following Sebastian who is in the lead. As the group soars over, they point their wands at the darkness, throwing them across the battlefield.

"We must provide all the support we can," Sebastian remarks as Kelvin spins his staff, hitting multiple incubuses with light as members of the vampire coven attack dark guards dragging them down to the ground and destroying them.

Nadia and Destiny stand back-to-back with their wands in their hands, projecting lightfields. As two dark incubuses attack Nadia, Dawn raises her wand and drops them to the ground. She smiles at her daughter, then spins her hand and launches orbs of light at the darkness. A pop rings out as Michael and Kells appear, carrying multiple dwarfs.

"Lady Nadia, Lady Destiny, we are emptying the dungeons now. Be ready to get everyone out of here," Michael says as he begins to walk away, then disappears. Suddenly, Kells reappears walking away from the same spot from which Michael disappeared, carrying more Arcane.

Balimore appears on the battlefield, picking up boulders with his magic and throwing them at multiple elves, dwarfs, and fairy soldiers. Then, he is lifted off the ground.

Walking across the field and causing the darkness to explode with every step is Noel, furiously dragging an incubus behind him. He drops the incubus and, retrieving his wand, points it at Balimore, who begins to wither. As the incubus gets to its feet, Zander runs a sword through the side of its neck. His eyes green, when Zander pulls his sword out of the incubus, he spins it backhanded, killing three dark guards, and, finally, taking the incubus's head clean off.

"Noel, whatever you are going to do, you better do it now," Zander yells as Noel's eyes turn white and he flies into the air.

Suddenly, Isabella, Michael, Kells, Willow, Sophia, and Peter arrive carrying dwarfs to the portal. The six Ignatius siblings no sooner arrive then they disappear again, only to reappear, this time with Rose, Ethan, and Oliver, The group is carrying the remaining prisoners from the dungeon. Flying up, Sebastian jumps from his broom, throws a wand to his mother, who has just arrived, as she catches dark magic and redirects it into the ground.

Merlin appears and begins throwing dark magic at Sebastian. Then, Liam appears out of the ground, catching Merlin's magic in his palms as he is pushed backward.

"You will die like the rest of them," Merlin sneers at Liam but is suddenly flung backward as Nimuway appears.

"I see that you still have not learned, Merlin," Nimuway says as Balimore appears to her right, throwing dark magic at her and causing her to drop to one knee, sliding backward until Zander catches her.

"By the power of all magic," Nimuway declares as the dark magic begins to bounce back, and Balimore flies off his feet. The darkness continues to grow in numbers and the Arcane start to fall back toward the monument when, suddenly, a wave of magic rolls over the battlefield, taking out all of the dark in one quick motion.

Stopping, the Arcane observed the area cautiously as Noel walks across the ground and incubuses fly backward whenever they approach him. Furious, Merlin throws magic at Noel, but Noel absorbs it on the spot. Stopping, Noel gazes at Merlin, then he tilts his head slightly and snaps his fingers as Balimore and all of the dark council members instantly dissolve into dust.

"You will never win. You may destroy some of them, but my copies will continue. You will never get all of them," Merlin sneers as he throws magic at Noel. When the magic freezes in mid-air, everyone notices Rose standing across the field, hands raised, with her brothers at her side, their hands raised as well. The three spin their hands and their wands appear. In one gliding sweep, they blast the frozen dark magic out of the air.

"How is that possible? How?" yells Merlin as he throws dark magic again. Again, it is stopped in mid-air.

"You see, Merlin, we have learned not only to stop time but to control it," Rose remarks, strolling up to the frozen magic and tapping it as it falls to the ground and explodes like icicles falling from the edge of a roof.

"Something you do not realize, Merlin, is that the three of us, have several things you do not have and will never have," Oliver explains, coming up behind Rose.

"What is that?" Merlin asks, spitting angrily on the ground.

"We know," states Ethan as he blasts Merlin with light from his wand.

"We have family," says Oliver, following his brother.

"We have love," declares Rose as the three grab each other's open hands and magic flies around them, the darkness disappearing, the fallen Arcane who have been killed reawakening, and magic spinning around Merlin. When he tries to move, he is slammed into multiple invisible barriers.

"You see, Great Granddad, we are in charge. Not you. Your magic is evil," the Magical Three say in unison as they raise their hands, and the magic whirling around Merlin picks up speed. Nanofairies fly across the ground and join the magic, spinning a helix around Merlin. Noel appears in front of the Magical Three, his hand extended, and the pocket watch floating above his hand.

Striking the invisible barrier with blast after blast, Merlin yells, trying to raise the darkness, but nothing happens. Everyone begins talking amongst themselves as 15 magical grimoires appear, flying around Noel. Lowering his hand, the watch remains floating as Noel thumbs through the various Curpendulums as they continue to fly around him.

"Merlin, you have committed crimes against the Arcane and Mundane alike. You have sought out these grimoires with the intent of using their magic for your gain and to enslave all," accuses Noel.

"You will not win," Merlin screams as he begins to transform into an incubus, but Noel raises his hand, preventing him from doing so.

"Merlin, I, Noble Elder, at this moment, strip you of your magic and sentence you to a Mundane life. Oh, and Merlin, heed this warning. If you raise a finger against anyone or anything, I will be back. I will break and shatter every rule of time to return," Noel declares as the pocket watch flies up into the air.

The watch begins to spin rapidly as bright light rays explode from the clouds. As the area grows brighter and brighter, the light lifts, and the Magical Three, their friends, and family find themselves standing in the courtyard of the Arcane Academy. As everyone looks around, they notice that the Ignatius 7 are gone.

"What happened?" Oliver inquires.

"It appears Noel stopped the battle," Rose replies as Mora approaches.

"Not only did Noel stop the battle, but he has altered the very path of time," she says, holding out her hand as an orb floats into the air, revealing the other timelines dissolving one by one.

"It looks like only one timeline remains, the present one," Nadia says as the members of the Arcane Parliament nod.

Peace falls over the land as the remaining remnants of Merlin vanish. The guardians of Avalon return to their post. Athena and her Hippolytes became permanent members at the Arcane Academy, and the seasons come and go. The Arcane and Mundane take the time to build bustling cities where everyone lives inclusively.

Twenty years have passed. Rusty is walking through the grounds of the school carrying a picnic basket. He approaches his siblings sitting on a blanket.

"Dear brother, let us help you," Hope and Vivian say, both grabbing the basket as Matthew and his girlfriend, Rebecca, join the group after hugging Sebastian and Ethan.

Oliver and Olivia serve the food as Zander leans on the stone wall. The group sits, talking and waiting for Rose, when a laugh is heard, echoing over the land and causing the entire group to jump to their feet. Wands are drawn and members of the Arcane Parliament appear. Dragons soar overhead roaring.

Chapter 24
The Story Continues

Dear Diary,

The summer is coming to an end, and we are transitioning into the fall season. Life is ever-changing and evolving here at the school. Years have passed since our friends and family members were kidnapped. When Noel restored the timeline in the battle and returned us all here to the academy, life went on, and none of us saw time-traveling older versions of any of our children again. Though we do not hear from the time-traveling versions of our children, we still have to deal with the darkness.

The students here at the school help keep Zander and me going as all five of our children are grown now and starting their own families. Ten years ago, Zander and I took in our grandson, Ambrose, to help raise him. Although Rusty and Meredith are excellent parents, Ambrose's powers have proven to be a challenge over the years. A child of his power requires one-on-one attention and extra support, which we can provide. While the other timelines do not exist anymore, we know, from our journeys through time, that Ambrose was going to end up with us. However, things were going to be very different. The

Ambrose who we saw during our journeys through time possessed magical power, the Ambrose who came to live with us gave up his power several years ago to become a Mundane.

Although Ambrose has been residing with Zander and I, he is off to college in two weeks, and then Zander and I will be here alone. The entire family is worried and will be watching to make sure he and everyone around him are safe. Ambrose will always be a part of this family, but a level of complexity occurs as he is now without his magical power.

Although Oliver has retired from his career and is looking for his next venture, Olivia still holds her post at the school, teaching Mundane studies. When Rusty was ten, Olivia accepted the post to teach at the academy and has been here ever since. In his retirement from magical investigations and searching for the next thing to do, Oliver became the President of the Arcane. Dad and Mom are still with us, pushing one hundred and fifty years easily. Dad is working as an advisor to Oliver, and Mom has decided to take up gardening when she is not busy being grandma and great-grandma and spoiling the kids.

Gwen went off to college, married an Arcane man, and started a family. Madeline and her wife became professors, teaching Archeology and are currently leading digs across Europe, tracking the Curpendulums.

Sebastian is still working and claims that he does not plan on ever retiring. He and Liam made up as siblings, but many believe that Liam would have liked to establish a *relationship with Raven. However, he went mad and his whereabouts are currently unknown. Mora retired from the academy over five years ago. When she stepped down, I took over as the head of the Academy. My job is rewarding but I miss the days of being in the library.*

I must wrap up here. I have much to get done before the new term begins. This school does not run itself.

~Roslynn

❧

Several days later, walking down the hall, Ambrose is carrying a journal in his hand as he looks around.

"I am going to miss this place," he says aloud, as he continues down the stairs and out the back door of the grand estate. Strolling down the walkway, he acknowledges Cedric, then sits down on the bench overlooking the pond. Mr. Cee approaches meowing.

"Mr. Cee, what are you doing?" Ambrose inquires.

"Meow."

"I know. Right, Mr. Cee? You are going to miss this place too. But think about this, we will have many new adventures together."

Ambrose smiles as he scratches the cat's head. Then, he clicks open the clasp on his journal, pulls out his pen, and begins writing.

❧

Dear Journal,

This is my last official entry before the new chapter in my life begins. College! A moment none of us thought would ever come. Yet, here I sit, writing, looking out over the grounds of my family's estate, and wondering if I will ever see this place again.

I have come to learn that the visions of time have changed and altered. Growing up in this truly mystical place has been amazing, and it has made life interesting. I have learned many things and understand the true power of the magic of time. Time was restored to perfect working order over twenty-five years ago. Grandma has said that, without the Ignatius 7 and the Lord Dalton Time Yule, that could not have happened. For me, it is still hard to believe that my siblings did step in to help but you know the challenges I have with them.

Time has twisted, transformed, and changed, in this case, for the better. I have come to learn of the past, the present, and the future, as well as the role of Noel in the lives and times of the Arcane. Although I, at this time, do not know what tomorrow holds, I do know and carry with me the stories of time, the Curpendulums, and the various timelines. When I was ten, the Lady Time Yule, herself, took me to the Priory of Time and granted me access to the time orbs. It was in that moment, that my understanding of my destiny changed forever. My studies never ended, and, in some ways, you could say that I did not have a normal childhood.

Grandmama made it a point to teach me everything she knew about time and the history of the Arcane. She said I could do anything I put my mind to, and, while I agree with her, she still does not understand or comprehend the fear I live in everyday even without magic. I do not want the responsibility that has been placed on my shoulders. It is my hope by heading off to college, things will change.

Many of the Arcane—okay, 99.9% of the Arcane—have normal magic. I am the other 0.01%. My magic is rather bizarre and, truthfully, I am not a fan of it. That is why I gave up my magic.

Noel, who I have learned about in the many stories, had the Lord Dalton Time Yule, who was his life partner. I have not had Lord Dalton Time Yule here, so I look at things differently. Growing up with my siblings around had its challenges. Believe me when I say we have had our moments, some good and some evil. While I am close to Willow and get along with Sophia and Kells, I do not care for Pete, Isabella, and Michael. I find my dear, charming, eldest sister, Isabella, to be a pain and Miss-know-it-all.

I begin college in less than two days. I am excited to start this new chapter, but I also know that some significant challenges lay ahead. One positive thing about college that I am excited about is that my lifelong, best friend, Amelia, will be living across the hall from me. We are excited to have many of the same classes together. Although Mundane, she is a truly gifted scientist who can build anything she puts her mind to. Mr. Cee will be going with me, and I am excited to see what this new journey holds. Oh, and I got a job on campus as a barista. Yes, you can laugh now. It is at Dwarf Brews, so now Isabella can get that discount she has always wanted. She remarks that this is one perk for coming to visit me.

Mom, Grandmama, Grandpapa, and Willow are coming along to take me to college. Dad and I are still not speaking. So, he is not joining the others for my send off. Grandmama did not find me funny, when I said that I would take a dragon to school. Grandpapa thought it was funny but had to look stern when Grandmama insisted on accompanying me. I am hoping her duties at the school will keep her busy and out of my hair. I know that Mom and Grandmama are secretly worried that me going off to college will mean I am ditching my powers and will not help the Arcane

Secretly, the thought has crossed my mind multiple times. I have thought of escaping and going to live in the mountains somewhere, in a cabin completely off-grid, or in the city where no one can find me.

For now, I will smile and keep them happy. But then, it will be nice to get away and try something new.

Yours Truly,

RJ

Closing his journal, he looks around, then rises to his feet. Looking out over the water, an arm rising out of it catches his attention. The hand is holding a letter.

Epilogue
The Ignatius 7

What do you mean a Mundane is the answer to defeating Merlin? Well, you will simply have to wait to find out. Join the Magical Three and their friends as they help the Ignatius 7 prevent Merlin from enslaving the world. The House of Phoenix Chronicles, Volume III, *The Ignatius 7*, is set twenty-five years after the *Secrets Echoed*. Now, grandparents themselves, the Magical Three's incredible journey continues but in a very different way. When RJ, a Mundane archeology graduate student, is mysteriously injured, he makes a discovery that uncovers one of the greatest secrets of the Arcane and Mundane worlds and forever alters how he understands the battle between good and evil.

Learning the truth of Merlin's darks plans and discovering that magic can happen even for those born with no magical power, RJ now holds the key to stopping the destruction of the Mundane across the globe. As time continues to unravel and missing relics of the past emerge, a bizarre, twisted fate, in which the Knights of the Round Table are at the heart of Merlin's plan for total power, is revealed.

RJ and his roommate, Dalton, set out to discover their college's history while meeting resistance every step of the way. RJ's journey quickly takes an interesting turn when he receives help from unexpected allies, including the Ignatius 7.

Growing frustrated with the endless echoes of time, RJ must formulate a new approach to handling time's bizarre game by channeling the power of technology, mind, magic, and love to bring an end to the battle and save both the Arcane and Mundane, all the while listening to his heart, falling in love, balancing the complex life of a college student, and dealing with his estranged family.

Afterword
Chronicles of Phoenix

Words have the power to transform a person's life in many ways and are one of the most transformative art forms known to man.

~Wilhelm P. Ostir

I knew the journey in The House of Phoenix Chronicles, Volume I, *Rise of the Magical Three* was just the beginning. With the growing success of Volume I, I understood that I had to keep things going, and ten months after the release of Volume I, it gives me great pleasure to share with all of you, my readers, Volume II, *Secrets Echoed,* of this epic and fantastic series.

As a writer, the journey of developing the storyline, the characters, and the lives becomes an art form in itself. As I noted in the Afterword of Volume I, my writing is very much influenced by my career as a licensed therapist. My experience working with mental health, life coaching, and helping the LGBTQ+ community, combined with my love of history, has influenced my story themes, characters, and relationships in the House of Phoenix Chronicles.

When asked to summarize the series, I would say this. It is a fantasy love story that includes some exciting characters along the way. One of history's greatest wizards, Merlin, is at the forefront of the story but with a bizarre twist, which brings magic, time travel, mystical creatures, technology, and the challenges of growing up to life in this epic tale.

As readers and writers, we are aware of many literary themes one of which is the most popular—the *Hero's Journey*. Unfortunately, society has taught us that most of the time, the female heroine is cast as the "damsel in distress," who is saved by colorful companions, usually a man. As a gay man and as the father of a teenage woman, I feel there are not enough stories with female heroines in the literary world. The House of Phoenix Chronicles explores the life of a young heroine, her two brothers, and their struggles with love and power that will shape their destinies. I hope this series inspires the next generation with a love for reading, our fellow humans, and values that redefine the role and acceptance of all people.

Although I grew up in a family of readers and academic scholars, I hated books with a passion as a young person. It was not until my high school years that I began to enjoy reading and became engrossed in fantasy fiction. In college, I discovered that I am dyslexic, a severe reading disability. Once I had that under control, I thrived in my college education far beyond what I could ever have expected. As the late Ruth Bader Ginsburg said:

> Reading is the key that opens doors to many good things in life. Reading shaped my dreams, and more reading helped make my dreams come true.

In developing the House of Phoenix Chronicles series, I live by Ginsburg's words. My goal as an author is to write a series that helps open doors to many good things in life: enjoyment, happiness, amusement, a sense of awe, adventure, and an overall love for reading. At first, for me, reading was my enemy. Coming to love reading opened the doors for many opportunities in my life, opportunities that I hope others will experience through my writing.

Sincerely yours,

Kurt W. Oster

Character List

The Noble House of Phoenix

The House of Phoenix continues to be the pivotal character line of the series. The members of this house share Arcane, Mundane, and magical heritage. Members of the House of Phoenix have married into the Houses of Elder, Ignatius, Knight, and Drake. The Noble House of Phoenix is a critical member of the Arcane community and serves in high-ranking roles of the Arcane.

Merlin Ambrose Phoenix (Arcane of Mystical & Magical Experience, Sorcerer Warlock)

Merlin is the series' main antagonist. In his early years, he served as King Arthur's court advisor. He is the self-proclaimed King of the Arcane and one of twelve founders of the Arcane realm. Merlin continues to disrupt time with his thrust for power as he seeks out the Curpendulums.

The spouse to the Lady Nimuway. He is the father of Titus Phoenix and father-in-law to Flora Aine Phoenix. He is the grandfather to Kelvin, Wade, and Terra Phoenix. He is the great grandfather of Oliver, Ethan, Bethany, Daemon, Eric, and Roslynn Phoenix. Throughout his life he was the teacher to Morgana and later to Alezander for several years. He is half incubus (father) and half-human (mother, princess).

He is the second great grandfather of Madeline and Gwendolyn Phoenix, Matthew Knight-Phoenix, and Ari, Theo, Hope, Vivian, and Rusty Ignatius. [Appearing in books I-V].

Lady Nimuway Gwendolyn Phoenix (Arcane of Magical Experience, Mystic, Witch, Sister of Avalon)

A mystic with excellent knowledge and understanding of the living earth. She is the great Lady of the Lake who takes on this persona to confuse everyone with whom she interacts. She is the Queen of the Arcane and one of the twelve founders of the Arcane realm. In death, she becomes the Queen of Avalon and serves as its mystical guardian. Nimuway has worked behind Merlin's back to ensure he cannot succeed. Although a virtue of purity and light, many mysteries remain around the great lady. She is the co-leader of the Sisters of Avalon.

The spouse to Merlin Ambrose Phoenix, she is the mother of Titus Phoenix and mother-in-law to Flora Aine Phoenix. Grandmother to Kelvin, Wade, and

Terra Phoenix. She is the great grandmother of Oliver, Ethan, Bethany, Daemon, Eric, and Roslynn Phoenix. Nimuway is the best friend of the Lady Mora Elder.

She is the second great grandmother of Madeline and Gwendolyn Phoenix, Matthew Knight-Phoenix, and Ari, Theo, Hope, Vivian, and Rusty Ignatius. [Appearing in books I-V].

Lord Kelvin Chadd Phoenix (Arcane of Magical Experience, Sorcerer, Arcane President)

He was born the high Prince of the Arcane realm and became the Third King of the Arcane realm upon his father's death. He is the first and current President of the Arcane and serves as the leading Magical Ambassador of the Arcane to the Mundane. Upon his retirement, he serves as an advisor to his son, Oliver Phoenix, who becomes President after his father. He utilizes a wand or staff, interchangeably, as his primary weapon of choice.

He is the eldest child of the late King Titus and Queen Flora Phoenix. He is the eldest brother of Wade and Terra Phoenix. He is the eldest grandson of Merlin and Nimuway. He is the spouse of Nadia Freya Drake. He is the father of Oliver Phoenix, Ethan Knight-Phoenix, and Roslynn Phoenix Ignatius. He is the uncle of Bethany, Daemon, and Eric Phoenix.

He is the grandfather of Matthew Knight-Phoenix, Madeline and Gwendolyn Phoenix, and Esther, Ari, Theo, Hope, Vivian, and Rusty Ignatius. In addition, he is the great grandfather of Isabella, Peter, Michael, Kells, Sophia, Willow, and Russell Ignatius. [Appearing in books I-V].

Lady Nadia Freya Phoenix {Nee: Drake} (Arcane of Magical & Mundane Experience, Diviner, Witch Goddess)

High Princess of the Arcane. Member of the House of Drake. Upon Nadia's reunification with her children, she becomes the wise mother who is always there to guide them on their journey. She utilizes a wand or staff, interchangeably, as her primary weapon of choice. However, Nadia has been known not to need a weapon to be able to fight or cast magic.

Eldest sister of Hawke Drake and Emma "Destiny" Drake-Phoenix. Daughter of Fortis and Dawn Drake. Spouse of Kelvin Phoenix. Mother of Oliver, Ethan, and Roslynn Phoenix. Witch Goddess, highest witch of the realm. Child of two realms. Second leader of the Arcane Resistance. She serves as the advisor to her children. She is the grandmother to Matthew Knight-Phoenix, Madeline and Gwendolyn Phoenix, Esther, Ari, Theo, Hope, Vivian, and Rusty Ignatius. In addition, she is the great grandmother of Isabella, Peter, Michael, Kells, Sophia, Willow, and Russell Ignatius. [Appearing in books I-V].

Oliver Kelvin Cuinn Phoenix (Arcane of Mundane Experience, ArchSorcerer)

High Prince of the Arcane when his parents were heir to the throne of the Arcane realm. Currently works in Magical Law Enforcement and serves as an advisor to his father, the President of the Arcane. ArchSorcerer. Member of the Magical Three.

He is the eldest son of Kelvin and Nadia Phoenix. Grandson of Titus and Flora Phoenix and Fortis and Dawn Drake. Husband of Olivia. Great grandson to Merlin and Nimuway Phoenix. Twin brother of Ethan Knight-Phoenix and older brother of Roslynn Phoenix Ignatius. Father to Madeline and Gwendolyn Phoenix.

Brother-in-law to Sebastian Knight-Phoenix and Alezander Ignatius. Uncle to Matthew Knight-Phoenix, Ari, Theo, Hope, Vivian, and Rusty Ignatius. Great uncle to Esther, Isabella, Peter, Michael, Kells, Sophia, Willow, and Russell Ignatius. [Appearing in books I-V].

Olivia Madaline Phoenix {Nee: Pendragon} (Mundane of Arcane & Mystical Heritage, Advisor to the Arcane Parliament)

Is a member of the House of Pendragon. She is a descendant of King Arthur and Queen Guinevere. Non-magical but lives among the Arcane. Loved by the covens. Serves as Mundane Advisor to her father-in-law, President Kelvin Phoenix. She is the wife of Oliver Phoenix. Mother to Madeline and Gwendolyn Phoenix.

Sister-in-law to Ethan and Sebastian Knight-Phoenix and Alezander and Rose Ignatius. Aunt of Matthew Knight-Phoenix, and Esther, Ari, Theo, Hope, Vivian, and Rusty Ignatius. Great aunt to Esther, Isabella, Peter, Michael, Kells, Sophia, Willow, and Russell Ignatius. [Appearing in books I-V].

Madeline Heidi Phoenix (Arcane of Magical & Mundane Experience, Witch)

Works for the Arcane Parliament in magical artifacts. Travels the world with her husband. Daughter of Oliver and Olivia Phoenix. Granddaughter of Kelvin and Nadia Phoenix. Niece of Ethan and Sebastian Knight-Phoenix and Alezander and Rose Ignatius. First cousin of Matthew Knight-Phoenix, and Ari, Theo, Hope, Vivian, and Rusty Ignatius. [Appearing in books II-V]

Gwendolyn Theresa Phoenix (Arcane of Magical & Mundane Experience, Witch)

Arcane writer, teaching Arcane about the Mundane. She writes on the history and times of the Arcane. Daughter of Oliver and Olivia Phoenix. Granddaughter of Kelvin and Nadia Phoenix. Niece of Ethan and Sebastian Knight-Phoenix and Alezander and Rose Ignatius. First cousin of Matthew Knight-Phoenix, and Ari, Theo, Hope, Vivian, and Rusty Ignatius. [Appearing in books II-V]

Ethan Ambrose Kenrick Phoenix {Married name: Knight-Phoenix} (Arcane of Mundane Experience, ArchSorcerer, Professor)

High Prince of the Arcane when his parents were heir to the throne of the Arcane realm. Currently works as the Potions Teacher of the Arcane Academy of Magical Teaching. ArchSorcerer. Member of the Magical Three.

He is the second eldest child of Kelvin and Nadia Phoenix. Grandson of Titus and Flora Phoenix and Fortis and Dawn Drake. Husband of Sebastian Knight-Phoenix. Great grandson to Merlin and Nimuway Phoenix. Twin brother of Oliver Ignatius and older brother of Roslynn Phoenix Ignatius. Father to Matthew Knight-Phoenix.

Brother-in-law to Olivia Phoenix and Alezander Ignatius. He is the father of Matthew Knight-Phoenix. Uncle to Madeline and Gwendolyn Phoenix, and Ari, Theo, Hope, Vivian, and Rusty Ignatius. Great uncle to Amelia Pendragon, Martha Pendragon, and Esther, Isabella, Peter, Michael, Kells, Sophia, Willow, and Russell Ignatius. [Appearing in books I-V].

Sebastian Nolan Quid Knight {Married name: Knight-Phoenix} (Arcane of Magical Experience, Sorcerer, Necromancer)

Sorcerer and Necromancer. He is the head of the Arcane Magical Law Enforcement division. Son of Aden and Divinity Knight. Older brother of Liam Knight. He is the husband of Ethan Knight-Phoenix. He is the father of Matthew Knight-Phoenix.

Brother-in-law to Oliver and Olivia Phoenix and Alezander and Rose Ignatius. Uncle to Madeline and Gwendolyn Phoenix, and Ari, Theo, Hope, Vivian, and Rusty Ignatius. Great uncle to Amelia Pendragon, Martha Pendragon, and Esther, Isabella, Peter, Michael, Kells, Sophia, Willow, and Russell Ignatius. [Appearing in books I-V].

Matthew Nolan Kenrick Knight-Phoenix (Arcane of Mundane Experience, Sorcerer, Necromancer)

Sorcerer in the series who serves the Arcane Parliament in an undisclosed position only known by his father, Sebastian, and his uncle, Oliver. He was discovered during the Mundane Realm Siege. He is a necromancer and utilizes a wand as his primary weapon of choice. He has had multiple love interests throughout his life, both male and female.

He is the son of Ethan and Sebastian Knight-Phoenix. In addition, he is the grandson of Aden and Divinity Knight and Kelvin and Nadia Phoenix. He is the nephew of Oliver and Olivia Phoenix and Alezander and Rose Ignatius. He is first cousin to Madeline and Gwendolyn Phoenix, and Esther, Ari, Theo, Hope, Vivian, and Rusty Ignatius. [Appearing in books I-V].

Wade Brennon Phoenix (Arcane of Magical Experience, Wizard, Member of Arcane Council)

He was born the Prince of the Arcane realm and was the second heir to the throne of the Arcane realm behind his brother until the birth of his nephews and niece. He works for the Arcane Parliament and serves as an advisor to his brother, Kelvin, when he is President of the Arcane. He utilizes a wand or staff, interchangeably, as his primary weapon of choice.

He is the second child of the late King Titus and Queen Flora Phoenix. He is the younger brother of Kelvin Phoenix and the older brother of Terra Phoenix. He is the second eldest grandson of Merlin and Nimuway. He is the spouse of Lady Bethany Phoenix. He is the father of Bethany Minerva Phoenix Fae. He is remarried to Emma "Destiny" Drake. He is brother-in-law to Nadia Phoenix. He is the uncle of Oliver, Ethan, Rose, Daemon, and Eric Phoenix. [Appearing in books I-V].

Lady Emma Destiny Phoenix {Nee: Drake} (Arcane of Magical & Mundane Experience, Witch, Historian)

She is the Magical Three's protector who resides in the Mundane realm. She was a high school teacher to Mundane students and later took a post as the Head of History education for the Arcane Academy of Magical Teaching. She is the leading living Arthurian historian among the Arcane and Mundane. She is the daughter of Fortis and Dawn Drake. She is one of the three heads of the Arcane Council. In addition, she serves as an advisor to her sister, Nadia, and her niece, Roslynn. She is the second spouse of Wade Phoenix. She is the stepmother to Bethany Phoenix Fae. She is the sister-in-law of Kelvin Phoenix. She is a friend of Mora Elder Ignatius and Alexander Ignatius.

She is the younger sister of Nadia and Hawke. She is the aunt of Oliver, Ethan, and Rose. She is the great aunt to Madaline, Gwendolyn Phoenix, Matthew Knight-Phoenix, and Ari, Theo, Hope, Vivian, and Rusty Ignatius. [Appearing in books I-V].

Deceased Members of the House of Phoenix

Titus Marvin Phoenix (Arcane of Magical Experience, Wizard)

Second King of the Arcane. Spouse of Flora Phoenix. Son of Merlin and Nimuway. Father of Kelvin, Wade, and Terra Phoenix. He is the grandfather of Oliver, Ethan, Rose, Bethany, Daemon, and Erik Phoenix. (Deceased). [Prequel].

Flora Aine Phoenix (Arcane of Magical Experience, Witch)

Second Queen of the Arcane. Spouse of Titus Phoenix. Mother of Kelvin, Wade, and Terra Phoenix. She is the grandmother of Oliver, Ethan, Rose, Bethany, Daemon, and Erik Phoenix. (Deceased). [Prequel].

Terra Discordia Phoenix (Arcane of Magical Experience, Witch)

Late Princess of the Arcane Realm. Daughter of Titus and Flora. Granddaughter of Merlin and Nimuway Phoenix. Sister of Kelvin and Wade Phoenix. Mother of Daemon and Eric Phoenix. Aunt of Oliver, Ethan, Roslyn, and Bethany Phoenix. Member of the Dark Guard. Killed by Cedric. (Deceased). [Book I].

Daemon Merlin Phoenix (Arcane of Magical Experience, Conjurer)

Baron of the Arcane realm. Son of Terra Phoenix. Grandson of Titus and Flora Phoenix. Great grandson to Merlin and Nimuway Phoenix. Member of the Dark Guard. Brother of Eric Phoenix. (Deceased). [Book I].

Eric Marvin Phoenix (Arcane of Magical Experience, Conjurer)

Baron of the Arcane Realm. Son of Terra Phoenix. Grandson of Titus and Flora Phoenix. Great grandson to Merlin and Nimuway Phoenix. Member of the Dark Guard. Brother of Daemon Phoenix. (Deceased). [Book I].

&

The Mysterious House of Drake

The Mysterious House of Drake is an Arcane family of vast power and serves as the protectors of the ancient Arcane village. Academy of Magical Teaching, which was founded initially by the Lady Mora Elder. Members of the House of Drake have married into the House of Phoenix and other notable Arcane families. The members of the House of Drake are all of Arcane and Mundane

Experience as the Drake Family remained behind in the Mundane realm when Merlin created the Arcane realm. Members of the House of Drake have exceptional magical power, with the origins of their magic still a great mystery to date.

Dawn Rhiannon Drake (Arcane of Magical Experience, Witch, Sister of Avalon)

Spouse of Fortis Drake. Mother of Nadia and Hawke Drake. Grandmother of Oliver, Ethan, and Roslynn Phoenix. Is a member of the Sisters of Avalon. Turned back to the side of the light. [Appearing in books I-V]

Deceased Member of the House of Drake or Whereabouts Unkown

Fortis Mael Drake (Arcane of Magical Experience, Knight, Wizard)

Knight of the Court. Chief of the Guards of Light the Ancient City. Spouse of Dawn Drake. Father of Nadia and Hawke Drake. Grandfather of Oliver, Ethan, and Roslynn Phoenix. (Deceased). [Prequel].

Hawke Adie Drake (Arcane of Magical Experience, Wizard)

Son of Fortis and Dawn Drake. Uncle of Oliver, Ethan, and Roslynn Phoenix. Brother of Nadia Drake Phoenix. Member of the Dark Guard. [Whereabouts unknown].

The Dark House of Knight

The Dark House of Knight is an Arcane family of magical experience. A long-standing house of the Arcane community. After it was discovered that Lord Aden was in league with Merlin, Morgana, and the dark council, the House of Knight took on the mantle of the Dark House and because of the actions Lord Aden, the Lady Divinity divorced her husband to live among the Arcane people. A powerful Sibyl, she is considered the supreme mistress of divination among the Arcane. The Members of the House of Knight are Arcane of Magical Experience.

Divinity Macha Knight (Arcane of Magical & Mystical Experience, Mystic, Sibyl, Sorceress)

Sorceress. Head of the Arcane Council of Light, one of twelve founders of the Arcane realm. Head Sibyl. Mother of Sebastian and Liam Knight. The ex-spouse of Aden Knight. Friend of Kelvin and Nadia Phoenix. Current teacher of Arcane. [Appearing in books I-V].

Liam Tarlock Knight (Arcane of Magical Experience, Summoner, Warlock)

Warlock. Summoner of Darkness. Second Head of the Dark Guard. Son of Aden and Divinity Knight. The younger brother of Sebastian Knight. He is a leading member of the Dark Army under Merlin and Raven. Whereabouts by the end of Book II is unknown. [Appearing in Books I-V].

Whereabouts of the Members of the House of Knight Unknown

Aden Duncan Knight (Arcane of Magical Experience, Summoner, Warlock)

Warlock. Summoner of Darkness. Head of the Dark Guard. Father of Sebastian and Liam Knight. The ex-spouse of Divinity Knight. Whereabouts at this time are unknown. [Whereabouts unknown].

The Extraordinary House of Ignatius

Considered to be the eldest and largest of the Arcane Houses, The Extraordinary House of Ignatius is an Arcane House and the Royal Family of the elves. The Extraordinary House of Ignatius has been the ruling family over the Aelfdene village for centuries. A family known for their beauty and grace, all the members of the House are known as incredible wielders of elemental magic, archery, weapons, and healing abilities. The Extraordinary House of  Ignatius has married into the other notable Arcane Houses, including the Houses of Elder and Phoenix.

Lady Mora Ignatius {Nee: Elder} (Arcane of Magical & Mystical Experience, Elder, Witch Goddess)

Dowager Queen of the elves. Headmistress of the Arcane Academy of Magical Teaching until her retirement. Mother of Alezander Elderchild Ignatius. Spouse of the late King Caspar Ignatius. Grandmother of Ari, Theo, Hope, Vivian, and Russell Ignatius. Great grandmother to Esther, Isabella, Peter, Michael, Kells, Sophia, Willow, and Russell Ignatius. Witch goddess and sorceress. The eldest living Elder she became the only living original Elder upon the passing of Noble Elder. [Appearing in Books I-V].

High King Alezander Elderchild Ignatius (Arcane of Magical Experience, Elder, Elf, ArchSorcerer)

Reigning king (upon father's death) of the elves. Former student of Merlin. Youngest member of the Council of Elders. Spouse of Roslynn Phoenix. Brother-in-law of Oliver and Olivia Phoenix and Ethan and Sebastian Knight-Phoenix. Uncle to Madeline and Gwendolyn Phoenix and Matthew Knight-Phoenix. Father of Ari, Theo, Hope, Vivian, and Russell. Grandfather of Esther, Isabella, Peter, Michael, Sophia, Kells, Willow, and Russell Ambrose Ignatius. Teacher at the Arcane School of Magical Teaching. Member of the elf royal family. Cousin of Avery, Maria, Alvina, and Lukas Ignatius. Nephew of Otta Ignatius. Weapons Master of the elves. Known for his skill with the long sword. [Appearing in Books I-V].

High Queen Roslynn (Rose) Sophia Nadia Ignatius {Nee: Phoenix} (Arcane of Mundane Experience, Arch Sorceress, ArchSeer)

Former High Princess of the Arcane realm. She became the queen of the elves upon her marriage to her husband, King Alezander. ArchSorceress. Member of the Magical Three. She serves as the Assistant Headmistress, and Head Librarian of the Arcane Academy of Magical Teaching. She will become the Headmistress of the Academy upon the retirement of her mother-in-law from the position. Daughter of Kelvin and Nadia Phoenix. Granddaughter of Titus and Flora Phoenix and Fortis and Dawn Drake. Great granddaughter to Merlin and Nimuway Phoenix. Sister of Oliver and Ethan Phoenix. Aunt to Madeline and Gwendolyn Phoenix and Matthew Knight-Phoenix. Mother of Ari, Theo, Hope, Vivian, and Russell Ignatius. Grandmother to Esther, Isabella, Peter, Michael, Sophia, Kells, Willow, and Russell Ambrose Ignatius. ArchSeer and Time Cycler. [Appearing in books I-V]

Ari Torion Ignatius (Arcane of Magical Experience, Elf, Wizard)

Eldest son of King Alezander and Queen Roslynn Ignatius. Spouse of Amber Detlar Ignatius. Father of Esther Ignatius. Nephew of Oliver and Ethan Phoenix. Grandson of Kelvin and Nadia Phoenix and Caspar and Mora Ignatius. Uncle of the Ignatius Seven. Cousin of Madeline and Gwendolyn Phoenix and Matthew Knight-Phoenix. Time Traveler. Leader of the Elfish Guard. Member of the Elf Royal Family. [Appearing in Books I-V].

Amber Ignatius {Nee: Detlar} (Arcane of Magical Experience, Elf, Witch, Seer)

Wife of Ari Ignatius. Mother of Esther Ignatius. Daughter-in-law of King Alezander and Queen Roslynn Ignatius. Elf Seer. Member of the Elf Royal Family. [Appearing in Books I-V].

Esther Ardulriina Ignatius (Arcane of Magical Experience, Elf, Grand ArchSeer, Witch)

Elf Witch. Daughter of Ari and Amber Ignatius. Granddaughter of King Alezander and Queen Rose Ignatius. Cousin to the Ignatius Seven. GrandSeer. Member of the Elf Royal Family. Head of the Magical Nexus. [Appearing in Books I-V].

Theo Merlion Ignatius (Arcane of Magical Experience, Elf, Wizard)

Second eldest son of King Alezander and Queen Roslynn Ignatius. Nephew of Oliver and Ethan Phoenix. Grandson of Kelvin and Nadia Phoenix and Caspar and Mora Ignatius. Uncle of Esther Ignatius and the Ignatius Seven. Cousin of Madeline and Gwendolyn Phoenix and Matthew Knight-Phoenix. Time Traveler. Leader of the Elfish Guard. Member of the Elf Royal Family. [Appearing in Books I-V].

Hope Fenmenor Ignatius (Arcane of Magical Experience, Elf Healer, Witch)

Third child and eldest daughter of King Alezander and Queen Roslynn Ignatius. Niece of Oliver and Ethan Phoenix. Granddaughter of Kelvin and Nadia Phoenix and Caspar and Mora Ignatius. Aunt of Esther Ignatius and the Ignatius Seven. Cousin of Madeline and Gwendolyn Phoenix and Matthew Knight-Phoenix. Time Traveler. Leader of the Elfish Guard. She is an Elf Healer. Member of the Elf Royal Family. [Appearing in Books I-V].

Vivian Shazorwyn Ignatius (Arcane of Magical Experience, Elf Priestess & Warrior, Witch)

Fourth child and second eldest daughter of King Alezander and Queen Roslynn Ignatius. Niece of Oliver and Ethan Phoenix. Spouse of Bridgett Agarvran. Granddaughter of Kelvin and Nadia Phoenix and Caspar and Mora Ignatius. Aunt of Esther Ignatius and the Ignatius Seven. Cousin of Madeline and Gwendolyn Phoenix and Matthew Knight-Phoenix. Time Traveler. Leader of the Elfish Guard. She is a elf priestess and warrior. Member of the Elf Royal Family. [Appearing in Books I-V].

Russell (Rusty) Ambrose Alezander Elderchild Ignatius (Arcane of Magical Experience, Elf, Heir to the Aelfdene Throne, Grand Sorcerer)

Fifth child and third eldest son of King Alezander and Queen Roslynn Ignatius. Nephew of Oliver and Ethan Phoenix. Grandson of Kelvin and Nadia Phoenix and Caspar and Mora Ignatius. Uncle of Esther Ignatius and the Ignatius Seven. Cousin of Madeline and Gwendolyn Phoenix and Matthew Knight-Phoenix. Spouse of Meredith Amser Elder. Father of Isabella, Peter, Michael, Sophia, Kells, Willow, and Russell Ambrose Ignatius. Time Traveler. Leader of the Elfish Guard. Member of the Elf Royal Family. Heir apparent to the Aelfdene Throne. Grand Sorcerer. [Appearing in Books I-V].

Meredith Amser Ignatius (Arcane of Magical Experience, Sorceress)

Wife of Russell Ambrose Alezander Elderchild Ignatius. Mother of the Ignatius 7. The extent of her magical power is still unclear. [Appearing in Books II-V].

The Ignatius 7

The extraordinary seven siblings who shape the story of time. The seven are exceptionally gifted sorcerers and sorceresses whose magic is the strongest of all Arcane. The seven are the allies of Noel and Lord Dalton Time Yule. The seven are the children of Russell and Meredith Ignatius and grandchildren of King Alezander and Queen Roslynn Ignatius. The seven have the gift of time travel and jump in and out of the various timelines, influencing the outcome of the story.

Isabella Roslynn Ignatius (Arcane of Magical Experience, Elf, ArchSorceress) [Appearing in books II-V]

Michael Cunnings Ignatius (Arcane of Magical Experience, Elf, ArchSorcerer) [Appearing in books II-V]

Peter Kelvin Ignatius (Arcane of Magical Experience, Elf, ArchSorcerer) [Appearing in books II-V]

Kells Ingálvur Ignatius (Arcane of Magical Experience, Elf, ArchSorcerer) [Appearing in books II-V]

Sophia Ilivhrae Ignatius (Arcane of Magical Experience, Elf, ArchSorceress) [Appearing in books II-V]

Willow Lillian Cemno Ignatius (Arcane of Magical Experience, Elf, ArchSorceress) [Appearing in books I-V]

Russell Ambrose Alezander Elderchild Ignatius, Jr. (Arcane of Magical Experience, Elf, ArchSorcerer) [Appearing in books II-V]

Aelfdene Village House of Ignatius

Archduke Lucas Ignatius of the Glen Sheldon (Arcane of Magical Experience, Elf, Member of the Aelfdene Royal Court, Sorcerer)

Aelfdene Village

Serves as the overseer, Archduke, and head of the Aelfdene village. From the elfin tribe of Sheldon. Succeeded his father as regent of his family's glen. Appointed by King Alezander Ignatius to oversee the Aelfdene village. Cousin to the King through the paternal line. Lukas' father is one of the younger brothers of King Casper Ignatius. Cousin to Alvina, Maria and Avery. Nephew of the Lady Otta Ignatius [Appearing in books I-V].

Countess Alvina Ignatius of Glen Sprite (Arcane of Magical Experience, Elf, Member of the Aelfdene Royal Court, ArchSorceress)

Member of the Ignatius Royal Family at the level of Baroness. Serves as an overseer to the Aelfdene village. From the elfin tribe of Sprite. Head of the Sprite Library. Sister of Maria and Avery. Daughter of Otta Ignatius. Cousin of Lucas Ignatius and King Alezander Ignatius [Appearing in books II-V].

Countess Maria Ignatius of Glen Sprite (Arcane of Magical Experience, Elf, Member of the Aelfdene Royal Court, ArchSorceress)

Member of the Ignatius Royal Family at the level of Baroness. From the elfin tribe of Sprite. Serves as an overseer to the Aelfdene village. Sister of Alvina and Avery. Daughter of Otta Ignatius. Cousin of Lucas Ignatius and King Alezander Ignatius [Appearing in books II-V].

Duke Avery Ignatius of Glen Sprite {aka Duke Sprite} (Arcane of Magical Experience, Elf, General, Member of the Aelfdene Royal Court, Sorcerer)

Serves as the second overseer when the Archduke Ignatius is not present. From the elfin tribe of Sprite. Member of the Ignatius Royal Family. Succeeded his father as regent of his family's glen. Appointed by King Alexander Ignatius to help oversee the Aelfdene village. Cousin to the King through the paternal line. Avery's father is the second eldest brother of King Casper Ignatius. Youngest child of Duke Ignatius and Lady Otta Ignatius. Younger cousin to Alvina and Maria. Master horseman. Highest ranking elf Archer Commander [Appearing in books II-V].

Lady Otta Ignatius (Arcane of Magical & Mystical Experience, Elf, Seer of Aelfdene)

The seer of the Aelfdene village. Is a member of the Ignatius Royal Family. Wife to the Duke. Mother of Alvina, Maria, and Avery. Stripped of her powers by Lord Time Yule. Concerns around prophecies and loyalty. Sister-in-law to King Caspar and Dowger Queen Mora Ignatius [Appearing in books II-V].

Deceased Members of the House of Ignatius

King Caspar Ignatius (Arcane, Elf, Wizard)

Deceased King of the Elves. Father of Alezander, Raven and (Brother) Ignatius. Spouse of Mora Elder. Grandfather of Ari, Theo, Hope, Vivian, and Russell Ignatius. (Deceased). [Prequel].

The Divine House of Noble

The living house of the Elders also known among the Arcane as the "Nobles." The Nobles are an extraordinarily gifted group of Arcane appointed by the Celestials to serve as the leaders of the Arcane. Formed the first council of Arcane. Govern the rules of magic. The Nobles are thousands of years old and live among the Arcane.

Noble Elder (Arcane of Magical & Mystical Experience, Elder, Grand ArchSorcerer)

Member of the Arcane Council of Light. Most powerful living magical being. Father of Elder Light. Grandfather of the Lady of White [Appearing in books I-V].

Elder Light Noble (Arcane of Magical & Mystical Experience, Elder, Wizard)

Member of the Arcane Council of Light. Grandfather of Mora Elder. Son of Noble Elder. Husband of Lady Elder Noble. Father to the Lady of White Noble [Appearing in book I].

Lady Elder Noble (Arcane of Magical & Mystical Experience, Elder, Witch)

Member of the Arcane Council of Light. Grandmother of Mora Elder. Daughter-in-law of Noble Elder. Wife of Elder Light Noble. Mother to the Lady of White Noble [Appearing in book I].

Lady of White Noble (Arcane of Magical & Mystical Experience, Elder, Witch)

Mother of Mora Ignatius. Daughter of Elder Light Noble and Lady Elder Noble. Grandmother to King Alezander Ignatius [Appearing in book I].

Lord Count Vladimar Dracula (Arcane of Mystical Experience, Vampire)

The first vampire. Member of the Council of Light. Possesses magical power. Father of the vampires. Ally of Noble Elder and Elder Yule [Appearing in books II-V].

Anwina, the Luminous (High Arcane, Immortal)

Celestial who powers are unknown. Is immortal. Known as the Luminous Being of Light [Appearing in books II-V].

The Elegent House of Yule

Elder Yule (Arcane of Magical & Mystical Experience, Elder, ArchSorcerer)

The Master of Time. The origins of Elder Yule are unknown. One day, he just showed up, appointed by the Celestials to the Council of Light. Controls and manipulates the power of time. Creator of the Timekeeper [Appearing in books II-V].

Lady Nova Astria Yule (Arcane of Magical & Mystical Experience, Elder, ArchSorceress, Sister of Avalon)

Wife of Elder Yule. Mother of Lady Citrine Time Yule and, Lord Dalton Time Yule. Is considered one of the most powerful seers. She is the co-leader of the Sisters of Avalon. Foretold many of the prophecies of the Arcane and Mundane alike. Parents and lineage are unknown [Appearing in books II-V].

Lady Citrine Time Yule (Arcane of Magical & Mystical Experience, Elder, ArchSorceress, Master of Time)

Keeper of Citrine's Antique. Master of Time. Tinker of clocks. Older sister of Lord Dalton Time Yule [Appearing in books II-V].

Lord Dalton Time Yule (High Arcane, Arcane of Magical & Mystical Experience, Elder, Grand ArchSorcerer, Master of Time)

Successor of Elder Yule. Upon his father's death became the Master of Time. Spouse of Noel. Younger brother of Lady Citrine Time Yule [Appearing in books II-V].

Noel (High Arcane, Elder, Grand ArchSorcerer and Necro Sorcerer, Master of the Curpendulums)

Successor of Noble Elder. Grand ArchSorcerer, Immortal. Unable to be killed. Elemental Sorcerer. Known as the Master of the Curpendulums. The only Arcane who uses nanofairies in battle. Spouse of Lord Dalton Time Yule. Ally to the Houses of Phoenix, Ignatius and Elder. Best friend of Cedric and Willow [Appearing in books I-V].

Mr. Cee (Arcane of Magical & Mystical Experience, Familar)

Cat of Russell Ambrose Elderchild Ignatius, Jr. Is an shapeshifting animagius. All black cat. His right eye is blue and his left eye is green. Serves as the protector of Noel in panther form [Appearing in books II-V].

House of Dragonne—The Dragon Guard

King Drago (Arcane of Magical & Mystical Experience, Dragon)

Second eldest dragon, Father of all dragons, King of all Arcane beasts. Spouse of Belinda. Ally to the Houses of Phoenix, Ignatius, and Elder [Appearing in books I-V].

Dragon Guard

Queen Belinda (Arcane of Magical & Mystical Experience, Mother Dragon)

Eldest dragon. Mother of all dragons, Queen of all Arcane beasts. Spouse of Drago. Ally to the Houses of Phoenix, Ignatius, and Elder [Appearing in books I-V].

Autumn (Arcane of Magical & Mystical Experience, Familiar)

Princess dragon. Child of the king and queen dragon. Ally to the Houses of Phoenix, Ignatius, and Elder [Appearing in books I-V].

House of Fae

Queen Amaryllis Fae (Arcane of Magical & Mystical Experience, Fairy)

Queen of the Fairies. Mother of Phineas. Friend of the House of Phoenix. One of twelve original founders of the Arcane realm. Serves as the guardian of Oak Glen. Head of the Fairy Council and Army [Appearing in books I-V].

Phineas Fae (Arcane of Magical & Mystical Experience, Fairy)

Prince of the Fairies. Son of Queen Amaryllis. Second of the Fairy Nation. Husband to Lady Bethany Phoenix [Appearing in books I-V].

Lady Bethany Minerva Fae {Nee: Phoenix} (Arcane of Magical Experience, Witch)

Princess of the Arcane. She is the cousin of Oliver, Ethan, Daemon, Eric, and Roslyn Phoenix. She is the best friend of Sebastian and grew up in the Arcane realm. She is the spouse of Phineas. She is a Professor of Arcane Studies. She is the daughter of Wade and Bethany Phoenix. She is the granddaughter of Titus and Flora Phoenix and the great granddaughter to Merlin and Nimuway Phoenix. She is a member of the Arcane Council [Appearing in books I-V].

Arcane of Mystical Heritage

Lord Count Conrad, The Second Dracula. (Arcane of Mystical Experience, Vampire)

Son of Vlad Dracula. The second Lord Count Dracula. The head of the Vampire covens. Prisoner in the Priory of Dark. Good friend to Lord Dalton Time Yule. Ally of the House of Ignatius and the Magical Three. Sworn enemy of Merlin [Appearing in books II-V].

Conway (Arcane Mystical Experience, Vampire)

Second of the vampire coven. Prisoner in the Priory of Dark [Appearing in books II-V].

Cedric (Arcane Mystical Experience, Vampire)

Vampire. Butler to the House of Phoenix. Protector of the family. Age is unknown. Feared by Merlin. Friend to the Houses of Phoenix and Ignatius. Keeper of many of the secrets of the Houses of Phoenix and Ignatius. Protector of the Ignatius children [Appearing in books I-V].

Leo (Arcane of Mystical Experience, King, Creature)

The king of the forest. Lion. Spouse of Lucy and one of twelve original founders of the Arcane realm. Member of the Arcane Council [Appearing in books I-V].

Lucy (Arcane of Mystical Experience, Queen, Creature)

The queen of the forest. Lion. Spouse of Leo and one of twelve original founders of the Arcane realm. Member of the Arcane Council [Appearing in books I-V].

Leaf (Arcane of Mystical Experience, Wizard)

Animagus. Friend to the Magical Three. Member of the Arcane Council [Appering in books I-V].

Athena (Goddess, Immortal)

The great goddess of all knowledge, warfare, and strategy. Serves as advisor to Queen Roslynn Ignatius and the Lady Mora Ignatius. Keeper of the Library of Knowledge [Appearing in books II-V].

෪

The Faculty

Lady Marybelle (Arcane of Magical Experience, Sorceress)

Teaches reading at the Arcane Academy. Has the ability to animate texts and make them come to life. Head of Arts and the Humanities [Appearing in books II-V].

Professor Giggle (Arcane of Mystical Experience, Dwarf)

Eldest living dwarf. Teaches Economic Education. Has a temper. Best friend of Mr. Bruin [Appearing in books II-V].

Mr. Wolf (Arcane and Mundane of Mystical Experience, ½ Vampire)

Teacher of Physical Education at Arcane Academy. Co-chair of Physical Education [Appearing in books II-V].

Mr. Terran (Arcane of Mystical Experience, Centaur)

6'8" Centaur. Teacher of Physical Education at Arcane Academy. Co-chair of Physical Education [Appearing in books II-V].

Ms. Hoot (Shapeshifter, Arcane of Magical & Mystical Experience, Sorceress)

Teacher of mystical creatures. Creatures Mistress. Shapeshifter from human to owl. Taught Lord Leaf when he was a child [Appearing in books II-V].

Ms. Adwin (Arcane of Magical Experience, Sorceress)

Teacher of Art and Choral. Known as the Art and Choral Mistress. Has the ability to animate paintings and works of art. World-renowned artist. Type of Arcane is unknown [Appearing in books II-V].

Ms. Tulip (Arcane of Magical & Mystical Experience, Fairy)

Garden Fairy of earth and environmental magic. One of several fairies who can take full size and walk among the Arcane and Mundane. Teacher of Elemental Magic for Arcane Academy [Appearing in books II-V].

Lady O (Arcane of Magical Experience, Witch)

Assists around the Arcane Academy. Oversees nourishments for the students of the Arcane Academy [Appearing in books II-V].

Mr. Bruin (Arcane of Mystical Experience, Dwarf)

Second in charge of the Academy Library. Dwarf Warrior. Best friend of Mr. Giggles. Queen Roslynn's right hand assistant in the library [Appearing in books II-V].

Other Characters

Morgana (Dark Arcane, Sorceress)

Dark Arcane Sorceress. Self-declared Queen of the Arcane. Continues to be brought back to life by the Council of the Dark. Seeks the Curpendulums. Enemy of Merlin and the House of Phoenix [Appearing in books I-V].

Lady Raven Helegella Ignatius (Dark Arcane, Summoner, Witch)

Dark Witch. Summoner of Darkness. General f the Dark Army. Love interest of Liam Knight. Younger sister of High King Alezander Ignatius. High Princess of the Elves [Appearing in books I-V].

Lord Balimore Oblivion (Arcane of Magical Experience, Warlock, Head of Dark Council, True Origins are Unknown)

Serves as the head of the Dark Council. Sworn enemy of the Houses of Noble, Phoenix, Yule, and Ignatius. Servant of the incubus King. Acts of a teacher and mentor to Merlin. His true origins are unknown but is believed to be as old as Anwina, the Luminous. Adopted father figure to Merlin. [Appearing in books II-V].

Father Francisco (Arcane of Mystical Experience, Spiritual Leader)

Serves as the head of the Priories of the Arcane. Is the keeper of the certain texts and Arcane artifacts. Spiritual advisor of the Arcane communities. Head of the covens. Serves as an intermediary between the Arcane and Mundane communities. Member of the Arcane Council. [Appearing in books I-V].

King Arthur Pendragon (Mundane, King)

King of Camelot. Head of the Knights of the Round Table. Spouse of Gwenivere. Friend of High Kind Alezander Ignatius. Ancestor of Olivia Pendragon Phoenix [Appearing in books I-V].

Queen Gwenivere Pendragon (Mundane, Queen)

Queen of Camelot. Spouse of Arthur Pendragon. Ancestor of Olivia Pendragon Phoenix [Appearing in books I-V].

Sisters of Avalon (Arcane of Magical & Mystical Experience, Mystics, Seers)

Sisters of Avalon are a magical & mystical group of Arcane women whose duty is to protect all earthly magic, the knowledge of the Nobles and the Celestials. The Sisters serve as advisors to the Noble Elder, Elder Yule, and Arcane of Light. The Sisters are protectors of mystical artifacts held in Avalon. Mystic Healers. The Queen Nimuway serves as one of the two co-leaders of the sisters of Avalon. The other co-leader of the Sisters of Avalon is the Lady Nova Yule. When Arcane women pass or ascend many of them become Sisters of Avalon swearing an oath to continue to protect magic, the Arcane, and the Mundane. Immortal upon becoming a Sister of Avalon. [Appearing in books II-V].

Council of Light {aka Arcane Council} (Arcane of Magical & Mystical Experience)

The Council of Light (aka the Arcane Council) is the governing body of all magic associated with the light. The Arcane Council has a love of life, Arcane and Mundane alike, earth. Work to protect all life. The term Council of Light if used to define the members of the ancient times the Nobles, and Elders appointed by the Celestials to guard and oversee magic. The use of Arcane Council was adopted by the new Council and serves as the current governing body of the Arcane. [Appearing in books I-V].

Council of Dark (Dark Arcane of Magical & Mystical Experience)

The Council of Dark is composed of Dark Arcane who left the Council of Light or are Dark Arcane who seek to control the Curpendulums. The head of the Council is Lord Balimore Oblivion. [Appearing in books I-V].

Vampire Coven (Arcane of Mystical Experience)

The Vampire Coven is the last remaining coven of pure vampires. Over the centuries, Merlin turned many of the vampires to his side. Angry Merlin locked the Vampire Coven away in the Priory of Dark as it is known by the Dark Arcane or the Lost Priory as it is known by all other Arcane. The Vampire Coven aides the Sisters of Avalon and anyone seeking to protect the Curpendulums. [Appearing in books I-V].

About the Author

Kurt W. Oster, LICSW, LCSW, MAT, RPT™ is a gay author, clinical social worker, and educator who advocates for the needs of children through his practice as a clinical social worker and as a Registered Play Therapist™.

His writing is devoted to encouraging the transformation of children with attention deficits, autism spectrum disorder, anxiety, OCD, ODD, learning challenges, and coming out issues. He explores these traditionally unspoken topics and brings awareness to neglected groups via his literary works and bibliotherapy that features neurodivergent and LGBTQ characters.

Kurt obtained his Bachelor of Arts (BA) from Rutgers University, a Master's in Social Work (MSW) from the University of Pennsylvania, and Master of Arts in Teaching (MAT) in Elementary Education from the University of Southern California.

Through his writing, Kurt aims to demonstrate that anything can be achieved while making storytelling enjoyable and changing how it is done.

Other Publications from Perceptions Press

Perceptions Press

CASTLE
CARRINGTON

TRANSGENDER
PUBLISHING

Available now from All Genders Press
https://allgenderspress.ca/

Rise of the Magical Three (2021, revised 2023
Kurt W. Oster, LICSW, LCSW, MAT, RPT™

Raised by a mysterious grandmother and believing their parents to be dead, Roslynn and her older identical twin brothers, Oliver and Ethan, had only read of magical beings and creatures. But, transitioning into young adulthood, the three embark on an incredible journey as they are introduced to the riddles of their family's past that will forever change who they are and are yet to become.

As the three siblings discover the ways of the magical arts, they quickly learn that they are not alone in their quest. Finding help when and where they least expect, the three develop friendships, confront the darkness, work together to save their family from an ancient curse, and learn of a mysterious and ancient bloodline that will forever shape the fabric of time and love.

Their fight becomes more significant than even they had anticipated and forces them to make decisions about whether they can effectively save the world, the multiple realms, and magic as they know it. Learning that magic is driven by passion, knowledge, bloodline, and time, will they be the ones to save time, or will they become mere echoes of time? (https://allgenderspress.ca/echoes-of-time/)

The Ignatius 7 (2022, revised 20223)
House of Phoenix Chronicles Book III
Kurt W. Oster LICSW, LCSW, MAT, RPT™

When RJ, a Mundane archeology graduate student, is mysteriously injured during a walk across campus, he makes a discovery that uncovers one of the greatest secrets of the Arcane and Mundane worlds and forever alters how he understands the battle between good and evil.

Learning the truth of Merlin's dark plans and discovering that magic can happen even for those born with no magical power, RJ now holds the key to stopping the destruction of the Mundane across the globe. As time continues to unravel and as missing relics of the past emerge, a bizarre, twisted fate in which the Knights of the Round Table are at the heart of Merlin's plan for total power is revealed.

RJ and his roommate, Dalton, set out to discover their college's history while meeting resistance every step of the way. RJ's journey quickly takes an interesting turn when he receives help from unexpected allies, including the Ignatius 7 and others.

Growing frustrated with the ongoing echoes of time, RJ must formulate a new approach to handling time's bizarre game by channeling the power of technology, mind, magic, and love to bring an end to the battle, save both the Arcane and Mundane, all the while listening to his heart, falling in love, balancing the complex life of a college student, and dealing with his estranged family.

(https://allgenderspress.ca/the-ignatius-7/)

Mystical Way of Time (2023)
Kurt W. Oster, LICSW, LCSW, MAT, RPT™
(A children's book)

In a moment of boredom, young Lord Time stops, thinks for a moment, then gets out his paintbrushes and starts creating.
What emerges is a beautiful village, with many people, all different but living and working together in harmony.
Take a magical journey with Lord Time and his sister, Citrine, as they stroll along the Mystical Way.

Here everyone is welcome, all are accepted, and each person celebrates the ways in which each one is unique.

When a new library opens, Lord Time and Citrine help create a memorable moment of acceptance for the new librarian in town.

(https://allgenderspress.ca/mystical-way-of-time/)

Bibi The Happy Trans Girl (2023)
Karla May-Strange

Bibi is a vibrant young transgender 7 year old who love everyone, especially herself. Perfectly Trans.
(https://allgenderspress.ca/bibi/)

Eli The Happy Trans Teen Takes Testosterone (2023)
Karla May-Strange

Eli is a tween, a transgender boy tween. He is just starting out on his journey to become a young adult.
(https://allgenderspress.ca/eli-the-happy-trans-boy/)

Norm As I Am! (2023)
Cy Nelson

Late spring brings larvae to the garden. Some are pink and some are blue. However, Norm does not conform to these expectations. Follow the journey to find Norm's rare and beautiful authentic self.
Available in French Norm Comme Je Suis!
Available in Spanish Norm Como Soy!
Available in Chinese Norm Jiu Shi Wo!
(https://allgenderspress.ca/norm-as-i-am/)

PUBLICATION EXPECTED IN 2021
The Gospel of a Witch
Diana Bishop
The 200 angels who procreated with human women and fathered the Nephilim were cast out of Heaven. Their Nephilim children were ordered by God to be destroyed because of their destructive and corruptive behavior on Earth, but not before they fathered children of their own. These children of Nephilim came to be the witches, vampires, and werewolves of lore. It was generally believed by these supernatural beings that God disapproved of them, although they were three-fourths human and were left untouched by the purge. Lena's parents were such Nephilim offspring. They suffered under the same assumption until they met Jesus when he was physically among humankind. They became a part of his discipleship and Lena was born in his presence. They, and, in turn, Lena, were charged by Jesus with the mission of spreading the message among the Nephilim decedents that they were loved by God and were welcome in Heaven upon their death, contingent on the life they had lived. *The Gospel of a Witch* is a part of Lena's story as she endeavors to complete her mission.
(https://allgenderspress.ca/the-gospel-of-a-witch/)

Coming soon from
All Genders Press
https://allgenderspress.ca/

PUBLICATION EXPECTED IN 2024
Things are Not What They Seem
House of Phoenix Chronicles Book IV
Kurt W. Oster, LICSW, LCSW, MAT, RPT™
Shifting, altering, and replaying over and over, one timeline after another is acting up. When fifteen timelines act up all at once, a new, rebellious Noble Elder must calm the chaos and re-establish the balance of time, magic, and everyday life. Noble Elder grows into their new role despite moments of wanting to throw up their hands and walk away. Traveling through time and meeting hiccup after hiccup along the way, Noble Elder collaborates with six, headstrong Ignatius siblings, learning to navigate complex and, at times, downright awkward relationships with them.

Working together and, sometimes, against each other, the Ignatius 7 quickly learn that things are not what they seem when they discover a truth that rocks the very core of what they know about magic. Noble Elder, tired of the growing attacks of darkness, seeks the help of Arcane and Mundane alike in a battle between light and dark.

When magic stops working because of time disruptions, RJ, Amelia, Minnie, and Dalton return to help and must learn to navigate complex friendship with the Ignatius 7. Will their epic journey to find the Curpendulums, restore time, and bring normalcy to the earth succeed? Will time break the spirit of Noble Elder, and stop time altogether? Or

will Noble Elder discover new ways to handle the challenges of life, magic, and darkness?
(https://allgenderspress.ca/things-are-not-what-they-seem/)

PUBLICATION EXPECTED IN 2025
The Curpendulums
House of Phoenix Chronicles Book V
Kurt W. Oster, LICSW, LCSW, MAT, RPT™
(https://allgenderspress.ca/the-curpendulums/)

The **House of Phoenix Chronicles** *is planned as a series of books filled with wizards, witches, fairies, elves, dwarfs, centaurs, mermaids, and dragons in the fight of their lives to protect their ways of life, their families, and the earth. The Phoenix siblings, Roslynn and her older identical twin brothers, Oliver and Ethan, embark on a remarkable journey of friendship, romance, hatred, and mystery as truths are revealed, challenges faced, and battles with ancient darkness fought. Bending magic to their will, Roslynn, Ethan and Oliver, step in and out of time, breaking the rules at every stage of their remarkable journey. Along their way, they meet friends from the past, present, and future, and discover an ancient secret that could forever change the fabric of history, including our understanding of Medieval times and the Knights of the Round Table: a curse sent by darkness to unravel time as it is known. One minute, magic was at its height, the center of life and the community. In the next, cities and villages lay in ruins, a mere echo of a time that was. Can the three siblings channel their family's magic, one of the most powerful magical bloodlines ever to live, for good? Or will their efforts backfire, leading to the destruction of all magical beings? Will they be able to break the curse that affects their family? Can they save their bloodline and the ways of magic? Will they help bring magic back to earth, or will they become the continuation of the curse?*

PUBLICATIONS EXPECTED IN 2025
The Two Princes
Masters of the Curpendulum Book I
Kurt W. Oster, LICSW, LCSW, MAT, RPT™
(https://allgenderspress.ca/the-two-princes/)

PUBLICATION EXPECTED IN 2024
Dancing Dylan is a Happy Non-binary Child
Karla May-Strange
(A children's book)
Dancing Dylan is a self confident, non-binary teenager. They/Them, Dylan, is enjoying the freedom of being genderqueer and learning how to experience life with an open heart. (https://allgenderspress.ca/dancing-dylan/)

Publications from other divisions of Perceptions Press
Perceptions Press www.perceptionspress.ca
Stephanie Castle Publications www.stephaniecastle.ca
Castle Carrington Publishing www.castlecarringtonpublishing.ca
TransGender Publishing www.transgenderpublishing.ca